MW00774583

SUPER
SONIC

ALSO BY THOMAS KOHNSTAMM

Lake City

Do Travel Writers Go to Hell?

SUPER SONIC

A NOVEL

THOMAS KOHNSTAMM

COUNTERPOINT ▪ CALIFORNIA

SUPERSONIC

This is a work of fiction. All of the characters, organizations, and events portrayed in this novel are either products of the author's imagination or are used fictitiously.

First Counterpoint edition: 2025

Library of Congress Cataloging-in-Publication Data
Names: Kohnstamm, Thomas B., author.
Title: Supersonic : a novel / Thomas Kohnstamm.
Description: First Counterpoint edition. | California : Counterpoint, 2025.
Identifiers: LCCN 2024043766 | ISBN 9781640096813 (hardcover) | ISBN 9781640096820 (ebook)
Subjects: LCGFT: Novels.
Classification: LCC PS3611.O3695 S87 2025 | DDC 813/.6—dc23/eng/20240920
LC record available at https://lccn.loc.gov/2024043766

Jacket design by Gregg Kulick
Jacket image © iStock / urbanglimpses
Book design by Laura Berry

COUNTERPOINT
Los Angeles and San Francisco, CA
www.counterpointpress.com

Printed in the United States of America

10 9 8 7 6 5 4 3 2 1

For Johnny McGlocklin. My older brother in spirit.

And, as always, for Tábata, Benício & Bettina.

All history was a palimpsest,
scraped clean and reinscribed
exactly as often as was necessary.

—ERIC ARTHUR BLAIR

A hundred years ago, perhaps, another man sat on this spot;
like you he gazed with awe and yearning in his heart at
the dying light of the glaciers . . . He felt pain and brief joy
as you do. Was he someone else? Was it not you yourself?

—ERWIN SCHRÖDINGER

SUPER
SONIC

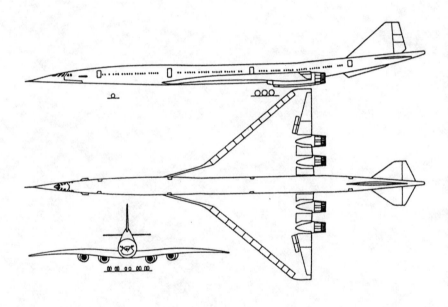

PROLOGUE   *1852*

Seagulls circle as the pale, bearded men return in larger boats, this time with elaborately dressed women and children and a variety of unfamiliar four-legged animals.

The birds watch through their yellow eyes as the newcomers saw down trees and plow earth into the tideflats once rich with crabs, sea stars, and young salmon. Not the highest tides or darkest storms could produce such change.

The gulls learn to compete for food with a fresh desperation. In time, they are relegated to scavenging refuse and carrion.

Many birds retreat along the shoreline. One small colony of gulls follows families from the longhouses as they flee inland.

They fly up to a wooded hilltop crowned with a large gray boulder. There they find mice, soft roots, and even some smaller birds to eat.

The gulls sit atop the rock, biding their time until the newcomers go back to wherever they came from and things return to the way they used to be.

PART I   *1856*

Si'sia, "Little Chief," as his friends tease him, stands shoulder to shoulder with the other children as they carve the pit from the wet winter dirt. They dig with sticks and the three metal shovels they borrowed from settlers' empty cabins. Hot rings of raw skin on Si'sia's palms become water-filled blisters and then collapse into weeping holes of their own.

The children work through the night without water, light, or pause. All the dead must be buried before the Bostons, the white men from the East, return from the safety of their stone long-house and the metal boat just offshore. Before the settlers can further disrespect the bodies of the tribal warriors strewn about the stump-studded hillsides and crooked streets of mud.

Si'sia's family are among the few *dxʷdəwʔabš*, or Duwamish, to disagree with Chief Si'ahl and his attempt to appease and cohabitate with the advancing settlers. Every circle of the seasons they are told to give up a little bit more. And what do the Duwamish get in return? Chief Si'ahl, at least, got the settlement renamed after him, or something close to it. The earlier name of Duwamps was plowed under along with everything else.

The Bostons' new chief, the man called Stevenson, forced this uprising by ignoring promises, murdering other tribes, and calling for a war of extermination. Of course, Si'sia respects the bravery and sacrifice of his father, his uncles, and all the other warriors. But even at his young age, Si'sia knows that this won't end well for the tribes, including the Duwamish who stayed out of the fight.

Stevenson doesn't care that Si'sia's people have inhabited this land since the Changer walked down from the mountains, defeated the great monsters, and brought seeds and fishnets and canoes, transforming the world so the $dx^wdəwʔabš$ could live in it.

Perhaps the Changer has returned. This time in the form of the Bostons. That's what Chief Si'ahl has said. Or maybe the Changer is Stevenson himself, as his mother guessed while talking around the cook fire.

Si'sia is not so sure, but his greatest fears were confirmed the moment that the metal boat's guns came to life with flashes of fire and thunder that pummeled the hillside and the forests beyond.

A handful of Duwamish women, including Si'sia's mother, drag the bodies on mats of bark to this secret burial site atop a wooded hill. The one crowned with a large oval boulder. Where Si'sia's uncles took him to climb and play as a younger child.

As the mass grave is hollowed out in the dirt beside the rock, the women carefully blanket the bottom of the pit with sand and pebbles carried up from the beaches in baskets. The dead, both whole and in pieces, are stacked in the grave under the dim midwinter moon. Si'sia wants to be sad, angry, vengeful, something... he knows he should be, but all he can do is focus on the pit before him and the pain boring its way ever deeper into his hands.

No one knows how many have been killed, so the children keep plunging sticks and shovels into the ground over and over for as long as the bodies keep arriving. Si'sia vomits when he sees the first of his uncles, much of his face torn away. He never sees his other two uncles, but his mother confirms that she helped pull their corpses up the hill. Her brothers were but three of her countless trips.

When his father's broken body is placed beside the edge of the grave, Si'sia cries to himself in the dark but does not stop digging.

As a headman, a *siab*, and one of the leaders of the doomed revolt, Si'sia's father deserves a burial befitting a man of his stature. But the sun will arrive soon, along with the Bostons and their guns.

Si'sia and his mother roll his father into the ground, atop the pile of rebel Duwamish and fallen men from other tribes. There is no time to mourn.

Without sharing a word, the women and children start to cover the bodies with the nearly black dirt and pack it down into the ground with their hands, feet, and stones. Once the soil is again firm, they push with all of their might against the boulder. It doesn't move.

They recruit more children and more of the exhausted women, slicked in sweat and viscera of the dead, and summon the strength to push even harder. The rock tips and then leans, exposing the edge of its rounded base.

Si'sia's mother sends two women back down the hill to fetch a rope. They return with more Duwamish who'd initially stayed out of the fight and a thick cable used by the settlers to secure boats. They wrap the cable around the top of the rock. Together, they pull while the others push from the opposite side. The boulder starts to give. It rolls over, landing with a soft thud atop the grave.

"It looks like an egg now," Si'sia says to his mother, blood and dirt drooling from his palms.

"What matters is that they're safe," she answers. "Until the Changer comes again. And the land returns to us."

They work together to disguise the area around the burial site with sticks, leaves, and pine needles. Before the morning sun climbs over the mountains, the Duwamish disperse. Some return to longhouses that will soon be taken from them and burned. Others flee inland to the forests and mountains.

At dawn, a group of seagulls returns to the rock.

ONE *2014*

Sami keeps an eye on her digital watch until it reads 1:00 p.m. sharp and then delivers three knocks on the new principal's door. She times them on a tight cadence, hoping that the knocks will convey a sense of efficiency and professionalism. First impressions and all of that.

She's no stranger to the school, though; that's for sure. Each of her four children attended Stevenson Elementary over the last decade and a half, and she's been into the main office for everything from tardy slips to forgotten brown-bag lunches to checking on stomachaches—real, exaggerated, and outright fabricated.

Sami's also been here as a student herself, back when principals were more concerned about mushroom clouds than active shooters. Not to mention that she's put in innumerable hours through four terms as head of the PTA to the point that a gag proposal was once circulated to change the school mascot from the Super Seagulls to Sami the Seagull, complete with a hastily drawn bird wearing the white orthopedic running shoes that somehow, for better or for worse, have become her personal trademark.

It's hard for Sami to fathom that, after an entire lifetime at Stevenson Elementary, this is her final year. Her youngest, Macy, will start middle school next September—and that will be that. Most importantly, Sami knows this is her last chance to do what she needs to do: the reason she sunk so many years into this often thankless work... if you can even call it work, as she was surely never compensated with anything more than fleeting parental appreciation and an end-of-the-school-year bottle of Chardonnay from the neighborhood Food King.

While she waits at the principal's door, Sami inventories the two envelopes, the large one and the small one, in pockets of her blue rain jacket and runs through the kids' pickup and drop-off schedule for the rest of the day in her head. She then uses her thumb to clean a scuff mark off her new white shoes, which are made from a more finicky material than her usual brand but were on sale at a very persuasive price at her favorite off-retail big-box store.

As she stands back up, she winks to the framed photo of her grandmother among the other dust-covered Stevenson Elementary portraits, awards, and Native American–inspired trinkets in the main office's glass-fronted cabinet.

The simple caption etched in her grandmother's frame gives her married name, Masako "Macy" Hasegawa, and the length of her multi-decade tenure. It forgoes the crucial details that her grandmother survived incarceration—or internment, as they used to soft-pedal it—at Camps Harmony and Minidoka to become one of the first, if not the first, *nisei* Japanese American teachers in the Metro Public School system and played an integral role in establishing the longest continuously running elementary music program in a city that once prided itself on such things.

And the caption definitely doesn't indicate that prior to incarceration, most of this hilltop neighborhood including all the land under the school itself was a dairy farm owned and operated by the Hasegawa family—land for which they were also surely never compensated.

After Sami gives a second series of slightly louder knocks, a voice shouts, "Jesus. Hold your horses," followed by some elaborate rustling. The principal opens the fireproof wood door with an empty coffee mug in his free hand, the brown dye job in his comb-over not quite syncing with whatever backup plan he employed on his beard.

"Principal Doucette?" Sami shakes his moist palm and tries to not be judgmental about the crumbs on the paunch of his maroon sweater-vest, the hint of stale flatulence in his office, or the general state of chaos creeping from his desk across the chairs and to the floor.

She grounds herself by looking out his office window at the large boulder across the street. Kids graduate. Principals turn over. Teachers move on and retire. The Stevenson Rock remains all that it is and ever will be: a huge stone crowned with a frosty white peak of seagull crap.

He rubs his brow. "I wasn't expecting—my secretary, she didn't tell me—"

"Millie never misses her Cherry Coke and Camel Lights late lunch, you know." Sami motions with her head back toward the main office. "I've been telling her about Nicorette since the nineties. But she's what now? Seventy and still working?"

Doucette shrugs.

"Watch her outlive us all." She tries to give him a convivial nudge in the shoulder but doesn't quite connect. "Me? People say I'm like my grandmother: a control enthusiast, if not zealot. Probably worse for you than smoking, right? But it keeps me on top of the pandemonium of family life. Usually. Anyway, I let myself back."

She laughs. He doesn't.

"Sorry, who are you?" He returns his hand to the door handle.

"Sami." She holds her smile for what feels a bit longer than reasonable.

Doucette moves his bearded chin slowly from left to right and back again.

"Sami Hasegawa-Stalworth. New president of the Stevenson PTA. Or the new old president all over again. I took a couple of years off but . . . guess what? I'm back."

"Ah, right. PTA." He makes his way to his desk, sitting down behind a low skyline of binders and unopened mail.

She follows him into the office, leaving the door ajar for aeration's sake. "I think it's safe to say, on behalf of the school's parents, that we all hope you'll be joining us for longer than the last interim principal."

"Here. Take a seat." He motions to a chair stacked with manila folders and then locates and passes to her a blue vinyl ring binder with *PTA* written in Sharpie on its spine.

She clears the seat and flips through the binder's pages. There's nothing much of value, and she can't say that she's a huge fan of its shambolic organization. But Monica, her friend and the current Stevenson music teacher, always says that she needs to remember that others have different approaches to doing things. That there is no one right way. And that Sami needs to learn to let go a bit and share responsibilities if she's ever to expand beyond what she can manage directly by herself. No matter how determined she is, Sami is still only one person.

A single PTA application form is stuck in the front of the binder. It's from a guy named Bruce and it looks as if it were written in crayon. Sami wonders if there are any kids named Bruce these days or if all Bruces are born directly into middle age, reflux, and credit card debt.

Either way, she welcomes poor penmanship over the last year's Bay Area transplant who used her tenure as PTA president as a platform for her performative social media activism and fringe health theories, only to skip back to California before the end of the school year, leaving no successor, no budget, and no log-ins to any of their online accounts.

Sami searches the binder for other paper applications or even a basic sign-up sheet, but they are nowhere to be found.

Doucette refills his mug from the stained Pyrex carafe of a

twelve-cup coffee maker behind his desk. "I remember now. You're the one my secretary said is pretty plugged in around here."

"Maybe once upon a time." She folds her hands atop the binder on her lap. "My older three kids are in middle and high school now. None of the PTA parents I used to be able to count on were crazy enough to have a fourth child." She forces another laugh to obscure the persistent shadow of feeling stuck.

She's more than aware that she forsook the career that she might have had to be a parent. Again and again and again . . . and then again. She once thought she might be, at least, a locally renowned newspaper reporter by this point in her career, but instead, her life exists in a five-to-ten-block radius, and she can barely fit in her best pair of jeans that already went out of style after she had her third child.

Like a space shuttle, a long-term stay-at-home parent must time their reentry into the career world at a very specific angle. She knows that her window of opportunity has likely closed. She has no résumé beyond the PTA, and what major accomplishment does she have to show for it?

Well, she is going to change all of that. Right now.

Sami fishes the smaller envelope from her jacket pocket. She removes a single sheet of paper, smooths it flat, and slides it across the narrow canal of free space on Doucette's desk.

It reads:

PETITION FOR SCHOOL NAME CHANGE:
MASAKO HASEGAWA ELEMENTARY

He glances over the page, takes a loud sip of coffee, and asks, "What's wrong with Stevenson?"

"Where should I start?"

"I dunno. I didn't really read that plaque out in the front hall there."

"First governor of the state. Before it was even a state."

"That's not nothing."

"He accomplished things, no doubt. He was a general in the Civil War too. Killed leading a charge. It's more about *what* he accomplished: like forcing the Duwamish to sign a zillion BS treaties and still doing his best to boot them out of the city, championing what today we'd call ethnic cleansing, raising his own personal army, declaring martial law, arresting his political opponents, and then pardoning himself. That's a lot of nasty behavior for a guy who didn't even live here for a full four years."

"Gotcha." Doucette puts back the coffee like it's water.

"So, this is it. My PTA grand finale. My special purpose." She removes the second, larger envelope from her jacket and opens it to flip through a stack of papers with thousands of names handwritten in blue and black ink. "It's taken years of email requests, neighborhood cookouts, pestering shoppers in the Food King parking lot, and stapling fliers on telephone poles, but I've finally got enough faculty and community signatures. Now I just need to finalize school board support. And, of course . . . get the John Hancock of the sitting principal."

She feels an inward warmth at the impending public proof of her contribution. For posterity. Yes, evidence that she existed and was an indispensable member of this community. But more importantly, it will be an enduring testament to the fact that her family made this place what it is today. That they existed. Here. And kept and maintained this land. Their names will not be washed away or lost to history. Just as she promised her grandmother before she died. Literally, on the old woman's deathbed.

Doucette sets his coffee mug atop the petition and uses the handle to rotate it in circles. He takes a protracted exhale and says something to himself about his big mouth. "Look, Sami. I'd love to help you out—"

"Please don't tell me you're about to move on too?" Doucette doesn't strike her as the ideal fit for the job, but this game of principal musical chairs isn't good for the kids, the teachers, or the wider community.

"The city's really starting to boom again, right? All this internet Monopoly money. The district needs to modernize. Better resource the key school buildings. Build some all-glass magnet flagship whatever downtown."

"Geez. I mean, I don't think a single floor tile's been updated here since my grandmother's days."

"See, that's the thing." He drops his voice. "I'm not supposed to share this, but I'm trying to be transparent with you here, so you have to promise to keep this to yourself: they're gonna need to absorb some of the smaller, more outdated elementary schools next year."

"Absorb?" She is hit with an overwhelming urge for a cigarette even though she hasn't had one since before the kids were born.

"Yeah, like consolidate with other schools."

"Consolidate? Meaning? Share some resources? Some students?" His point is not lost on Sami. As usual, her mind goes straight to the worst-case scenario. But she hopes that, if only she can keep tap-dancing through enough questions, he'll eventually admit that it is all a simple misunderstanding, if not an ill-timed joke.

"The students will be reallocated to a variety of other locations. All the students." He leans back in his chair and looks out the window toward the rock, his gut rising and falling with each breath like a sleeping dog under a blanket. "Stevenson has debt, declining enrollment, failing infrastructure, a weak neighborhood tax base. The list goes on. I mean, it doesn't even have space for a real playground."

"It has a playground."

"On the roof. And that play structure is Tetanus Central."

Sami knows quite well that Stevenson is almost, but not quite, poor enough to qualify for federal support as a Title I school and too small, too old, and its art programs too irrelevant to the new version of this city to continue to be deemed of great value to the accountants, consultants, and other hired killers now running the show. But outright closure had never crossed her mind.

She hesitates too long to keep feigning new denials. "And the building itself?"

"All these tech dorks gotta have their new condos, right?" He slouches. "Whether they actually sleep at the office or not."

"That can't... it can't..." Sami grabs the PTA binder and gets to her feet, her mouth suddenly lacking saliva. "Without a school, the whole neighborhood... all that my family did... it'll be... buried."

"I'm not saying anything's for sure." Doucette refuses to meet her gaze. "If the school puts its best foot forward, you know, the PTA plugs some debts, throws a few buckets of fresh paint on the walls... who knows? It could all be fine."

She stares out the open door, back into the main office where the secretary, Millie, now grinds down Ticonderoga No. 2s in the hand-cranked, wall-mounted sharpener. Sami makes out the contours of Grandma Masako's jet-black 1970s hair and oversize glasses in the portrait and thinks about all that has gotten the school to this point.

Sami is careful to not raise her voice as much as she would like. As much as someone more experienced at expressing their rage might. "So... OK... wow. Let's think... I'm the PTA person. You're the principal. What can we do to fix this, Bill? Can I call you Bill?"

He doesn't answer.

"Can you talk to somebody? Can you help me talk to somebody? There must be something we can do. Together, right?"

"This isn't some heartwarming nineties movie." He belches

softly. "I've overseen the closure of two failing schools in the last three years. Apparently, I've got a knack for it."

Sami considers fleeing. Dead-ended, once again. Maybe she shouldn't have even tried.

As she gathers up her stack of papers, she looks over the thousands of signatures. The initials of the bagger at the grocery store. The cop's name and rank. The nurse with the ornate middle initial G. All of those parents and teachers. Former students.

Sami realizes that all she is asking Doucette for is one more signature. A quick bit of ink to add to the legions.

She channels Grandma Masako, stands up, and calmly places a ballpoint atop the petition. "Hasegawa Elementary is not failing. We won't let it fail—I can't let it fail. Please, Bill."

TWO *2014*

Sweat beads under Bruce's green 1996 SuperSonics NBA Western Conference Champions hat. The fraying cap his wife says smells like a wet dog. Or a dead dog. Some kind of dog. The one he wears every day to conceal the fact that his blond ponytail is adrift on the rising seas of his scalp, no longer part of a contiguous landmass.

He and his eight-year-old daughter, Sierra, push the shopping cart out of the elevator and down the endless rows of the parking garage to the dented, bumper-stickered back of his prized '87 Volkswagen Westfalia van, the Westy. He curses himself for having let his disabled parking permit lapse. But now's not the time to dwell on that.

Sierra devours sugar-encrusted gummy creatures from an oversize bag, her lips and fingertips stained bright red. Between bites, she puffs on a translucent plastic recorder and shows her dad some of the melodies she recently learned at school. "See: if I play a major scale from the top down, it's a Christmas song. Eight, seven, six, five—four, three, two, one. What song is that?"

"No idea."

"C'mon, Bruce. 'Joy to the World.' I gave you a hint. It's the C major scale. Backward. Here, try to guess another . . ."

Bruce is proud of his daughter. She's rarely spoken this much, even to him. They—the experts, whoever—say it's some sort of an expressive language developmental delay. But Sierra's come so far since discovering her love of music. She's doing so much better at

Stevenson Elementary and has even stopped her morning melt-downs to avoid class.

Although Bruce's wife is still pressuring him to join the PTA and "better advocate for Sierra's special needs," he knows their daughter will grow out of her challenges without the additional evaluations, individualized education programs, therapists, speech-language pathologists, ongoing social stigmas, and all of that BS.

He does his best to listen to Sierra's every word, but it's hard to remain present as searing pulses of white electricity fire down the length of his spine, lighting up the soles of his feet in his duct-taped sport sandals. Bruce wishes he could take a nice, dank bong hit. That'd help. It always does. But alas, he doesn't smoke weed anymore.

OK, he still does. Pretty much every day. But he's strictly a social smoker now, as he explains to his wife every single time she returns to her old hobbyhorse of how he needs to quit. He's steadfast in his commitment to only smoking when he has someone else to smoke with, and she should accept that as significant progress.

Bruce tries to remove his aluminum medical cane from the shopping cart. It's wedged under the fold-out baby seat. As he grips the cane's cream-colored foam handle and attempts to rock it free, Sierra loads their purchases—two plates, a coffee mug, a children's animated movie–themed plastic cup, the largest-size container of instant coffee, two forks, two spoons, three frozen pepperoni pizzas, and a nine-dollar braided bathroom rug—into the back of his VW bus.

"Remember? Mommy said three," Sierra tells him as she jumps in through the sliding side door and buckles herself into the back bench seat.

"Three what?" Bruce slams the tailgate, winces, and makes his way with his cane around to the driver's side. He holds on to the top of the open door as he raises himself into the seat and then grabs his shorts by the cargo pockets to pick up and swing his legs into the vehicle. The cane claims its spot in the passenger seat.

"Home by three. No excuses. For a change," she says through a mass of chewed sugar, cornstarch, and Red 40. "Mommy said that last part, not me."

"Yes, yes. I remember. Three." It's no secret to anyone who knows Bruce that he rejects servitude to the almighty clock. Time is a man-made construct, anyway, as he has explained to Sierra so many times before. It's but one way to measure planetary motion, and only relatively recently, during the Industrial Revolution, became an effective tool for capital to squeeze more productivity out of the working class at the expense of their leisure and joy.

Bruce has no idea what time it is and would normally claim that he doesn't care. He left his flip phone at home—on purpose, he tells himself. He'd prefer to not own the damned thing in the first place. And the Westy's clock hasn't worked since he can remember. But the sun is already heading toward the horizon; it still sets early this time of year. It seems to him a reasonable part of the day to get Sierra home, but he doubts that his wife, Wren, will agree, especially during this unforgiving period of trial separation when his every action is up for subatomic scrutiny.

He edges the Westy out on to Stevenson Way, the main drag with its strip malls and semi-completed six-story apartment buildings crowding out the remaining dive bars and warehouses from yesteryear. As the van climbs the hill like an old mule, he watches in the rearview mirror as his daughter tips the bottom of the candy bag into her mouth. "I told you to slow down." He raises his voice. "You're gonna gag."

"You told me to finish it before Mommy sees it."

"You know what I mean."

"To lie?"

"Don't say that. That's not what—I'd never encourage that.

Mommy and I still agree on everything when it comes to you." He pauses a moment to consider. "Sometimes it makes sense to not call unnecessary attention to certain things."

"OK, Pops."

"Make sure to lick your fingers clean too." Tardiness plus a sugar overdose would be a step too far for Wren. He could always try to blame their late arrival on the unreliability of the Westy's four-cylinder *wasserboxer* engine. Over the years, he'd regularly tried to convince Wren that they needed to spring for a Subaru engine replacement. That the *wasserboxer* didn't have the horsepower, durability, or dependability for such a heavy vehicle. But Wren never prioritized maintaining Bruce's beloved Westy.

Last time he used the "car didn't start" excuse, he followed with, "It's a well-known mechanical issue. And you refuse to let me get a new engine. What can I do?"

"Remember when the neighbor got a job in Hawaii? And practically gifted us her Camry? And you gave it back because a Camry wasn't your 'thing?'" She raised her voice. "You could have done that. That's what you could have done. You could have been willing to change. Or improve your situation, our situation, in some small way. Rather than drive our kid around in a thirty-year-old tin can."

He profoundly disagreed and still disagrees with that assessment. He's changed plenty. More than she appreciates. Isn't he a stay-at-home father? Isn't he only a social weed smoker now? The Westy is just about all he's got from back in the day. And maybe his ponytail. And his Sonics hat. And a few other things. But that's not the point. The point is that maybe she's got it backward, and he actually needs to change less and be more Bruce.

Bruce Jorgensen, better known in his younger years as Loose Bruce, achieved two glorious decades of living life on his own terms, chasing fresh powder across the Cascades in the Westy, wearing his legendary racoon roadkill cap that, unlike one of those commercial Davy Crocketts, was all head and no tail. Offseasons were spent surfing in Westport, mountain biking in Bellingham, and building grow operations throughout Washington State.

He lived with no drama. No regrets. No kowtowing to El Hombre. Always under the radar of banks, the government, doctors, and all other forces out to kill his vibe. Not only did he not own a tie—expected—but Loose Bruce rejected belts, zippers, laces, buttons, and flies of all categories. Wake and bake over caffeine and alarm clocks. Reggae and deep-dub cassettes on the Walkman all day.

When Bruce and Wren fell in love and he moved into her grad student housing, he promised himself and her that they wouldn't live on autopilot and become one more pair of domesticated androids. They would bend squareness to their will. They'd be Loose Bruce and anthropologist Wren playacting as typical members of society and would enter that world as curious tourists on open-ended visas, without becoming full, flag-waving citizens of normalcy. Although, it now seems that she might've just been humoring him. Or lying to herself. Maybe both.

As she abandoned academia for corporate direct deposit and his spinal issues became chronic, the couple beat a rapid transition into unequal business partners in the child-rearing and homemaking industry. Between lack of sleep, diaper changes, somewhere around twelve million bong hits (only after Sierra was sound asleep for the night, of course), and a steady diet of painkillers, Bruce couldn't hope to keep up with the shifting tectonics below his feet. Neither Bruce nor Wren noticed their conversions until they were full-fledged.

And now, Bruce must keep believing that this trial separation thing, whatever it is, that he and his wife are going through is not the end but a correction. A helpful slap across the face that will snap them out of this sleepwalking and get them back to the way things used to be.

He whips a jolting, hard right in the Westy, or as hard as one can turn in such a lumbering, top-heavy vehicle, and pulls into the lot of the old bar and grill on Stevenson Way. Plywood covers the ground-floor windows of the building. The lot plays home to a handful of parked and abandoned cars including an old minivan, caked with spray paint. There appears to be a large, blond man napping, if not living, inside the minivan.

"Daddy?" Sierra asks, hesitancy returning to her voice.

"Just one more thing."

"But we're so close to home."

"Real quick, honey."

"Mommy's not gonna be happy."

He noses his van into a spot next to the only nice car in the lot, an immaculate white Cadillac, which idles with a man distractedly smoking in the driver's seat.

Bruce knows he is pushing his luck but focuses on his greater goal of slaying the Great Satan known as money that he's convinced inhabits the Ninth Circle of his marital inferno. Wren has long denied this charge, stating for the record, whatever record that may be, that what she can't deal with is Bruce being trapped in a self-imposed existential funk.

And also, for the record, he never believed her. About the money thing, that is. And he doesn't understand why being a dedicated stay-at-home father is not enough in itself. Castrating the rest of one's lifestyle, personality, and desires is not sufficient. He also has to be happy? Like smiling and making small talk with strangers at PTA meetings kind of happy? Fuck that.

He grabs his cane, gets out of the car, and walks with purpose in his sport sandals over to the driver's-side window of the white Cadillac. He is going to be more Bruce. The most Bruce anyone can be.

Mel sits inside the car wearing a plush white sweat suit and a yellow-gold crucifix necklace. He has gained a few pounds, but his hair still looks bulletproof, with a nice coat of black dye. He lowers the window a few inches and puts out his cigarette in the ashtray without looking up at Bruce. "I called your cell like five times. I was about to bounce."

"It's perfect." Bruce assesses the old restaurant, appreciating all that nice stonework, right up to a chiseled square-and-compasses design with the big letter G.

"It's a teardown."

"Not for me, Mel."

"Don't call me that. Nobody calls me that."

"Nice to see you too."

"My name is Melchor. Not Mel."

"You've been Mel your whole life."

"I've been Melchor, the same crazy-ass Pinoy, my whole life, bro. Melchor's what my mother . . ." He takes a moment to cross himself and peer skyward. "That's what she named her only son. I dumbed down my name in elementary school to make things easier for you white boys. But you know what? If I had to learn that Peggy is short for Margaret or how to spell Aaron or Sean, you can say fucking Melchor. Two syllables and it sounds just like it's written. Saddest part is that it isn't even originally Filipino. You can say it, if you make a tiny effort outside of your comfort zone, you fat Viking fuck. And what's that on your face? A soul patch? Since when you been playing jazz trumpet?"

"Look at you all grown up and fancy these days. To me, you're still the short kid trying to fool the girls with your fluffy grandma perm." Bruce pulls an envelope from his jacket and passes it to Melchor through the open window. "You staying out of trouble, dude?"

"Every day I don't do cocaine is a blessing from God, my brother."

"Always told you that shit was poison. How long's it been?"
Bruce thinks better of his original plan that they smoke a quick
bowl together.

"Seven years sober, thank God. Just collecting rents for my
family and betting on the ponies. A little fishing on the weekends
when I can squeeze it in."

Melchor exhibits the relatively relaxed air of someone who op-
erates in an extended family subeconomy that takes care of its own.
He'd inherited a chunk of change in his early twenties from his
grandfather's auto detailing business and went on to lose it all on
blow, poker, and vanity investments in a Texas barbeque restaurant
and a stake in a used-luxury-car dealership. Fortunately, Melchor's
aunts and uncles never quite let him hit bottom.

Melchor weighs the envelope in his hand. "You know my mom
always taught me good manners, and I hate to be rude . . . but I'm
gonna have to count this in front of you."

"It's half of the first month. More like a quarter. Or fifth. Look:
consider it a down payment. I'll get you the rest." Bruce holds his
breath and tightens his sphincter as he waits for his old friend's
response.

"Get the fuck outta here, dude. I should've known you were
gonna pull some bullshit."

"The place is just sitting here collecting rats and spiders." He
waves toward the restaurant and tries to smile. "C'mon. You know
I'm good for it."

"No, I know you're not good for it. You remind me of my Uncle
Arnulfo. Remember what happened to him?"

"I still don't like to think about that. Listen, I had to invest the
rest of my budget in my master plan. To make this whole thing
work. Lots of parts. Moving parts. I've made my own sacrifices too.
You should see the place I'm living in off the side of the freeway."

"Your master plan..." Melchor shakes his head and tries to hand the envelope back to Bruce. "I know we have some history, but..."

"We got a lot more than 'some history,' Mel...chor." Bruce taps his cane on the ground. "I'm ready to keep layering on specifics until you do the right thing."

"I know the story. But it was divine intervention that, at the very moment the cops showed up, I stepped away to piss behind the dumpster."

"They kicked me in the back and ribs, literally, until they got bored. And you drove home with a trunk full of weed and slept in your own bed that night. You remember that part of the story?"

"God wanted me to urinate at that very moment. All part of His grand design."

"Look, man. I never blamed you. In fact, I was happy for you. But fair is fair."

Bruce can barely wrap his head around the fact that, now, more than a decade later, these two men exist in an alternate dimension where the state's Liquor Control Board is holding a lottery to allocate recreational marijuana retail licenses to a handful of lucky winners. It won't be easy to prevail, but the biggest hurdle is finding an elusive qualified location within the city limits that doesn't run afoul of distance standards from any restricted entities.

"If anybody is going to sell legal weed around here, it's gonna be Loose Bruce and Mel—I mean, you," Bruce tries. "You know we can't let it be some Eastside suburban trust-fund twats."

"My aunt wants to sell this lot to a developer to build apartments above one of them toasted sandwich chains or those spots with like fifty frozen yogurt pumps and all the crushed Oreos and colorful sprinkles."

"When I win the retail lottery, you can double the rent. Triple it. I'm gonna remodel the place, everything. I told you. I got a plan.

Foolproof. Shit's gonna take off like a supersonic jet. Check the name. You ready for it? . . . SuperChronics."

Melchor nods to Bruce's green '96 Sonics hat. "Bring 'em back. I mean . . . Oklahoma fucking City Thunder? Does Oklahoma even have a city? We drafted Durant and now he's MVP, putting up thirty-two a game? You seen these chumps cheering on TV? Waving their fake-ass Thunder signs. How can they steal our city's history, slap a new name on it, and dance around all goofy and shit pretending like nothing happened?"

"Can't let the motherfuckers win, right? I'm telling you: Super-Chronics. In our own way, we're gonna unite the past with the present to become the intergalactic weed lords of the future. Me and you. Reclaim what's rightfully ours."

Melchor lights another cigarette and waves the ash in the general direction of Bruce's cane. "I'll talk to my aunt. That's the best I can do."

"Thank you, dude. Thank you. I promise you won't regret this."

"Weird."

"What?" Bruce asks.

"I feel like I've heard you say that before."

"Yeah, and who ended up regretting it?"

Melchor rolls up the window, waves the envelope at Bruce, and shouts through the glass, "I'm taking this straight to the track. No refunds. No matter what my aunt says."

Bruce places his palms together, dedicates an ersatz prayer to his old friend in his departing white steed, and then jogs back, or as close as he can come to jogging, to the Westy.

"Whatcha smiling about, Pops?" Sierra considers his profile through the rearview mirror.

"You'll see, Toots. Soon enough." He hadn't been sure that Mel would go for the partial payment. Yes, he'd hoped for it, but they hadn't seen each other in person for ages. A warm feeling of postorgasmic afterglow pulses through his veins as he allows himself to see the realistic contours of a path by which he could stabilize his finances, if not become incredibly wealthy, and simultaneously reconnect with his true self—on his own terms. This could fix, will fix, everything for Bruce. For Sierra. He feels something forgotten and unfamiliar: a sense of genuine excitement radiating its way out to the tips of his fingers, toes, nose, and eyelashes. Most importantly, this will help him win back Wren. It could even allow her to take her foot off the gas at work. Quit, if she pleases.

As he gets closer to their ... her house, Bruce decides that he should tell Wren about his victory in this pivotal battle that will help him win the greater war of financial success and self-actualization: his struggle to reintegrate Loose Bruce into his present Mr. Bruce Jorgensen reality. He'll explain it all to her right now, when he drops off Sierra. Let his grand future be known. Give Wren something to pen into the *Get Back Together & Live Happily Ever After* column of her *Divorce?* ledger.

Bruce rounds the corner and pulls up in front of his old place. Wren paces on the front porch, phone to her ear.

As he parks, she pockets her phone and stares at him, tapping the back of her left wrist with increasing intensity.

"I'm sorry," he mouths to her and then raps the top of the dashboard with his knuckles. "The engine?"

He recognizes her expression. Too well.

After a swift reassessment of the emotional situation on the ground, he opts to bid farewell to Sierra inside the van. He'll update Wren about his impending personal and professional breakthrough at a more advantageous time.

Bruce gives his daughter a kiss on the cheek, confiscates her near-empty bag of gummy garbage, and waves a hesitant goodbye to Wren. His wife dismisses him with a shake of her head and marches Sierra toward the front door.

THREE   *1971*

Ruth spins in her bed. Her feet flying up past her head. Folding herself in half, coming back around. Rag-dolling in circles. She's not used to drinking this much. Not used to drinking anything, really. All that rum and pineapple juice and the whipped cream and maraschino cherry and whatever else they put in that tall, ridged soda-shop glass giving it the innocent look of an ice cream float. She barely knew it had alcohol except for the metallic aftertaste.

In the moments between spins, she slows down just enough to be hit with a combination punch of regrets. Regret that she disobeyed her mother, Masako, who tolerates no insubordination. Regret that she lied to her. Or nearly lied, anyhow. Which she had never done before. Regret that she kept her mom up late worrying, anxiously rosining and re-rosining all her violin bows at the living room table.

When Ruth got home, her mother yelled at her or as close as she ever came to yelling—her tone more upsetting than her actual volume—and sent her to her room. And Ruth went. Without an argument. Not that it meant much to send an adult to their room at almost midnight on a weeknight.

"Yes, Mom. I'm sorry," she'd said upon entering the house, watching the floor. Masako craned her neck to see Larry sitting atop a beat-up motorcycle in the middle of the wet street. He didn't have the wherewithal to wear a jacket, let alone a helmet. A lit cigarette dangled from below his wispy mustache primarily grouped in the corners of his top lip. He tried to wave hello to Masako, but she slammed the front door and turned to her daughter. "What did you call me?"

"Yes, *Okasan*." Ruth opted for the more formal term. They only speak English with each other. How could they not? Ruth was born and raised here. She understands Japanese reasonably well and can conjure some fifty to a hundred words in incomplete sentences but can't conjugate a single verb. Her American-born father didn't really speak Japanese either, even though his parents were from Wakayama Prefecture. Yet Masako becomes all about traditional values when she's upset. Fumes about how American children have no standards. No morals. No structure. And it's not worth reminding Masako, or Macy as she is known around town, that she too was born here. And that Masako even addressed her own mother as "Mom."

Sure, it had been a mistake to get a ride home with Larry, to accept that long hug from him when Ruth could feel his warm breath on her neck. When she started to think he might try to try to kiss her. Or, even worse, if he was getting a, you know. And, worse than that, she had hoped for all of that to happen. Even the last part.

This thing, whatever it is or could be with Larry, it won't go anywhere. Can't go anywhere. She shouldn't have given him her home number. What had she been thinking? She will apologize again to her mother in the morning, plead for forgiveness, and won't answer Larry's phone call—if he ever even calls her, that is.

Now she tells herself that she's just drunk, but no matter how hard she tries, she can't ignore a second emotion: that she also feels bad about feeling bad for disobeying her mother. For considering it disobeying at all. Ruth is twenty-five, after all, and a few months away from her master's degree in education at the university. She is over this arrested adolescence where her mother has near-total control of who she is and what she does.

When she got to her room, she kicked off her shoes but didn't remove any of her street clothes before lying down atop the neatly made bed. That's a major infraction in her household. Not to mention the excessive drinking. Going out on a weeknight, period. Setting foot in a bar of all places and, especially, getting a ride home on a motorcycle with an unknown white guy.

Is Larry white? Masako called him *aitsu*. "What are you doing out with *aitsu*?" Ruth was unclear on the full meaning but took it to be rather harsh and dehumanizing, if not a little bit racist—which she wouldn't put past her mom. She had only heard Masako use the word once before, with a Native American panhandler at the Greyhound station. Upon reconsidering that the term was below her, Masako corrected to the cold yet relatively classier negative *ano hito*.

Regardless, first thing in the morning, she will apologize to her mother again. To reassure Masako that all their plans are still on track. That nothing happened with Larry. And nothing will, whether Ruth wants it to or not, which is ultimately beside the point.

There is a thump on the glass of her second-floor bedroom window, like a sparrow flew into one of the long, aluminum-trimmed, sliding midcentury panes along her wall. It's happened before to the poor birds but never in the middle of the night. She considers looking out the window to see what it was, but that would require raising her head, and that's too nauseating of a proposition at the moment.

There has never been any question about Ruth's next steps. She will become a music teacher just like her mom. Ruth has only ever been an extension of Masako and the family, not an individual with her own dreams and goals and path to follow. And it's not fair. Her mother had her own path as one of the first—if not the first—*nisei* teachers in the city. And as the woman who essentially built Stevenson's reputation as a music powerhouse.

And that was all Masako needed and desired. She was happy to have a steady toehold in American society, to make an impact through the school and prove herself as a person of merit, but she didn't care to go further. She didn't want to become too much like them. Whites may control the levers of power in the United States, but Masako still recognized them as boorish, self-promoting, and generally unhygienic people. And she wants her daughter to succeed in a prescribed role in American society but never fully give herself to it. Ruth could follow in Masako's footsteps right out to the preapproved limit, but that was it.

Although it has never been openly discussed, Ruth knows that her mother is waiting for her to transition into the job so that she can eventually retire. Masako will hold on like a dying Supreme Court justice, waiting for the right opportunity to be substituted by her handpicked successor. Ruth even student-taught under Masako, which was atypical within the school district and likely went against some bylaw about nepotism. But it is what Masako desired. And nobody was going to cross her, especially not within her fiefdom at Stevenson Elementary.

It's not like Ruth is even particularly good at any musical instrument. Music has always been a central part of her life, Masako made sure of that, but in high school she gave up on being exceptional at anything after rotating through flute, oboe, and most devastatingly, the violin.

She remembers, some years back, performing a snippet of Brahms's Violin Concerto in D major in the living room. The recital was met with a long, dragging silence from her mother, who doubled as her live-in tutor. Masako looked as if she wanted to say something but kept her lips drawn tight. Her focus aimed just above Ruth's head.

This home performance was the culmination of years of study

and months of specific practice. Rather than ask how it was, Ruth got straight to apologizing. "Sorry?"

Masako's lips started to move two or three times before she committed to words. "No, I should be sorry," she said and went to her bedroom for the night.

After that, Ruth dabbled with instruments but focused on music education rather than trying to become a musician herself. She went back to school for her master's, not because she was or is particularly interested in education either, but she needed to buy more time.

Her mom had meticulous plans for every other aspect of her life too, including marrying a junior version of her father, Sammy Hasegawa, or at least of the man who her mom now imagines Sammy was or would have been or could have been some twenty-five years after his death. And even though Masako's handpicked suitor, Beckham Wong, is a perfectly good prospective husband, he's about as appealing to Ruth as a career as an elementary school music teacher, attending her mom's church, or for that matter, anything else her mother has planned for her without her insight or consent.

Ruth tries to get a handle on her spins and these unruly thoughts, these further betrayals of Masako's Master Blueprint. She reaches for her water glass, but swipes it with her wrist, knocking it to the floor. Fortunately, the clatter doesn't wake Masako or there would be double hell to pay for prying her mom out of bed after her ornate insomniac's bedtime routine—which involves tea, music, mediation, a hot bath, and God knows what else—and has already been stalled out for hours after its fixed 8:30 p.m. deadline.

The water is everywhere. It'll evaporate, Ruth thinks, surprising herself with uncharacteristic nonchalance. She refocuses on the drumbeats pulsing in her head and wants to put on the album. But the record player is in the living room, so that's a nonstarter regardless of the hour. Ruth can play her music only when Masako is at work, church, or the Food King. Her three reasons for ever leaving the house.

The first and only concert Ruth had ever attended was James Brown at the Spectrum in Philly a bit over one month ago. She had to travel all the way across the country, get thousands of miles from her mom, to make it happen. It was during a trip with her master's cohort to go to a conference about education and race, see the Liberty Bell, and all that tourist business—with chaperones, of course.

The show was unlike anything Ruth had ever experienced. All the people, people of all backgrounds, dancing. Sweating. Having fun. It completely changed the way she understood music. The way she felt music. In her marrow. She couldn't even tell her mom because she would dismiss it outright as "not real music." She could barely tell her mom about the conference itself. Even considering Masako's groundbreaking role as a public school teacher, she thought it ridiculous to observe any connection between race and access to education, scorning it as Americans complaining too much and always trying to find new ways to do things worse.

Upon her return to home, Ruth went to a record store near campus during lunch one day and bought three LPs. The rail-thin record store guy with the dirty glasses and the hooded sweatshirt that smelled like an ashtray recommended a few other albums while finding inventive ways to tell her about all the recent concerts he attended, even though she hadn't asked.

Now the three LPs live in the back of her closet, under two folded blankets. Even when her mom is out of the house, Ruth rarely works up the nerve to listen to the music and always worries that Masako will burst through the front door at any moment, scolding her for becoming a *sansei* degenerate. But Ruth does spend a lot of late nights looking at, if not studying, the album covers. She has a new James Brown album; *Led Zeppelin IV*, which appears to have occult elements; and the *Sticky Fingers* album with a full view of Mick Jagger's denim-swaddled penis, a word she can barely even say in her own head.

Ruth would never deny that Masako loves music. Just not in a fun way. It is not a joyful love. It is a demanding love based on technical prowess. She's never once seen her mom dance. Or listen to popular music. She imagines her mom has heard of the Beatles and Elvis and maybe even the Rolling Stones, but she's never once talked about a specific musician who has lived in the last century. To her, music is the pursuit of divine perfection.

When Ruth got home with Larry, she wanted to scream at Masako. She can admit that now. Scream that she's an adult. That not once in all those years has she disobeyed her, wronged her, deceived her. Nothing. Not once. She has every right to go out to have drinks and eat cheeseburgers at the Dirty Bird with her grad school classmates as they near the end of the term.

And Ruth is even disappointed with herself for feeling like just one more woman of unknown and possibly unlimited talents becoming a teacher, nurse, or secretary, well, because that's what women do. She knows the job is important. Teaching and nursing are noble professions, although she doesn't have much of an opinion about secretarial work. And she knows there are expectations for her to be the next Masako Hasegawa, public school stalwart delivering daily excellence into unrelenting juvenile mediocrity.

But it all feels a bit underwhelming. Maybe she would have liked to be a lawyer for the ACLU. Did anyone ever ask her that? Well, she wouldn't, but nobody asked her. Or play in a band if music had been a more expressive and less exacting undertaking in her life. She'd like to play drums, perhaps. How about that? She could get behind that. Some way that her music could be seen and enjoyed by other people, not just a bunch of dumb kids and their dumber Stevenson parents. She'd never say that out loud. Just like she'd never admit out loud or even to herself that she'd like to go over to her closet and look at that *Sticky Fingers* album cover right now. Press it against her cheek.

Something else hits the window. Bigger this time. Like a seagull or small owl. Ruth tries to look. As she sits up, hot bile rises in her throat, and she has to lie back down to avoid a torrential vomitous disaster.

Even though Ruth has never voiced her career and other reservations to her mother, she is pretty sure Masako knows they're there. Her mom has always worried about her. That she is one step away from an inexorable slide. Something that could be triggered by a solitary misstep or momentary lapse in judgment. Maybe that is Masako's fundamental insecurity of being the daughter of penniless immigrants. Of working as a child laborer in a strawberry field during the Great Depression, whose only escape and joy was practicing music under the relentless tutelage of her own mother. Maybe it is the lingering trauma of getting married and starting to build her own life only to have it all ripped away when they were sent to the idyllic-sounding Camp Harmony and then on to a veritable concentration camp in rural Idaho, with twenty-four hours' notice and a single suitcase per person . . . losing their home, their dog, the family farms. And then, for good measure, losing her husband to an untimely accident. Ruth knows that few people would have the strength to start from scratch as a pregnant widow after the war.

Masako wants Ruth to be proper, respectable, and diligent. She wants Ruth to stay close to home and have a quiet, organized life like her own. She has also voiced interest in Ruth and Beckham buying the house, moving in, and taking care of her. And voicing interest is as good as being a done deal in this household, regardless of the fact that Ruth has met Beckham only once or twice in passing at her mom's church.

Ruth feels guilty again for exploring her doubts. There is no doubt that life has been hard for Masako. And Ruth's mom sacrificed everything for her. Of course, she will take care of her. Of course, she will do whatever must be done.

And after all of Masako's searching and striving to make arrangements with Beckham and his family, she is more than slightly upset to see her daughter come home drunk with Larry, that same loser Ruth got into trouble with that one time when she was an eighth grader at Stevenson and he called the house looking to talk to her like she was some sort of common louche girl.

Masako knows Larry didn't go to college. Knows that the most Japanese thing about him is his crappy old motorcycle. Even worse, he might be part Southeast Asian. He did mention that he has a talent for gardening. That it ran in his family. Ruth's mom might kind of like that.

Beckham, on the other hand, is almost done with dentistry school at the university. There's the small issue that his father was Chinese, but that's offset by the fact that his mother was Japanese, and he grew up in the care of his *nisei* aunt, an important benefactor of Masako's church. He's a near-perfect future husband, as Masako has assured Ruth—so long as they don't think too much about the half-Chinese issue or his Anglophile first name. Masako is all in. And Ruth has nothing against him. But he's also exactly what is expected of her.

She notes the distance to the wastepaper basket on the other side of the room. Just in case. It's 1971, and she is still a virgin. Who is a twenty-five-year-old virgin in 1971? Ruth is. Maybe she'd marry Beckham, but what if she had wanted to join the Peace Corps first? Or protest the Vietnam War. Is that an option for a dentist's wife?

All through 1968 and 1969, she lived at home and did homework and kept out of trouble. She would still like to try smoking a marijuana cigarette, at least once.

She slowly raises her head enough to see what appears to be a pine cone on the outside windowsill. Ruth manages to get to her knees atop the bed and peer out into the yard but can't see anyone or anything out there and then lowers herself back down carefully enough to avoid any mishaps.

She and Larry knew each other from way back. From Stevenson, when the school went all the way up through eighth grade. They almost held hands, or kind of brushed the backs of their hands against each other, once in the library when they were thirteen or fourteen. He tried to call her at home and Masako shut it all down. Scared off Larry. Embarrassed and grounded Ruth and went as far as asking some of the other teachers to keep tabs on her at school. That was the closest Ruth came to having a boyfriend her whole life. And she doesn't remember Larry during high school and isn't even sure they went to the same one. She has some vague, perhaps fictive, images of him smoking in the parking lot, maybe freshman year, and hanging out in front of the shop class. But he hadn't really crossed her mind in years, until tonight.

And there he was, wearing a black Jimi Hendrix T-shirt at the Dirty Bird's bar. He told her that he was mourning the death of the world's greatest musician. Yes, there was potential. And there was and is desire if she allows herself to feel such a thing. Is it so wrong that she wants to explore this one moment of adventure before she goes down the lane that's been paved for her, has kids, and then eventually dies? Just to see? To know for sure? How can you know that you are a Christian if all you have ever known is Christianity? Or know that you only like vanilla ice cream if the only ice cream you've ever eaten is vanilla?

And Masako has surely predetermined her thoughts about

Larry. But she is wrong. He has a job working for America's Pre-eminent Aerospace Company. An important job. And he is interested in Ruth because of Ruth. Not because someone else organized it.

You know what? She is going to go on a date with Larry. Even if it's just once. It's her life. Ruth doesn't want to sneak around or disrespect her mother any more than she already has. But she has every right to go out with a guy she might like and to explore that feeling. She will bring it up casually. Tomorrow. And her mom will have to be understanding and supportive. Yes, she promises herself. She will do it. First thing. Or second thing, right after she apologizes again.

Then she hears another thump. But this is not on her window. Shoot. Something must have hit her mom's window, one room over.

She jumps back up to her window and sees Larry, or someone who looks a heck of a lot like him even though there is only a splash of streetlight on his face, outside near the big rock between their house and the school, as he pitches another pine cone right at her mom's window. She wants to scream for him to stop but catches herself before the sound escapes her throat and makes things worse.

She loses sight of him for a moment as he wanders into the dark trees at the perimeter of the yard. Suddenly, he is running toward the house with his arm back, ready to deliver an overhand strike to the glass just a few feet from her sleeping mother. Ruth scrambles to open her window and signal for him to stop, but as she fumbles with the lock, she realizes that she is going to vomit.

The pine cone nails her mom's window, responding with a deep concussion. Possibly cracking the glass.

Ruth retches right into her hand and then, as she sprints across her room, she does it again, into the wastepaper basket, so tidy and clean that she doesn't even have wastepaper in it. She can taste the pineapple's acid coming back up. And is that blood or maraschino?

Through the gap below her bedroom door, she sees the hallway light flip on. She hears her mother's racing footsteps between her own dry heaves.

"Ruth," Masako yells, marching toward her room. "Ruth Hasegawa? What is the meaning of this?"

FOUR   *1971*

Prime rib. Saturday, while it lasts. Larry holds his index finger over the text on the plasticized menu. While it lasts, he repeats to himself.

"You waiting for someone, hon?" the red-faced waitress asks him, a thin stripe of sweat rolling down from her temple.

"Yes. Yeah. Uh huh." He looks at his watch and says in his most forced, most proper diction, "Just my friend. Ruth. She's only a minute or two late, but I'm sure she'll be here any second."

"Alright then. Just let me know." The waitress trots on to the next table.

Larry checks the prime rib details again. He even came by the other night and studied the menu. It was just like this one but taped up in the front window. He stood outside the Broiler, smoked two cigarettes, tried to figure out the weird compasses and letter G masonry at the roofline, crushed the butts under his boots, and rode his motorcycle home.

He really hopes that the menu in the window and the menu he has now are the same. He made an assumption. But he could be wrong. He checks again. Prime rib. Saturday. Prime rib. That's the thing right there. While it lasts. That's what he invited Ruth for. Saturday. He checks his watch again. She's now more than five minutes late. Six, in fact.

It's not like he is always the most on-time person. "Being

punctual . . . not your greatest strength," as his manager, Gerry, says at work. But this is a special occasion. A first date. Or first formal date. The first formal date of his life at twenty-six, not that she knows that. It's not like he'd come right out and say that to her. She wouldn't laugh in his face. She is too classy for that. The laughing part. But she might realize that he is nothing. Nobody. Has nothing. No manners. No education. No history. He's never even met his own father. Larry wrote him, perhaps, a hundred letters over the years, and his dad didn't bother to respond. Not once. Larry's not even sure if he had his father's right address, or name, for that matter.

In fact, Larry considers his whole life to have been unexceptional to the point of near invisibility. A nonevent. He looks at himself in the reflection in the plasticized menu and sees most other interchangeable guys who might paint your fence or rotate your tires. He has medium-brown hair, an attempt at a mustache, a medium build, and no other distinguishing features beyond a bit of acne that's persisted past his teenage years.

He isn't obviously Duwamish. Every once in a while, someone asks where he comes from, which he takes as a roundabout expression of doubt about him being white. He gives them the same puzzling answer of, "My family has been here since before this city was a city." But most people don't go out of their way to talk to him in the first place.

He hasn't stuck with any jobs or hobbies for long and hasn't made many lasting friendships or had any great romances. It's not that he doesn't want to share experiences and to engage with other people, but he lacks confidence and spends most of his time in his own head.

But he's leaving that person behind. Starting today. Right now.

Eight minutes. He's tempted to check with the waitress to be sure there's prime rib left. That's why he picked the Broiler for dinner in the first place. Prime rib is the nicest dinner he knows of.

And the Broiler is the nicest restaurant he knows of, not that he knows of any other restaurants that serve dinner. Well, the Peking Castle. But the rest are just burgers and fries. And fish and chips, of course. To be fair, he hasn't been to a real restaurant for dinner since he was a little kid.

He has no idea what people do on real dates either. The closest he'd come to a date before is sneaking into the movies with Jo, his next-door neighbor's blond niece. He had four cans of Rainier jammed into his jeans pockets and another two in her purse. And she'd taken his virginity behind the neighbor's backyard toolshed where they kept the lawn mower. They'd had sex a few other times when she came to visit, meaning stayed with her aunt and uncle for a few months when her dad was off fishing in Alaska, sometimes for months on end.

There had been a couple of girls while he was in the Navy, but dates weren't really part of that whole equation. Since then, there were a few ladies here and there. But dating consisted of lucky timing and outlasting everyone else at the bar. She, no matter who she was, would inevitably leave before falling asleep, even though he often found himself wanting more.

Ten minutes late. He should have picked Ruth up at her house. He has a motorcycle. She doesn't drive. It only makes sense. He offered, but she said no thank you. Her mom is not happy about him dropping her off late the other night after they ran into each other at the Dirty Bird.

She even brought up how they once held hands at lunch or in the library or somewhere. He remembered exactly where it was, in Mrs. Stone's fourth-period English class. Back-left corner of the room. It was one of the most important and inspired moments of his entire youth. But he pretended to also be vague on the details, so as to not scare her off.

They got older, and lines around class, family, and potential became clearer. They never spoke in high school. Not once. To be honest, he figured she'd never noticed him in high school. Few did. Or that she was too smart or sophisticated to want anything to do with a kid like him. And she said the same thing: that she didn't think anyone remembered her from high school. He bought her some fancy drink she wanted with pineapple juice in it. She put it down like a champ.

He wonders if her mom thinks he's trash. Ruth assured him that she doesn't think that, but he's not sure if she's just being polite. That's a good word for her. Polite. Even Gerry at work, with his hairy neck moles, told Larry he eats like he was raised in a barn and that it's hard to look at him during lunch. He doesn't know how to do things or why to do things.

The personnel manager at work, Larry forgets his name, called him into his wood-paneled office with the big windows once and gave him a lecture about "giving people space" and "comfort zones" and "appropriate interactions" after he'd tried to ask the dishwasher girl in the cafeteria on a date for the second time. How was he supposed to know she was deaf? He just thought she was shy. And, if she's deaf, how did she even report him? He's still convinced that it was the lumpy old Scandinavian cafeteria boss lady who had it out for him.

But he knows that the "space" thing is hard for him. How does he go from running into Ruth at a bar, speaking to her for the first time since eighth grade, to giving her a ride home and then blowing it by going and throwing pine cones at her window? What did he expect? That she was going to spontaneously come outside and have sex with him behind a backyard toolshed? No, that's not even what he wanted. To elope? For her to save him in some broad and unspecified manner. From whom? Most likely himself. From ordinariness. From loneliness. From nothingness.

Twelve minutes. He rolls down his shirtsleeves to cover the

seagull tattoos on his forearms. An old attempt to give himself some distinguishing marks. The physical representation of just another bad decision. But what else do you do when you live on a naval air station with a bunch of other young dumb men, spending your days following orders, tightening nuts and bolts, masturbating until you ejaculate air, and wondering when you're going to ship off to Vietnam.

He half stands to tuck in his shirt again. He is not going to give up like usual. OK, he messed up with the pine cones. He called her the next day, apologized, and invited her out for a real date. One he researched and prepared for. He looked at the prices on the menu and set aside the right amount of cash for the prime rib. Two prime ribs. Maybe the Captain's Platter for good measure too, just to show her he was serious. Women really like all that seafood stuff. And all of it deep-fried, who can resist? Add a salad too, with that nice iceberg lettuce. They love that. At least, that's what Gerry told him. Thirteen minutes.

He'd thought that joining the Navy and maybe even going to Vietnam would give his life some significance. That and the fact that he was able to get out of multiple grocery shoplifting charges by enlisting. He wasn't proud of the legal drama and didn't do it for sport like some of the other kids in high school who stole beer and candy and baseball cards. People don't steal uncooked hot dogs, dry spaghetti, or bricks of cheddar cheese for kicks.

Anyway, the main point was that enlisting would show others he could do something big. Make a real commitment. But again, he came up short. His first big step toward building confidence, what allowed him to ask Ruth on a date, is that now he has a job. A union job. A real job. A career. A machinist at America's Preeminent Aerospace Company. Headquartered right here in town. And he is on his way to financial independence, homeownership, maybe with a small vegetable garden, and so much more.

Fourteen minutes. He mulls over the menu, bouncing his knee under the table, folding and refolding his secondhand, oversize sport coat next to him on the plush red booth seat.

Choice of soup or salad and potato.

He knows tonight will be more than he has ever spent on dinner. But it's a special occasion. He did some budget estimates. Added it all up. Went to the bank to make sure he had enough cash in his wallet. He didn't want to mess up a big night by having to ask her if she could chip in. No, from now on, he thinks things through. That's what smart people do. Established people. Like the engineers at work.

Prime rib with soup. No, soup would be ugly to eat in front of her. Too much chance for slurping. Or spilling. Or having something stick around in his mustache while he tells her all about his job and future plans. And the homeownership thing. His mom has barely been making rent her whole life. Women like guys who own houses or will own one someday.

He feels almost decadent eating out at a restaurant like this. Most days, he eats at home with Mom. When the seasons line up, they get much of their food from their own small backyard. He's always had a green thumb. Especially for potatoes and tomatoes. Otherwise, his mom makes toast, scrambled eggs, hot dogs, and spaghetti with butter and sometimes some melted cheese. Rice with ketchup. Not all at the same time. TV dinners on Fridays. And burgers on Saturdays. Cooked on the frying pan and served on toast, like he likes them.

The waitress didn't bring bread to the table. He's going to ask for bread. Maybe hunger is fueling his nervousness. He's sure Ruth has a good reason for being late. Even if she doesn't seem like the kind of person who'd be late. Not at all, but he doesn't want to dwell on that. Not yet. He just needs to eat.

On an additional perusal of the back page of the menu, including

payment options, he reads that rolls are served upon request. He is
going to ask. No, he's going to play it cool. He needs a cigarette. No,
he's going to sit tight. He doesn't know if she smokes. She seems
like someone who doesn't smoke. Doesn't drink coffee. He was surprised when he ran into her drinking alcohol at the Dirty Bird last
week. Either way, he's heard that women, even some men although
he doesn't know any guys who fit that bill, don't like smoke when
they are eating. He wouldn't make that mistake. Not with Ruth.

He half stands and re-tucks his shirt. Larry thought about a tie.
But he didn't want to come on too strong. Also, he doesn't know
how to tie a tie. Also, he doesn't own a tie. But, yeah, after the whole
pine cones thing he needs to keep relaxed. Not overwhelm her with
"let's live happily ever after" appeals, although, he must admit, they
are pinballing about his brain.

He rereads the menu, fixating on the Captain's Platter. It in-
cludes cod fillets, prawns, and scallops. It also comes with coleslaw
and a choice of soup, salad, or potato. That sounds like they might
be ordering too much with the prime rib and all. But she can take
any leftovers home in a doggie bag. Share with her mom. Maybe
that will help him to win back over her mom. He could even send
some prime rib home. Let her know that he's a guy who will spare
no expense. Perhaps she'd prefer some scallops. He's never had
them before, but he thinks they're some kind of fancy clams. And
clams aren't intimidating. Shit, he and his mom used to dig them in
the tideflats outside of town. They might've been a bit too close to
heavy manufacturing, but you can justify a lot of things when you
are hungry.

At the Dirty Bird, he told Ruth he worked for America's Preeminent Aerospace Company . . . and savored her glowing response.
Most of the city works there. Anyone who is anyone, anyhow. But
he didn't have as much time as he would have liked to explain all
about his work on the second most important national aerospace

project this side of the Apollo mission: the Supersonic Transport. The hyper-speed future of air travel and the endeavor that is guaranteed to give global significance to this whole city and to one Larry Dugdale. Ruth should know every detail. She will know every detail. Soon after she arrives. He will work it into his pre-rehearsed introduction.

Larry was hired almost two years back. The Aerospace Company was growing by leaps and bounds and they were taking anyone with a pulse; even better if that person had a touch of experience. He told them about his work at the naval air station, maintaining actuators and whatnot. The timing was right because they offered him the job before anyone had time to figure out that he earned himself a dishonorable discharge from the Navy and never went to Vietnam.

But that's all beside the point. It was and still is boom time, and Larry Dugdale is going to be at the center of it. Jet City, U.S.A. It's a big moment. He's spent most of his short adult life working on planes, but he'd never once flown in one. Nobody knew that at work. He's terrified of flying, not that he'd ever had the option, but that's between Larry and himself. But he is working on the company's crown jewel . . . the very first made-in-the-U.S.A. Mach-speed jet that will dominate the skies of the twenty-first century. The Soviets are working on one. The Europeans have the Concorde. And with Larry's support, America will be not only next, but America will be the best. Again. And his company will become the World's Pre-eminent Aerospace Company.

This supersonic jet will fly at Mach 2.6, or nearly three times the speed of sound. Faster than the Concorde and with twice as many passengers. The city is so inspired that it named its first professional sports franchise, a basketball team, after this jet that still has yet to be built. Larry is in on the ground floor. He is going to be somebody and play his part in something huge and make sure that Ruth knows all about it.

It's not an overstatement to say that getting the job saved Larry's life. After his untimely exit from the Navy, he'd fallen back in with old neighborhood friends, acquaintances really, who convinced him to drive for three different convenience store robberies. He'd never had to handle a gun or anything. But he also made less than a hundred dollars between the three jobs while facing a very real prospect of taking one in the face from the cops or an angry clerk or spending the rest of his twenties in jail.

Larry refocused on what he knew: actuators. Or, more specifically, fabricating and maintaining pieces for actuators. Before he started on the Supersonic Transport, he worked on old 727 actuators, fixing their tail-door opening mechanism. Now he takes a piece of metal about the size of a bedside lamp and shaves it down to spec, usually to function as a lever bar with two holes in each end to fit into the gears to move an actuator. Then the actuator uses hydraulics to move a mechanism or system like wing flaps, doors, and eventually the nose cone on the Supersonic.

And by doing his bit in making that nose move up and down, he has a chance to take someone like Ruth on a date. To a real restaurant. To be a real part of this city. He thinks of the future. Of what all this could be. Destiny. Him with a real girl. A nice girl. Someone he looks up to and considers himself lucky to be with. Someone he could build something with. A family.

Living with his mom and playing it straight had helped. Over the last couple of years, it had been impossible to find an apartment for rent in town. Hiring numbers were through the roof. The Aerospace Company hooked up some of the new engineers with apartments: East Coasters, a handful of Brits and Canadians, even a guy from India. Larry heard they were paying a full $150 per month for engineers to stay in furnished, one-bedroom apartments downtown.

He was doing OK for someone who had been dishonorably discharged for eating four or five liberty caps he found growing in the mulch flower beds in front of the mess hall and joyriding in a commander's Jeep.

It wasn't Larry's fault that his own building key worked in the ignition of the Jeep. A voice in his head told him while tripping that he needed to take the Jeep out of the Naval air station and drive to an ancient burial site somewhere back in town. There he could commune with some seagulls who knew the history of the land going back to the time of the Changer or some crazy shit. The fact that the key slid into the ignition was destiny. He told himself that if it turned on the Jeep, he must go. It didn't turn over smoothly, but, by forcing it a couple of times, the engine roared to life.

He drove out a back gate and rolled the Jeep into a ditch less than a hundred yards off the base. He couldn't figure how to get it out, so he wandered back onto the base with the conviction that honesty was the best, and only, policy. With his pupils overtaking the whites of his eyes, Larry asked the master-at-arms for a six-pack of Rainier, oranges (preferably not those bullshit ones that are hard to peel and full of seeds), and a menthol, although any tobacco product would do, and explained that he'd only borrowed the Jeep because he was summoned to speak with some seagulls, who may or may not have had some information to share about his ancestors. It took a tow truck, wooden ramp, and four men to extricate the Jeep, which was surprisingly undamaged beyond a bent axle. And Larry is still fairly certain that they messed up the axle with the tow winch.

He was convinced they were going to ship him straight to Saigon. He peaked while handcuffed in the brig, inventing nonsensical faux-Indian chants while mucus-laden tears careened off his chin.

After a hasty psych evaluation that noted "likely schizophrenia," he was still nailed for the gross misconduct of stealing and damaging the Jeep and soon found himself right back with his mom just off Stevenson Way, never again to be an enlisted member of the United States Armed Forces.

Twenty minutes late. Should he try her from the pay phone over by the bathrooms? He sprints from the table to where he can see the pay phone. There's someone using it. He waits and tries again. Still busy. On a third attempt, he finds it free. OK. He makes up his mind to do it. But first he wants to let the waitress know where he's going in case Ruth shows up while he is at the phone.

Larry stands at the edge of his table and waves down the waitress. Before he gets to the phone call logistics, he asks if there's still any prime rib. Just to be sure.

"Prime rib's Saturday," says the rosy-cheeked waitress with an obligatory smile.

"Of course, prime rib. Saturday. As longs as it lasts." He holds up the menu and points to the text, clarifying that he too knows what he's talking about.

Before excusing herself to grab a new round of plates at the kitchen window, she says, "Yeah, well, today's Sunday. Day late and a few dollars short, hon."

FIVE *2014*

Sami drops the bag of groceries while rushing into the house. The brown paper cracks open, ejecting zucchinis and a carton of milk onto the front porch. A cantaloupe bounces down the three front steps, adding a new bruise with each impact.

She curses under her breath. Too much going on at once. Like usual. If only her kids would make a little bit of an effort. Even pretend to participate.

At least Sami didn't drop the envelopes with her prized signatures, which now include the latest addition from Principal Doucette. He had sighed for effect while scrawling out some illegible initials. Made sure to clarify that "none of this name stuff has any impact on the school's future operational status." But he signed it. Probably just to get her out of his office. And now, after Sami's chauffeured a series of tightly scheduled drop-offs and pickups, she's rushing to get dinner underway before her call with Kim, her eminent, and correspondingly elusive, sister-in-law.

Most of the lights are off in the house. A set of sheets and a half a load of whites hang drying on the backs of dining room chairs. Her husband, Percy, went through his big sustainability phase over the last few years. Still seems to be in its thrall. Insisted on going fully solar. Now the amount of power in the house is dependent on the Weather Gods, and in the Pacific Northwest they can be fickle and vengeful deities. She wishes they could afford a backup generator, but they simply don't have the money for it after their layout for the panels and installation. Also, Percy is quick to remind her that generators run on fossil fuel, which would make the whole endeavor one step forward and three steps back.

Once in the kitchen, she inspects the maimed groceries in the afternoon light from the window. With a chef's knife, she surgically removes the soft spots from the zucchinis and dices the cantaloupe into ever-smaller pieces as she knows that, otherwise, her kids will use the imperfections as an excuse to not eat any fresh fruits or vegetables. Her youngest has recently claimed to be vegetarian, but Sami is battling to make sure she does not subsist on a diet of only candy, carbs, and dairy fats.

To make matters trickier, one of Sami's sons is a vegan, her other daughter is affectedly blasé about "eating whatever, so long as it's all in moderation," and since getting dumped by his first girlfriend, her eldest son has become insecure about his boyish slenderness and has set about mass consuming red meat, raw eggs, whey protein powders, and a variety of sketchy supplements with names like Mega Beast Gainer in neon font–emblazoned jeroboam pill bottles which he buys off the internet and which she frets will lead to future maladies.

It's important to Sami that the kids eat some sort of clean protein and a real, green vegetable every night. No "organic" chicken nuggets or prepackaged baby carrots masquerading as nutrition. Getting a healthy dinner for six on the table every night, day in, day out, is no small undertaking. But it must be done.

She thought it was tough before to have four young kids at home with an endless rotation of needs and diapers and feedings. Then teaching them to read and tie their shoes and basic manners. But at least in retrospect, there was something intimate and fulfilling about all of that. Now she's an unpaid taxi driver who runs a free boardinghouse: room, three square meals per day, laundry, and Wi-Fi... when there's sufficient electricity. Nobody ever told her that this would become the job description of "mother." At least Macy is young enough to still give her a good hug, here and there, between shouting "I hate you" as a more forceful euphemism for "I'm frustrated."

As a matter of fact, Macy is still sitting in the car having a temper tantrum because her mother cut her off from screen time tonight until she finishes all homework, as per her conversation with Macy's teacher about lack of follow-through with her work on fractions and long subtraction. Sami knows she should have left the softball backpack in the car for Macy to bring in and learn some lessons about independence and perseverance. But she also knows Macy would leave the bag in the car, which would be OK, except for the fact that it has a water bottle in it that's going to end up all mildewed and scummy inside.

Like clockwork, Percy comes through the front door in his cycling gear, helmet atop his head with a small, dentist-looking mirror attached to its side and holding his commuter roll-top bag. His clip-in cycling shoes click and scrape each of his steps through the midcentury flagstone entry.

She holds up her phone and says to her husband, "I'm about to have an important call—can you please get Macy from the car?" But Macy materializes right behind him. They're having an apparently hilarious conversation planning family game night for after dinner. Sami does her best to not resent the sincerity of his laugh. She reminds herself to try to appreciate Percy's easy rapport with the kids, but frequently she can't, as she's the parent locked in an infinity war with all four of them to eat their meals, brush their teeth, put on clean clothes, get places on time, go to bed, and wake up in the morning.

Percy gives Sami a quick kiss and moves past her dinner preparations to the fridge, where he pours himself a pint of cider from a big glass growler. It's likely from the batch he brewed with his new best friend Hank, the apple farmer from Eastern Washington, whom he met in some online home-brew hobbyist group and who seems to own only one pair of fruit-stained coveralls.

As Percy goes to change, Sami gets to marinating the chicken thighs and the tofu, using separate knives, separate cutting boards and dishes—not a mistake worth making twice. She remembers that her vegan son has become convinced that he has a soy allergy, and she starts to brainstorm some alternatives to tofu. With a bit of refrigerator magic, Sami could pull together a substitute. But screw it, she thinks. She'll cook it, and he can eat it or go without. Zucchini and rice for dinner won't kill him.

From one moment to the next, there are children everywhere. On the couch. In the kitchen. They're at the table, yelling, messing up the place settings that Sami asked them to do, but they didn't do, so she did them herself even though she knew it established a bad precedent or maintains a bad pattern or charts a poor course—but she just wanted it done and done right.

Percy returns to the kitchen in his post-ride leisure attire, always a fleece, lightweight hiking pants, and knobby trail running shoes. "Decent ride home today. Not quite the mileage I want to hit yet this week. But I got in some solid uphill, at least." He extends one of his legs in front of him, curling the toe of his shoe upward. "Might feel it a bit tomorrow."

She smiles in response to his fitness update but offers no comment. A small act of rebellion in the face of what she knows is good for him but can't help but feel is an extravagance she doesn't get to enjoy. The vegetables, all cut on the bias and drizzled with extra-virgin olive oil, are laid upon a silicon mat on a baking sheet and ferried into the oven. Percy retrieves his glass and pours himself another cider as she gets the chicken and tofu into the top rack.

They stand in the dim kitchen for a few minutes without saying a word. Not knowing where to start or how to continue.

He goes first. Somebody has to. "Macy and I were thinking Kings in the Corner for game night tonight. I know it's kind of for younger kids, but it's a classic and—"

"Sorry. I have to tell you something," she cuts in.

"That sounds serious," he says and takes a drink, staring down the length of the glass. "Wait . . . you're pregnant?"

She looks around to make sure the kids are out of earshot and lowers her voice. "I hate to break it to you: but we have to have sex to get pregnant." She cocks her head to be sure he knows she's staying on the humorous side of long-term monogamy humor.

"Glad you think that's funny." He fake-laughs into an exaggerated cry. "What then? You're gonna leave me? Please don't do it . . . unless you take the kids too."

"I heard that, Dad," Macy says from the other room in an unimpressed monotone.

"Kidding, honey," he responds, trying to match her drone. "Kind of?"

Sami grabs the pint from his hand and takes a long swig of the bitter cider, which he tries to explain away as dry. She tries to pass it back to him but thinks better of it and finishes the glass in one go. "Take the kids?" She wipes her lips with the back of her sleeve. "I'm not letting you off the hook that easily, Mr. Stalworth."

"OK. That covers my primary concerns. I think I'm ready for whatever it is you need to tell me."

"I took back over as head of the PTA."

Percy pours himself another drink, takes a sip, and considers his words. "Didn't you tell me you were done with the Stevenson PTA like, I don't know, forty-two million times? And what about your Grandma Masako–renaming grand finale? What was it . . . your 'special purpose'?"

"I know. But they need me. And I can do both things. I think."

"OK. Just be careful about trying to solve everyone else's problems. Like last time. And, let's see . . . every time before that."

"Oh yeah, also, I had to call a last-minute PTA meeting." She washes her cutting boards in the sink. "Tonight."

"What about Kings in the Corner?"

"Things are complicated. Or they could be. I'm pulling together a chocolate bar fundraiser."

"Seems a bit 'high sugar' for you."

"Leftovers from last year's PTA debacle. It's the easiest option. Probably the only option, considering the time frame."

She avoids a further conversation by checking again to be sure that her phone battery is charged and that she has sufficient reception. Kim's late. She should have called already. Sami shouldn't be surprised. She too is running behind on time to make rice and opts for pasta instead. Sami sets the water to boil just as her phone rings.

"Hey, Kim," she answers, reminding herself to breathe and not hold her tension in her jaw.

"This is Kim Stalworth's assistant. Elise."

"Hi, Elise. It's Sami."

Elise doesn't respond.

"Remember: We've spoken before. Like twenty times. I'm Kim's sister-in-law."

"OK."

"And met like twice. At least."

"OK. Hold for Kim Stalworth."

As Sami waits, Percy makes a point of crossing his eyes on his way out of the room.

"How's it going, sis?" Kim greets Sami as if she held warm feelings toward her or considered her any sort of peer. But making you feel important and the object of her prized attention for a short, fleeting moment is Kim's superpower, if not a studied imitation of her late father.

Kim proceeds to not listen to how Sami is doing and begin venting about herself. "Just the usual shitstorm. Nonstop, you know. Well, you can try to imagine, anyway." Sami's sister-in-law is an executive VP and head of giving at Mothership who will soon make official her widely anticipated run for mayor. When not working or running for political office, she is competing in, training for, or recovering from triathlons. If you give her an opening, she'll tell you all about it.

Sure, Sami can imagine Kim is busy but doubts that Kim can imagine her life either. Kim's one son is now away at college in New England, but, even when he was at home, she was armed with a full support staff of nannies, house cleaners, private chefs, landscapers, and tutors. By the time Kim's male human child experiment in exceeding all developmental key performance indicators was twelve years old, he slept in a queen-size bed facing a wall-size television, had his own full bathroom and a private trainer for his predestined college rowing career. Sami's four kids share two bedrooms and a single bathroom. First-world problems, for sure. But still . . .

"You're so lucky to be a stay-at-home mom." Kim slathers on a layer of pandering disingenuity that, considering the obviousness to anyone who has met Kim before in person, is borderline, if not wholly, insulting to Sami. "It's brutal out here. Being at home sounds sublime."

"Grass may just be greener, after all," Sami says, increasingly convinced that she has no real choice in the matter and that her years out of the workforce are an insurmountable obstacle at this point. But when people find out that she is married to a Stalworth, they often assume she is set for life. Truth be told, the family name has more imagined heft than any remaining assets. Only Kim has rebuilt a fortune for herself. And, having seen how money and power putrefy family relationships, Percy has pretty much run in the opposite direction from The House of Stalworth legacy, which he considers to be a curse.

"Careful what you ask for." Percy pesters Sami from the doorway to the dining room.

"Just a sec." She covers the phone with her hand and tells him to stop.

"Just looking out for you," he says.

"She's like your dad: a being of pure ambition. But what you see is what you get." Then Sami removes her hand and says into the phone, "Sorry, Kim. Am back."

"Hi, big brother," Kim almost shouts. "Thought I heard you creeping around back there in your spandex." Kim refocuses on Sami. "Listen. I know my brother's a bit of a dork and a hippie, but you should focus on what you two have got. A nice, straightforward life."

"Yeah, thanks. Very empowering stuff."

"Promise you won't get mad about this, Sami? When we talk about 'average voters' during strategy meetings, I always envision you and Percy. Right down the middle. Not poor. Not exactly. And not stressed all the time by fluctuations in the stock market or how to not get reamed by the IRS. I envy that."

Percy sees it that way too. But earnestly so. Perhaps it's the one way in which he and his sister somehow agree. He is a pious devotee of his daily schedule that has been strategically assembled over the years to maximize his personal time for hobbies and inessential routines. Exercise in the morning. Commute. At work from eight to four. Home by five. Sharp. He participates well during evenings and on weekends, but as soon as the kids go to bed, he is down to his safe space in the basement to play with his new cider yeasts or whatever he does.

It's not that Percy is a bad guy or that they have a bad relationship. Quite the opposite. Much of Sami's wider annoyance with Percy is his persistent good nature based on his acceptance and even appreciation of life as it is. He does his thing and is both positive and kind. The kids adore him.

Percy is more than content with his job as a social worker and sometimes shop teacher at the high school. She always thought he'd eventually become some sort of private therapist. He has all of the credentials but feels that he has greater impact in the public system. In fact, he downright loves it. When not exercising or brewing something, he fills his free time tinkering with open-source designs for folding bicycles that have never caught on in North America.

Only due to the fact that they inherited the house, taking on a reasonable remainder of the original mortgage, Sami didn't have to work when the kids were babies, and he could pursue his altruistic career without having to compromise for money. So long as they were OK to live forever on the same budget that they had lived on in their twenties before they had kids. People used to live like that in this city. Not so much anymore.

Percy could have been an administrator by now, at least, but he says that management is all about dealing with other employees' work bullshit and will only take him away from making a direct difference in young people's lives—what he most enjoys about his job in the first place. He says that the last thing we need in modern life is more inane work drama and more noise in people's heads.

On paper, she respects everything that he says and, after all these decades, still appreciates his idealism. But she can't help but feel that it's the idealism of someone who grew up with money. Maybe more noise in people's heads is worth it for more cash in their bank account. Sure, he gets the summer off, but going on a weeklong vacation with four kids costs close to the average annual American salary. Especially with the way prices are heading around here. Yes, they could always go on another camping trip, but unless there is an affordable restaurant nearby, Sami just ends up doing the same cooking for six, but in the woods on a rudimentary gas stove. She's not one to let her kids settle for hot dogs and s'mores all weekend. Of course, she also has an eye on the long term. Their eldest, Cooper, is taking the PSAT in a few weeks, and even the thought of the impending financial quicksand of four university educations feels like it's going to trigger one of her migraines.

And what about the fact that Percy's sister is going to be mayor of the whole damn city? She knows Percy would ask her to take a deep breath. Point out that Kim is getting under Sami's skin, intending to make her feel insecure, if not insignificant. The woman is as competitive as the day is long. But sometimes Sami does let it get to her and becomes an uneasy mix of irritated, self-doubting, and jealous—all while kicking herself for knowing that Percy is right, and she shouldn't fall for it.

Sami checks her watch. Shit. She puts her hand over the phone again and turns to Percy. "Time got away from me."

"When do you have to be there?" he asks from just beyond the doorway.

"Now." She spoons the not-quite-ready pasta into bowls and tosses them to her husband.

As Kim goes on about voter statistics and fundraising targets, Sami interrupts, "Listen, Kim... sorry, but I need to know about that thing."

"Yes, that thing... so many things... so many people asking for so many things..."

"You were going to talk to the superintendent."

"Yes, of course, I saw him at a golf tournament today."

"I know. That's why I asked to talk to you. Remember?"

"Right, yes, the naming thing about your grandfather."

"Grandmother... no—well, it's related, and I still want to talk about that, but what about the other thing?" She waits until Percy is delivering food to the dining room and can't hear. "The school closure thing?"

"Well, sis, my sweet little Macy is going to be in middle school next year, right? Maybe it's time for you to move on."

"One sec." With the phone cradled between her ear and shoulder, Sami pulls on her blue jacket, waves goodbye to her family eating around the table, tries to ignore her own hunger, and jogs out the door toward the school. She says to Kim, "Please. I'm scrambling to pull together an emergency fundraiser. And I don't even know if this closure rumor is real or not. Probably all a false alarm."

"We're all in this together, sis. Family, right?" Kim again cameos her personal warmth playacting that has always made Percy want to shoot himself in the face. Then she turns serious. "This can't blow back on me. Not one word. But they've narrowed it down to a list of contenders."

"And?" Sami pauses in front of the big rock.

"And, unfortunately, Stevenson is a front-runner."

"Like neck and neck? How many others?"

"OK, there aren't any others on the list. It isn't even a list."

After an aborted first attempt, Sami tries to steady her voice and says, "But there's so much history—my grandmother, she—"

"Pro tip, sis: sentimentality gets you nowhere in this life."

Sami's frontal cortex, or something in that vicinity, flutters. Her vision swoons. She thinks that she thanked Kim before hanging up the call to burst into heaving tears.

But there is no time for this emotional extravagance. Sentimentality gets you nowhere.

Sami wipes her face clean on the sleeve of her jacket as she forces one impossibly heavy footstep after the next toward the school.

SIX *2014*

Bruce licks French vanilla creamer from the blond soul patch beneath his bottom lip. He should've known better than to drink coffee later in the day. Especially the twitchy rotgut from the gas station. But he had to haul ass back here from the state capitol and still be awake enough to make a positive impression. Or some sort of an impression. At least awake, present, and more or less engaged, considering that one of the main points of him attending this meeting is for a good word to make its way back to his wife.

He has never set foot in the school at night like this. The lights are lower than their usual postwar public-building flicker. He paces alone in the front hall. It seems rather cavernous for such a small building, with the squeals of his sandaled footsteps bouncing off the hard angles and buffed butterscotch-colored floor tiles.

The PTA lady told him she'd meet him here. Right inside the front door, he swears she said. Or did she? Either way, she's nowhere to be seen. He doesn't have a watch, but he's probably late. He can be confident in that. He feels the expanding agitation that she is going to scold him. She's gotta be one of those overachiever type-A professionals whom he can't abide. Whatever people call middle-aged yuppie parents nowadays. Running the PTA as a trophy hobby or bragging right between deposing defendants or closing major real estate deals. Fuck her and everybody like her.

He already sees how this is going to go poorly, and will make him look even worse to his wife. He should cut his losses and leave right now.

He turns around and considers walking back out. But the front door pulls open, and a woman enters dressed in mom jeans, cheap sneakers, and a rain jacket. Her hair is unadorned and worn straight back over her head into a simple ponytail. He probably wouldn't give her a second look on the street. For all he knows, he's met her before at drop-off and didn't bother to hold on to the memory. Not that Bruce is known for his powers of recollection or for interacting with other parents at drop-off. But this lady's just another everyday school parent, not the PTA boss.

"You Bruce?" she asks.

He nods in guarded affirmation.

"Sami." She shakes his hand with a grip that seems to be trying to make up for her defeated posture. "Were you able to print out the forms I sent you?"

When his phone rang earlier in the day with a number he didn't recognize, he wasn't sure if he should answer it or not. He receives few calls from anyone not related to him. His initial thought, of course, was: bill collector. But it could also have something to do with his weed plan. Or it could've been the school calling about Sierra. He answered, and before he understood what was going on, he found himself committing to some sort of PTA project. Sami, or whatever her name is, assured him it would take only a few days. And it was important, if not essential, for the school. If he could "hit the ground running," she'd owe him a favor.

She said she'd follow up with some "emails with attachments" to print up for the first meeting. Bruce didn't mention that he's never opened an attachment, let alone printed one. Or the fact that he doesn't have a computer and doesn't know his email password. Fortunately, his daughter was able to log on to his old account on her mom's computer, print the forms for him, and leave them in their mailbox so he could grab them in a quick drive-by.

Wren saw him retrieving papers from their mailbox and came out to ask why he was at the house outside of their agreed-upon parenting plan. He was forced to come clean that he'd committed to a PTA project. Her brow and cheeks softened, and she said, "Good job, Bruce." Words he hadn't heard in a long while, maybe since some of his more involved bathroom cleanups in Sierra's toddler years.

Now Bruce waves the small stack of email printouts at Sami and says, "Got 'em right here."

"Wonderful. Thanks. Please go make the copies in the office like we talked about. And then come find me downstairs when you're done," she tells him, straining to be motivational but wiping at her eyes and already heading down the hall. "Millie, the secretary. She's still here. She'll point you in the right direction."

He makes his way to the fluorescent lights of the main office and finds the receptionist doing some sort of large-print word search game at the front counter.

"You the PTA's fresh meat?" Millie asks, chewing on the stem end of a blue Bic pen cap and twisting a curl of her gray hair around an ink-stained index finger.

Acid churns in Bruce's stomach, caffeine charges through his bloodstream, and drops of cold sweat run down his sides.

"Yeah, I'm, you know, helping out. Uh, photocopies. For a chocolate bar sale?"

"Machine's over there." She points him to a side room.

He mouths a "thank you" and makes his way toward the side room but is unsure of why she keeps staring at him with a dogged grin. "Everything OK?" he asks.

"All these years," Millie says. "I've never seen anyone like you in the PTA."

"A guy?"

"There's been a few guys. I just never seen a grandpa."

"What?"

"It's so nice."

Bruce doesn't know what to say so he unfurls his spine as far as he can force it, attempts a theatrical twirl of his cane to demonstrate its total and complete triviality, and speed walks his maximum of three to four quick steps into the other room. Best to pretend that he didn't understand her, although he heard her on levels she can't fathom.

He stares long and hard at the gray box of a photocopier, his anxiety and technological self-doubt sweeping him downriver from any methodical assessment of how and where to start. He gives in and calls Millie to come over and show him how to coax it to life.

First, she hits power. She laughs in an overstated fashion that may or may not be sarcastic and then places the sheet face down on the glass, closes the top, and hits the big yellow button that says copy.

"You want to do five copies? Hit the button that says five. Want six? Hit six. See where I'm going with this?" She walks back toward her desk in the main room.

Bruce waits a moment, triple-checks that she's not watching him, and then removes his additional paperwork from his coat. He'd never admit this to Sami or his wife, but he jumped on the chance to make photocopies for the PTA today because he had no idea how he was going to deal with all of the other copies he needs to make for his business applications and background checks. And, God knows, he needs to get all of these bureaucratic forms copied, signed, and submitted before Melchor changes his mind or his aunt does it for him.

Today Bruce hightailed it to the state capitol and picked up all of the LLC formation and other paperwork that he'd originally intended to get at some point over the next few weeks. He puts the first page on the photocopier glass and shouts to Millie through the door, "How do you do twenty?"

"A two and then a zero. That's twenty. Two and a zero just like we teach the kiddos here at Stevenson Elementary," she says from her desk and then mutters, "Tits on a bull."

"What'd you say?" he asks, having heard but daring her to repeat herself.

"You just remind me of my husband," she says. "My recently deceased husband."

"Sorry for your loss?"

"He was a looker. Thank God, 'cause he wasn't good at much else. I mean, he was amazing in bed too, I guess. He did this one thing with his index finger and thumb—"

"OK. Great, hold on. I have to focus in here." Bruce prints twenty copies of the first page of the LLC application and arranges them on the tabletop. He copies and stacks the second page on top of each and admires his organizational handiwork, priding himself on his collating system and the fact that he is maneuvering free photocopies. And not only for one company. For SuperChronics LLC. Loose Bruce Brands LLC. Legalized It LLC. The list goes on. He is going to make this work. Not just because he has a plan. Because he deserves it.

Bruce sacrificed his youth and body to build the region's cannabis culture, starting as a teenager lugging backpacks of weed across remote stretches of the Canadian border. Then it was on to all the concrete, masonry, framing, electrical, irrigation, and drywall work he did on grow operations in attics, basements, back corners of warehouses, old barns, and a couple of retired school buses over the years. He even customized a group of buried railway cars in the eastern part of the state.

There's no Guinness World Record for it, but he built the first hydroponic grow op in the city in the eighties. Probably the first in the state. If only he'd done it for himself and not for some prick who had little more going for him than cash on hand, he'd be sitting pretty now. *Uff da*, as his mom's family used to say in dismay. And the Jorgensens had plenty to be dismayed about.

But Bruce had never been a player of what some call the long game. This was justified by his reflexive disdain for money and the power it exerts over people's perceptions of reality. He saw all of his work as a means to the end of living the unencumbered, rad life. God forbid he ever had a bank account with enough money in it to be flagged by the IRS. Loose Bruce was not down with that. Just living life one day at a time had always been his motto. And, according to some (formerly) close to him, a coping mechanism.

"Planning to sell a whole lotta chocolate bars, huh?" Millie asks, back in the doorway and straining to read the titles atop the stacks of Bruce's papers.

"Just being thorough." He tries to look like he's still engrossed in making copies but monitors her out of the corner of his eye.

As she moves closer to pick up the articles of incorporation for the recently stapled Sierra's College Fund LLC, Bruce blocks her with his cane.

"Right. Sure . . ." She winks.

One more doubter. Add her to the pile. But he will prove Millie and the rest of them all wrong. It's not like he came up with this weed plan out of nowhere. Bruce has had other big ideas in the past. Some of them went on to be huge successes—just not of his making.

He'd come up with the idea for a cell phone for kids with GPS and only the ability to call home or 911. Thought of that, years ago. He'd thought of a condom with some sort of numbing gel in it for the premature ejaculators out there. Not that Loose Bruce ever needed something like that, or even normal condoms or seat belts or helmets or any of that bullshit. But for some reason, he had that idea sophomore year of high school, and now they're for sale in the family-planning aisle in your average drugstore. How about a calendar that lets you know when your wife is PMS-ing? Wren was unnecessarily dismissive of that one. How about fixed-amount credit cards for people who don't have credit or to use on the internet for porn or other sites you don't want to show up on your bill? That crossed his mind a few years back, and now he sees them next to the beef jerky and vapes and other impulse buys at the convenience store. Don't get Bruce started on vapes.

Beyond his big cannabis retail idea, he has one other good one also currently in the works. But it is too far ahead of its time, and he'd need the capital from the cannabis idea to make this other happen. In the future, cameras will be everywhere, and facial recognition technology will be pervasive. He read all about it. It's already happening in China and England, or the United Kingdom or whatever it's called now. He will invent a pair of simple, affordable plastic glasses that work as a scrambler or jammer. Kind of like those plastic license-plate covers with a diffusion lens in them so that red-light cameras can't read your plates. One of those for your face. But nobody is really going to care about that for another ten years, even as the state further erects the scaffolding of the surveillance state all around us. He can see that we are the frog in the pot with the water getting warmer and warmer by the minute.

As for his weed plan, the first challenge is that the properly zoned locations are near impossible to come by. And that was done on purpose. The city wants these dispensaries to exist only in specific areas around town. The minimum buffer distance as outlined in RCW 69.50.331(8) requires licensed marijuana producers, processors, or retailers to be located at least a thousand feet from playgrounds, recreation centers, schools, childcare centers, public parks, public transit centers, libraries, or game arcades. The thousand-foot buffer distance is measured as the shortest straight-line distance from the property line of the proposed business location to the property line of the off-limits entity.

The old restaurant doesn't look like much, no, but it has street access to a busy thoroughfare, a storefront, and abundant parking, and most importantly, it is a thousand-plus feet from any off-limits community locations, a rare feat in the increasingly dense city. To the best that Bruce could tell, and God knows he did his research, there were no other eligible locations in this whole part of town. This is the spot. The one.

Having an eligible spot and clean application was the first big hurdle. But that left the challenge of winning a number-out-of-a-hat lottery pick. That led to Bruce's big innovation. One way or another, he was going to make sure he was front and center when this city did for weed what it had done for coffee, software, and airplanes: taken something that already existed and given it that fresh restart in this fresh little corner of the world where anything is possible and dreams can be realized without regard for the baggage of the past or even of the present. All that matters is the future. Here, on the very far end of the world, we can reach out and almost touch the future.

Bruce had chopped and reconfigured a hundred commercial spaces over the course of his life. The restaurant has two floors, which—after smoking a fat nug of particularly dank sativa, back when he did such things by himself—he had the epiphany to subdivide into five units per floor. Cheap drywall and a few non-load-bearing two-by-fours would do the trick. Then he'd assign separate unit numbers and submit applications as a different LLC for each space.

When he read and reread the fine print of the law, he found

out that there are two applications allowed per spot, so in the one building with the ideal location, he could submit a total of twenty applications and dramatically improve the chance of winning that Willy Wonka golden ticket. It was also rumored that the city intended to have some degree of regional distribution among vice zones, so twenty applications from this one part of town was as good as a lock.

Wren told him that he had to connect with something that had meaning to him and value in wider society, and he sure as fuck had found it. And, now, right now, with all of these photocopies laid out on the countertop in front of him, Loose Bruce is taking the steps to tie back together his whole life.

Millie further applies the weight of her midsection against Bruce's flimsy cane barrier. "You're giving the ol' girl a workout there, eh?"

"What?" He drops the cane and uses his forearm to sweep all of his LLC paperwork into a single pile, placing it beyond her view. Sweat runs down his sides again.

She nods at the machine. "She's no spring chicken. Not used to taking that kind of load."

He smiles at her with as much sincerity as he can muster, doing his best to keep things in the realm of professional camaraderie as he perspires under his hat and inhales the sharp, burnt-ink smell of the copies. He also gathers the chocolate-sale papers into a folder and taps the end on the countertop to even them out.

He offers Millie a quick, chaste thank-you and goodbye while turning his back to squeeze past her in the doorway.

"Hey, wait. Come back, ol'-timer," Millie shouts after him. "You even know how to get to the basement?"

"I'll figure it out. Thanks," he says, appreciating the reminder to head downstairs and regretting his decision to risk an extra few hundred throbbing, exploratory steps. After pacing the ground-floor hall from end to end, he discovers the staircase right next to the main office and works his way down, stepping sideways on each stair, to find Sami.

There aren't many places she could be on this windowless subterranean level. There is a row of storage closet doors, and he finds her midway down the line, under a bare bulb hanging from the ceiling. She doesn't turn around and keeps rummaging through thickets of rakes and push brooms to get to old cardboard boxes.

"Bruce. Yes, good thing you're here. I'm gonna need some help moving all this damn chocolate. When I find it. Should be a whole mother lode of it."

"Where's everyone else?"

"Everyone else who?"

"PTA."

"We're it. Need to keep this small for now."

Sami gives up on finding the chocolate in this closet, steps back out into the dim hallway, and gives Bruce a look up and down, noting his cane. "Oh shoot. I forgot."

"It's OK, I can help you move stuff. Or I can try. Anything for the PTA, right?"

"You print those photocopies?"

"Yes, ma'am." He hands her the folder, quickly checking that he still has his LLC papers separate inside his jacket.

"Great. We'll get this organized and then put the students to work. Community effort. Get this wrapped up ASAP."

Bruce knows that, in this quiet moment with nobody else jockeying for Sami's attention, he should pick her brain with a bunch of questions about his daughter's special education plan. That's what his wife would want him to do. In fact, Wren even gave him a handwritten list of specific questions, not that he brought it with him.

"Hey, Sami, I was wondering—"

"Yes?" She grips her folder to her chest, looking at him.

But he draws a blank. Bruce chases the questions down the nether regions of his mind, but they retreat into ever-darker territory, always a few steps beyond apprehension. He doesn't know what to say, so after a few garbled false starts that trigger hints of skepticism, if not concern, in her increasingly downturned mouth, he holds out his hand, signaling for her to pass the door keys. "Here, let me check the next one."

"You sure?"

"Of course, I'm sure." He twirls his cane again to show its insignificance.

She hands him the big janitor ring, gripping it by two of its dozen or so keys. "Try those last two doors. Gotta be one of them."

He attempts one, turns on the light, and finds the room stacked with old typewriters, a piano, and a midcentury-looking rusted-out floor buffer. No boxes with chocolate bars.

He tries a few more keys and finally gets one that works in the last door.

The bare bulb doesn't turn on, but he thinks he can make out the outline of boxes atop a wooden pallet. He's pleased about his discovery. Such precision. A surgical strike. Maybe he can still convert this into a productive conversation about improving support for Sierra's special needs at the school. Help budge the whole bureaucratic logjam. Bruce feels his confidence rising. "Here we go. Looks like it says *World's Finest* or something on the side. Those're them?"

"Should be, yeah. Awesome. I was getting worried there for a minute that they got thrown out."

"You got a flashlight?" he asks over his shoulder and sees her starting to skim through the photocopies.

She turns on the light on her smartphone and passes it to him.

And with that, he remembers all that Wren told him. The long waitlist for the school speech therapist. The trouble qualifying for an individualized education plan and other school services because Sierra's standardized tests are poor but passable. And, especially, the fact that their insurance company doesn't recognize speech therapy as a health care service. Not without the school providing robust supporting documents that spell out exactly why they require private speech therapy too.

He'd promised Wren that he'd work to get Sami's help with those supporting documents. That was the first goal as they waited out the rest of the bureaucratic thaw.

"Our daughter needs us to get this done like last year," Bruce's wife had said with mounting frustration.

"It's not my fault that she is having these challenges, Wren."

She nodded in affirmation but not convincingly so, at least not as Bruce saw it. "They all said, hold tight—she'll grow out of it. And now, here we are. But with years wasted."

"And it's not your fault either for not being around as much as you might have wanted."

"I know that," she said with bloodless affect.

"Sierra's having some challenges. We know that. But she loves music. And she's starting to talk more sometimes when she's with me."

"Don't rub it in, Bruce."

"It's gonna be OK, Wren."

"Maybe. Maybe not. It's up to us to fix it," she said. "What I know is that if you can help dislodge this process, it would mean a lot. To Sierra. To me. A lot."

Now Bruce surveys around the side of the chocolate boxes with the light. "While we're here, Sami, I meant to ask you a couple of questions about special—"

"Sorry, are these the copies I asked you to print? Or the ones from the first email?"

His impulse is to ask if she sent him more than one email. He has no idea. But he has enough sense to determine that that question will not go over well. And it's not a good look to tell her that he had his daughter print the emails or blame it on her. So, he does what he learned from marriage and pretends that he didn't hear her.

"Did you check these, Bruce?" She flips through the papers, her voice increasingly desperate. "Before printing up a stack of them?"

"Yeah, of course . . ." He is distracted by a hole in the side of the cardboard box. A puncture a little smaller than the circumference of a can of soda. Multiple holes in the boxes. All the boxes.

That's when he smells it: sweet. Sickly sweet.

He looks to the floor. As the phone light sweeps back and forth, he sees it. First, one or two. Then, everywhere. Like black hail. Rodent feces. Yes, everywhere. And there, behind the door with one foreleg in a snap trap, is a bloated rat carcass, heaving with the tiny writhing pins of white maggots.

SEVEN   *1971*

Ruth has never once lied to her mother. Sure, she's omitted a detail here and there, but she's never intentionally misled Masako on anything of great importance. It is the two of them, Ruth and Masako, against the world. Making life work, together. Their relationship is based on total dedication, total trust, total everything.

Some weeks on from Larry dropping off Ruth on his motorcycle, Masako continues to make it known that he, *ano hito*, is unworthy of her daughter's attention. And Masako doesn't even know about him standing up Ruth at the Broiler. Again, she didn't lie. Ruth told her mom that she was going to campus to study. Yes, even though it was a Saturday, and she always studies at home over the weekend. But she did go to campus that day, and she did study. Kind of. And applied makeup in the library bathroom and spent a bunch of the afternoon imagining what she and Larry might talk about. So what if Ruth stopped by the Broiler on her way home and Larry happened to be there? She did go as far as telling Masako to please not worry about her for dinner, that she'd eat elsewhere. She was primed to give her mom a vague "probably on campus or on my way home," but Ruth made sure to inform Masako of her plan when her mom was busy practicing her violin, and she didn't ask any follow-ups.

Ruth spent an agonizing and humiliating hour at the Broiler, occupied with slowly sipping ice waters, biting at the corners of her fingernails, checking the door, asking other diners for the time, and apologizing to the waitstaff. It became clear that Larry wasn't going to show. She considered that he might have set her up as a joke or a dare, with all of the self-lacerating dread that entails. She walked home in the rain and silently ate a country-style miso and tofu with Masako. Sure, it hurt to be stood up. She assumed that, at best, he had thought better of hanging out with someone so square, boring, and sheltered. At least his nonappearance meant that, technically, she had not broken her lifelong honesty streak with her mother.

Then came the calls. The notes hand-delivered by him as she stepped onto the bus. The Hendrix album left at the front door with a note that said, *I hope you like it*, but she could also see under the lettering where he'd written and then erased, *My favorite. For my favorite.* There were many letters mailed to her—with no return address to tip off her mom. No matter how many times he asked for another chance to take her to dinner at the Broiler, she demurred. Being stood up once was already too much. She wouldn't let herself be embarrassed or hurt like that again.

Then he asked to meet her for a walk. Simple. Innocent. Straightforward. Masako begrudgingly cleared her to go on a stroll, in exchange for a promise that Ruth would be on her best behavior when she met with Beckham, her mom's chosen suitor, at church in a little over two weeks. Masako justified that five minutes on a walk with Larry would help Ruth "realize how foolish she's being" and "get him out of her system." She also stipulated that it had to be during daylight, and they had to stay in the immediate neighborhood, within view of the house and school.

Ruth said, "We'll just meet up by the rock to talk or something."

Much to Masako's displeasure, they've walked together every Thursday since. And a couple of Tuesdays. Under the guise of friendship. And getting fresh air. Plain and simple.

Today's the first day in a few weeks that the clouds have given way to spots of near sun. They pause to admire the top fringe of the downtown skyline, only a big hill or two away. Sometimes it surprises Ruth to remember that there's the rest of the city out there, beyond her otherwise-isolated hill neighborhood.

She dresses conservatively, with her down jacket zipped all the way up to her neck. No makeup when her mom is signing off on her appearance. But she tries to show her more spontaneous side with a colorful earring or by wearing sneakers. Larry, for his part, seems to be trying hard to be the perfect gentleman. Instead of arriving on his motorcycle, he shows up in his mom's old Datsun. He wears threadbare sweaters under his ill-fitting sport coat that must have belonged to his grandfather.

If anything, he's been too deferential and too gentlemanly for Ruth's taste and overly honored to be in her presence. She is intrigued by his risk-taking side, or what she envisions of it, and wants to see more.

A gigantic passenger plane flies low overhead, going somewhere exciting and possibly international. A place with real history and culture. A place that is not here.

"What's that one?" she asks as they tilt back their heads to observe the sky above. She comes close to casually leaning up against his shoulder. Close enough that they both pause for a moment to recalibrate.

"747," he answers, sounding semi-confident to her. "It's new. Biggest plane to ever fly."

"That's the one you work on?"

"Nah, trust me, those things're a fad. All the top engineers, guys I know . . . friends of mine . . . they say they're just regular planes. But made way bigger." Larry pauses in front of the giant rock. "The future, our future: it's supersonic."

He details his role in bringing the four corners of the world within a few hours of one another spent in a reclining leather seat in which "you simply kick back, smoke a cigarette, and can't even feel that you're moving, let alone faster than the speed of sound." Ruth allows her imagination to run wild, an exercise with which she is not well acquainted: visualizing the two of them, Larry dressed like the dapper bad guy in that *French Connection* movie that she didn't tell her mom she went to, sitting hand in hand in the first-class cabin or whatever the fancy part is called, hopping over to London or Tokyo and back while reading a copy of *Rolling Stone* or *Vogue* with a cold martini. Not that she reads those magazines or has ever had a martini, cold or otherwise, or even really knows what's in it. But she'd be open to try one.

For now, the extent of their travels is walking within view of the school and her house. Tonight is the first time that Ruth doesn't spot Masako supposedly working late and watching from her class-room in the school building. Ruth can't help but be pleased that she seems to be making progress convincing Masako that she was get-ting anxious about nothing. That she and Larry are purely platonic.

And she further elaborated her most winning point to her mother, that Larry is a company man, a union member, and a pro-fessional who is playing an important role changing the future of international transportation and shrinking the planet. He is part of something monumental. And she and Larry are doing nothing but talking on their little walks anyway.

As they circle the school, she tells him about university and teaching and never having deviated from the plan. He, for reasons incomprehensible to her, seems impressed with the steadiness and relative normalcy of her life, explaining that he always felt he had to be his mother's parent. He says that he can only imagine the luxury of a stable home with resources and plans and expectations and a mom who takes an active, daily concern in his well-being, let alone a mom who plans for his future.

But Ruth prefers not to talk about herself. She is convinced that she is the antithesis of interesting. She likes to listen to his stories about forging his own path to find his way in the world, all the way to something that will give his life significance and change the lives of so many people in so many places.

"Sure, the 747 will democratize existing air travel," he tells her, sounding rehearsed. "Soon normal people will be able to fly to here and there around the country, even for the weekend. But supersonic travel is going to collapse our very understanding of time and space. We're gonna be living like *The Jetsons.* Just like everything we were talking about in the World's Fair back in, what was that? Sixty-two?"

As they continue their walk, the backs of their hands brush up against each other. Ruth tires of avoiding the inevitable and grabs his hand. His palm becomes hot and damp with sweat. She likes the feeling of gripping his hand. A prickly burn rises up the skin where her shoulders meet with the back of her neck. They walk without speaking. Focusing instead on the small point of physical contact between them. She lets go as soon as they come back around in view of Masako's schoolroom window, even though it appears to be empty.

She asks him questions. "Have you ever had sex?" "Have you ever smoked marijuana?" "Have you ever been in a fight?" "Have you lied to someone you love?" "Have you broken a law?" "Protested the war?" "Taken acid?" "Humphrey, Nixon, or Wallace?"

He gives her one-word answers. All yeses except for the last one. She imagines that he's trying to spare her the details, but it only makes her more intrigued. When she pries on where he protested the war, he answers, "Leaving the Navy was a form of protest, I guess." But that's all he'll say about that.

They walk another half block to the corner of her street, where he always parks his mom's car in the same spot. She gives him a quick, chaste hug, turning her side toward his torso. She's late to get home, and finals are next week. The sun is going down. But, most taxing, Masako has been organizing for her to meet Beckham and his aunt for a more involved opportunity to talk and get to know

each other after this Sunday's services. There are outfits to pick out
and conversations to rehearse.

"You OK, Ruthie?" Larry asks, betraying some concern that
the bottom is about to drop out of his sojourn into this world of
happy normalcy.

"Just family stuff, life stuff, you know."

"You'll do great." He pats her on the shoulder as if he were an
older uncle by marriage.

"I'm not sure."

"Not sure about what?"

"Everything."

"Everything? You have everything you could ever want or
need." He motions, palms up, and turns around, waving past the
school and her house and stopping to smile and bring the focus
back on himself.

She offers a tight grin. "It's not that easy."

"OK, so what do you want then?"

"What do you mean?"

"I mean: What do you want to do with your life?" A question
she has never been asked.

She doesn't know where to start and, instead, wraps her arms
around him. Pressing their bodies together.

They stand there holding each other. A federation of misfits. She
smells cigarettes and peanuts, perhaps a Snickers. She wants more.

Ruth looks around again for her mom. She is nowhere to be
seen. The shades are drawn on the front of the house as is typical for
Masako near sunset. Yes, this is progress. And she has an idea why.

While she and Masako never spoke directly of the incident the
night that Ruth and Larry met at the Dirty Bird, earlier today, after
a couple of weeks of serious consideration and angling, she had decided to directly address the details of the evening with her mother.

Ruth acted as if it were a non-incident, but "just in case" it was of interest to Masako and she wanted to know more about her friend, she told her that he was quite a gentleman. That Larry had thrown the pine cones at the window to let her know that she'd left her purse on his motorcycle. He was concerned she wouldn't have it for class the next day.

Ruth was surprised and exhilarated by the power of her misdirection. How it was plausible enough that, even if it didn't fully convince Masako, it sowed enough doubt in her mom's mind that it softened her position. Ruth's second fabrication, that she had suffered food poisoning from the Dirty Bird, was less successful. She'd told her mom that Larry sped her home in the best interest of her well-being. But it seemed that Masako was trying hard to believe that one too. Deceit was much easier and far more useful than Ruth ever imagined.

She pulls back to look into Larry's dark, shining eyes and then reaches toward him with her lips. She feels her face brush against the corners of his mustache and then meet with his mouth and start to kiss him. Not that she knows exactly how to do that, but she moves her lips and then tongue, and it comes at turns clumsily and then more naturally, like early adventures in dancing by herself in her bedroom to make-believe music. Effervescence froths through her chest and head. She worries that her hands are shaking, only to realize that they are his hands that tremble atop hers in a firmer and firmer clinch.

She feels nauseous, but knows that it's probably nerves too. Over Larry's shoulder, Ruth sees the porch light flash on at her house. Once. Twice. Three times.

EIGHT   *1971*

Larry strolls down the aisle of Food King, right past the oils, vin-
egars, spices, and other stuff in jars and bottles that he's never
bought or considered buying. It's the first time he's been to this
store in a while, as it's the same place where he was busted as a teenager stealing two frozen Salisbury steak TV dinners. He probably
could've gotten away with one down the back of his pants, but the
second one up his shirt was the giveaway. The box had been too
cold against his bare skin, so he kept shifting and readjusting its
placement. But what was he going to do? It was his mom's birthday,
and she deserved better than standard food bank fare.

"That was the worst decision of your life," a plainclothes store
security guard said as young Larry rounded the corner from frozen
foods and into cereals.

"Man, I wish," Larry responded, sagging under his own shame,
before being taken without any resistance to the manager's office
in the back to await the arrival of Officer Wayne and the neighborhood squad car.

Now, all these years later, he has gradually started to return
to the Food King. His initial visits were quick, exploratory affairs
to buy a single item: a beer, a pack of Winstons. He kept his head
low and tested the reaction. At first it was nerve-racking, thinking
that he'd be persona non grata, blackballed forever. He is just now
starting to live a bona fide life with a good job and the woman of

his dreams in his sights and was disinclined to be treated like a common criminal again.

But Food King is the only store in the area, and getting groceries on a motorcycle in the rain from the next neighborhood is borderline ridiculous. Fortunately, the security guard is gone. Heart attack last June, Larry heard. Dead before he hit the floor in the dairy aisle. Many of the same cashiers are still there or are former bag boys, but they are just going through the motions of life and work.

Larry now walks to the mouth of the aisle, and there she is, Masako Hasegawa. His future mother-in-law. At least, in his unfolding vision of the future.

OK, he saw her car at the edge of the parking lot, took a U-turn on his bike, and then followed her into the store. He watches her from a few yards away. Her cart is empty. She wears a clear plastic head covering to protect her ink-black hair from the rain, and she has what appears to be water droplets and some steam on her big plastic glasses. Larry walks toward her.

As he gets close, he starts to nod his head as if to greet her and register his surprise to run into her at Food King at 7:40 in the morning on a weekday when he should be on his way into work. Just a totally unexpected run-in and a spontaneous chance to get to know each other a bit better, right some misperceptions about him, and reset the course for their forthcoming familial relationship.

He stops, sets his feet, and parts his lips to say hello. She looks right through him, as if he were an apparition, a feeling with which he is more familiar than he would like to admit. He bails out of his salutation mid-word, and Masako goes about putting a bunch of carrots and a red onion into her cart as he passes her, like any other stranger.

He shouldn't have done this. Stalking his girlfriend's mom, the one who he is pretty sure has it out for him, is exactly the kind of reason he's never done well in polite circles or related well with teachers or bosses or commanding naval officers.

Larry hits the eject button and starts walking as fast as he can without quite breaking stride toward the front door of the Food King. His body makes this decision for him before his brain can understand it. But he does glance back over his shoulder for a brief moment, long enough to see Masako turning to look at him.

Fuck. He knows he should keep moving. They can both pretend that they never saw each other or didn't realize who the other one was. What do they call that on *Perry Mason*? Plausible deniability? It's early in the day, after all. It could be dismissed with some "hadn't had my cup of morning joe" maneuver. And Masako has that clear plastic thing over her head, making her harder to recognize. Furthermore, she can argue that her glasses were fogged up, so she couldn't see him from afar. Each would have an out, and Larry could try again at a later date.

But they both did see each other, and that is fact. If he slinks off, he is accepting relegation to being a fringe element in Ruth's existence, someone who doesn't merit a simple hello from her mother during a (seemingly) random encounter in the grocery store at a very sober and civilized hour. Larry will continue his fate of surviving in the shadows just beyond the warmth of the campfire of respectable society.

This is hardly the first time Larry's missed his moment. When he was sixteen, he saved another boy from drowning at the lake. The son of some important family, who claimed to have had a cramp or something but was likely drunk. Or Larry didn't exactly save the kid. He saw him floating face down in the water and considered grabbing him. But, instead, he shouted to Matty Donahoe, one of the lifeguards, who saved the drowning Stalworth kid.

Matty was a lanky mouth breather whom Larry knew from earlier years at Stevenson Elementary. Prior to the rescue, Matty's greatest claim to fame was that he sometimes smuggled a choice selection of his dad's nudie magazines to school to let other boys look at them in five-minute increments in exchange for chewing gum or quarters.

Larry saw that Matty's feet were still on the bottom when he grabbed the kid and carried him to safety. He then watched in abject horror as local TV did an interview with the two boys and Matty was elevated to a local celebrity. Parents lavished him with praise. Girls were all over him. He was interviewed in the newspaper. More than once. They literally asked him what it felt like to save a life. The two boys were even in the Maritime Parade together waving from a float to passersby. People wanted to get close to Matthew Donahoe, "the hero lifeguard" who saved the Stalworth boy. They wanted to share in his courageousness and his example of how order was preserved, rich kids were protected from undesirable outcomes, and the world would go on being OK.

While Matty started dating all of the popular girls and bragging about his conquests to anyone who would listen, nobody even thanked Larry. Not once. Matty told the newspaper about how he "had a feeling that something was wrong, and then I just sprang into action, without time to think about my own safety." There wasn't even an asterisk about Larry in any of the articles. And who knows—without Larry—Matty might have let the kid go under. Just as easily, he could have been the negligent lifeguard who let the Stalworth boy die on his watch. The same Stalworth boy, Bobby, now the youngest member of the city council, is already married with two young kids and people talking about him becoming mayor someday.

Or, with a slight change of events, Larry might have waded further into the water and grabbed Bobby himself. He knows he could have done it. He's not the strongest swimmer. Actually, he can't swim. Nor was he as tall at Matty, but he probably could've also stood on the bottom, saved the future politician, and made a name for himself in the process.

Larry now stands in front of the Food King, fishing in his pocket for the motorcycle key. What if he had saved the boy? What if he had snuck back into his barracks and pretended that he had no idea how his commander's Jeep ended up in that ditch? What if he hadn't been scared off so easily when he called Ruth in eighth grade and wanted to ask her if she would "go with him"?

Fuck it. He turns around and heads back inside the store. He's not going to fail again. Not this time. Larry returns to find Masako near checkout, walking toward the front door. She seems to have abandoned her cart. He worries that their near encounter rattled her to the point that she gave up on her carrots and red onion. Why did he follow her in the first place? He has such a talent for making things worse than they have to be. That, in fact, is arguably his greatest talent. But now they are facing each other, and there is no backing out this time.

"Hi. Hello. I was, I mean, I was about to go to work, and I thought maybe it was you I saw back there and just wanted to introduce myself," he borderline shouts at her. "I'm Larry."

"Yes?" Masako is polite if not distant.

"Ruth's friend."

"Oh, yes?"

"Yes." He blanks on what to say next, wishing he had more practice with these sorts of interactions or at least more confidence to roll with things and say whatever comes to mind. To be natural. But he can't trust his natural self. What comes to mind right now is professing his love for Masako's daughter and begging her to accept him as a worthy person, a good guy, a boyfriend, if not husband material. *I just want to be part of your family forever,* he thinks. *Be the father of your grandchildren. Likely be the person who helps you through your later years, drives you to old-person* doctor appointments and to the lake to feed breadcrumbs to the ducks, and holds your hand on your deathbed. I might even play a central role in organizing your funeral. I can and will do all of that for you. Happily. Deal? But all he can muster is, "Ruth is great. She's super nice."

Masako can't even give him a courtesy smile. "Yes. OK . . . have a good day then," she says and tries to move past him toward the door.

He almost lets it go again but then pursues her.

"Mrs. Hasegawa," he tries, "you know, well, I'd like to get to know Ruth better, and I was hoping that—"

"Why are you in the store at this hour? Are you following me?"

"Wait, what? Why would you think that?"

"It all seems odd. But OK, can I help you with something specific? I'm in a rush."

"I just wanted to tell you that I really enjoy spending time with your daughter. She is a very special person."

"I know that. And you basically already said that." Then she softens. Only a bit. "But thank you."

"And . . ." He balks at going deeper into the conversation.

"And?"

"And I thought maybe I could tell you a bit more about myself. That maybe you had the wrong idea. Not that you have a bad idea. Or bad ideas, in general. But just that I could give you more information. A better, fuller picture. I too have a close relationship with my own mother. I'm from the neighborhood. And I am working on, well, do you know anything about supersonic flight?"

She shrugs.

He looks around the store. Are people staring at him? A cashier, who may or may not be on break, makes fleeting eye contact with Larry. OK, maybe not eye contact, but she seems to be looking in his direction. Does she remember his indiscretion all those years ago with the Salisbury steaks? Larry slouches down into his shoulders but is still able to deliver his set piece that he practiced in front of the mirror for an occasion like this. "The 2707. It's a jet. It'll seat two hundred fifty to three hundred passengers traveling faster than the speed of sound, which does depend a lot on air temperature, but at sixty-eight degrees Fahrenheit is roughly seven hundred sixty-seven miles per hour. Twenty-five airlines have already ordered over a hundred jets. It's the future. The future for this city. The future for the world. And I am involved in that future. Right at takeoff, if you know what I mean."

"Don't I know you from somewhere else? Did you go to Stevenson?"

"Yes, Mrs. Hasegawa."

"Were you ever a student of mine? I like to think that I remember the faces and, at the very least, the first names of all of my students over the years."

"No." He had, in fact, been a student of hers for a few months but changed out of music after getting his ass beat at the bus stop by full-time bully Paul Petersen and everybody's favorite lifeguard Matty Donahoe for daring to play something as emasculating as the flute. They smacked and prodded him with the flute until it broke, and, since reporting his assailants was not a viable option, Larry's mom had to pay back the flute's value to the school by working extra night shifts for almost four weeks.

He could also remind Masako that he was the kid who called her daughter once in the eighth grade, the boy she promptly chewed out over the phone. But he decides to let that be.

"But you did go to Stevenson?" she asks. "Do you not appreciate music education?"

"I do, it's just that . . ." He wants to explain to her about getting borderline sodomized with a nickel-plated wind instrument and what it was like to grow up without a dad and have to keep a running tally of every price sticker at the grocery store to make sure you can afford checkout and to be called a filthy Indian by people who don't know you and had recently moved to here from wherever, for her to understand who he is and who he could be and that even if he has made mistakes and had his fair share of shortcomings that his motives are, and will always be, pure.

"Wait, I remember. Weren't you the child who vandalized his instrument?" she asks, her face widening with recognition. "The school's flute?"

"Yes, that was me. But, no, I didn't vandalize anything. I mean, it was much more complicated than that."

He is spared further explanation as a big guy with a store vest and name tag enters the aisle. He's bald and, even from a distance, appears to have a cleft lip scar and billowing neck hair. But what makes the man stand out is the fact that he wears a white collared shirt and a tie under the scarlet Food King vest. Every alarm bell in Larry's brain rings: manager.

"I gotta get to work," Larry tells Masako. "The future doesn't wait . . ."

"Hey, you," the man says in a steady but raised voice as he starts toward them.

Larry quickly offers his hand to Masako. She turns, instead, to see what's the issue with the employee coming down the aisle. Larry grabs the back of Masako's hand, gives it a momentary, self-conscious squeeze, and then sprints out the store in the other direction.

PART II *1897*

Si'sia is no longer "Little Chief." He's full-grown Siab to those who know him and Old Sam or any number of other nonsense nicknames to those who don't.

He works in the shadow of the boulder in the middle of his small hilltop farm, packing his potato harvest into burlap bags and loading them onto the back of his well-brushed and expertly shod mule.

Siab pretends to not notice the white man who stumbles into the far edge of the clearing. The man takes a moment to catch his breath before taking an unenthusiastic kick at the flock of gulls that dare obstruct his path. The birds spiral skyward.

"Indian Sam," the man shouts at Siab as if they were at twice the distance. "Yes, you boy."

Siab eats his feelings about being called "boy" by a Boston some twenty winters his junior. The man, Erasmus, pays Siab and his wife an unsolicited visit every few days at varying levels of intoxication. Asking for this or that. Taking other things. Talking about his big ideas for the future. Coveting every bit of the farm with his yellow, blood-shattered eyes.

Erasmus claims to have once been a man of influence but dresses in the same moth-eaten, shiny-kneed suit, unbathed but still bragging about being a Mason and Knight of Something-or-Other and his journalism career back in the cities of stone and brick. But he never has any money. Or food. And what money he does have, he's known to spend smoking Chinese poppies in town.

At first, Siab had some sympathy for Erasmus. But that has long passed. The man's hardships were always trivial compared to the monumental upheaval Siab has witnessed in his own life. The loss of almost everything and everyone in the world he once knew. Yet Siab maintains his honor. His pride. And his defiance—even if he must keep it discreet so as to avoid the gallows.

No matter that he is, perhaps, the last Duwamish landowner in this ancestral Duwamish land, tilling the earth as a simple potato famer: He knows he is still a headman. A *tyee*. A *siab*—which was hammered into his nickname of mock deference by childhood friends, who are all now either dead, disappeared, or barely surviving in exile.

Siab and his wife, Tietsa, known around town as Indian Marie, will always carry themselves with pride. They will never beg. Never grovel. And never step off their property without their smart peacoats and hats whose cuts pay subtle tribute to their heritage, without getting undue attention from people who have a problem with their continued existence on this land.

Erasmus makes his way toward the boulder and says to Siab, at the same elevated volume as before, "What say you about my offer from the other day?"

Siab doesn't answer.

"The tubers."

Siab hoists another sack from his harvest onto the back of his mule. "I don't know what you mean."

"Tuber. From the Latin for bump, lump, or swelling. An Old World term for a New World staple. Spuds. Potatoes, my boy."

Siab wishes the man would go away. That all of them would go away.

"OK, I see your negotiating technique. Let me refresh your memory about my unrefusable offer. I will take these potatoes and trade them, the lot of them, to a colleague of mine in Chinatown, a very savvy businessman indeed, considering his own racial pedigree. In return, he will give me a superior imported good from the Orient, which I shall then resell to my professional and social colleagues for a duly superior price and share back with you at a fair and predetermined flat fee, worth at least what you would make for selling these tubers directly to your other... shall we say, coarser associates. Let us dare to consider it a partnership."

Siab and his wife worked without rest to harvest the potatoes, and he is not interested in this man's scheme. It is true that, as a *tyee*, he was never destined for the life of a farmer. His family had once had slaves of their own, captives from the inland and river tribes, to do that sort of work. But these days, Siab does what he must. And he's found that he has a talent for farming. He and his wife don't owe Erasmus any favors and have already shared many things with their neighbor—from chickens to bricks to free labor—in the man's barren dirt patch on the far side of the hill.

A couple of the seagulls return and land atop the dark gray rock, getting ever closer to the remaining loose potatoes. Siab knows they're hungry. Their beaches have been polluted and built over with piers on creosote piles. Their shellfish consumed by the ravenous human scavengers, who leave filth and open sewage in return. Siab is not concerned about the birds eating his bounty. He knows them, and they know him. It's the unpredictable Boston whom he keeps in the corner of his eye.

Siab can accept the fact that Erasmus is always taking, and there is no sharing in return. Since his earliest memories, when the first white settlers arrived by ship and proclaimed the ancestral Duwamish land to be *Alki New York*, or roughly "New York Someday" in Chinook trade jargon, he had come to understand the new nature of things. This nature of the growing Boston territory that continues over the mountains and on to another ocean that he would never see.

Most Duwamish adults had been killed by smallpox or sent to reservations. Children were shipped off to Indian boarding schools, never to be heard from again. Even Chief Si'ahl died across the water, packed onto a bit of unfarmable scrubland with other uprooted tribes competing for any meager hunting. The Great Chief's passing didn't earn a single mention in the local newspapers.

Some Duwamish survive in this changing place, working in brutal jobs at hops farms, timber mills, and brothels, living precarious lives on the streets or, in some cases, quietly intermarrying with white men. But Siab alone had figured out how to own land like a Boston.

He bides his time in quiet resistance, maintaining his toehold on this one little hill of territory with its big stone marker, as he waits for the settlers' wave to break and finally recede. And now, after all of these winters, it appears that it will. Ever since the fire.

It was, by far, the biggest blaze Siab had ever witnessed. Some dumb yellow-haired kid was said to have knocked over a flaming glue pot into a bunch of sawdust. And, sure enough, half of the stolen city built from the stolen forests was repossessed by fire and wind. The smoke blocked out the sun, and ash rained over Siab's farm.

Siab had always known, as his mother had told him, that the Changer would return, and the entire undertaking of the settlers would eventually collapse in on its own recklessness, greed, and predation. Besides, he had always figured that the proximity and the height of their wood structures, which they'd nailed together at ever-faster speed, were an unnecessary risk. The Duwamish, for all of their supposed savagery and lack of technical knowledge, never would have built their longhouses on top of each other like that. It made no sense.

Food has become harder to find in the few circles of the seasons since the fire. Some of the white people are still living in tents along the waterfront and competing with the gulls for the dwindling clams. Many don't know how to search for shellfish and end up exhausting themselves digging holes to nowhere in the sand. They also don't know how to read the tides to understand when the snails menstruate and the clams can't be eaten. Some get very sick. Some die.

If he and Tietsa can hold on a bit longer, he knows that the world will start to change and change back to how it was. Siab needs to sell the potatoes at the market in town so he can make his land payments to the city bank with its ever-hungry iron vault. There is some sickness with the money, having to do with mistakes made by other, faraway banks. He finds this all laughable. Their money is just another story these demented people tell each other. But story or not, it still means that he must sell more potatoes to make more money so he can pay even more for this small bit of land that has always belonged to his people.

Alas, seasons always change. And the season of the settler is passing. The forests will grow back over the plowed fields and burned buildings. Salmon will return to the bay and rivers. The Duwamish people will come out of the shadows and return from exile. And their martyred ancestors will finally get proper burials. This will be the fulfillment of Siab's purpose.

In order to make Erasmus go away, Siab decides that he will, once again, give one sack of potatoes to his bothersome neighbor. Of course, he won't share the whole harvest, which is what the man desires. But one sack is still substantial. Siab would like to see Erasmus learn to grow a whole bag of potatoes.

As Siab decides how to best explain his offer without entering deeper negotiations, Erasmus picks up a half of a broken brick from the nearby construction pile, mutters something about "infernal sky vermin," and lofts the fragment in the general direction of the gulls on the rock.

Siab watches the path of the brick as it peaks and then curves downward, achieving an improbable yet direct hit on a bird's head, instantly killing the animal in a spatter of red blood, white feathers, and splintered yellow beak.

The two men stand in silence as the other gulls squawk and fly from the boulder.

Siab feels the blackest of voids opening under him. He must get away from this man. Get the man off of his property. Unsure of what to do next, Siab marches toward his house to grab his shovel, avoiding looking at his neighbor.

"Shit." Erasmus shakes his head, a bit sheepishly. "Oh well. Just protecting our harvest, right?"

Siab returns with his shovel, the old one he's had since he was a kid and has painstakingly maintained, thrice replacing the wooden handle and brushing and oiling the metal to keep it rust-free. He is tempted to give the tool a nice, arcing swing and remove Erasmus's oversize head with the edge of the blade. Or at least give the man a solid spank across the jawline with its broadside. Teach him a lesson about his place in this world.

Instead, Siab leans the shovel against the rock and collects the limp bird, carefully tucking its wings under its body and nudging salvageable pieces of the beak back into place with his thumbs.

"That's quite an erratic rock, huh?" Erasmus motions toward the boulder with his chin.

Siab pretends he can't hear him. He rolls the gull inside of a scrap of torn burlap and lays it on the ground.

"Likely carried here by glacial ice. Hundreds of miles from the mountains up north. Maybe even Alaska. You believe that same ice was more than half a mile thick? Carved the lake here, the Sound, this hill, everything."

Siab can do without this traveling beggar and bird murderer explaining to him the history of this land. Before he'd lost his child teeth, when he was still little Si'sia, he could recite from memory the story of how Storm Wind and his mother drove North Wind away, melting the ice and flooding the valleys with fresh water.

As his shovel breaks ground, Siab finds himself slicked in a cool, sticky sweat. Killing the mystical, if not obnoxious, seabird, even if done unintentionally, has convinced Siab that Erasmus will bring calamity and suffering on all those in his path. This is not a typical Duwamish conviction; his people esteem the crow much more than the common gull. But it falls under Siab's personal cosmology of beliefs after a life spent as the region's most sought-after boat guide on and about the saltwater inlets and numerous freshwater lakes.

To make matters worse, this gull was killed right here. On the rock. On this sacred land.

"So, what say you, my boy?" Erasmus gathers himself again and motions toward the unclaimed potatoes.

Siab turns his back to the man. He pauses for a moment to build resolution toward his decision, wipes the dampness from his neck, and continues digging. "Not today, sir. I see now that you will bring misfortune to others for the rest of your days."

Tietsa comes out the front door of the house to see who is on their property. Before she is off the front porch, Siab gives her the whistle. The specific three-part whistle that they have rehearsed together. It says: Go inside and put the heavy fir beam across the door. Load the rifle and stay away from the window. Do not open the door for anyone until I return.

When she hesitates, Siab whistles again.

Erasmus tries to walk around in front of Siab, but the Duwamish man keeps rotating away. "I could care less about your irrational superstitions. But it's hard to not take your miserly, misguided, and, dare I say, shortsighted refusal to participate in the grand opportunity that I offered you as an affront. A very personal sort of disrespect at that."

"Leave my property." Siab puts on his wide-brimmed hat and tightens down his mule's straps for the trip into town. "Now, please."

Erasmus surveys the length of the farm in a sweeping, speculative gaze and wanders back toward the woods. "Things change. They always do. Watch yourself, Old Sam."

Siab waits to be sure that his wife is inside with the door closed and that Erasmus has retreated beyond the perimeter of their property before leading his mule to the trailhead. He made his wife promise that, if she must shoot, to wait and be sure the man is standing inside the house before pulling the trigger. And then to make sure he dies. There can be no debate, doubt, or discussion with the police, as the white man's word will always win. Siab watches the house in silence, long enough to finish an entire one of those new, machine-rolled cigarettes he'd bought when last in town. Then he and the mule proceed up the trail.

No more than five minutes into hiking the first hill, Erasmus reappears, shuffling, coughing, and swearing down trail from Siab.

NINE *2014*

The house is a glass and steel affair with an *ipé* tropical hardwood deck cantilevered out over the lake and a view back across the water to the city skyline. It's the house that Mothership built. Kim and her husband, Zafar, have both worked at the company on and off since forever, leaving here and there to have a short tryst with a competitor and then negotiate a bigger compensation package upon their returns.

"C'mon, Percy, what happened to my upbeat, positive husband?" Sami says as she pulls the car into the semicircular driveway in front of the lakefront home. "Zafar will be here. I bet he's not making a big deal about it."

"He has to be here. He lives here."

"He still doesn't huff and puff the whole time."

"Yeah, he steps out every five minutes for a work call."

"He's got a big job."

"What's the income threshold at which 'oppressive gender roles' or 'absentee workaholic' changes to 'he's got a big job'?"

"Can we please not go there?"

"I'm not going anywhere. I wish I were, but I'm right here. I'm just saying."

Sami parks and sets the emergency brake with expressive force. She always drives and cannot abide Percy's frequently distracted driving, much in the same way that he is distrustful of her convoluted directions. Long ago, they decided that she is the family's official driver, and he is the navigator. It's one of a handful of core compromises that keeps them married.

The four kids fill out the back two rows of the food-crumbs-and-discarded-packaging-strewn Land Cruiser, which is an unrepentant gas guzzler—a source of ongoing shame for Percy, but there are no car payments left on it, and Sami's long resisted getting a minivan and, thereby, giving up on the last hints of existence beyond her maternal persona.

"Ma? Mommy?" Macy calls from the third-row seat as they start to get out of the vehicle.

"Don't worry, we're not fighting. Just discussing."

"Can we play video games on their giant TV?" Macy asks. The other three kids second the notion with a variety of affirmative grunts and agreements of "Yeah, Mom."

"This is the first time your aunt has invited us over in what? Three years? You are going to go inside and be polite. Nice manners. Not be feral. And you are not going to obsess over video games."

"But?" the kids all seem to say at once.

"Or sugar. Don't embarrass us. Please." Sami gets out of the SUV, feeling a bit too aware of her lackluster, budget-conscious attire, and Percy begrudgingly follows. The kids are already heading up the stairs.

Kim's assistant Elise opens and holds the front door. A generic yet attractive college grad from somewhere out of state with short, straight hair and neutral business attire full of clean lines, she offers the family little more than a nod as they pile into the house.

Sami has always felt like a guest at her sister-in-law's. And not a welcome family guest sort of thing—more like another professional assistant getting an invite to the boss's place, where you are hesitant about the quality of your small talk and about where you can and cannot set your drink.

No matter how frequently Kim refers to Sami as "sis," it feels more like an infantilizing nickname than an indication of familial warmth. But maybe Sami is overthinking things. She is aware that she tends to do that. Plus, not everyone gets the chance to have a holiday dinner with the honorable Kim Stalworth, likely future mayor of the city . . . these days, not even her close family members.

Percy only attends the odd holiday or family dinner like this because his elderly mother is still alive, and he knows it's important to her to keep propping up the image of a functional family that enjoys, or at least can tolerate, each other's company. Once Grandma Stalworth is out of the equation, Percy won't be attending any more events at his sister's place. Even now, he will be physically present, but Sami is sure he'll retreat into thinking about a seasonal fresh-hops cider or how to best reroute a bike hand-brake cable around a folding headset.

The kids, on the other hand, love to go to Kim and Zafar's house, as there are any number of huge screens, a pool table, air hockey, and endless fountain drinks from a programmable soft-drink dispenser behind the bar.

Elise directs the kids downstairs and Percy and Sami into the living room.

"That's so nice that you're joining us," Sami says to Elise. "Is your fiancé coming too?"

"Right." She checks the time on her smartphone and then walks them into a second living room beyond the first living room. "Kim and Zafar will be out in a few moments. I've got to get back across the bridge."

The space is attached to the long dining room that then conjoins with floor-to-ceiling accordion windows opening onto the outside deck over the water. Sami is stunned by the view, even though she's been here before. She stops staring out over the water to notice Percy's mom in her wheelchair, rolled right up to the edge of the twenty-foot-long hardwood table. Grandma Stalworth's eyes are closed, and a wine spritzer is cradled in her left hand, her gunmetal-blue perm nodding slightly with each inhale. These days her drinks get only a dash of wine in them, but she still managers to act blacked out after two.

As Elise excuses herself and leaves, she turns back to Sami. "I have to come back and take Grandma Stalworth to her nursing home after dinner."

Sami apologizes that they only have one car and can't fit all of the kids plus the wheelchair. "We could do two trips?"

"Just do me a favor and remind Kim to call me with a civilized amount of lead time. Not like a 'come get her right this second' thing. My parents are here visiting for the first time. They flew a long way. They're meeting my fiancé for the first time. Can you do that for me, Sandy?"

"Sami."

Elise gives her a thumbs-up and continues back toward the front of the house.

Percy and Sami each give Grandma Stalworth a kiss atop her hair that smells of dye, perfume, and baby powder. They leave her to rest and can see Zafar out on the deck, talking into a headset with a mic, pacing, gesticulating, and arguing in what Sami knows to be Urdu.

Kim bursts in from the kitchen shouting Zafar's name. She is dressed in upscale athletic gear with no shoes. She wears no makeup at home but has her hair sculpted back into a sleek blond bob that showcases her high cheekbones and tidy jaw. Sami admires the lack of lines in her sister-in-law's smooth face. The definition in her upper arms. Dermatologists and triathlon coaches go a long way. Not to mention nutritionists, personal chefs, and probably a small brigade of plastic surgeons. But Kim's competitive nature prevents her from ever admitting to such support. To her, it's all a balance of natural talent and the character-defining discipline.

"We have to get moving, right to the entrées," Kim announces to her brother and Sami without greeting them. "My chef tried to claim she had today off, but, c'mon, what am I supposed to serve my guests? I made a deal with her for early in, early out."

Sami simultaneously hates her sister-in-law and worships everything about her. Kim was groomed for success since childhood. She and Percy's father, legendary former mayor Bobby Stalworth, would talk about city council meeting minutes with the kids at the dinner table. While he was a good ole boy who had never worked with a female above the level of secretary, Mayor Stalworth recognized early on that more passive and idealistic Percy was not moving in his direction and started coaching younger, hardheaded Kim to go into business and then politics. An engineering degree followed by an MBA was the plan of attack. He encouraged her to wait to go into politics until she'd proven herself as "a competent contributor in the private sector." This would help her to better line her pockets than he had as a career public servant and give her a more dynamic résumé to eventually break out beyond city politics and onto a national stage.

Even now, walking across the dining room and delivering directions, Kim carries herself with the regal posture of a former synchronized swimmer. She was on two of Stanford's collegiate national title teams, was a near miss at the Olympics, and credits the sport for her self-control, teamwork, and ability to navigate the complex process of subjective judging. When given the opportunity, she will buttonhole Sami, or anyone else in her proximity, about how synchronized swimming—or artistic swimming, as she now calls it—gave her a thick skin and taught her how to never give up when the odds were stacked against her as the only woman in the room during her business education or the early years of her career. In fact, it's made its way into her recent stump speeches.

Upon completing her MBA, Kim had her pick of industries and was recruited by Wall Street, defense contractors, and management consulting but went straight into tech, which was still a Wild West where she could make a name for herself. Kim bet on the relative backwater of her hometown over the Valley because she was looking to make a big impact, and Mothership was still in enough of a formative phase that she could carve out her own little principality. Plus, she was able to coattail off the regional name ID of her mentor and father.

In her estimation, and now in her campaign collateral, this city is the future of the country—New York Someday. The next act: keeping America relevant as the East Coast ossifies from state taxes, infrastructure decay, political gridlock, and, most glaringly, a lack of innovation.

This far into her career, she'll admit that San Francisco retains a bit of a lead in the tech gold rush. Or, as she likes to say, is the Florence of this American Renaissance. But with the right leadership, Kim is sure her hometown will be remembered as the Milan or the Venice.

Kim slides some platters onto the table. "I said no appetizers with dairy. Clear as day. No dairy. And, instead, I got no goddamn appetizers. Not one. You believe this shit?"

"Great practice for city politics." Kim's husband, Zafar, enters from the deck. He has the frosted-templed, patrician air of someone who might have been a national-team cricketer or politician himself had he grown up back in Pakistan but instead was ignored, if not marginalized, as an immigrant teenager in the small-town Midwest and retreated into the relative safe space of computer science and business. Nobody ever mentions it, but Kim recruited him out of Harvard Business School for his first job at Mothership, where she was his boss.

Percy wakes Grandma Stalworth with a series of firm pats on the back and shoulders. As she comes to, the rest of them exchange awkward pleasantries and down a couple glasses of wine. Sami wants a third drink but doesn't want to outpace her hostess. "What about the kids?" Sami asks.

"I said hi to them downstairs. They have pizza, ice cream, Xbox. Everything they ever needed or wanted. Problem solved. They're all looking so grown up and handsome these days."

Sami offers to help Kim ferry the rest of the platters from an island in the kitchen to the dining room table. Percy does the same, but his sister ignores him.

As they all sit, Kim picks at a purple carrot from a vegetable dish, takes a quick bite, and registers her displeasure with the temperature. "Never should have agreed to let my cook go early. Once you start to get soft, people take advantage. "

Zafar places a hand on the back of her arm. She pulls it away.

He then holds up his wineglass with water in it and makes a toast. "To Kim Stalworth. The next mayor of this city. She is going to need the whole family's support on this."

Percy laughs, and everyone stares at him. He likes to remind Sami that even though the family's doctor told the newspapers that the great Bobby Stalworth's demise was an unintentional interaction between acetaminophen and warfarin, which might have been somewhat true, he left out the dozen alprazolam and most of a Costco house-label bottle of single malt. Not that downing a bottle of whiskey was a great challenge for the former mayor.

Kim works through her brother's slight and initiates some halting small talk about the kids and Mothership and how hard it is to find good help these days. But this has never been about an attempt to host their cold, emotionally disabled version of a family dinner. Or catching up with Sami, Percy, and the kids. It'd been so long since Sami and Percy had been invited to the house that they took a wrong freeway exit on the way over. As they near the end of the rushed meal, Kim turns to Sami. "Let's get to it then: What's going on with the school?"

Sami explains that things are complex and that she had hoped to talk about the school situation with Kim and pick her brain for some ideas. She stops short of saying that she'd prefer not to do it in front of the whole family. In fact, she wants to beg Kim for help but doesn't want to grovel.

"Fortunately, I've developed a very actionable plan for you. Very strategic. Because tactics without strategy—"

"—Is the noise before defeat." Zafar cracks his knuckles.

"Sun Tzu." Kim and her husband beam at each other in a moment of mutual admiration, bordering on a public display of affection.

Percy looks nauseous. Sami stops chewing her cold, but otherwise excellent, lamb cutlet with horseradish sauce. Her blood starts to carbonate with excitement and potential. She forgets to breathe. "Wait . . . really?"

"The school is known for the arts, right?" Kim plays with her fork on her plate.

"Look at my kid sister, doing her research," Percy says.

"I had Elise do some googling. The bar for basic research is awfully low these days."

Sami wipes her mouth with her napkin and readies herself for a long-awaited turn in her string of tough luck and bad breaks. "Yes, music. Stevenson always had a good music program. It used to have the best—"

"That's the problem right there," Zafar says, leaning forward. "You need science. Technology. Engineering. Math. That is all that matters nowadays. STEM. Art exists in service to hard sciences. Think about a music scholarship. Who pays for that? A musician? Come now. That is paid via value-generating work in engineering or math or chemistry. These other pursuits have value too, of course. But personal and emotional value, as hobbies."

Sami senses that this roller coaster has already reached its peak and is starting to career over the far side. Short trip. She keeps her head down to avoid any I-told-you-so looks from her husband.

Kim presses in over the table. "How many dedicated elementary STEM programs do you think there are in the city?"

"I dunno." Sami holds a tight smile. "How does an elementary student even know what they want to study, let alone technical stuff?"

"Yes, if their parents want them to have a life. A career. That's how they know," Zafar continues. "And who are a school's customers anyway? You always have to think about your audience. It's not the kids, that's for sure."

"Customers are, well . . . I think you're thinking more in terms of a private school situation, not a public—"

Kim interrupts, "The answer to my question is: there's one other dedicated STEM elementary program. I was a little bummed to find that out that there's competition. But, and it's a big 'but,' it's on the opposite side of town."

"Stevenson has no dedicated technology or engineering classes. Math. The regular kind, sure. No real science. Kind of. Maybe. But all that stuff isn't in line with the school's culture or history," Sami says.

"Don't get me wrong. I love music as much as the next guy," Zafar says, waving his arms toward the adjacent room. "Obviously, you have seen my collection of vintage Pearl Jam memorabilia?"

Kim nods at him affectionately.

"What's your second-favorite band?" Percy groans. "Golf?"

Zafar pushes through, unfazed. "Kids can learn music after school, for God's sake. What percentage of people become professional musicians?"

"I don't know about all this math business," Grandma Stalworth cuts in. "Way too many nerds in this city already."

"Yeah, Mothership is a veritable Asperger's convention," Kim adds. "But it also veritably prints money."

Grandma Stalworth continues, "This place used to be all loggers and fishermen. My first husband was a longshoreman. Broke as hell, but you should've seen the muscles up and down his arms. Like Manila rope."

"You had a first husband, Ma?" Kim looks at Percy for the first time since they sat down at the table.

"Why do you two think you have such different personalities?" Grandma Stalworth winks to her adult children, finishes her spritzer, and taps the edge of the glass. "Can somebody do right by an old lady and keep 'em coming?"

Kim does her best to ignore her mother and move back to stable ground. "Here's what you need to do, sis: Establish a STEM program at Stevenson, even something small before the end of the year. Pump the offerings a bit. I'll help with the school's overall rebrand. Then, I'll personally make sure you get an exemption for the closure. We're not going to ask the district to change their minds just because they have a soft spot for kids playing the recorder. No, we're gonna get a firm, legally binding exemption for this essential coursework."

Sami finishes her wine and focuses intently on her plate although she can sense Percy shaking his head in disagreement. She takes too long to answer, and Zafar jumps back in. "Start with a few dedicated tech and engineering classes. Easy."

"PTA doesn't hire teachers or create classes," Percy replies, stepping in for Sami, who's still trying to process everything.

"So, push the administration to make a few creative cross listings," adds Kim. "Call some of the third-grade math classes 'Intro to Engineering' or, I don't know, 'Innovation Station.' It's all spin. You can fudge a lot of it. The key is that you need some dedicated space for the STEM program. A real lab. Something tangible to showcase to the district. No way we can get an exemption for pure vaporware."

Sami tries to reengage, her head swimming with permutations. "I want to save the school, of course. There are just so many layers."

"Don't fear change, Sami. Change is inevitable. Disruption is what we do in the tech industry. What looks like a monopoly today is simply a commanding market position that will be overtaken tomorrow. We're constantly adapting. If you stand still, you die." Kim pushes her plate away from her, having barely eaten. "In my first job, I spent two years building up a product I loved, then I spent two years trying to kill it by building its free online competitor. Within the same company. But free. Well, we hit you with the auto-pay fees after you're locked in and afraid of losing all of your data. But that's the mentality you need to survive these days. Move fast, break things, and keep moving."

"Breaking things is different when talking about a school with real children, not some goddamn app," Percy offers.

"See, that's a failure of vision right there. Don't be a prisoner to the past," argues Zafar. "A school is not just a school. Why can't we think about schools more like apps? Or, more precisely, like start-ups. Nimble. Innovative. Customer-first. You need to always employ a data-driven growth mindset. In everything you do. We did it as parents. We do it in our marriage." He removes his smartphone from his pocket, opens a colorful pie chart on the screen, and pushes it in Percy's face. "Kim and I track and optimize the total time we dedicate to our partnership in order to consistently hit our quarterly targets. And look at the abundance we enjoy."

"I'm just the head of the PTA. There's only so much I can do." Sami feels a sharp cramp in her stomach.

"Who else is in charge there? Wild Bill Doucette?" Kim gives a dismissive laugh.

Sami fires Kim a quizzical look, wondering what her sister-in-law actually knows about all of this.

Kim builds momentum, seeming ready to jump atop the table. "Let's open the kimono here. Sorry, Sami, is that PC? It's OK, my husband's Asian. South Asian? Either way, Zafar and I will make it work. Right, love?"

Zafar crosses one calfskin slip-on loafer over his knee, thoughtfully scratches his temple, and nods in confident affirmation.

"And what do you expect in return, Kim?" Percy asks.

"C'mon, Percy." Sami's cheeks flush.

"No, it's OK," Kim says. "He's always doubted my successes and resulting generosity. Look, I want to see the school flourish."

"And?" Percy tries again.

"To help out my wonderful sister-in-law, Sami, over here."

"And?" asks Grandma Stalworth. "Be honest, Kimberly."

"Well, it's more of a lucky by-product or knock-on effect. But—just spitballing some preemptive risk mitigation for the primaries—I can't let myself get outflanked on the left by that broke-ass bitch on the school board who is starting to get some traction with her Facebook screeds calling me out for not living inside the city limits."

"You most definitely don't," says Percy, rotating his head to take in the ample gathering spaces in the suburban mansion and, out the windows, toward the water and hills that stand between them and the skyline.

"We own an apartment. Right smack in the middle of downtown," Kim hits back.

"Uh, that's Mom's," Percy says.

"Uh, she lives in a nursing home, Percy."

"I'm just visiting the nursing home. To see if I like it." Grandma Stalworth scours the room for someone to corroborate. "That's what you told me. Remember?"

The best she gets is a sympathetic hand on the shoulder from Sami.

Kim doesn't lose her stride. "I'm a local no matter my current mailing address. Our great-grandfather put this city on the map. Look, I even keep one of his most prized possessions over there on the mantel." She points a small golden statuette of a Roman god with wings and winged boots. "And our father was one of our most celebrated mayors, goddammit. My local credentials are a nonissue. But that commie school board candidate is also attacking me for having sent my son, our son, poor little Tucker, to private school. What a vicious low blow. He's twenty-two now. When I chose his private kindergarten, I didn't know I'd be running for mayor. Jesus. We need to come together as a family to prevent any more of these petty ad hominem attacks. Attacks on our children. Your own nephew."

"You totally knew you'd be running for mayor back then," Percy says.

Kim ignores her brother. "This school board lady claims to be some sort of a feminist. Wanting to be a role model for other women. But when it comes down to it: she's a total cunt. And the whole holier-than-thou public school self-righteousness is so pedestrian and tedious."

Percy laughs. "Too bad you can't simply ask your public school union card–carrying brother to go on the campaign trail with you."

"Too bad. Yeah, that'd be all too loyal." She turns back to Sami. "Here's the deal: Let's come up with a doable budget, and Zafar and I will bankroll the STEM facility. Do it right. And fast. Let's save this school from closure."

Sami's mood brightens. The roller coaster is headed back up the track. Don't look a gift horse in the mouth, she tells herself. Grandma Masako said that her mom, Ruth, looked every gift horse in the mouth, searching for Greek soldiers but ultimately rejecting any possible good fortune over a cavity or inflamed gum. She doesn't want to do this as Kim's proposed. She doesn't want to give up on music, but there must be a way to still navigate this. To creatively compromise.

Zafar uses his hands to frame out an invisible marquee. "How do you like the sound of *The Stalworth STEM School*? Nice alliteration, no?"

Sami chokes. "Wait. But my grandmother—all those signatures. That took years."

"You're a Stalworth too, right?" Zafar grins. "The campaign tieback is essential."

"It's a slight pivot off the groundwork you've already done, sis. I'll lean on the principal. The superintendent. It'll be more straightforward than you think."

"Renaming this school was my idea. I told my grandmother. I promised her."

"Evolution equals survival. Twitter was a side project at a podcasting company. You think those guys said, 'Great idea, but too bad we can't do it because we're a podcasting company'?"

Sami slumps forward in her chair. Her face feels hot. She has to pee. Or vomit. Or both.

"You do want to save the school, right?" Kim pries.

"It's tacky," Percy says, "naming something after yourself. You still being alive and all."

"First off, it would be named after our esteemed great-grandfather, Erasmus Stalworth. Although, true, most people would only remember the last name."

"Poor bastard died in an experimental dirigible accident," Grandma Stalworth says to no one in particular.

"That's probably just what they said when it was syphilis." Kim clears her throat and stays focused on her brother. "Second, in terms of me still being alive: I bet you wish I weren't around anymore, so your shortcomings as my sibling weren't so glaringly apparent."

Grandma Stalworth weighs back in, "He did try to smother you with a pillow from the davenport when you two were kids."

"I bet he was too lazy to follow through." Kim finishes her drink and tips the empty glass toward Percy. "Brother, go make yourself useful. Get one for Mom too." Then she pinches her index finger and thumb to within a centimeter of each other and mouths "just a splash," nodding toward their mother.

Percy half stands from his chair, a rare rage shaking his lean, bike-commuter frame.

Zafar steps in from the side, putting an arm around his brother-in-law's shoulder. "Easy. This is a family conversation. In the best interest of everyone in this family. A rare win-win. It will save the school. All those poor kids wanting nothing more than a shot at a future in a productive career. And, yes, we'll get a couple of press cycles out of it. A good talking point or two. Good photography, of course. A way to deflect and counterpunch in the debates. And, to be honest, I don't give a shit about the name after the election. You can get new signatures. Try to change it to Grandma whatever. Or Chuck E. Fucking Cheese, for all we care."

"I can see it now," Percy says, wriggling out of Zafar's half embrace and mimicking his marquee hand motions. "The *Vote Kim Stalworth, Corporate Democrat for Token Disadvantaged Public School Students* Elementary." He then excuses himself, saying something about needing to go to the bathroom and disinfect his conscience.

Grandma Stalworth laughs through her nose.

"What?" Kim stares at her mother.

"He's always had your number." Grandma stares back with no intimidation. "Since you first ran for seventh-grade class president."

"That was sixth grade. Thank you. And I won too." Kim redirects. "I was thinking more along the lines of the Erasmus Stalworth STEM Center. STEM Academy? Lab? Workshop? What do you think, Zafar? Incubator? That sounds more current. More bleeding-edge."

Zafar sits back down and kicks his feet up on Percy's empty chair. "We also have to be mindful about SEO and how those keywords play in search. I can tap my agency support for some focus-group market research. Get a word cloud of terms that resonate with likely voters. Also, Sami, we can supply a few laptops and digital projectors to the STEM program. Software licensing, of course. That's easy. And by 'we,' I mean Mothership. Deal?"

"Look, I appreciate all of this." Sami tries to look up but then sinks her head back down as her nausea increases. "It's all a lot. A lot to think about."

"Give Elise a call." Kim stands up. "She'll walk you through the next steps."

"I mean, we'd be transposing something else atop generations of school culture. History. I'm, I'm not sure that's in our best interest."

"The school's best interest or your personal best interest?" Kim slams her palms down on the table. Her eyes go wide, scanning left and right and then settling again on Sami. "Let me help with that. When I become mayor, with my own mother as my witness here today, I will give you the job of your choice in city hall. I will punch your fucking ticket, sis. Like it's never been punched before. God knows, whatever my brother is doing to your ticket, he ain't punching it."

Sami straightens up and tries to match Kim's titanium gaze but can't maintain it for more than a few awkward seconds. She has to double-check that her mouth is closed while she processes the information.

"Deal then? OK. Settled." Kim hits a button on her phone and puts it to her ear. "Elise. Yes. Come get my mom." Kim starts pacing. Grandma Stalworth raises her glass again, signaling for a refill with a new urgency. Kim waves it off. "Yes, now. Of course, right now. When else would it be?"

TEN   *2014*

Sierra sits in the back seat of her dad's Westy, trying to understand a minor scale she learned from teacher Monica at school. She has it written down in pencil on a piece of lined paper as *1–b3–4–b5–5–b7*. She balances the sheet on her knees and tries to play the scale. It's still too hard for her, but she did learn that what makes it sound so cool is the minor third sound of 1–b3, 1–b3, 1–b3 and 5–b7, 5–b7, 5–b7.

If only talking with adults and other kids could be based on such rules and structures. She takes a break and makes another attempt at sketching her dad's head, ponytail and all, from her back seat vantage point while he waits for his chance to take a left turn across Stevenson Way, into the busted-up restaurant's parking lot.

Even though things are difficult between her parents right now, at least Sierra is doing a bit better at school. She's feeling slightly more comfortable, able to talk with some other kids and no longer spending recess and lunch all by herself. Learning music gives her a focus, something to talk about with other kids, and makes school not suck quite so bad.

"You should call back the PTA lady, Bruce," Sierra reminds her dad as he pulls the car into one of the spaces on the edge of the lot along some blackberries and a grassy ditch full of standing rainwater and empty aluminum cans.

"It's way more than I bargained for." He grabs some papers, a pen, and his cane.

Bruce already told Sierra's mom that he was going to do something with the PTA. And Sierra had thought it a good idea to back him up and make sure her mom was frequently reminded of the fact that Bruce had taken that big step. The big step that her mom had long wanted from him. "But Bruce, I told—"

"Anyway, bigger fish to fry now, honey," he says, slamming the door.

"Bruce. Wait," she shouts to him through the window as he makes his way over to the parked white car with the cigarette man inside. "I'll organize the papers for you. Let me help. I can do it. I can do it all."

When he doesn't answer, she goes back to coloring in her dad's ponytail in her drawing. She spells out his name below the caricature in big bubble letters. She calls him by his first name not because she feels distant from him but because he has always been a Bruce kind of guy. Not a normal dad. Never a normal anything, really.

She puts down the pencil and notices a protuberance of dried chewing gum on the rear side of the driver's seat. Down in the footwell, she can still see the red paper French fries holder thing that led to her parent's fight about what Bruce was feeding her, back when they all still lived together. Back when things were better at home. Bruce is also not the kind of guy to spend a lot of time vacuuming his ancient Westy. In some ways, it is surprising that he has a car, a real car . . . one that runs at all.

She is also tempted to clean it for him. She could do that for him too. She likes to have a job. A chore. A purpose. Something to put her mind to when she doesn't get to do the things she likes to do, like music and doodling and eating candy. Anyway, she knows she could clean the whole car for him and make it look nice for Mommy, so maybe they would get along better.

But Sierra won't do it because she learned the hard way after

Mommy came home from a work trip to San Diego and Sierra had been trying to do the laundry and fold it. She had been hoping that Mommy would come home in a good mood and not be mad at Bruce, for a change. But Sierra didn't know how much detergent to use, what could go in the dryer or not, and ended up making things worse. Mommy wasn't mad at Sierra but was mad at Bruce for not doing it himself. Same thing with making dinner. Cleaning the house. A long list of other things. And Sierra knows that waiting until someone else cleans the car for him would fall in the same category.

Not that her mom says all of this to her. Mommy and Bruce try not to fight in front of her. They go outside. They go in the basement. They used to go into their bedroom when they still slept in the same room. But she heard some stuff anyway. Even if Sierra has problems talking sometimes, or a lot of the time, she can hear just fine. She knows that her mom thinks Bruce is frustrating. Because Bruce is not like most dads. Bruce can only be Bruce. Her mom knows that too. She used to be OK with it. Until she wasn't.

Sierra is like her mom in many ways. But not in every way. She is like Bruce in lots of ways too. She wishes her parents could get along better and start living together again. She doesn't like going back and forth between the houses, and nobody seems any happier now, even though her mom keeps telling her that it is for the best.

The sweat suit man now gets out of the white car to talk with Bruce. He still wears a big gold Jesus necklace and Nikes so white that they must have come fresh out of the box. Sierra wishes she had a sweat suit like him. But it would be hard to keep clean. Especially while traveling around in a van her mom calls "a mobile junk drawer."

Bruce told Sierra not to get out of the Westy. Made her promise that she would stay put. He and the other man are having an adult conversation. And Bruce almost never says things like "stay put" or "promise" anything or especially "adult conversation." He believes in Sierra making decisions for herself. He always told her that she could listen to any music she wanted or see any movie she wanted . . . that it was not his job to judge these things . . . and it was up to her to decide if a movie was too scary for her or not.

While Bruce is talking to the man in the sweat suit, Sierra decides to go ahead and start sorting the PTA paperwork into piles on the back seat. She's not sure what she is doing or supposed to do with all of these papers—Bruce probably doesn't know either—but she doesn't want him to go back on his word and let down her mom, again.

Bruce and the man put a sheet of paper up against the outside windshield of the van. The man takes the pen from Bruce and removes the cap but then slows to read something and starts talking to Bruce in a loud voice. Suddenly, Bruce and the guy are having an argument. Not a fight. Not exactly. But it sounds like they don't agree. And the man is raising his voice at Bruce and swearing and moving his hands around in the air with the pen between his fingers.

As the argument gets louder, Bruce grabs the paper and does his awkward attempt at fast walking back around to the driver's side of the Westy.

"We had a deal," he yells back at the man.

"You expect me to bend over backward on rent. And remodeling. But you won't work with me on nothing?" the man responds. "You're still the same stubborn Viking asshole."

"I prefer that you say 'Norwegian American asshole.'"

"Go fuck yourself."

"Fine. You know what I'm gonna do? I'm gonna go talk to your aunt. Without you."

"The hell you are."

Bruce unlocks the van's door with his key. "I don't care. This is bullshit." He sees Sierra watching through the window and motions, with a shooing-away swipe of the back of his hand, for her to stay out of the discussion or, at least, not be so obvious that she is paying attention to it. The two men start to talk again, but no one looks happy.

She goes back to sorting the paperwork and finds that not all of it, maybe not even most of it, is for the PTA. There's also all sorts of stuff about something called cannabis for the State Liquor Control Board.

Bruce promised her that the new business will change their lives in positive ways. Sierra wants to tell her mom about this big news and make sure she knows Bruce is working hard to make things better for their family. But he made Sierra swear to not talk about it. To anyone. Maybe because he wants it to be a surprise? She's not sure. And even if she did break her promise to him and told her mom, she knows nothing about the business or what kind of work it would be. She only knows the fact that it is going to be a huge success.

Bruce returns to the van for a second time, opens the door, and gets in. He doesn't usually have much of a temper, but she can tell that he is angry from the way he squeezes the steering wheel, scrunches up the paperwork still in his hand, and punches the wheel when the car doesn't start on the first try.

She wants to ask him about liquor and cannabis but isn't even sure how to pronounce the second word. And it doesn't seem like the right moment. As the car makes a long grinding noise and finally rumbles to life, he looks in the rearview mirror and seems to notice her distress. "You OK back there, Toots?"

"Sure." She pauses for a minute as her nerves interfere with her ability to think. "You?"

"This guy is, well, he's gone from me having to convince him about the business to him trying to steal my idea." Bruce starts to reverse the van out of the spot. "Son of a bitch. We had an agreement."

The man jogs up to the window and taps as they are about to

pull out of the lot. Bruce's window doesn't work, so he opens the door a crack. "What?"

"Let's work it out. Between us. My aunt won't understand," the man says. "Sixty percent."

Bruce shoots back, "I already told you, forty-nine is the highest I can go without giving up control of the business. This is my business. My thing. For once. I won't be the junior partner."

"So? I have the property, right? I can do this without you, but you can't do this without me."

"Story of my goddamn—that's not fair, and you know it. This was my idea. I need this, Mel. Melchor. I need it. For me. For once. For me."

"This is business, Bruce. Not therapy. If you need support, come to AA with me. Or church. C'mon now, dude." The man looks further into the Westy and almost flinches when he sees Sierra in the back seat. "Shit. Sorry for the language. Did you hear any of that?"

She wants to respond but can only nod.

"Sierra, say hi to Melchor. Melchor's an old friend." Bruce leans into the final word in a way that makes her feel as if it is still to be determined.

"Really didn't see you back there." Melchor nods to her.

"Mr. Melchor . . . Bruce, needs this." She struggles to get the words out. To form the r's and the s's. To not get laughed at. Her volume trails off. "We need . . . this."

"Pulling out all the stops, huh?" Melchor says to Bruce and then crouches down next to the car to rest his legs, while not letting his nice clothes touch the dirty vehicle. He takes a moment to watch traffic speed down Stevenson Way. "I want to help you, Bruce. But let's be reasonable here."

Sierra grabs the paperwork and moves up behind her father's seat, pushing her face up by his ear to whisper.

Bruce turns to Melchor and says, "She told me the building

doesn't look like it's worth fighting over. Not to her. It was her dad who's the guy with the special idea."

"Young lady, sometimes adults have to—"

She considers trying to answer directly and then leans to her father's ear again.

He repeats, "She said you made a promise, and a promise is a promise, right? And you have to share with friends. That's part of being a good friend. That's what everyone says in elementary school."

"Jesus, Bruce, stop making this up."

"Must've gotten the diplomatic gene from her mom." Bruce maintains as serious of an expression as Sierra has ever seen on him. But she then notices the birth of a smile twitching in the corners of his mouth. He is proud of her. She can feel it.

"Fifty-five." Melchor gives a pointed exhale.

"Dude . . . honestly, what's the six percent to you?" Bruce bashes his forehead twice against the steering wheel. "Forty-nine for you, fifty-one for me or I'm gonna talk to your aunt. Win or lose. I'm all in."

"If we get this—"

"When we get this . . ." Bruce corrects.

"Couldn't we sell to the highest bidder? Someone who actually has a background in retail. Make a quick buck and get out?"

"It's not about a quick buck. Not really about the money at all."

"Not about the money? Oh my God, Bruce. Are you fucking kidding me?" He takes a moment to cough. "Sorry again for my language, kid."

"We'll sell over my dead body."

"That can be arranged." Melchor says and looks at Sierra. "Just kidding?" Then nodding yes to Bruce. "Uncle Arnulfo: dental records."

Sierra talks for a good moment in her father's ear as he nods along. She then shakes a registration form up in his face and holds her finger to the text.

Bruce says, "The paperwork. It's all due tomorrow. If there's no deal, then there's no time for anything else. No other options. This is it. See?"

She says some final words into Bruce's ear.

"Keep promises to your friends, Mr. Melchor," Bruce repeats.

"It's more complicated than that, kid."

"Like she said: we sign now, or we miss tomorrow's deadline," Bruce concludes.

Melchor pauses to light another smoke.

"OK," says Sierra, surprising even herself with her volume. "Let's go, Bruce."

Her dad closes the partially open door and starts to drive off.

Melchor grabs at the door handle, the cigarette between his lips. "OK, whatever, fifty-fifty. Final offer. Straight-up equal partnership. Fuck me . . ." He wipes bits of ash from his sweatshirt and signals for the contract.

Bruce looks back to Sierra for her approval. She shrugs. She is only eight, after all.

"Fuck me's right." Bruce places the paper on the dashboard, touches up the percentages with his pen, and then cracks the door to pass the wrinkled signature sheet to his once and future coconspirator.

Melchor signs the contract against the side panel of the Westy and passes it back to the new business owner.

Bruce reads Melchor's looping signature on the paper. "Not gonna tell your aunt, huh?"

At first, Melchor refuses to answer and then says, "Things went so smoothly last time we worked together. What could go wrong?"

Bruce sticks his cane out the open door and nudges his business partner in the thigh. Melchor wipes at the contact point on his sweatpants to preserve their gleaming spotlessness.

"Take my advice, Bruce: whenever you need to negotiate something, take this kid with you." He raps his knuckles twice on the side of the Westy and walks back toward his car. "Goddamn, I'm a sucker at heart. Get outta here before I change my mind."

As they head out onto Stevenson Way, Bruce punches the interior roof with joy. A joy Sierra has seen even less than his seriousness of a few minutes ago. "Hell yeah. Nice work, Toots. I swear I've never heard you talk like that. Even if it was only to me. I'm taking you out for a soda," he shouts.

She is pleased to finally see her father happy but confused about what they've gotten themselves into. "Bruce, what's *can-na-bis*?"

"Well, it's a, I want to explain, but can we talk about that another time?"

"Can I get a Red Bull?"

"Let's stick with a root beer. Just finish it before you get to your mom's."

"And you get those papers in the mail." She pulls a sheet from the bottom of the stack that reads DEADLINE EXTENTION. "Before Mr. Melchor realizes . . . they're not due now for another week."

ELEVEN   *1971*

Ruth and her mom work their way down the buffet line in the church basement. The fluorescent tube lighting reflects a white glare off the aluminum-foil food containers. The room smells of charred pork, a recently backed-up laundry sink, and folding plastic chairs.

She is aware that today's offerings have more of a Hawaiian bent than Masako would prefer, from the macaroni salad that always manages to roil her stomach on to the chicken drumettes in the too-rich homemade teriyaki sauce. Her mom prefers food more to the point, fresh vegetables, lean meats and, seafood without these filler calories and sugar-laden flourishes. Not that Masako considers macaroni salad or teriyaki to be real food at all.

Beckham and his aunt are on the opposite side of the buffet, a few churchgoers ahead of Ruth and Masako. The young dentist looks sharp in a well-fitting Sunday church suit that doesn't appear to be a hand-me-down or have been purchased for a funeral. He is even wearing a tie, which Ruth is sure pleases Masako and gives her some hope for this new generation.

Before serving himself, Beckham slowly pushes Reverend Saito's wheelchair down the length of the buffet. Ruth knows this is the kind of son-in-law Masako believes she deserves. The kind of person who could reclaim some of the Hasegawa family stature. Ruth wants to respect her mother and their family's well-being, she really does, and has promised to navigate this event with an open mind.

"Please don't embarrass me about my food choices," Ruth whispers to her mother as she heaps yakisoba noodles, macaroni salad, rice, and a slice of cold pizza onto her paper plate. She immediately removes the pieces of pepperoni from the pizza and puts them to the side.

"I'm just pleased you're here at church," Masako says to Ruth as she arranges some ashy carrot sticks, uncooked broccoli, and a single grilled chicken breast with a plastic fork. But as Ruth takes a hasty bite from the rigid pizza, Masako can no longer help herself. "Ruth Hasegawa: you know better."

Ruth rolls her eyes and pointedly chucks the slice of pizza into the garbage can. "I always come to church when you ask."

"Yes. When I ask." Masako looks dismissively at her daughter, still chewing the crust. She looks quickly to Beckham and his aunt, making sure they haven't taken note of Ruth's unladylike dining behaviors. "But I want you to be motivated, on your own, to come to church. To really believe. To rediscover your spiritual center. And, of course, your manners."

"I'm trying my best, Mom . . ." She pauses to evaluate Masako's expression. "I mean, *Okasan*."

Masako motions to Beckham with her head and whispers to Ruth, "He's a handsome young man."

"Sure. Better than that terrible Arthur guy you tried to—"

"And better than that terrible Harry guy you—"

"It's Larry. You know that. And I told you, he's a friend, OK? But at least, I can be myself around him—"

"'Be myself' . . . what does that even mean? You know how I feel about your flights of fancy, Ruth. Not now, please."

Ruth knows the lecture. She heard a variation of it on the drive over to the church. "What is happiness? There is fleeting, surface happiness. And then there is fulfilling, sustainable happiness. The kind of happiness that one must work for. One with lasting benefits over the long remainder of life, even after the initial passion has subsided."

Masako loves to tell anyone who will listen that she knows a thing or two about self-denial and sacrifice. That she is the most professional sufferer out there. That she has suffered her way to a sort of self-anointed moral purity. That she has unique insights on things that Ruth's silly, selfish, sex-crazed generation will never know.

Masako worked her way from backbreaking child labor in strawberry fields to marriage to a near stranger and rising in the greengrocer business; through displacement and inconceivable loss, becoming a widow in her twenties; through single parenthood and into becoming a respected teacher, proponent of the classical music training, and stalwart member of her church. When in doubt, she worked. She made the right decisions. The hard decisions. She was consistently disciplined in her tastes, decisions, and actions.

Ruth has told her mom, in as respectful and tactful a way as possible, that she is a holdover from another era. No fun. Square. A grinding perfectionist. But Masako simply answers that that is how she has been able to survive, raise a daughter, play a valued role in her community, and—Ruth assumes—continue to make sense of the world around her. Masako can't abide low standards and won't fake them in order to spare anyone's feelings. In her opinion, that is the path to ruin and, most unfortunately, the current trajectory of wider society.

It's as if Masako feels that she has sacrificed too much of her own chance at joy in this life to let Ruth enjoy life enough to even risk screwing things up for herself. Her daughter is going to continue the family legacy of teaching music at Stevenson and marry someone Masako approves of, preferably this Beckham gentleman. And that is that.

It's in Ruth's best interest and in service of her greatest long-term happiness, whether her young mind can currently appreciate that or not. And, as she's told her daughter many times, if Ruth wants to experience true elation, she should work harder and learn to play Bach, Beethoven, Bruch, or Brahms. Not just be able to play the music but learn to channel the emotion and feel it as the composer must have while delivering that level of perfection into an imperfect world.

In an unspoken and unchoreographed, yet precise, dance, Masako and Ruth arrive at the end of the buffet table at the same moment as Beckham and his aunt.

"Good afternoon, Mrs. Noguchi. Didn't see you here," Masako says to Beckham's aunt, who Ruth knows to be a somewhat beastly woman of a small, cynical mind and gluttonous appetites including a flair for conspicuous consumption, with her fur shawls and tinted-windowed BMW sedan. But she is important in the church, which is important to Masako, and she isn't even Beckham's real mother, after all.

"Wonderful sermon, don't you agree, Mrs. Hasegawa?" the aunt inquires.

"Ah, indeed." Masako had paid little attention to the sermon, instead harassing Ruth with advice on posture, manners, the right amount to talk, and taboo subjects to avoid during this impending faux-spontaneous lunch introduction.

"You two should sit down and eat," the aunt says to Beckham and Ruth. "Come along."

She shepherds them into folding chairs along the wall, and the two older women bookend them on either side. Ruth shares a self-conscious hello and focuses on her plate. Beckham responds with little more than a head nod.

Ruth doesn't know what to say so she starts to eat, but her mom's scrutiny effectively kills her appetite—which is likely Masako's intention. When Ruth fills the uncomfortable void by pushing her food around the plate with a plastic fork, she can sense her mother's building rage at this etiquette peccadillo.

Beckham earns a pass as he gnaws the drumettes off the bone and eats sticky rice, at least holding his chopsticks well toward the back ends as Masako prefers.

His aunt nudges him with a stiff finger in the rear of his arm. He straightens up and asks Ruth, "You're getting a master's?"

"Yes, I'll be done soon." She works at smiling and gives up on sculpting her rice into tiny mounds. "Education."

Beckham's aunt jumps in to preempt any lull now that the conversation has begun. "I'm happy to see you at church. I noticed you weren't here two or three times, no, three, in the last month."

"I study a lot. Even on weekends."

"Beckham does too, but he still comes to church. It's very important to him." The aunt doesn't have a plate of food and concerns herself with touching up her red lipstick.

"Hmm. Yes. Me too?" Ruth tries, imagining the old woman's frog lips and then whole putty-filled face slowly sliding down and off the front of her skull and dropping, *splat*, on the floor like a plateful of room-temperature, congealed eggs.

The aunt speaks up, her face somehow still affixed to her head. "Don't study too hard, Ruth. Once you have children, you won't end up using that degree anyway." She winks to Beckham. "Work ages a woman in unflattering ways."

"It's 1971, Auntie." Beckham sets his plate on his lap, adjusting his shirt cuffs within the sleeves of his suit jacket. "Her degree could also be very useful as a parent. In the home, if nothing else." He locks on Masako's dark, attentive eyes, trying to convey solidarity. Now it's Beckham's turn to fill in the silence. "I'm in dentistry."

Ruth puts up a flat hand to cover the food in her mouth. "I know."

"Sorry, I'm—I'm not much for small talk; I'm not so practiced at it—should we discuss something else?"

"I don't know. You tell me."

Masako intervenes. "Do you play a musical instrument, Beckham?"

"He was a concert-level pianist," his aunt answers. "Starting at a very young age. Although he's now focused on more professional concerns."

Masako nods her head in approval even though she surely already knew this about him.

The aunt continues, "How about you, Ruth? You must be a musician too? Let me guess, violin?"

"I'm less a musician than, I don't know, I guess a music educator. A music educator-to-be . . . I'm figuring it out, you could say."

"'Those who can't . . .' right?" Beckham says.

If Masako is upset by his commentary, she disguises it behind a mild smile.

"Who're your favorite composers?" Beckham manages his way back into the conversation while wiping at his mouth with a paper napkin.

Ruth considers angling. She wants to service her family's needs. Her mother's desires. But she needs to be honest with herself, especially if she is to potentially spend the rest of her life with this man.

"Really, I've been exploring more contemporary musicians lately."

"Like who?" asks Beckham's aunt.

Ruth looks to Masako as if she is about to ask for approval but then runs with it. "Zeppelin. James Brown. You know, some Stones. You ever heard Hendrix? He is, or was, a genius."

The aunt turns to Masako to arbitrate. "Sounds profane."

Masako feigns unfamiliarity with her daughter's burgeoning interest in popular bands, but her look to Ruth says, *We are going to have a serious conversation about this the moment we step out of this room, young lady.*

"Commercial music, Auntie. Radio stuff." Beckham moves to appease his elder relative. "What the younger generation is listening to."

The aunt crosses herself, and Ruth hopes that she accidentally smears the still-open lipstick in her right hand across her lumpy visage.

Ruth imagines the content of the impending conversation with her mother. That Ruth has been educated in Dvorak, Wagner, Mahler, and Ravel since her birth. How she could have easily listed those composers and moved on in the conversation even if she is currently dabbling in cheap, transient popular music trends. Stuff that isn't music so much as the untrained sonic exhibition of youthful rebellion and needless cultural agitation. How Masako doesn't understand why Ruth has to assert some sort of imagined honesty or contrarian individualism in a moment when that is clearly not what is required.

As expected, Masako steps back in before Ruth can continue any sort of deluded and prideful martyrdom mission. "Well, dentistry is a very stable career, yes, Beckham?"

"It is. Yes. Or it was." He sits up straighter in his chair, having found his lane. "As of last year, socialists forced fluoride into the public water, which will not only lower IQ and likely birth rates, but will, unfortunately, constrain the number of future dental patients."

"Isn't that a good thing? Stronger teeth?" asks Ruth. "Not the IQ part. But, I mean, that and the birth rate issue honestly sound a bit suspect. Don't tea and raisins have naturally occurring fluoride?"

"The problem is that there are only so many good patients to go around, and they only come in once or twice per year, tops. Sure, there are some people who need a lot of work done, but most of them are poor. Or don't care about their dental health. Usually, those two things intersect. So, there are a few more solid years of dentistry as a good moneymaker here, but unless the city starts growing faster or people stop drinking tap water, we're going to hit a tipping point in terms of supply and demand in the next decades. That's why it's important to be very focused now, so I can retire by forty and concentrate on investing. Let's hope President Nixon can get capital gains down below this ludicrous thirty-four percent."

Ruth asks about the legions of people who've moved here to work at America's Preeminent Aerospace Company, and how we're becoming a city of the future and changing the way that people connect with each other.

"This town's always been on a boom-and-bust cycle, reaching high and then falling low. I don't see any reason things won't continue that way."

"Even with the Supersonic Transport? We've never had anything like that before."

"Another silly gold rush. My dentistry school adviser, he golfs with his patient, an aerospace exec. The guy says, off the record, that the supersonic thing is a government boondoggle, at best. He bets it'll never make a single flight. And, then what? Who's gonna foot the bill for all those wasted government resources and all that graft? Not the bloated, profit-sucking machinists' union. The already-overburdened, hardworking American taxpayer, that's who."

Masako's expression slackens and she leans forward, concentrating on moving the toe of her shoe back and forth on the floor.

Ruth shifts in her chair. "Maybe this town is about to really put itself on the map with a mix of engineering, fresh ideas, optimism, technology, all that stuff coming together and changing the world in new and unexpected ways."

Beckham laughs as if her thoughts on the economy are the best joke he's heard in a while. "You should ask my auntie to teach you how she makes these chicken legs. They're the best."

"Thank you, but I'm a vegetarian."

"Is that a political party?" asks the aunt.

"She doesn't eat meat." Beckham glances from his aunt to Masako again, burning right past Ruth. "You do know that meat and seafood remineralize teeth and balance oral pH, right? Eating a vegetarian diet for a prolonged period of time creates vitamin D and calcium deficiencies, eventual gum disease, and tooth loss. Look no further than rural China."

Masako is locked on the noodles and rice on Ruth's plate. *See, Ruth? I told you.* Ruth swears she can hear her mother's thoughts. The pinpricks of her billion criticisms over her choices.

"That's how it works, right?" Beckham is somewhere between complaining, ranting, and joking, but Ruth can't quite tell. Maybe she is simply hoping about the playful part, as nothing else about him has suggested a particularly ripe sense of humor. "Socialists convince people to become vegetarians against their nature, and then they 'need' to put fluoride in the water to save the same people's teeth. Next thing you know they'll 'need' to take over health and dental insurance too. It's all a race to incentivize dependency and mediocrity, if you ask me."

"Show me a woman's teeth." The aunt tries at some levity. "And I'll guess what kind of car her husband drives. Not just the make and model but sometimes even the year."

Beckham and his aunt both laugh. "She's right. She's so good at it," he says. Masako offers a polite, pursed-lipped smile of her own. Her hands resting symmetrically on her knees throughout the conversation.

Ruth looks at the self-satisfied expressions of both Beckham and his aunt. *What are you thinking, Ruth? Do you really believe that you, a silly girl, know something that we, people with money and confidence and insurance and retirement plans and a connection to that great intangible power of "what most people know and think and should know and should think," all somehow just overlooked? That the United States of America doesn't know? That Richard Milhous Nixon himself doesn't know?*

Ruth has noticed that she is tired and dizzy with increasing frequency. She's had a few mystery bruises and did taste a slight bit of blood when eating toast this morning. She doubts it's from vegetarianism. It could be anemia. Or lethargy from a life frequently devoid of agency, if not actual hope. But are those things caused by vegetarianism, if not her broader political outlook? Creeping deviancy? A general lack of morale (and morals)? Consorting with men of dubious parentage?

But maybe she knows nothing. Nothing about taking care of oneself. Or the right way to live. Or God. Or what is happening in the present or the future. Or careers. Whatever makes the world go around.

Maybe she is just that after all: a silly girl. An Asian girl, at that, who should smile and be quiet, or at least stay quiet and stick to the plan that her mother fought so hard to create for her. A plan that her mother, and likely Beckham's aunt, never had handed to them when they were young women. A plan with guarantees that millions of girls around the world would leave it all behind and float across shark-infested waters in patched-up old inner tubes to even get a fighting chance at seizing. The rare opportunities like a steady career, like a house, like healthy and well-educated children, like Beckham.

Her mother's thoughts pile atop her, weighing on her chest. *Listen to the people who know what's best for you. Hardworking people. Serious people. The good kind of people. The right kind of people.* And then there are the deeper thoughts, the ones that Masako would never give voice to, but that Ruth imagines lie somewhere in her mind. *Find stability at any cost. It might not be what you want, but it's what you need. And all I want for you now is a life better than my own. A life with less hardship. Less pain.*

Sure, Ruth never met her father. His absence gives a certain sense of murky incompleteness to her life, and Ruth wishes she'd had the chance to get to know the great Sammy Hasegawa of family lore, wishes he'd been there to comfort her as a child and to be a domestic counterbalance to her imperious mother, to spoil her with chewing gum, extra TV, flexible bedtimes.

She watches Masako considering the room blankly and tries to feel compassion for her. To be fair, in Ruth's twenty-five years she had never directly experienced extreme emotional pain. Real pain of any sort, that she remembers. Masako had shielded and absorbed it all. And, maybe, therefore, Ruth cannot understand the treachery and imbalanced uncertainty of the world in the same way as her mother.

Ruth mashes down and demolishes the rice mounds on her plate with the back of her fork and re-forms them into a new topography. She concentrates to unearth a nice smile and project it toward Beckham and his aunt and then her mom. You can do this, she tells herself. You might have to do this.

She stares at the double doors across the room that lead out to a loading dock or somewhere that's not here.

Suddenly, she imagines Larry blasting through the doors on his motorcycle, a lit cigarette dangling from his lips. The smoke's cherry burns lava red. Black Sabbath plays over the PA system, or possibly from the heavens, as he whips doughnuts around the room, leaving dark rubber skids, choking smoke, and overturned tables with flying bowls of macaroni salad and Chex Mix.

Without sharing a word, she vaults atop the back of the bike. As they accelerate past Beckham's screaming, frantic aunt, Ruth gives the woman a solid slap across the ass. Then they head off into the bright white light beyond the doors.

Or maybe not.

Ruth stares at the door. Waiting. Nothing happens. She blinks and tries again. Still nothing.

TWELVE   *1971*

Larry stands to welcome Ruth to the Broiler's red plastic–lined booth where he has been eating bread and drinking ice water with single-minded focus. Even though he's pretending to be absorbed in the basketball game on the color TV, he's barely watching the shapes on the screen.

Ruth walks in looking stunning in her creased denim pants, nylon jacket zipped up to the neck, and dangling feather earrings. Her glossy ponytail swings as she walks closer to the table. He feels the whisper of something shifting in his gastrointestinal tract and then a competing reaction in his groin. Can she see the cold sweat on his neck and forehead? The shine on his nose? The terror in his eyes?

They greet each other with a quick hug and congenial pat on the back. Lukewarm by his estimation. Her hip point meets matter-of-factly with his crotch. Not quite the level of emotional and physical connection he had hoped for. But he's sure that he is coming off as repulsively anxious, that she can smell it on him.

He doesn't know what to say, and their eyes drift up to the television on the wall.

The game's announcer says, "If the SuperSonics lose this game to the San Diego Rockets, we'll be jockeying for second to last in the division."

"Our top scorer tore his Achilles three games into the season,"

Larry elaborates. "They've never had a winning season. But next year will be our year, I can feel it."

"All sorts of supersonics trying to take off around here next year, huh?" She smiles at him, but he doesn't know if it's sincere.

"That's the plan." He keeps pretending to watch the game, so he doesn't have to ask how it went when Ruth met with her officially sanctioned suitor at her mom's all-important church. The guy is probably some sort of professional. A well-spoken young gentleman with real money and real plans and real degrees. A nice family that eats dinner together. Table manners. No dishes in the sink. Matching socks. No lint in his navel. No bled-out blue-ink seagull tattoos. No dishonorable discharge. Never played a supporting role in an armed robbery. Fuck, he's probably even circumcised.

Ruth's mom finally got to her. He's sure of it. It wouldn't take much. Just a quick nudge at the right moment to send Ruth careening into the yawning chasm of obviousness that she is light-years out of Larry's league, class, caste, team, cohort, universe, and whatever else. That she's only experimenting with him in a moment of last-gasp rebellion or even just simple curiosity prior to giving into overwhelming natural momentum and becoming the person she was always supposed to be.

Since they reconnected at the Dirty Bird, Larry knew that the probability of him and Ruth living together happily ever after was always going to be a million-in-one outside chance. But he still allowed himself to imagine that it is was possible. At the least, he was hoping for a longer run at it. But now he'd be willing to bet all of the $46 in his bank account that she only agreed to a second attempt at prime rib dinner at the Broiler because she came here to break up with him. To let him down gently. That's the kind of person she is. A kind person. Caring. Thoughtful. Honest. Genuine. Really everything he wants in a woman. And now it looks like it is coming to an end before it ever took flight.

Indeed, she told him ahead of time that they have "something important to talk about." Are there more nerve-racking words that can be uttered in a relationship, or a friendship with potential, or whatever it is that they have? She insisted that they must meet up in person. He suggested the Broiler because, again, their prime rib is the nicest dinner he could think of, and the nicest dinner he could think of is the best way to convince her to not break it off with him.

Larry offered to pick her up, but she said she would meet him there. He took this renewed delineation of boundaries to be another bad omen.

The same ruddy waitress as before is suddenly talking to Ruth. Asking about drinks. Larry extricates his focus from the basketball broadcast and tries to be mature, ordering a martini, which only comes in an intimidating "executive" size. When he double-checks the executive's price and realizes that a martini has hard liquor in it—which he's never before tried and probably shouldn't test out tonight—he quickly downgrades to a bottle of Rainier.

Ruth orders a wine. Sophisticated. Like he thought.

"Red or white?" asks the waitress.

"Um, you pick." Ruth unfolds and refolds her napkin.

"I'll be back to take your order." The waitress speeds off to the next table.

Larry is tempted to escape back into the safe mindlessness of the television but finds himself studying her makeup-free, yet still dramatic, eyelashes and the reflection of the overhead lighting off the dark center of her pupil. If prodded into conversation, he prefers to talk about basketball or planes or something, anything else beyond what she needed to see him about. Here. Now. But his worries flame over, and suddenly words are coming out of his mouth before he can properly avoid or even edit them. "So just say it. Tell me. No, sorry, I meant to start with, 'You look very pretty.

And thank you for meeting me out tonight.' But, yeah, what did you want to talk about?"

"Let's get our drinks first."

"Oh my God. No, tell me now." Shit. She recoils, and he can feel that he is being too pushy, his nerves getting the best of him, like usual. "Please," he follows. "I didn't want to bring it up, but I did exactly that. Sorry. But please."

"How're things with you? At work?"

He assumes she is worried that he's one clumsy move away from backsliding into predestined intergenerational poverty, his greatest inheritance. Perhaps his only inheritance. "Who'd you hear that from?"

"Hear what?"

"From your mom? No, the guy she wants you to be with? The church guy?"

"No. Maybe. It doesn't matter. Listen, there are rumors about the Supersonic—I wanted to warn you. As a friend."

"As a friend?"

"Yes, as a something. I don't know . . ."

"If you ask me, the only problem is that damned 747." Larry leans into the table, unsure of where he should put his hands. Elbows on the table or not. He busies himself with his napkin, imitating her. He realizes now that she may not see him as anything more than a friend in the first place. They did kiss. It was arguably the highlight of his young life—maybe not even arguably. But did she see it differently? "The airports around the world were not ready for such a large plane. Runways are too short. They were gonna make dozens of 747s per month. Now they're doing about half of one per month. That's bad news, but not the end of the world."

He does his best to project straight-backed, wide-eyed confidence, attempting his best mimicry of "Hero Lifeguard" Matty Fuckface Donahoe waving in the parade.

The waitress returns with her order pad and pen at the ready. "What can I get you while you're waiting on those drinks?"

"We'll take two prime ribs." Larry leads with chivalrous buoyancy, needing to remind himself to breathe.

"Easy, Larry. I'm a big girl; I can order for myself."

"I just wanted to get you the best. Like you deserve." He thinks it might be cool to wink to the waitress or back at Ruth then but spends too long considering the options and potential outcomes and loses his opportunity.

"I don't eat meat."

"What do you mean you don't eat meat?" Larry asks.

"I don't eat meat. I'm a vegetarian."

"Are you allergic to it?" the waitress asks.

"No. I love animals."

"I love them too," says the waitress. "To eat."

Larry asks, "What about the Captain's Platter? You eat seafood, right?"

"Nope."

"Fish isn't an animal."

"Mammals aren't the only sentient beings." She turns to the waitress. "Do you have any vegetarian options?"

"Salad, I guess."

"Anything else?"

"You know you're at the Broiler, right?" asks the waitress. "And in America."

"Yes."

"Take another look at the menu. I'll be back."

Larry tries to maintain enough of an upbeat expression to mask his confusion: his realization that he knows so little about her. His realization that Ruth and her mom still know so little about him and, most importantly, that everything else that they learn about him will only tally up to her running the other way as fast as she can.

"You should still get prime rib," she offers. "Don't let me stop you."

The waitress returns with the drinks. Ruth's red wine in a stout glass and Larry's beer in a longneck bottle. Ruth takes a sip. Her mouth screws tight as she chokes it back and then orders the green salad.

"And you, hon?" The waitress points her order pad at Larry.

He thinks a moment. "Make it two."

"You don't have to, Larry," Ruth pleads. "I mean it."

"I want to," he says, not offering that he is concerned about the cost and effectively killed his appetite with two baskets of bread and butter and a half gallon or so of ice water. He hopes the waitress won't rat him out.

"You sure, kid?" the waitress asks, as if she's seen every manner of awkward decision play out on dates in these plush booths or maybe fearing a two-appetizer total order on a four-top during the weekend dinner rush and its commensurate tip or lack thereof. "She said you don't have to."

"I'm fine. Thanks." He sets a constipated smile and holds it until she jots down the order and moves along to the next table.

After the waitress leaves, they are unsure of where to pick back up the conversation and sit in momentary silence. Larry is convinced that her next words will be her breaking up with him.

"Who is he?" he preempts.

"Who's who?"

"You know: the guy."

"Nobody. Not nobody. Somebody. Somebody from my church. Or my mom's church. My mom likes him. Not me. But I'm still trying to figure out if my preferences even matter. It's complicated."

"And he gave you these ideas? Trying to make you doubt my future. I'm sure your mom loved that."

"I heard, you know, stuff about the Supersonic. I—I care about what happens to you, so I thought, you know." She downs another acidic slug of the wine. More easily now that all of her taste buds are blown.

He is tempted to ask her to elope with him. He can feel the alcohol working its way through his system. In spite of his hammering anxiety, the muscles in his neck start to relax. His hands and feet radiate a light warmth. His mother always tries to remind him Dugdales and alcohol don't play well together. But it's never stopped him before.

The thought of covert matrimonial flight works its way from his brain down to his tongue but fails at the last moment. Don't put her on the spot, he tells himself. He knows he'd die if she rejected him. Instead, he regurgitates one of Gerry's standard rants from work.

"Canards. If anything, it's the goddamn canards. They set us back. But that's temporary."

"I have no idea what you're talking about." She guides her lips to the rim of her glass and finishes the last mouthful of wine.

He explains that they never should have put canards—those little baby wings that make the front of the jet look like some sort of mutant catfish—behind the nose. The canards were supposed to decrease lift up front and cut down on flex to the plane's fuselage at high speeds, but they only added more weight, the Achilles injury of the supersonic dream.

Larry erupts, "Everyone knows it was originally designed to have a swing wing, a variable-sweep wing that changes positions during takeoff and flight. You know what I'm talking about, right? And you know what made the wings move? An actuator. And you know who makes the pieces so that actuators work? Me. But the damn five-thousand-pound titanium pivots were too heavy, so rather than finding a way to fix that issue, and had I been on the job then I would've found a way, without a doubt, but what'd they do: They bailed on the swing wing, opened a whole new can of worms, and went for a delta fixed wing. Making the jet into a big-ass triangle. But then they needed to add the canards up front for stability. And again: weight issues. And now we're behind schedule. But what does a small schedule issue really, truly matter when we are destined to change the future of the world?"

He memorized all of that in the past days so that he could speak intelligently about work. He doesn't want her to think he is just another monkey who turns a wrench. A stooge who lucked into a job by being in the right place at the right time . . . much in the same way that he feared that he was only in her fleeting presence because he'd stumbled into the Dirty Bird that night. He must do everything in his power for it to not all pass right through his fingers.

The salads arrive: each a sad mélange of damp iceberg lettuce, a quarter wedge of a hard tomato with a remnant of its stem, thinly sliced raw white onion, and a mysterious off-white dressing on the side in a metal ramekin.

"What about you, Ruth? Have you thought about my question? What you want to do?"

"Teaching. I guess."

"Not what your mom wants you to do. What you want to do. If you could do anything. I mean, you really can do anything."

"In an alternate reality or if I were dreaming, I guess, I'd, well, I dunno."

"Tell me."

"I think I'd like to write. Be a journalist."

"Write about the war and news like that?"

"They say 'write what you know.'" She blushes, stutters, and then gets it out. "Maybe I'd like to try my hand at becoming a music journalist?"

"That's amazing."

"Is it? From what I understand . . . which is very little, it's a totally unpredictable career. And I have so much more to learn about popular music. I'd have to change so much and learn so much, already now when I am an ancient, unmarried twenty-five-year-old. Most importantly, my mom will never let me do it."

"You should do it."

"I can't."

"I'll help you. However I can. Seriously."

"Don't be silly. That would stand in the way of you following your dreams."

He decides that vulnerability and authenticity are the best policy. "I'm already there. I came from pretty much nowhere, and now, here I am having a salad at the Broiler with you."

She starts to respond. Larry slows down time and tracks the formation of her lips. Guessing at what she is about to say and if it will make or destroy his life. But, *oh shit*, here comes the big bald manager guy from the grocery store. Dammit. Larry has just enough time that he could excuse himself to the bathroom and then slip out the door. But ditching Ruth a second time at the Broiler would guarantee that she never speaks to him again. He puts his hand across his forehead in an attempt to mask his face and braces for the worst.

Ruth starts talking, but he's having trouble paying attention. She says something about her mom. Her family. Music. Did she say fluoride? Her dreams. Even though Larry keeps his head low, he can only see the man coming closer and can only hear his blood crashing against the inner walls of his own skull.

"Don't you think?" Ruth asks.

Larry sees the cleft lip scar. The neck hair.

"Larry?" She looks at him with a concerned stiffness in her brow.

"It was, I didn't mean to. I just ran into her," he stammers.

"Ran into who? You OK, Larry?"

"Yeah, no. It's nothing," he says as the big man stops at their table, standing over him, evaluating Larry's face.

"You're the young fella who was at the store the other day?"

"Me? No. Not me. What store?"

"Yeah, it was. It was you. Who hightailed it outta there. I'm sure of it. I recognize that smudge on your upper lip."

Larry feigns ignorance, looking at Ruth with a shrug, and then runs his index finger under his nose, self-consciously checking for density.

"I kicked her ass out. That old oriental broad." The man stands to his full height with pride and turns to Ruth as if to apologize for his words but doesn't. He continues, "Can't have her following a customer. Spying around."

"Spying on who?" Larry asks.

"You, kid. I seen her sitting out there a few mornings in a row in her car. At first, I'm thinking she's stealing stuff. You never know who's a thief. One granny lifted so much kitty litter and apricot preserves the other month that I had to charge more for cold cuts to offset the shrink. And she was in a goddamn wheelchair. You believe that? Some of these old-timers no longer know where a good deal ends and where petty larceny begins. Anyway, I was getting to work, and I seen her again, and then I seen her following you. Then again, inside the store, pretending to put stuff in her basket. I told her to get the hell out and never come back."

Larry balls his hands together and doesn't respond.

"I was thinking maybe you could tell me what that's all about." The man gives Larry a knowing look of camaraderie. "I seen others like her taking cans out of our food drives for veterans."

"Other old ladies?"

"Not her age, her kind."

"No. Sorry, don't remember what or who you're talking about, no."

"Right..." The manager shakes his bald head and observes Ruth for a moment. "OK. Have it your way." He pauses again as if he were about to say something, shakes his head again, and then leaves.

Once the manager is back at his own table and firmly out of range, Ruth says, "I need you to please be honest with me."

"About what?" Larry asks.

"My mom. This is about my mom, isn't it?"

"No. No way. He must be confused. Thinking of someone else."

"Is my mom following you? Oh my God." She puts her head in her hands. "She is. Isn't she?"

Larry turns up his palms. He can't lie to Ruth but also wants to steer away from drama rather than put a cinder block on the gas pedal and speed straight toward it.

"Oh my God. She's impossible. This is my life. Not hers. Not hers and mine. Mine. I'm so sorry, Larry."

"No, I didn't even realize . . . I barely remember what that guy is talking about." He watches her face flush a deep red, almost purple. "You OK?"

"Yes. Maybe. Just a bit dizzy. And furious. And totally fucking embarrassed. Wow, I can't believe I said that."

"Me neither."

"But that's how I feel. How I actually feel."

Larry looks up to the TV just in time to watch the SuperSonics lose to the Rockets for their second game in a row. This one by a single, measly point.

Ruth climbs onto her knees on the seat. "This has to stop. Something has to change. Right now. And I'm the only one who can do it. Yeah, fuck it."

"What?"

"Yes, this, what she did, it's actually a good thing. She's gone too far. She always goes too far, but now it's out in the open."

"What does that mean?"

"Pay the bill."

"You haven't finished your lettuce."

"Let's go to your car. I want to lose my virginity."

"You what?"

"With you."

"With me?"

"Now."

PART III

1897

Siab and his mule start to climb the last hill that separates them from the charred, battered center of the city. He's pretty sure that he's gotten away from Erasmus, leaving his derelict Boston neighbor back on the trail. The man barely eats or works; how could he ever hope to keep up with a Duwamish headman of Siab's hardened abilities?

The moment that Siab thinks that question, the universe answers. His mule stumbles and spills some of its potatoes to the ground. Siab moves as quickly as possible to repack the load, but suddenly Erasmus appears at the bottom of the hill.

The man is persistent, Siab will give him that. No matter what happens, he must not fight him. The Changer is returning, and the Bostons' city has burned. Siab must stay focused on what is about to happen. The Duwamish will finally be able to reclaim their ancestral land.

"Indian Sam. Yeah, you. Looks to me like you've got so many potatoes that they're weighing you down," Erasmus shouts up to Siab.

"I said, 'Not today, sir.'" In a lapse of his better judgment, Siab stops, waits, and looks the man dead in his sunken face, his other concerns be damned. He wants to let him know that he is not to be challenged, especially not by a sickly Boston. As Erasmus gets closer, it becomes apparent that his pupils are tiny pinholes, a sign of the Chinese flower poppy that Siab knows to be prevalent with sailors, professional girlfriends, and degenerates alike throughout the city. "I am going into town to do my business. Please go about your own business too, Mr. Erasmus."

Erasmus tries to spit on the ground with put-on Western bravado, but the saliva does not take proper flight and runs down his chin. "Your overinflated self-regard is not becoming of you, Indian Sam. Nor is your parsimoniousness. A gentleman must always exhibit a degree of humility. And generosity. Although I gave you the benefit of the doubt, but you are no gentleman. And a thoroughly unaccommodating neighbor to boot."

Siab returns to the trail ahead of him, avoiding any additional exchange, and picks up his speed, driving the mule to the top of the hill. He knows that if Erasmus were to try to steal the potatoes, no policeman in this city would dare consider the complaint of anyone known as Indian Sam. And if he were to put up a fight, God forbid if he were to hurt this overeducated, inconsiderate parasite—Siab would go straight to prison, or worse, and have his land confiscated before the day was over.

"Indian Sam?" Erasmus calls again from down the trail. "Perhaps I took too forward of an approach with you before. Let's permit bygones to be bygones. What actually matters is that I am a man of action. As you may know, I am a Knight of the Order of St. John of Jerusalem, a Knight of the Red Cross of Constantine, a Knight Templar, and, of course, thirty-third-degree Scottish Rite Freemason. I am accustomed to finding solutions where ordinary men determine none are to be found. And I shall therefore improve my proposal by offering you a percentage of the profits, say, three, no, five percent. Instead of the flat fee, of course—not on top of it. I'm a charitable man, but a businessman must always mind the bottom line."

Siab and his mule navigate switchbacks toward the top of the hill. His neighbor walks behind on the zigzagging path.

Erasmus calls again, "This is a rare opportunity, Old Sam. When is the last time you collaborated with a graduate of Yale University? Are you familiar with Skull and Bones? Scroll and Key? Wolf's Head? I'm not a gambling man. At least not since, well, since the Panic of 1893 forced me to trade my nana's wedding china for a loaf of stale bread and two sticks of Jewish butter. But even I'd be willing to take a wager that this opportunity is a first for you, Sammyboy."

Siab had been in many partnerships and had many supposed opportunities with the settlers. That's how he got the name Sam. Sam Dugdale was the name his employer, David Denny, the lucky younger brother of one of the original settlers of this city, foisted on him.

When Siab complained that he didn't care for the name, Denny told him that he should be honored as "Samuel was the last of the tribal leaders of Israel and God's chosen voice in a time of change." Siab asked how Denny recognized all that in him, and the wealthy Boston responded, "No, I just think you look like a Sam. And Dugdale was the street I was born on."

"Sam Dugdale" knew he had been particularly useful to the white man, and not only because he was a born noble and natural leader who knew how to fake acceptance of the settler's religion and customs and had proven himself adept at learning at least six dialects of Lushootseed, Chinook Jargon, English, and a serviceable amount of Norwegian, Russian, Spanish, Japanese, and Cantonese.

His most important skill, at least in the white men's appraisal, grew from his extensive childhood explorations of the lakes, rivers, and bay. Before they were killed, Siab's uncles, who were all upriver Duwamish, showed him how to navigate the entire region. He'd memorized each rapid and sandbar and where to best carry a canoe across the mudflats from lake to lake. And he knew how to fish and fashion his own wooden tools from the abundant nature around them, skills that this supposedly more advanced form of man from lands afar did not seem to have.

Siab was paid almost nothing over the years except food rations and the sunshine of Denny's benevolence. At first, he had not wanted their coin anyway. He did not trust the money. Why was it any different from any other promise or treaty? He wanted one single thing: land, a specific piece of land.

It lay on the edge of the city, just over a couple of hills. When Siab propositioned Denny about it, the affluent settler seemed bewildered why anyone would want an unusable dirt pile crowned by a big stone, a dumping ground teeming with refuse and an exasperating number of gulls.

Denny joked that Siab must be in some sort of mental decline, an old fool obsessed with a rocky garbage patch. But he still granted his aging Duwamish beneficiary this one special wish. It probably wasn't even a big deal to Denny, who was riding high as the wealthiest man in the whole new city.

Siab retired from guiding and carefully tilled the hill's crest, turning it into an unassuming, if frequently fecund, potato field. As he was one of a few Duwamish living proudly and openly in town and the only one who owned land, the area was soon called Little Duwamps and then Duwamps Hill.

And it was a good thing that Siab got the land when he did, as Denny promptly went bankrupt. Siab didn't wish that fate upon the man. Denny wasn't the worst of them. The two men had even shared a tent once in a rainstorm on a lakeshore. Denny offered his coffee and even went as far as apologizing to Siab for the volume of his snoring. His financial downfall had something to do with building too many iron trolley cars with borrowed money. Goals and concepts that Siab found laughable. But after what he had already witnessed during his lifetime, he knew that you should never assume that you understand the boundaries of human existence and the greater powers that act upon it.

He looks back down the trail to see that he and the mule have again put some distance between themselves and that deadbeat Erasmus. The man did not look particularly strong, after all. But then again, Siab knows that rodents are plenty successful even without much in the way of physical force. And now that David Denny is living modestly in the care of his daughter on a dairy farm, he worries that people like Erasmus are liberated to steal more than just his most recent potato crop.

Siab takes note again of Erasmus's distance. This is the main way into town, so it is possible that the man would follow the same path regardless of his refusal to share his crop with him. However, this final wooded section before the ridge of the second hill is the last place that they would be alone, and Siab would be the most vulnerable before entering the public spaces of the city.

He can't be sure, but it now appears that Erasmus is gaining on him. Siab looks again to see that the man has something in his right hand, tucked back and steady against his side. Perhaps a knife. Or a blackjack. A pistol?

Siab gets a better look, and the man has what appears to be a rock in his hand. Still large enough to kill him if well placed. In fact, it looks reddish and could be a piece of a brick. Yes, he has seen what the man can do with a brick. The irony of the last Duwamish landowner in the city getting killed with something taken from his own garden is not lost on Siab. He had already come too close to this man. Entered his path. Looked him right in the face even after he had known better.

He could turn around and kill Erasmus now. Likely with his bare hands. But it would only cause another and greater loss. His hanging, yes. But they'd execute Tietsa too, just for sport. And

maybe hang their grown children, who live in exile. And, most devastatingly, Duwamps Hill would be desecrated with their houses,
roads, and pit toilets. This cannot happen. Especially now, when
they are so close to the long-awaited return of the Changer.

Siab emerges from the trees and onto the final hilltop, the
city center now opening out below him: the platted blocks of low
houses and mud sloping down to the denser knot of burned and
semi-reconstructed buildings and on to the bent fingers of faded
wooden piers grasping into the bay.

He hears his neighbor near hyperventilating as he too summits
the trail. Siab turns around to face him. "I am going to attend to my
own business. Please do the same, Mr. Erasmus."

"You are making a grave mistake, Indian Sam," Erasmus pants,
one hand on his hip, the other now fully behind his back. "This opportunity. You'll regret this. Maybe even sooner than you imagine."

"If you are going to steal my crop, take it and leave me and my
farm be."

Just then a group of young white men crown the trail from the
other side, heading toward Siab and Erasmus. This could be better or worse for Siab. Based on his experience: probably worse. He
considers running but would have to abandon his mule. He decides
to stand still and hold his breath. The men pass Siab as if he were
another tree on the hillside.

"Erasmus, you hear the news, you old fop?" The boys greet
Siab's tormentor with unbridled joy.

When Erasmus shakes his head, they point down to the city
and harbor below. Both Siab and Erasmus creep forward to see a
throng of men all crowded along the waterfront. It's people for as
far as their eyes can see. Along the pier is a large metal ship, the
kind with round chimney pipes that point to the sky, coughing out
steam. The kind that can travel to seas beyond where Siab has ever
considered venturing, even at the pinnacle of his seafaring days.

The ship is swarmed by these tiny, faraway men like ants on spilled honey.

"What happened down there?" Siab asks.

The men continue to ignore Siab.

"What is it, boyos?" Erasmus follows.

"Gold. A ton of it." The leader of the group laughs and bounces on the points of his toes. "A literal ton."

"Where from?" Erasmus asks, turning an ear to the younger men.

"Alaska. Someplace like that. The goddamn mayor quit on the spot and's already on his way to start panning. I'm just heading over to say goodbye to my ma. Well, and borrow her savings for gear."

"Gear, yes . . ." Erasmus looks into the sun.

"Alaska?" Siab asks, having heard the Boston name for the land to the north before but not able to associate the north with anything other than the source of pestilence, raiding tribes, and the North Wind that brings ice and snow.

The men all laugh. "Old Injun doesn't know his way past his own nose."

Erasmus takes a bite from the half-eaten crab apple in the hand that was behind his back. "Bad news, Indian Sam. Deal's off. I shall reorient my efforts elsewhere. Opportunity costs, dear boy."

Siab is at once relieved and disgusted to see what's in Erasmus's hand. He could have shown the man much sweeter and more edible fruit than the bitter, grainy deer food he grinds between his molars. But Siab has bigger problems now.

He tries to count the number of people in the harbor. Their bodies bleed together into a single mass of pulsating, gold-fevered humanity. He tries and tries again to count. He attempts to count their hats.

Indeed, the Changer has returned. But this is not the way it was supposed to be, Siab repeats to himself.

He has never enjoyed the hard, yet nasal, sound of English, its over-prescriptive naming conventions, limited verbs, and unimaginative vocabulary. Although he has found use, if not entertainment, in its rich glossary of expletives.

Siab gives up on his tally of hats and feels his hopes falling away. "Fuck me."

THIRTEEN *1958*

Even though this is Masako's first day as a teacher, she is no longer a young woman. Starting a new career and maintaining this kind of grueling output of energy and attention for this many kids is a young woman's game. Sure, older women still do the job, but most of them have years of experience under their belts and know the routine well, if not spend half the time on autopilot.

Teaching is not what she ever intended to do with her life. Alas, this is where she has arrived, and she is going to make it as meaningful as possible.

Now, in the final period of her and Stevenson Elementary School's inaugural day, Masako—or Mrs. Hasegawa, as she is known to the students—welcomes some thirty fourth graders, including the one Asian student also known as her daughter, Ruth.

The children file into the classroom. She leaves it to them to choose their own chairs. Children need to follow rules, but they also need to be allowed to develop their own independent decision-making skills. They will never learn to make good decisions unless they get the opportunity to make decisions. For themselves.

She watches through the open door as the new part-time janitor, the Black guy, one of the few she's ever seen in this neighborhood, moves his electric polisher machine thing out of the way of the stream of children. The janitor is more handsome than Masako thinks she should admit. Even to herself. He nods to Masako, which is more than Ruth does to acknowledge her mother upon entering the classroom and pulling closed behind her the heavy wooden door, with wires running in neatly crossed diagonals through the glass in its peep window. Masako's daughter passes by empty seats in the front and then the middle rows and heads all the way to the back. She sits in the worst possible location of all: right next to the two women.

That despicable duo had just returned from drinking coffee and gossiping. Or informing Stevenson's Un-American Activities Committee on Masako. Or whatever other petty business they were up to between periods. They reclaimed their two adult-size chairs against the back wall. Masako prays that they didn't see the janitor nod to her, as that could be unfortunate on multiple levels.

One woman has an aggressive, restless thinness to her while the other is round and slovenly. Both have bad, dull hair and derive their status from the newly minted Stevenson Elementary PTA run by the skinny one with small, gray teeth, Bev Donahoe. Libby Mintzer is her soft-edged sidekick. Masako wants nothing to do with either. But she has no choice. The parent group has concerns about Masako teaching at the school. She is currently undergoing a deeper evaluation to make sure that she is the right fit for the "Stevenson Elementary culture."

As for her qualifications, Masako is pretty sure she is the only one who's lived in this neighborhood since before the war. She started alongside her *issei* parents as a seasonal farm laborer, working for a dollar a day before she even got her period. She practiced music at night. Hoping someday to play at Carnegie Hall in New York. Or even with the lesser orchestra here in town.

The Hasegawa family farm had no electricity and, at first, had running water only in the main house. She worked her way up and married the *nisei* son of the owners right before the family became one of the biggest dairy and vegetable suppliers in the city. Only to lose it all, including her husband's life, during wartime incarceration.

Masako has spent the last decade finishing her education, working as a part-time secretary, caring for her daughter, and re-establishing a small house on the property that once belonged to the Hasegawas—all as a widow and single mother. And they want to know if she is a fit for "Stevenson culture."

"Did you ladies have a nice break between classes?" Masako asks Libby and Bev before starting the class. She gets a meek smile from one of the women. The other takes out her clipboard and one of those new pens with the click button on the back. She presses on the button a couple of time to be sure the pen is activated and starts scribbling her notes. Indispensable and insightful, to be sure.

Masako has tried her best to be polite. To engage these women in conversation. But they are taking their job very seriously. Observing from a detached distance. Masako wonders about their qualifications. Neither of the women seem to know much about music. Or hygiene. Or health. Or any art at all beyond maybe organizing family photo albums. Considering that this is the first day of the school, they probably don't know much about the school's culture, how the school is run or should be run. They may know a thing or two about teaching, although that is not clear either.

After some basic pleasantries and introductions to the students, Masako goes about sorting the class.

"All students who have instruments with them, please move to the left side of the room." About ten kids pick up their flutes, clarinets, and the odd cello and move toward the windows.

"OK then, who in here knows how to read music?"

A couple raise their hands. Ruth does, gingerly.

"How about sight-read?"

No one raises their hand.

It is going to be a long haul to establish a decent arts program at this school. If they even let Masako stick around. But the city is booming again, and these new schools need new teachers.

The growth proves that the Jet Age is upon them. All of the chatter among teachers and parents and the newspapers and radio is that some new commercial jetliner, the seven-oh-whatever, has six seats across. A row of three. An aisle. And another row of three. Flying is now for everyone. Or almost everyone. And America's Preeminent Aerospace Company is hiring.

There is no more farmland in the city limits now, Hasegawa or otherwise. And Masako, for one, will not miss the time of fishing, lumber, and farming. Especially dairy. Berries. And everything else she did in her early years. She can barely bring herself to eat any of those things these days.

She wants to ask these American people who drink milk with breakfast, lunch, and dinner to the point that the sourness wafts from their pores, "Have you ever actually milked a cow? It's like giving a hand job to a fat man. A fat man as big as a Volkswagen Bug, full of gas and chewing a mouthful of grass." Of course, she has never said that. She has never said the words *hand job* out loud, but she sure knows what it is. She was married before, after all.

Masako feels mental, physical, and motivational exhaustion settling in. Teaching is far different from what she imagined. Far different from a disciplined, isolated life of practicing music. Or even working in agriculture. One must be like an incandescent bulb that is turned on, at every moment. It is like hosting an ongoing holiday dinner where you must oversee the conversation and make sure that everyone stays engaged.

She had been nervous throughout the preceding summer, waking up at three and five in the morning. Sleeping had never been her forte. It didn't help that she received dozens of pieces of hate mail from concerned citizens about her teaching in the school, followed by a handful of death threats and even slashed tires on what was, in fact, her neighbor's station wagon.

Masako had hoped to move quickly this first day, to evaluate relative skill levels and get the different students on track to maximize their potential. And, of course, to see if there are any decent ones. But today was mainly rules, logistics, and paperwork. There wasn't much real teaching happening. With her grouping exercise, she tries to evaluate a few of the students as best as she can. She reasons that, even if she can't determine the decent ones, she should be able to designate the ones who aren't going anywhere. Like when they release baby sea turtles on the beach. If only one out of one thousand will make it to adulthood, the ones who are running in circles in the sand and can't even find their way to the water's edge aren't going to do well with gulls, not to mention the sharks. If nothing else, she hopes to recommend to them that they take physical education instead or not waste her time and the other students' time and chance to improve. She knows this sounds harsh. But it is also a realistic assessment of a world that is, well, harsh.

At lunch, the crew-cutted, chinless math teacher, Al Schneider, was amazed by Masako's "fork skills" and offered her two pencils "if that'd be easier." The whole room laughed, or so it seemed. Masako knew any reaction would be judged and decided to not react at all. Schneider then continued on about how he might soon leave teaching and go work for America's Preeminent Aerospace Company. Soon they'll have jets faster than the speed of sound. They've already started working on concepts. And they need ever-more people with math skills, you know, the only important skills.

The other teachers were all aflutter about how the city is becoming a real metropolis and how there's going to be a World's Fair here in a couple of years. It had been planned as the fiftieth anniversary of some big deal Alaska Gold Rush Expo that they had in the early 1900s, but the city couldn't pull it off in time. There is a sense that the future is coming and coming soon. Right here, of all random places on Planet Earth.

But Masako knows that technology and engineering cannot

sustain a place. This city needs music. Poetry. A sense of its cultural history.

These people have no nuance, she thinks. No appreciation of aesthetics. Look at her two classroom monitors, as case in point. Human tubers.

It will be her contribution to this city of the future to build a music and arts program in this new outpost within the Metro Public School system.

Masako will overcome her past and deliver beauty to the world in any way that she can. She knows that she won't become the concert violinist that she would like to be, it is too late for that now. But this is her small offering to the world, and she will do it as well as can be done.

Masako is the first woman of Asian descent to teach in the school system. It is a conditional short-term contract for an auxiliary elective teacher. She is not a full teacher. Not yet. But the position is something that is concurrently both mundane and revolutionary, depending on how one considers it, so the best approach is that it is not recognized or talked about. At least, not by her. It has to be done as quietly as possible. Masako feels like if anything is said about it, the school district will realize what's going on and the whole deal will fall apart. It will turn to dust in the light of day. That could still happen, depending on how things go with expert music, culture, and pedagogy critics Bev Donahoe and Libby Mintzer.

Masako prefers not to think about the fact that her own daughter, her prized pupil, has proved relatively unteachable at home. It's not that she is bad so much as she crumbles under Masako's expectations. OK, she is bad too. Especially at the violin. Masako should have known better than to get Ruth to play her favorite instrument. The standard is too high. But that doesn't mean that Ruth can't change. Can't succeed elsewhere. Being here at this school, surrounded by the other students, will hopefully give Ruth confidence to take on her training and destiny and become the musician she too could be. The musician that Masako never had the opportunities to become.

Ruth begged Masako to not make a big deal that they are mother and daughter. Her daughter seems to care only about what others think. But their relationship will already be obvious to anyone with functional vision. And to Masako, the deeper, potential political implications are irrelevant, as she would never give her daughter— or anyone, for that matter—preferential treatment. Her classroom will be based only on talent, discipline, and hard work.

"So, nobody can sight-read music?"

Again, no one answers. The quiet becomes awkward, at least in Masako's perception of it. One of the women clears her throat.

"How about you, young lady?" Masako points at Ruth, who grips a clarinet and trains her attention on the back of the head of the person seated in front of her. On the edge of her field of vision, Masako thinks she sees one of the boys hit another with a flute. But she can't be sure, so she lets it go and hopes the PTA ladies didn't catch it either.

She places the stand with sheet music in front of her daughter and says, "Why don't you try this?" This is a bit of a plant, as she knows Ruth can already play Glenn Miller's 1939 hit, "In the Mood," from memory. By introducing some more popular music from the big band and swing genres (not really Masako's favorite and a lesser form than her orchestral favorites), she figures that she can better engage the classroom, impress her evaluators, and maybe give her daughter some healthy encouragement in the process.

Ruthie needs to toughen up. The kids are sure to taunt her on the rooftop playground simply for looking different. Maybe a showing of some talent, however limited, will deter her critics. Or, at least, build a safe retreat within the girl.

Masako can hear the dryness of her daughter's tongue as she labors to wet the reed in her mouth. But one must fight through these things, and the only way to do that is to actually experience it. Ruth keeps working on the reed, adjusting and readjusting her finger placement on the clarinet.

One of the boys makes an obscene bathroom noise with his mouth. The children laugh. "Quiet," she says in an elevated, firm voice. As close as she gets to shouting. Her first time showing any cracks in front of Bev and Libby all day. A hot ripple of frustration climbs up Masako's chest.

Ruth inhales, holds her air so long that Masako is concerned that she will start to get dizzy. Her daughter then unloads into the clarinet. The reed screeches in a pitch that feels like a screwdriver into the ear. Ruth panics, apologizes, and starts murmuring something to herself while regrouping.

She is about to start again when the boy calls out from behind Masako, "Teacher's kid, and she still sucks."

Masako's daughter crumbles through the shoulders. She sets the clarinet upright, bell-down on the tiled floors, stands, and starts walking toward the door at a pace just short of running.

"Ruth, wait." Masako heads her off at the doorway. She jams the toe of her shoe against the base of the door right as Ruth's hand meets the handle.

"Sayonara," one of the boys shouts and is rewarded with a torrent of laughter. Others follow with taunts of "banzai" and "kamikaze" in exaggerated accents.

Masako hesitates, reflecting for a split second on her regret that she called on her daughter and how, after the first mistake, she should have let her leave. But it's too late to change course now.

She wants to say something but must show steadfastness in front of these hyenas. She sends the crying girl back to her seat, turning in time to see Bev Donahoe scribble out a detailed note on her clipboard.

FOURTEEN 2014

Sami unfolds the printouts that she made from her online research, mainly consisting of searching "how to negotiate." She slowly reads the bulleted list out loud. "Preparation and research, build relationships, active listening, know strengths . . ."

". . . and weaknesses," her friend Monica, the current music teacher at Stevenson, adds from across the table.

"I don't need any help figuring out those."

"And last but not least?"

"Compromise." Sami shuffles her salad lettuce around the disposable, biodegradable container without eating and watches out the window as Mothership employees walk up and down the sidewalk wearing their blue credentials affixed to their belts. Almost all are men in their twenties and thirties in loose jeans and long-sleeved T-shirts. Some stop and order from company-sanctioned food trucks and make brief small talk. Most keep their attention trained on their phones.

"The correct answer is, 'Know when to compromise and when to walk away.'" Monica takes a bite of her cheeseburger. "If you're not willing to walk, you're just bluffing."

"Right . . ." She prefers to not think about it and takes in her surroundings. The restaurant isn't much more than a brightly lit cafeteria with a handful of design overlays. This is not the domain of white tablecloths and two-martini power lunches. Contract vendors, the C-suite, and coders alike efficiently consume calories and then get back to their desks.

"I'm such a tourist down here," Sami tells Monica. "Everyone seems so smart. So focused. Like they were trained to do this stuff since childhood."

"Yeah, because they didn't have any friends and no girls would talk to them." Monica finishes chewing and swallows. "So, they spent all their free time defiling themselves and playing with computers."

Sami knew she was right to ask Monica to accompany her into Kim's work territory for this meeting. They might both be fish out of water in this part of town, but Monica's the friend who's sure to tell her, "Just grow some legs then, Sami."

Sami looks up to Monica Barrett; she always has. Monica too was born and raised in the city and is given to more direct advice, sometimes bordering on too direct, than most of Sami's other local friends and neighborhood acquaintances. Sami feels that may be some cultural difference because Monica is Black. Or maybe it's because Monica spent her early career as an executive assistant working for a local mortgage bank as it pursued aggressive national expansion—up until its spectacular collapse.

And Sami, in turn, was of crucial support to Monica while she tended to her ailing grandfather, Archie, through the end of his life—a role that Sami had experienced a few years prior with her own grandmother. Sami talked Monica out of many a tight and emotional spot in the pincers of childcare and eldercare. The two women bonded over long walks around Stevenson with vanilla lattes in paper cups and PTA meetings that were less about organizing anything tangible for the school and more about reaching for the branches of new friendships beyond one's own domestic quicksand.

Generally speaking, Sami appreciates Monica's matter-of-fact input she became accustomed to growing up with her grandmother, who, while politely *nisei,* also had the candor of a person who had come of age marginalized by mainstream society and took nothing for granted, suffered no fools, and took no one outside of her close circle of trust at their word. Sometimes the dance of indirect and deferential "that's nice, what do you think?" pseudo-Scandinavian culture in this city feels to Sami like death by a million limp, clammy handshakes. Even if she has some, if not too much, natural inclination in that direction herself.

"Just tell me what you think," Sami often wants to scream, but never does. "Say what you mean. Is it terrible? It is good? Let me know. Tell me. Let's get to the point." But none of that is necessary with Monica.

Sami folds up the printouts with the negotiating tactics. "You sure you can't do this meeting for me?" she begs Monica.

"This is your road to travel, my friend."

"Help me run the PTA then. We need the music teacher on board. I need you."

"You know my divorce is a mess. A very expensive mess. I'm driving Uber six nights a week. Full days on the weekend." She looks at her watch. "This meeting is setting me back at least twenty bucks in fares. Maybe thirty. Anyway, let's take some deep breaths and visualize this illuminati sister-in-law of yours. You're going to bend her skinny Pilates ass to your will."

Sami touches up her posture, mindful of her shoulders and neck, envisioning Kim walking through the door with her preening synchronized swimmer's gait. "I am willing to make compromises, but you have to make them too . . . Kimberly. It has to be STEAM, not STEM. Science, Technology, whatever else . . . and Art. Has to have art. This has always been a cornerstone of the school. Since it opened."

"What else?" Monica prods.

"The lab, sure. Space is tight. Too tight. Lack of space is likely one of the reasons they're trying to shut us down. So, we need to find additional space. The Stalworth Lab. Or incubator. Whatever. In the basement. Not in place of any existing programs."

"And? Most importantly?"

"Hasegawa. Have to stick with the plan. Rename the school: Hasegawa."

"And?"

"That's it. I mean, they can have the Staworth Lab at Hasegawa Elementary, but the name is—"

"Nonnegotiable." Monica wipes her mouth with a napkin. "Otherwise, you walk."

Sami takes a bit of salad but doesn't chew.

"Say it," Monica orders.

"That's when I walk?"

"Feel it." Monica goads her on. "Channel me talking to my ex."

Sami pulls her digital watch from her pocket and peeks at it. "Five minutes."

"I'm going to drink a coffee and sit at this table right over here. Make sure you don't implode. I won't let you be a pussy."

"She's Percy's sister. I can't . . . and Kim did offer me a job, after all." She again feels stuck.

"Listen, Sami. My family lived in the same neighborhood right in the middle of the city for three generations. Built the whole thing. And now most of the community has been pushed out by these overindulged man-children who don't know how to make their own ice cubes or change a light bulb. Oh hey, Brian. How you doing, sweetie?" She waves and winks at a bald, bespectacled customer with a blue credential dangling from his belt. "You think I let that get me down? You think I give a shit?"

"I don't know. Maybe?"

"Of course, I give a shit. I'm heartbroken. My grandma, remember my grandma? She was a fixture at her church bingo games for thirty years. Now she lives with my dad so deep in the suburbs that there're no sidewalks or buses or really anything unless he can give her a ride."

"How's your dad?"

"Ah, OK. I guess. Lonely. Still working around the clock, even though he's in his seventies. Anyway, I never should have let my granny lose her house. But I let it go because I was busy fighting too many other fights. That's what they do. Wear you down and wear you down until you roll over and give up. Letting go of that house is one of my life's greatest regrets. And now my grandma spends her days watching game shows, only looking forward to her Monday, Wednesday, and Friday baths."

"I can't let the school fall apart, not on my watch."

"That's right, Sami. What was the first thing you told me when we met?"

"That even after four children I'm not sure if I'm cut out to be a mom?"

"Nope."

"That my husband and I didn't have sex for over a year after our youngest was born?"

"No, but that's something you might want to talk to a professional about. Not that I even have a steady boyfriend. Never doing that shit again. I just use this app here." Monica shows Sami the face of her phone. "I get whatever I want. Whenever. Like, really, whenever. That's how I met tasty little Brian over there." She nods toward the Mothership employee hunched over his wrap. "I'll get you set up on it too. I know exactly how to write the profile for married ladies. Here . . . let me see your phone."

Sami squirms in her chair.

"I'm messing with you, c'mon. You know I don't sleep with strangers. Not during the school year, anyhow." Monica starts to pack up her stuff and bus the table. "The first thing you told me when we met was about your grandma. What she'd been through. What she meant to you. And your mom. To the whole community. Let's honor that, right?"

She gives Sami a quick kiss atop the head and moves to the adjacent table. Monica passes her hands over her own face, miming her expression wiped clean, and becomes just another restaurant patron.

Sami uses a paper napkin to clear the table of crumbs. She positions her chair to face the front door. She waits.

Nobody comes.

Five minutes later Sami is checking her phone for text messages and voicemails. Nothing.

"She gonna show?" Sami mouths to Monica across the tables.

"How should I know?" Monica mouths back. She shrugs and then says an audible, "What an entitled bitch."

Sami increasingly needs to go to the bathroom but holds it. "Been twelve. I can't be late to pick up my daughter at school. Call her at fifteen?"

"Call her now," Monica says. "Your time has just as much value as hers. Well, not in terms of money, but you know what I mean."

Sami picks up her phone and checks again for texts. "I think I should wait until fifteen—"

Just then she sees Kim's assistant Elise enter through the front door of the restaurant, typing on her phone.

"Elise, hey. Over here." Sami flags her down.

Elise looks up from her device and walks toward the table. She offers some generic pleasantries, sits down in the chair facing Sami, and finishes tapping out her message.

"Texting Kim?" Sami asks.

"No." She puts the device face up on the table, glancing back down to read and dismiss a follow-up response.

"Hmm, OK. Is she almost here? Because I can wait for her to

start. For a minute or two, anyway. I don't want to be pushy or any-thing, but I can't stay past the end of the hour because I have to pick up my..."

From the other table, Monica silently drags an index finger across her own throat.

"... have another commitment. Another meeting. After this. You know, can't go over."

"I thought you didn't work?" Elise asks.

Sami does some quick math to figure that Elise is closer in age to her eldest child than she is to her. "No, not exactly, Elise."

"I'm supposed to go over budget numbers with you."

"Wait, is Kim not coming?" Sami wants to turn to Monica for support but fights the urge. "Not at all?"

Elise shakes her head. "I'm not sure if there was an expectations gap there or what, but Kim is busy with some key meetings." She checks the time on her phone. "I actually only have a couple of min-utes myself. Normally, this kind of thing would be handled over email, but you're family, so she insisted."

"Well, I mean, thank you? I too have some key things to discuss with Kim. The STEAM thing. Remember, I emailed about it: put-ting 'art' in there. Keeping it in there, really, to stay in line with the school's history."

"Yeah, Kim said that was fine. She wants to consider adding ro-botics too, down the line. Don't really have budget for that now, but you know. So, STEAM it is."

Victory number one. Sami perks up and sneaks a quick nod to Monica. Optimism pumps through her veins. "The next thing is the placement of the lab or whatever you want to call it."

"From a cost perspective, a straightforward conversion of the main music room makes the most sense." Elise opens a note on her phone and skims down a list.

"We can't just replace the music room. That's the heart and soul of the school. It is the school. We can't replace any other existing class, for that matter."

"Kim's brand is innovation and growth mindset." Elise starts looking at her phone again, reading and seemingly indifferent to Sami's concerns.

"And?"

"Innovation and growth mindset. Not charity. She is about moving things forward. Not perpetuating some perceived past."

"What do you mean her brand's not charity?" Monica shouts from the other table. "She's the head of giving at Mothership."

"Sorry, that's my friend. Um, Monica. Just happened to be sitting right over there, eating, um, whatever she's eating." They all observe Monica's empty tabletop. "Small town, huh? Monica, meet Elise. Elise, meet Monica."

Elise is not impressed. "Yes, Kim's brand is supporting high performers to create their own success."

"Let's keep working on room placement. I have a good alternative in mind. We'll get you all the specs. What about the school name?" Sami asks. "The Hasegawa Elementary part. It's, well, that is not up for—"

"One step at a time. That's not me saying that. Kim told me to tell you that." Elise gets up and holds out a large legal envelope in front of Sami. "Here's the NDA. First, let's make the Stalworth Lab happen and save the school—and Kim's election, of course. Priorities. Right, team?"

"W. A. L. K." Monica mouths the letters to Sami.

Sami squeezes her eyes tight and presses on her temples. She thinks of her grandmother, the school, the neighborhood. Of Kim, the students, the lab. What is. What could be. What will be lost. Change. Compromise.

"What if—?" she starts to ask, but as she looks back up, the legal envelope is lying on the table, and Elise is gone.

FIFTEEN   *2014*

Bruce beats the sawdust off his Sonics hat against one of the five upright two-by-fours that he and Sierra sawed to length and nailed into place today. Most of the dust comes off the hat, but some holds defiantly to the sweat stain around the band.

Sierra sits a few feet away, doodling with a pencil on a spare piece of cardboard. Throughout the day, she's been perfecting her caricature of her father with his ponytail and raccoon hat. "Pretty cool, huh?" she says.

"Can't you make it slightly more, I don't know, handsome?" He holds out his hand, and Sierra lays another shiny 16-penny nail in his palm. He leans up against the upright board for stability, re-checks that he hasn't skewed anything, grabs his hammer, lines up the nail, and drives it through the board.

His phone rings. Sierra puts down her pencil and looks at it. "PTA lady. Again."

"Let it go. We're like . . ." He looks back at the length of the in-stalled wall framing, counting silently and moving his lips. "Half-way? A quarter? Less . . . than where we need to be today. Let's get back to it."

After the "rodent incident," as Sami had later described it in an email, the whole PTA endeavor looked a lot more complicated than he'd bargained for. It didn't help that she also didn't seem too pleased with the labor-intensive photocopy job he'd done for her.

He was hoping for a bit more appreciation. Even if it wasn't 100 percent perfect. It didn't look to him like other parents were exactly scaling the school's walls to do Sami's photocopying for her.

He never said he was quitting. But he assumed the whole thing was over with and went his own way, meaning that he stopped returning her calls. And most definitely not because he was afraid of rats. He'd seen plenty of those over the years. Little fuckers will gnaw down a full cannabis plant for no good reason. And it's not like they even get high off it.

What scares him is overcommitment. He's got enough commitments. Commitments coming out of his ears. His ass. Whatever other part of your body can hold commitments. Whether his wife, Wren, recognizes and appreciates that or not.

"How many more walls do we have to do?" Sierra asks him.

He waves the length of the room and then toward the banisterless particleboard staircase to the upstairs. Bruce knows there is little chance that he will have the space anywhere close to done in time to entertain the idea of an inspection by the Liquor Control Board. Not that in-person inspections are guaranteed, but they are rumored to be happening and Bruce needs to be prepared. It seems like the rules keep changing every day, and he has to stay ahead of whatever happens next. Especially considering he has hung his future on twenty cannabis lottery applications out of a single building. All eggs. One very rickety basket.

There's a knock at the door.

"Don't answer it." He shakes his head at Sierra, fearing a state inspector or, worse, Sami, on the other side of the entrance. The dead bolt is broken, and the door doesn't lock from the inside, only from the outside with the key. But Bruce thought ahead and leaned a low file cabinet up against the door to stop anyone from coming in and bothering their work.

"You sure, Pops?"

"Probably somebody asking for money." He has to get Sierra home soon. In fact, he pretty sure that she's already late again, but they got a slow start here, and he needs his daughter's support to get anything done. He can't do carpentry solo. Can't do much of anything solo. Not these days.

And on top of everything, the first hour was spent clearing garbage out of the space. Someone had been squatting here. Probably that tweaker everybody calls "Spazzy" who sleeps in the van on blocks out in the lot. It's possible that even a few people have been living here.

He'd originally thought about taking up residence here himself, but after removing the piss-smelling foam sleeping pads, newspaper used for various personal hygiene purposes, empty Four Loko tallboys, moldy Taco Bell wrappers, and hundreds of spent nitrous cartridges in a big gleaming silver mound, he's pretty sure that making the restaurant his primary address and Sierra's second bedroom would all but guarantee a divorce, if not outright loss of all custody rights.

Bruce has no plan of how to hoist up the drywall ceilings, let alone lift the board into place for the walls. Maybe Mel can dirty up his crisp sweats and do a little something more than just collect rent to earn his 50 percent.

There is another knock at the door. He hears whomever it is announce themselves but can't make out any details through the exterior brick and masonry walls. Bruce puts his finger across his lips and shushes Sierra. He whispers, "They'll go away."

The last thing he needs is somebody coming in here and trying to steal his idea. He's had enough of that for one lifetime. He didn't just build the first hydroponic grow operation in the city in '86. Or was it '84? But he was the one who came up with the concept after a season growing indoor orchids and tomatoes in British Columbia. Under the Loose Bruce budget-hydro blueprint, the plants sat in a floating tray with the roots dangling below into a channel with a constant flow of tap water mixed with nutrient solution. Standard stuff: mainly calcium nitrate, Epsom salts, and a blend of nitrogen, phosphorus, and potassium for both nourishment and aeration. Using cheap pumps bought from aquarium shops, the solutions passed through the root channels, and the runoff was then deposited into a big rain barrel where it was recycled back around the loop. And of course, this allowed the plants to be grown indoors where new Chinese-made lights could pump UV in lower 400-to-480-nanometer wavelengths into the plants eighteen or more hours per day, even in the dead of winter.

The whole thing was relatively simple. Rather ingenious but also straightforward when you think about it. At the time, it hadn't even crossed Bruce's mind to come up with the cash to build it himself or try to get a piece of the profits. He didn't have the tools, money, or skills to sculpt the hydroponic trays from plastics, so he was the one who had the idea to make do with repurposed polystyrene bumpers made to cushion the corners of furniture shipping boxes. He was a dirtbag skier trying to make ends meet and didn't realize at the time how this would change things beyond allowing people to grow expensive cannabis for a few deeper-pocketed connoisseur customers in places where it had been hard, if not impossible, to grow before.

Yes, there had been pretty decent weed in the city prior to that. This wasn't fucking Ohio or New England. But anything really chronic had to be imported from British Columbia.

But one after another, grow operations started to replicate that Loose Bruce blueprint. And the city began producing its own premium weed at such a scale that the price came down so that even high school students were going in together to get twenty sacks of fat, dense nugs frosted with trichomes. Not the schwag that made you tired, slovenly, and wanting to gorge on comfort foods. No, with this superchronic, you'd want to get off your ass and ski. Hike.

Engage with the world. And think about existence and what you should be doing with your life in a completely different way.

Was it an overstatement to say that the fruits of this labor influenced a generation of creative thinking that led this city from a backwater company town to one of the world's centers of music and then technological entrepreneurship? Probably, yes. And all of that had passed Bruce by. But it must have had something to do with it. It had clearly helped people approach the world, approach the future—from a slightly different angle.

And the dude who bankrolled Bruce's original blueprint (and aggressively under-negotiated his day rate) made millions. Billions? Bruce was partially paid for his labor in weed, a ski season pass, and a used Gore-Tex ski jacket. The money man, whose name shall never be spoken again by Bruce, went on to buy real estate throughout the city and invest in local tech and coffee companies.

Bruce went back to the mountains and got in a full season of uninterrupted skiing before he had to hustle up some new gigs in the early spring. It was a decent season with a glorious two-hundred-plus-inch base and steady temps under thirty-two, at least on the upper mountain. And nobody can take that from him.

He regrets things but also doesn't. OK, he regrets a lot of it—much more so since he became a parent in an ever-more expensive city and the stakes of his entire existence changed. But he doesn't regret the skiing. He lives, or lived, for the rhythm of the turns. The feeling of living a microsecond in the future where your ego, stress, and problems all drop away and you live by pure intuition, thinking only about the turn you need to make around the next tree and then the tree after that. He became a religious disciple of that flow state. It was the one thing that could consistently make him happy. Without fail. But to support his steady habit of absolutely fucking ripping pow, he had to go back out and make more and more money for just another run, another day in the mountains, another season.

There is another knock at the entrance and someone announcing themselves again.

"Shh," he says to Sierra. The door handle turns. He checks the file cabinet. It's secure. He's pleased with himself that he had the foresight to put in place such essential fortifications.

But the door opens outward—the cabinet tipping over and slamming down on its side, relieving itself of hundreds of ancient food and supply purchase orders and old menus. A bright triangle of daylight sweeps across Bruce's sandals and the detritus on the restaurant's uneven cement floor. He notices a yellowed Special of the Day menu that reads: CAPTAIN'S PLATTER $4.75.

"Jesus Christ, Bruce." His wife, Wren, enters the space, surveying the state of things from wall to ceiling to wall and back. "I've been calling you. Knocking. Have you been hiding from me? I mean, I can see your van parked right out front." She turns to her daughter. "Sierra? Seriously?"

Sierra doesn't know how to answer.

"Sorry. That's on me. I was occupied." Bruce takes the flak and then busies himself as if he is deep in thought studying his carpentry. He knows Wren is right. But sometimes he has to structure their days around his needs too. He's not going to go there, not going to say what he is really thinking, because they've had this argument so many times. But her entire point of view about this, while reasonable on its face, is predicated on the understanding that her priorities are the priorities. Her needs are the needs. Her schedule is the way things are, the oxygen around them, the one real and verifiable truth. And anything he wants to do that interrupts that in any way is an extracurricular, a favor, if not a misstep that blows a hole in the official calendar. He is the underpaid junior partner. The day laborer. Like always.

"Three o'clock, Bruce. How many times are we going to do this? God, I hate looking like the bad guy for just trying to maintain basic order."

"It's three?"

"I'm not your clock, Bruce. I don't do that anymore." He sees her purse her lips to start to say what he imagines to be "now that we're separated," but she holds her fire. They promised not to discuss those details in front of Sierra. They promised not to fight in front of her too. Wren readjusts. "I need you to stay on top of things yourself. That's the only way we can coordinate this intricate dance between two households."

"I'm doing a lot myself. More than you know. Plus, making this be between two households is a choice. And not my choice, right?"

Wren evades an answer by surveying the interior of the restaurant. She wrinkles up her nose at some perceived noxious odor and says, "I thought you needed Sierra earlier because you had a PTA meeting tonight?"

He shrugs.

"Don't tell me you already quit?"

It's Bruce's turn to ignore her question.

"You have important things to do in the PTA. For Sierra." She kicks a used nitrous cartridge with the toe of her shoe, and it spins across the floor into a shadowed corner. "So, this ... place. This is your newest scheme?"

"Not a scheme. A business. OK? You'll see." He retests an upright two-by-four for its fortitude and leans up against it, only adjusting his penis in his cargo shorts once. And almost imperceptibly, at that. "And how'd you even know about this place?"

Sierra hides her face.

"I agreed to a more flexible schedule because you were investing time in our daughter's school's PTA, not so she could do this. Whatever this is. Child labor? Does this have something to do with the privacy glasses again?"

"No. And, yes. Well, sort of. Over the long run. And, again, not a scheme." He tells himself to not take the bait. She had never been a believer in any of his more revolutionary ideas. The glasses, in particular, were too far ahead of their time for her. Especially now that she's increasingly co-opted by consumer life and the establishment.

"What about the PTA then?" She waits for him to dare not answer the question for a second time.

"Yeah, of course." Bruce clears his throat. "I'm just wrapping up some stuff before I head over. What do they call it? Multitasking."

"That's a new one." She purses her lips into an incredulous grimace and then laughs at Sierra's cartoon of Bruce in the coonskin cap on the cardboard. "Classic . . ."

"Well, today's all multitasking, to-do lists, serious business." He winks weakly at Sierra. "Gotta help the school. Gotta be a good father. Take my PTA role seriously. You know, for our daughter." He opens his flip phone, locates the numerous text messages from Sami that he's unsure of how to answer, not due to their content but the difficulty of the keyboard, and tries to put the evidence up in Wren's face. "Look, see: the PTA president. Simpatico. Right here. Getting the inside track for all that needs to get done. See?"

She squirms out of the way of his incoming phone. "OK, Sierra, grab your backpack and let's go. You've got music practice."

Sierra grabs the cardboard and her backpack.

"Leave that."

"I'm gonna keep working on it," Sierra says, stepping over the fallen cabinet and following her mom back out the door.

Wren pauses and says, "Bruce, please, go take a shower and change, or at least get that sawdust off your clothes before you go to a PTA meeting representing our family."

"Our family?" He stares at her, unblinking.

"You know what I mean."

SIXTEEN   *1971*

Masako opens the lid of the rice cooker and mixes in the mushrooms that have been steaming atop the rice. She makes sure to scoop from the bottom up so as not to break apart the fragile *matsutake* mushrooms. Just how her mother-in-law showed her based on the dish from her native Wakayama Prefecture, where the cool, damp inland red pine forests were ideal mushroom habitat. Not that Masako ever really liked her mother-in-law, but liking her was never an essential part of the equation.

She samples one of her mushrooms from her special, once-a-year rice, her *matsutake gohan*. It tastes like pine, ferns, and moss. Maybe a hint of dirt, or what people might call earthy. But in the best of ways. The texture of the mushroom is somewhere between meaty and delicate. Way more delicate than the overpriced, store-bought ones in the International District. And, interestingly, this part of the world and Japan are two of the only areas where such mushrooms grow in abundance.

The dish reminds her of *matsutake tori* foraging hunts as a teenager, those last few years before she was married. Masako could be remembering wrong, but she swears they were able to find the *matsutakes* in the wooded areas along the edges of the Hasegawa family farm that are all now covered with cement and houses. Albert, her former husband's cousin (whom she has only ever called Bert), still forages in secret mountainous areas that he won't reveal, even to family. He is sparing with his quarry but was willing to share the necessary amount with Masako as she told him it was for a very special occasion. She may have slightly exaggerated and said an engagement party for Ruth, or really a pre-engagement party, which was closer to fact. In exchange for the mushrooms, she offered a total of five hours of private one-on-one violin classes with Bert's youngest daughter.

Every family has their own traditional way of cooking *matsutake gohan*, seasoning the stock and some other key decisions around the quantity of bonito flakes and whether you serve the dish with or without chicken. Masako, due to her lifelong minimalism, not her daughter's passing vegetarian fad, is firmly in the no-chicken camp. The additional protein detracts from the full appreciation and flavor of the mushrooms.

However, today she has made half the dish without chicken and half with chicken. She did this to appease Beckham's aunt, who unsurprisingly let her opinions be known when Masako first volunteered to bring this dish to church this week. "*Matsutake gohan* without chicken is barely worth eating," she'd remarked with no interest in opening the point to further discussion. Masako could never accept that position, but she is willing to meet the woman in the middle, considering the bigger things at stake.

Masako knocks again at Ruth's bedroom door. She calls her daughter's name again and lets her know that the food is ready and if she doesn't get up now, not now but twenty minutes ago, they are going to be late for church.

"Ruth?" She raises her voice. "Ruth, don't be late. Let's make a good impression. Or, at least, a better impression this time."

When again there is no answer, she tries the doorknob to find Ruth's bed, tidily made as she insists of her daughter. Masako checks behind the door. Panic sets in. Could that Larry hooligan have abducted Ruth? This can't be right. She went out to dinner with a friend last night. True, Masako did not know the friend. But it was a classmate. One in Ruth's study group. Ruth had promised.

Ruth was home at a respectable hour. Not right after dinner, but within an hour or so. She had her books with her. "Ruthie, where are you?" she shouts, her voice bordering on panic.

There is no answer again, and she starts to run toward the bathroom; maybe Ruth slipped getting into the shower or something equally treacherous. Before she can make it there, she hears, "Here, Mom. I'm here," from back in the room.

Masako returns to the bedroom, enters, and looks around to find Ruth exiting her closet, fully clothed in that overly casual puffy jacket and those flamboyant feathered earrings that she disapproves of, especially for church or meeting with Beckham. "What were you doing in there?"

Ruth shrugs, staring off into the distance.

"Well, why didn't you answer me before?"

"I was meditating?"

"In your closet?" Masako doesn't know what to think other than hope that her daughter is not in another of her self-sabotage episodes. "Let's go. Hurry up. Beckham is going to be there."

Ruth walks across the room and sits down on the edge of her bed. "I'm sorry. But I can't go today."

Masako leans against the doorframe for a moment to take a breath and then straightens herself back up. "Yes, you can. I told you: Beckham is going to be there."

"I still can't."

"Why still can't you?" She takes a step into the room.

"I don't feel well." She tells her mom about her headaches. Her chills. Her lethargy.

There is a long quiet. Masako leans down to touch the back of her hand to her daughter's forehead.

"Feels fine to me."

"I'm telling you: I can't."

"That's not a choice, Ruth. Let's go. Now."

Ruth looks at her mother and considers her answer before speaking. "Sorry. No."

"Does this have something to do with Larry?"

"It has to do with me."

Masako laughs. "Of course, it has to do with you. This all has to do with you. I am doing all of this for you too. And you are coming to church with me. Right now. Did you brush your teeth?" She takes a hard look at her daughter's face. "I'm not sure about that jezebel makeup. I can forgive the outfit but not the makeup. Let's snap out of it."

"No."

"Excuse me? You don't get to say 'no' to me, young woman. Let's go before you embarrass yourself. And your family."

"What about you, Mom?"

"What about me, what?"

"Embarrass yourself?"

"Yes, if you refused to show. Did not meet that young man's expectations. His family's expectations."

"What about spying on someone? Following someone around a grocery store."

"I have no idea what you're talking about?"

"No?"

"No."

"Larry. Food King. Really? C'mon, Mom."

"Who told you this? That... man? He obviously can't be trusted. Someone at church knows his mother, and the rumor is that Larry was expelled from the Navy for being mentally unfit."

"That's not true. And anyway, it wasn't him who told me about the store. He defended you. The store manager told me."

Masako waves her off. "Who? Nonsense. Come help me get the

food ready to put in the car." She works to find a tone that conveys the issue has been settled. Time to move on.

Ruth starts to stand, but then stops. "I don't . . . I realized some stuff last night I don't think that I can ignore."

"Don't let that Larry get in your head that he is nice or whatever. A street dog may have puppy eyes but only brings fleas into your house."

"Mom."

"*Okasan.*"

"*Okasan,* that is so unfair."

"Again, I am only looking out for the best for you. You do not want to experience what I've experienced. I honestly don't think, with all due respect, my dear, that you have the strength to endure what I went through. I want the best for you. Larry is not the best. Not even good. Trust me."

"Can I really trust you, though?"

"How dare you even say that out loud? Even think that? I had to borrow two rice cookers and call in favors with every relative and church friend in order to make this batch of *matsutake gohan.* It took me the whole evening yesterday to make the dashi."

"What's that?"

"The stock, Ruth. Even white people know that. Get your head on straight."

"Sorry?"

"You and Beckham are going to meet with some of the other church elders today. We are planning another event, properly chaperoned of course, for the two of you next week. Do not sabotage yourself, Ruth. Do not sabotage us."

"I don't love him, *Okasan.* Maybe a different woman would. He's handsome and smart and successful. But I don't."

Masako laughs. "Who said anything about that? You want to experience true love? Focus on your music. Or try a little harder at church."

"But?"

Masako grabs Ruth by the arm. "Right now."

"No. I don't feel well. Not today. I'm sorry."

There is a ring at the front doorbell.

They're a little early, Masako thinks. "You better not be trying to stay home to meet up with Larry."

"No, of course not. But wait here, I'll get it."

Masako ignores the suggestion and walks briskly toward the front door. Ruth jogs behind her, sweat glistening on her forehead.

"I said, I've got it." Ruth tries to get around her mom to open the door first. As she edges around her mom, Masako nudges her out of the way. Not aggressively, but firm in that it is her house, and she will be the one to answer the door if she pleases.

She opens the door to reveal Beckham and his aunt standing on the front steps in their finest Sunday attire. The BMW is parked in front of their house.

"We were passing nearby," Beckham says. "Pardon the early arrival."

"And we thought we'd help you get all that *matsutake gohan* to the church," the aunt continues, craning her neck into the doorway to survey the main living area. "I can smell the chicken. Good."

"See?" Ruth mouths to her mom.

"Come on in everyone, please," Masako offers.

Once everyone is inside and busy organizing the platters for the car ride, Masako says she needs to check the mail. That she forgot to do it yesterday.

From the front porch, she can see Larry waiting on his motorcycle right past the corner. They make fleeting eye contact, and he tries to hide his cigarette. Larry backs up his bike with his feet, turns around, and peels off in the other direction.

SEVENTEEN   *1971*

Larry returns to Ruth's block after an hour or two of riding his motorcycle at top speed through side streets, once barely missing a parked school bus as he skidded out on the wet pavement—perhaps on purpose. And now, he waits for what he figures to be twice that long, shivering off the cold and fighting to keep his cigarettes lit. It's getting harder to ignore that he hasn't eaten anything since part of that salad last night.

He passes the time atop his beater Kawasaki Road Runner by watching the sharp, cold rain churn the surfaces of the mud puddles. Pine needles, pink coils of drowned earthworms, and bottle caps float along the curb and toward the overwhelmed drain at the corner.

Ruth promised that she was going to skip church. That they were going to get time together. Without her mom in the house.

He regrets that he fled. He should have learned his lesson from the grocery store. He should have made himself known. Made his intentions known. But he saw Masako and ran.

He thinks about last night in his car. The touch of her skin. The heat coming off of her neck and chest. The smell of her hair. The curve of her nipples under the streetlights. It was equally astounding and stupefying. Awkward. Rushed. And ultimately abrupt.

She had to be home on time to not raise the suspicions of her mother. He wanted Ruth to stay with him. To not run off. To give him a chance to try again and do better the second time. But she swore that they'd spend the morning together while her mom was out. Do it again. This time not so hurried and most definitely not in the passenger seat of his mom's Datsun.

Using his hand to slick back his hair and press out some of the water, Larry lights another smoke on the third attempt. Water runs between his pants and the seat of the bike, soaking his jeans and penetrating the perianal region of his yellowed tighty-whities. His wrist clears the rain from his eyelashes, just in time to see the gray BMW swing back onto the street and pull to a stop in front of Ruth's house.

The same guy as before is driving the car. The guy with the nice suit and the perfect, glossy, parted hair. An older lady, probably his mom, sits in the passenger seat wearing some sort of a dead fox over her shoulders. Ruth and Masako exit from the back seats of the car, crouching low to protect themselves against the rain.

They lean back inside the open car doors and gather big plates and some other things that look like white Crock-Pots, not that different from what his neighbors used for cooking dinner—those tangy, sweet meatballs with the chunks of pineapple and sesame seeds in there or the cocktail wieners with the sticky stuff that reminded him of cherry pie filling. Goddamn, it's been a while since he's eaten.

He watches Ruth and Masako struggling to carry the stuff in the rain and wants to help them. Maybe they'd promptly invite him in to dry off with a clean towel and have an early lunch, while Ruth explains her true intentions to her mother. Instead, the fancy man gets out and holds the umbrella over Masako's head, carrying an armload of platters and walking her to the door. Then he does the same with Ruth. And runs back and forth, bringing the additional Crock-Pots and such.

Larry stares slack-jawed at the action between the car and the house, this other, much-improved version of himself doing the job that he should be doing. His cigarette falls from his mouth, extinguishes itself in the mud puddle, and drifts off toward the street drain. Swearing to himself under his breath, he shakes his cigarette pack to determine if there's anything left but opens it to find only a booklet of wet matches.

With no more distractions, he returns to the main issue at hand and the dawning realization, if not terror, that no matter what happened last night, his window of opportunity is closing. It is now or never: he must intervene.

Ruth is being railroaded by her mother. By this BMW-driving Casanova or whatever the word is. By the man's ridiculous mother in the passenger seat. Larry knows that it is really he and Ruth who are in love. It is no longer a question. And he needs to make that clear to Masako before everyone involved makes a huge mistake that is embarrassing and confusing for them and heartbreaking, if not completely devastating, for him. And Ruth. Of course, for Ruth too.

At this point, he'd rather have the conversation with Ruth, the guy, the guy's mom, anybody other than Masako, who can pretty much decapitate Larry with a single look. He decides that as soon as the man has dropped off the last of the plates and Ruth and Masako are both inside, he will discreetly confront the guy as he walks back to his car. Not confront so much as go and talk to him and make sure that he understands what is really going on here and can no longer be denied. The man shouldn't be too surprised. He must recognize on some level that this is all forced. Playacting. That Ruth's heart is elsewhere.

He watches the guy wave to Masako and then give Ruth a stiff hug. He can tell by her body language that she doesn't love him. Can't love him. He is sure of it. But it still pains him to see her arms around another man. The other man who so clearly has Masako's favor. And the world's favor. Even if Ruth gives him a sturdy pat on the back like Larry gave to a union dude he worked with (and whose name he could never remember) after dry cupcakes and instant coffee at his retirement lunch.

The door closes, and the man returns down the front steps. Larry locks out the kickstand on his motorcycle and starts walking toward him. He hikes right through the puddle with purpose, clearing the water again from his hair and eyes. He closes in on the man, picking up his pace so that he will arrive before the man enters his German-engineered steel mobile fortress.

As Larry gets within a few yards of the man he realizes that he has no plan of what he should or could say or do. Sure, he could go right into explaining that he loves Ruth and Ruth loves him, but he doesn't want to be that direct. Or run that much of a risk of getting overly emotional in front of a man he's just met. What if he cries? What if the guy reacts poorly and tries to fight him? He thinks for a moment and comes up with nothing, so he settles on, "Hey."

"Hey," say the other man, showing off his flawless white teeth as he closes down a sizable umbrella and shakes off the water droplets. He opens the rear door and places it in the back seat of his car.

"I'm Larry."

The man looks at him, tilting his head to the side but still moving to open the driver's-side door of the vehicle. He says nothing.

"Dugdale," Larry says. "My name. It's Larry Dugdale."

"OK." He starts getting into the car and says something inaudible to the older woman in the passenger seat. The woman glances up at Larry with a look of practiced revulsion.

Larry has so much more to say. Does he start with himself or Ruth or Masako or how this man and Ruth's relationship is nothing more than a mother's desire to reenact her own youth or maybe he should start by telling him about the Supersonic Transport and how it is going to change the world? He wants another cigarette.

Would it take too long to track down and light another smoke? Could he ask this guy for one? Dude does seem to be in a hurry. He probably has some important work to do. And even looks like one of those health nut guys who thinks smoking is bad for you.

In the midst of Larry's deliberation, the man leans out of the car and places something in his palm. It takes Larry a moment to understand that it's a quarter. Before he can open his mouth to explain that he doesn't want money, the guy slams closed the car door and turns on the ignition. Larry realizes he is further losing his chance here. As he goes to tap on the window, the man does something that looks like a quick wave or a hand signal for Larry to get out of the way and accelerates out of the parking spot. Was that intentional? A threat, perhaps? He can't be sure, but he does know that the vehicle almost ran over his toes. Using his machinist skills, Larry estimates the car's curb weight at somewhere around three thousand pounds plus two full-grown adults. With a difference of a few precious inches, it could have been vehicular homicide. Easily.

He watches the red taillights on the vehicle as they disappear down the flooding asphalt and turn the corner. He smells wet grass, mud, and fungus under unraked leaves. Why did he spend the last hours here sitting in the rain and waiting? For what? One more missed chance. Another error. Another inability to follow through when it counts. Larry wishes he'd thrown himself under the BMW as it pulled away. That would have made a statement.

No, he can't do something like that now because, regardless of what Masako and BMW guy think, Larry is no longer alone in this world. He has Ruth. Or almost has Ruth. Almost had Ruth?

As he goes to slink back to his bike down at the corner, he looks up to the house and sees Masako in the window. Arms akimbo.

He offers her a sheepish wave and is not sure whether to go to the door to address her or admit defeat and scuttle off. He tries to turn away, but she has already made the decision for him.

The front door yawns open, and Masako marches down the steps, with no umbrella in the rain. Still dressed in her church clothes, but without having paused long enough to put her shoes back on, she carries a rolled-up newspaper in one fist. Larry braces for her to smash him like a housefly.

She stops a few paces short, unfurls the newspaper, and holds it above her head as a makeshift canopy. "What do you think you're doing here?"

He thinks of various excuses. None are particularly good. No, he won't miss his chance again. "I wanted to try to set the record straight."

"Larry..."

"Yes, Mrs. Hasegawa?"

"The record is straight."

Ruth comes out behind her. "What is? Oh..."

"Hi, Ruth," Larry says, standing taller, smiling, and unsuccessfully trying to melt her shock into a reciprocal smile—looking for any evidence that their alliance remains intact.

Ruth is unable to look directly at Larry and, instead, asks again what they were saying before.

"I was telling him that the record is straight," Masako says. "Straight as could be, if you ask me. All we have to do is keep it that way."

Larry stops his fruitless searching for angles and goes the only route he knows, his voice cracking with longing, fear, and desperation. "But I love her."

Masako waits an extended, agonizing moment to answer. "I'm sure you think you do." But even in her show of confidence, he can see her body rattle and compact—a potato bug curling up before a perceived threat. "But that only goes so far in this life, unfortunately, young man."

Larry turns to Ruth and then back to Masako, wiping the water again from his face with the back of his wrist. "I'm just trying to do the best thing for Ruth."

"You don't know the best thing for my daughter. Or yourself for that matter."

"What's the best thing then, *Okasan*?" Ruth takes another step out the front door.

Masako checks her bare feet in the wet grass. She shakes off the newspaper and replaces it above her head. "The best is for Larry to leave alone the natural progress of things that are beyond his control."

"What about me?" Ruth says to the two of them. The rain straightening her hair down the sides of her face. "What about what I want for myself? Do I get a say?"

Masako breathes deeply and pivots as if she is going to walk back inside. Clearly fighting back her instinctive answer of "No."

"Let her make her own decisions," Larry pushes.

"OK, Ruth," her mother finally addresses her daughter. Almost daring her to make a misstep.

Ruth pauses. She still doesn't know what to say.

"Tell her, Ruth," Larry nudges.

"Tell me what?" Masako holds her line.

Ruth shakes her head back and forth, eyes wide.

Larry verges on tears. "Tell her our plans. Our future."

"Your plans?" Masako asks. "Ruth?"

"No, I, I'm—"

Larry tries to help her out. "That's what we—well, last night, we talked and—"

"You told me you were with a friend last night, Ruth."

"I was . . . he is a friend."

The word hurts Larry down to the roots of his teeth.

Masako fumes. "What do you have to say for yourself, Ruth Hasegawa? You supposedly have all of these ideas. All these things to say to me. So, tell me: What do you want for yourself? To look at those filthy music albums in the back of your closet? To ruin your future over a momentary interest in someone you barely know? Tell me. Please."

Ruth stands quietly, rain running over her face. She doesn't clear it away and doesn't answer.

"That's what I thought. Inside. Now." Masako turns her back on Larry and walks to the house, grabbing her daughter by the forearm along the way.

Larry watches Masako draw the shades as rainwater streams down his legs and pools in his shoes.

PART IV   *1902*

Erasmus never thought his forties would be like this. The gold rush has come and gone, and he knows he should be thankful for all of his seeming successes. But he can't be happy. He feels pathetic, whiny, and desperate. He'd always believed that success would fill that gaping hole in him. And now that the money and prestige and accomplishments have arrived, he can't understand why he feels like an even bigger impostor. A hollow meat casing of a human who has led an objectively insignificant life, no matter how talented he has been at suckering marks and helping them part ways with their money.

"A fraud." That's what his wife called him. As she was leaving him and taking their children, she told Erasmus straight to his face that he did nothing but bring misfortune to others and would probably do so for the rest of his days. Those were the exact last words his wife, the mother of his children, ever said to him.

It can't be a coincidence. How could she choose exactly the same words as the old Indian's curse?

He spends his days in a mental loop, comparing himself to others who have done better than him. Made more money than him, yes. But, more importantly, lived more honorable lives. Given more to their families. To society. Indeed, he has been the cause of misfortune to so many others.

Is it the curse, or could he be suffering some sort of

neurasthenia or nervosism? He has all of the symptoms: fatigue, anxiety, headache, heart palpitations, high blood pressure, neuralgia, and depressed humors. His doctor told him that it is not uncommon among captains of industry and suggested an exorbitant blood electrification treatment. He declined. If nothing else, Erasmus knows another fraud when he sees one.

He knows he's not a bad person. Or doesn't have to be one. Not for the rest of his days or whatever the Indian told him. The real problem is his inner abyss. The lack of tangible center to the person known as Erasmus Stalworth.

He glad-hands and smiles his way around town, constantly aware of the fact that he never went to Yale, was never a Knight of Anything, and had never been engaged to Jefferson Davis's daughter—as he may or may not have told a few dozen colleagues during a moment of intoxicated bravado. His real name isn't even Erasmus. In some ways he's still little barefoot Bobby on the mud streets of Creede, Colorado, son of a failed silver prospector and some female human. He was on his own at somewhere between five and eight years old. Never even knew his own birthday or last name.

He sold newspapers on corners, taught himself to read, and fell in love with the idea of how those stories could travel over huge distances and shape people's understanding of the world around them. He would've killed to be a big-time newspaper publisher in New York or Boston. But that ship sailed. Sailed before the sperm even connected with the egg in some alley or unheated tar paper mountain shack.

Between hawking papers and then reading every day's edition from cover to cover, sometimes twice to study the layout, he learned from the local bunco men how to run a con. The primary industry in Creede was silver mining; the second was finding creative ways to liberate miners of their precious metals. He panhandled. Pickpocketed.

Led visiting businessmen to fixed card games. Told them stories about needing money for his sickly grandmother. Incentivized soap and perfume sales on the street with bogus raffle tickets. And, at night, he used to pretend to sleep in Ms. Jilly's straw crib so the john would have to tip him to get out. He'd split the take with Ms. Jilly, who made her little, dirt-faced autodidact promise to make something better of his life.

A few years later in Denver, he borrowed the name Erasmus Stalworth from a bankrupt land speculator who jumped to his death in front of the theater where young Bobby worked as the unpaid assistant for traveling showman Professor Mars.

By objective standards, his adult life has greatly improved. He owns a home. Land, with more on the way. He has a family. Or had a family. A wife known for her intellect and beauty—until she ripped out his heart or whatever it was that he had beating in his chest. He keeps company with esteemed businesspeople, newspapermen, politicians, and high-ranking Masons.

His ideas transformed this city. But he is still a man who takes more than he gives. Still bringing misfortune to others. And for that, his only respite is the poppy. And these days he has traded up from smoking pipes in Chinatown to injecting morphine from the city's finest chemists.

Not so many years ago, he was eating boiled shoe leather, stolen potatoes, and squirrels (often predeceased, as Erasmus has the hunting skills of a man who idolizes William Randolph Hearst). Now he looks across his mahogany desk, out the lead-paned office windows and across the mighty bay with its bustle of steamships heading out to the Pacific.

The harder he works to reach the shores of serenity and satisfaction, the further that distance becomes. He locks his office door and pulls down the blinds over the hall-facing window with his name in gold filigree on the front door, followed by his title: PRESIDENT. BUREAU OF INFORMATION.

That horrible lawyer, Sloot, will be here within fifteen minutes. He only tolerates the attorney's halitosis and poor sartorial choices because the man has the right connections and disposition to finally close the complex land deal that will cement Erasmus's legacy. That is why he must shoot up first. To cope. With the lawyer's shortcomings. His own shortcomings. With his role in this world.

Erasmus scratches at waves of symmetrical burning that run up and down his ribs and neck. He uses his gold-buckled leather belt to tie off his arm above the bicep and search for a vein in the inside of his elbow. After failing to get a proper bulge out of any of his traditional antecubital spots, he feels for possibilities in his neck. As a professional and supposed man of prominence in the community, he decides against such an exposed area, takes off his shoes and socks, and finds a serviceable blue line between his toes.

He had started this all off believing that the gold rush was a sucker's game. More than started off, he ran with it. Made a career out of it. Anyone with his level of street smarts could see that it was all hype. A lottery with a few lucky winners but legions who would buy tickets. And he capitalized on it, achieving his dreams at the expense of others.

He convinced thousands, many thousands, from all walks of life and from all over the country to make their way through the city's "Gateway to Alaska." Most lost their shirts. Many lost their lives. A good percentage blew all their savings on alloy-coated pickaxes and windproof, portable gas stoves, not to mention whiskey and prostitutes, before ever getting out of town and passing through those pearly gates to guaranteed, unimaginable wealth. Truth be told, it was Erasmus who coined the name "Gateway to Alaska." He first wrote it on a piece of the best new perforated toilet paper in the Chamber of Commerce bathroom while he was injecting sky-blue morphine between press meetings.

This town was not the natural or only gateway to Alaska. A

steamship had to travel some eight hundred long miles through the Inside Passage to Skagway. This trip took approximately three days. From Skagway, gold seekers crossed the White Pass or Chilkoot Trail to reach the headwaters of the Yukon River and, from there, they continued to Dawson City—a distance of another grueling five hundred miles. So, a gateway of sorts.

Tacoma, Vancouver, or even San Francisco should have been the jumping-off point for miners heading to the Klondike gold fields. Until Erasmus came onto the scene, San Francisco dominated maritime trade with Alaska and was home to many businesses with experience outfitting prospectors dating back fifty years to the California gold rush.

Vancouver was closer and perhaps the true gateway to the gold rush, and the all-Canadian choice presented fewer disputes with customs officials. Yet Canada was full of Canadians, which meant that rather than putting their backs into selling the dream, they expressed measured statements and caveats to prospective miners about the dangers of the adventure and the realistic chances of returning home broke.

Nobody else out there had Erasmus's verve. His hunger. His hole to fill. Whenever anyone pressed him to acknowledge the dangers of prospecting, he assured those considering the trip north that any and all risks could be duly mitigated by purchasing the right gear and new technologies here in town. They were not risks. They were situational challenges, problems in need of a solution. And that solution could always be bought for the right price. And the businesses, all of the businesses, that sold said solutions tithed a monthly percentage back to his Bureau of Information.

A scheme from someone in a jacket and tie is called a vision. As he told his Freemason brothers in the Chamber of Commerce, all that mattered was the story that they told and that they delivered it to as many people as possible. Again and again and again. In order to carry out that vision, he relied on a new technology called the telegraph. And he used it well, writing entire articles and letters to editors and sending them, faster than the speed of sound, to an ever-expanding network of newspaperman contacts back East and throughout the Midwest and South.

He leans forward and removes the glass ampule from below the ersatz gold telegraph on his desk. The telegraph is not hooked to anything. It's but a hollow spot to keep his morphine. He fumbles to get his medicine into the syringe before he can start to ponder how the fake telegraph is a metaphor for his life.

Erasmus pushes the needle between his toes, until it pops into his vein. He depresses the plunger on the glass syringe. The speed of everything slows. The waves of itching slow. His need to tap-dance through every moment of life to keep each lie balanced atop the stack of other lies slows. This city, which is moving faster and faster. The boats in and out of the harbor. Everything eases to a pleasant, manageable pace.

Erasmus feels a silky swell of nothingness wash over him. And that nothingness is all that he needs. All that he desires. He looks at the framed banner headlines and front-page stories covering the walls of his office. His first success had been to convince the *Post-Intelligencer* newspaper to print a special edition focusing on his "One and Only Gateway to Alaska" concept. They organized local businesses to chip in money for a massive print run of more than two hundred thousand copies for a city with a little over forty thousand people.

Then they mailed them to postmasters across the United States for distribution at local post offices. Twenty thousand were sent to newspaper editors and business organizations in the United States and Europe. Ten thousand were mailed to mayors, town councils, and librarians.

This then became his next great insight: to finance the Bureau of Information by taxing local merchants who stood to profit from the expected influx of population and increased trade. Businesses that paid dues received lists of prospective customers.

He devoted some of this money to advertising in newspapers and popular journals. He purchased a three-quarter-page ad in Hearst's *New York Journal* for $800, along with quarter-page advertisements in *Munsey's, McClure's, Scribner's,* and *Review of Reviews.* Originally, he framed all of them. But now there isn't enough wall space in his office.

He claimed the city to be the New York of the West. It mattered little to him that no major train lines went here but, instead, to the similarly sized hub of Tacoma and that there was little agriculture and no mining in the metro area.

For a week preceding the publication of the special Gateway edition, Erasmus placed advertisements announcing the upcoming issue and urging readers to send copies to friends and relatives in the East. It became the largest newspaper run ever produced west of Chicago. Take that, San Francisco.

In many ways, it was but a macro-version of what he'd learned handing out fliers to promote Denver doubleheader stage shows for Professor Mars, known for his oriental phrenology, mesmerism, and celebrated Mars Machine, a proprietary polished teak and wrought-iron table-mounted contraption for treatment of female hysteria via hand-crank, mechanized stimulation.

After all of the special editions were distributed, he started to follow up with more stories by telegraph. Erasmus wrote boilerplate feature articles about the city's virtues, which he distributed to editors throughout the nation. When asked if the articles were, in fact, advertising, he always responded, "Our fine city is not advertising the Klondike. The Klondike is advertising our fine city."

His next move was an old trick he'd learned from the stagehand union in Denver, or at least their attempt to set up a union. He convinced everyone with a stake in the city's success, from bosses to ministers to teachers, to get their employees, parishioners, and students to write letters about the glittering Gateway to Alaska to out-of-town friends and newspapers. The more spontaneous these letters could appear, the greater their impact. The result looked like a groundswell of unsolicited support.

Outfitters and other stores supplied Erasmus with the names and addresses of their new customers. He sent seemingly heartfelt telegrams, which he himself had typed, to the newspapers in those prospectors' hometowns, boasting of their impending success and encouraging everyone else to pull together what money they had and come to this city of endless opportunity. Erasmus took the liberty of signing each letter to the editor in the name of the local prospector.

But perhaps his greatest public relationships innovation, or "Erasmusism," as the Chamber of Commerce boys called it over rounds of top-shelf rye and Pacific oysters in the warmly lit back room of the Sea Maiden, was taking a semi-obscure comment by the Canadian Mounted Police that each miner arrives with enough gear to last a year and make that appear to be a legal prerequisite for heading north.

All who came here and hoped to find their fortunes in Alaska were inundated with what Erasmus coined "the one-ton rule." The rule obligated each man to purchase a literal ton of tents, packs, crystallized eggs, and evaporated beans. Merchants were soon selling prepacked one-ton "Klondike kits" for a whopping thousand dollars apiece. They could further mark up anything that bore the name "Klondike" and use it to sell everything from arctic underwear and frost extractors to insect-proof face masks.

And whether you were one of the handful who came back from Alaska with gold or the majority who came back with nothing, the Bureau of Information Office interviewed you, got a record of your story, and put a positive sheen on it before sending it out on telegraph, not just targeted to your hometown but to the whole country.

Wanting to know more, Erasmus commissioned a myopic math student from the recently established university, or "my Jew," as he fondly referred to the kid, to go up to the goldfields and perform surveys of the men. It was determined that over 70 percent of the miners had passed through town. And even now that the gold rush has wound down, the city has continued to grow. He figures that it has generated a million or more dollars. And Erasmus has profited too, but not like the Chamber of Commerce boys. The big merchants. The madams. The barkeeps. The landowners. And Erasmus knew, to the dollar, how much each of the successful miners had made. Indeed, his assay office weighed their gold and exchanged it for cash.

And he still wants more money, yes. But now he finds himself, in the aftermath of the gold rush, desiring something more. Something to prove his value to wider humankind. In the back room of the Sea Maiden, he announced to the Chamber that rather than future miners slogging all of that gear to future gold rushes by boat, mule, and sled dog, he intended to invent some sort of floating airship that would carry a ton of provisions over the water, mountains, and ice— straight to the source. Based on some early sketches, he envisioned using giant balloons, as some German count is said to have done, but adding birdlike wings, if not a large wooden ship propeller. Maybe, if the Chamber funded the effort, the ships would someday extend beyond mining and carry everyday passengers over great distances too.

The Chamber president laughed so hard that he blew rye out his nose. "You're a wonderful manipulator of the press, Stalworth. A downright master of the dark arts." The man dabbed the whiskey off his mustache with a white linen napkin. "Stick to your talents, son. Before somebody gets hurt. God forbid that person be an investor."

Erasmus is not sure if everyone in the room laughed at him, but it sure felt like it. He's certain he saw the bartender and waitresses laughing too.

A humbled and even more disgruntled Erasmus realized that,

as the city's most prominent booster, he should invest in local real estate so as to own more of what he'd been advancing. That's when he decided to revisit his other personal ambition: to turn all of Duwamps Hill into a grand Stalworth estate. If they were all going to laugh at him, at least he would create a physical tribute to himself that would ensure his name endured over the generations.

A knock on his office door snaps Erasmus out of his attempt at reverie. He uses a forearm to sweep his works back into the cubby below the golden telegraph and slam down the cover.

The hit of morphine was not sufficient. He had hedged so it wouldn't be debilitating for his meeting, but he only found it unfulfilling. It definitely wasn't enough to numb his lurking sense of being a two-bit fucking liar. Yes, his wife was right. He stands slowly, tests his balance, and unlocks his office door.

A besuited man enters the room and identifies himself as Sloot. His face reminds Erasmus of the interchangeable gluttony of Ms. Jilly's johns.

"Here you go, Stalworth." The man lays out a plat map of the area surrounding Erasmus's home and uses his stout, hairy finger to peg a contract down atop it.

Erasmus scans the document, trying to get his vision to focus. "This is for all of it?"

"Every square foot right up to the big boulder at the top of the hill."

"I thought Old Sam was still holding out."

"He was."

"Ah, progress. Excellent. So, what was his final price?"

The man sits down in the chair on the far side of the desk, intertwines his hands resting atop his gut, and cracks his knuckles. "We found legal cause to render his deed as invalid. No Indian can own land in the city limits. He was operating under a loophole that no longer exists. Frankly, I don't understand how he finagled the land in the first place. As the future owner of all the surrounding property, you will simply annex that land as eminent domain and expand your existing estate upon it. With my brother's construction company, to which you are contractually obliged."

"Wait, I pay Old Sam nothing?"

"You don't give hard-earned American dollars to good-for-nothing red Indians. They'll waste it on liquor, anyhow. But, yes, for navigating such an elegant solution for the property of..." He pauses to read the name from the legal papers. "Samuel Dugdale, also known as Indian Sam, and, not to mention, for the surrounding plats, you will owe our firm a few percentage points beyond what was outlined in our original contract. But I am sure you will still find these terms to be quite amenable."

Erasmus sits for a moment, not thinking about the specifics of the contract so much as what his wife said on her way out the door. Misfortune. To others. The rest of his days.

"Almost forgot." Sloot reaches into his briefcase to produce a small, winged golden statuette with winged boots and a caduceus. "Been holding on to this from the liquidation of the Denny estate. We managed the bankruptcy. What a disaster."

He slides it across the desk. Erasmus takes a closer look. It's painted with gold.

"Hermes," Erasmus comments, unimpressed.

"Mercury. Or that's what the auctioneer told me."

"Same shit."

"I thought of you. God of merchants, travelers, and—"

"Thieves?"

"I was going to say heralds, but..." Sloot smiles, a gold tooth glinting in the light. "You sure are a fountain of knowledge there, Ol' Stalworth."

The man says something else, but Erasmus doesn't listen. Another underhanded deal is not for him. He may have brought misfortune to others. But he doesn't have to do it for the rest of his days.

Erasmus needs to do something big. Something dramatic. Yes, damn what all of those Commerce bastards say. He will sink all of his talent, time, and money (and quite a bit more money that he plans to quietly borrow from the Bureau of Information, his Bureau of Information) into building the world's first flying air boat. He'll show them all. It will make this city into the true, unimpeachable "One and Only Gateway to Alaska and Beyond" and change the future of the world in the process.

If he puts his resources where his mouth is, he will no longer be an impostor or huckster. The two Erasmuses can become one. Duplicity to integrity. He still has time to change. To recover. To undo all of his deceit by personally proving that he meant everything he said to all of those poor, hopeful, lost prospectors—men not unlike his younger self. To prove that there is, in fact, no Stalworth curse. Even if he accidentally flattened that damned seagull.

He asks the lawyer to leave the papers in his office. Says that he needs to think it over. The lawyer looks deep into Erasmus's face, likely evaluating his sanity.

"Mr. Stalworth. As your legal counsel, I must insist that you do not squander this unique opportunity to own Duwamps Hill. The land seizure from the Indian will happen, sooner or later. Whether you comply or not. It is already in motion."

Erasmus doesn't answer and thinks on how he should also quit injecting morphine and will do so, but only after one more taste. Not even really one more. Just a roundup of the earlier one, if you will.

"It's best that you sign it," Sloot tells him, fingering the paper. "Now."

"It's best that you get the fuck out of here." Erasmus pulls the paper out from under the lawyer's finger and wads it up. "Now."

EIGHTEEN   2014

Sami stands in front of Stevenson Elementary in her blue rain jacket and white running shoes, watching the children stream out the front double doors. If only her grandmother could see the school now. Students of all national origins, colors, and creeds: playing, laughing, talking.

When Sami was in school it was mainly working-class whites, with a thin middle-class white crust and a sprinkling of Asian kids to cheat off of during tests and use as the punch lines for eye and accent jokes and other socially tolerated, if not treasured, racial humor. Now it's not quite so poor or quite so white, but it's still an area of the city that can accommodate immigrant and a few blue-collar families. Much of the rest of the town is working hard to price out everyone who doesn't work for Mothership. But never fear, Stevenson, it doesn't take an urban planner to see that the bourgeois armies are amassing to take this hill next.

She's also shocked by how few of the students she recognizes. None, really. Beyond a couple of kids she thinks she might know from her daughter's softball team. The faces are all starting to blur by child number four. Admittedly, she and Percy haven't made any significant investment in getting to know the parents of any of their children's friends since kid number two. And she's amazed by how the school, which occupies such a fixed place in her mind, is essentially a river. It flows by in a constant state of impermanence—never to be experienced the same way twice.

She spots her daughter Macy moving forward through the crush of children, weighed down under a heavy backpack to the point that she might be limping or walking with some sort of contrived preteen strut. But Sami's not here to meet her daughter today. She double-checks her digital watch.

She's the only one on time. No Doucette. The school's fearless leader has been expectedly noncommittal. No Bruce, who doesn't give off any sense of punctuality. And no Shawn, Monica's handyman father, who offered a no-charge assessment of their potential remodeling opportunities. At least Shawn had the decency to call and say that he'd be a few minutes late.

Principal Doucette comes out through the front door in a harried shuffle, his comb-over blowing sideways and bifocals swinging on a chain around his neck. Sami hopes, for the briefest of moments, that he's reprioritized and will be available for the walkthrough with Shawn, whom she'd asked to please refer to himself as a "building contractor." All she gets from the principal is a "Gotta run. Millie will lock up after you leave."

Sami asks where he's off to in such a hurry, but he has his phone to his ear before she can finish her question. He mouths "phone call" and heads toward his car in the lot next to the rock. From behind, she watches Doucette's soft wide ass with his belt not threaded through either of the back pants loops. Sami restrains an urge to run after him and give him a swift kick right in the middle of his ill-fitting Dockers. Not that she ever has or would ever do such a thing. But it can't hurt to imagine.

Sami is so in her own head that she only now realizes that her daughter has stopped to talk to her. She lowers herself down to Macy's height and explains that she left a snack of half a peanut butter and jelly sandwich and a glass of soy milk for her on the kitchen countertop at home. She tells Macy to walk home, wash her hands, eat the snack, do her homework as best as she can, and then get into her practice gear.

She warns her daughter that she won't be home until fifteen minutes to three. Ten minutes to three at the absolute latest, as they need a bare minimum of seven minutes to get to the playfields. She explains that she has her car keys with her, and they'll meet out at the car. At the car. Not in the backyard. Not in the TV room. Or Macy's bedroom. At the actual car. In front of the house. It's all on the handwritten note she taped to the back of the dining room table. Macy can't miss it.

The backpack with her bat, glove, and water bottle (with fresh water, of course) is already inside the trunk. It is essential that Macy is ready to go, or they will be late for softball.

And one last thing: Sami asks her to please not watch TV or anything else with a screen. That's a straight path to Sami coming home to find Macy still wearing her school clothes and in a state of hypnotized sedation—yet ready to spring back to life and massacre anyone who dares stand between her and the next minute of her show, game, video, or whatever other variation of boundless digital entertainment.

Sami squeezes Macy on the shoulder and sends her home. "Quarter to three. Remember." Then she checks her watch. "No. It's gonna have to be ten to three."

"Sami? That you?" An elderly Black man rolls down the window of his silver work van and parks it right in the spot of a departing school bus.

"Mr. Barrett? So nice to finally meet you. I've heard so much about you." She walks over to the van and shakes the man's hand through the window.

"Call me Shawn. Please." The man gets out of the van, straps on a leather tool belt, locks the door, and walks around the side.

The vehicle is immaculate. He strikes Sami as the kind of guy who could change your oil or rewire your electrical while telling you a story about his second tour in 'Nam.

"That's quite a rock," he says, pointing over to the lot.

"Been here as long as I've been here, which is a long time."

"Been here a lot longer than that. A glacial erratic like that's been here as long as this hill's been here. Actually, I was noticing on the drive up that it's more of a drumlin than a hill. It's got that inverted spoon shape, like half an egg. That's from the glacial ice pushing on the underlying, unconsolidated till. What do they call it? The ground moraine."

Sami nods like she is following along but is thinking that she needs to text Bruce again. As she starts to compose the message, Bruce rushes around from the other side of the school. He's moving about as fast as his body can handle, leading with his aluminum cane. In his other hand is a small stack of paperwork.

"What'd I miss?" Bruce says, sweat dripping from under his hat.

"Just talking with Shawn here about the rock." She motions toward the boulder with her head. "And this hill. The what's-it-called?"

"Drumlin." Shawn shakes Bruce's hand. "Why'd the school never pave the lot? Seems easy enough."

"Doesn't belong to the school. I think it belongs to the city or is part of that greenbelt with the creek behind it or something. For all I know, it's part of my property. God knows it was once upon a time." Sami opens the front door of the building and ushers the men inside. "Appreciate you all showing up today. Just need to make some assessments and calculations so we can figure out how to best accommodate the new lab space."

As they walk straight across the hall to the music room, Sami nods to the stack of papers in Bruce's free hand. "Got some notes for our walk-through?"

"Walk-through? No, uh, my wife . . ." He adjusts back his Sonics hat without removing it and wipes his brow with the back of his shirtsleeve. "When the time's right, she . . . no, we wanted to ask you about my daughter, you see, she . . ."

Sami glances at her watch.

"Everything OK?" he asks.

"No, it's not you. I'm just in a bit of a—what were you saying?" Sami opens the classroom door, with its small, wired-glass window, and ushers them all inside.

"I guess it can wait." Bruce shifts his weight foot to foot.

Shawn surveys the twenty-foot-high ceiling and large windows. "So, this is where my daughter works, huh?"

"Yeah, Monica was sorry to miss you," Sami says. "But had to get to her other gig."

"Never not working, my Moni." Shawn pulls out a tape measure from his belt and determines the width of the sills. "So, this is the prime real estate here, huh? Rest of the building looks pretty small."

"Yeah, this is what the investors want to turn into the lab. I'm pushing back on that. But we need measurements. Details. Potential costs. A workable alternative option to show them. Shawn, like I told you on the phone, we have some change coming. Whether we like it or not. You ever heard of a STEAM program, like Science, Technology, Engineering, Art, and Math?"

"Sure, if that's what they're calling it these days."

"Well, this school has always been more of a music and arts program."

Shawn looks at the electrical outlets and plays with the light switches. "My father was a musician. It's all he ever thought about. Wouldn't wish his life on anybody. I always wanted to be an engineer myself. Life got in the way. My father being a musician got in the way."

Shawn finds a water line that leads to a wall fixture for what could have been a drinking fountain or maybe a handwashing sink in decades past. He takes a small wrench out of his tool belt and uses the back of it to tap on the pipe.

"This pipe sounds good. No idea how much lead is in it." Shawn continues to move around the room measuring distances and picking at peeling floor tiles as he talks. "No gas line or suitable fire suppression in here for Bunsen burners, but you don't need any of that at the elementary level, anyway. This space seems good. Although I have to say, Sami, anything with the school district moves at a glacial pace. RFPs, authorizations, notarizations, legal, environmental reviews, asbestos, mold, community reviews, approvals. It's not anyone's idea of a good time. And it's expensive as hell."

"We're planning something different. Privately funded via the PTA. Just a gussy up, a facelift, so that we can make a good impression."

He shrugs. "Then this room could work. Where's the other space?"

Sami does an about-face on her white sneakers. "Follow me."

They go back into the hallway and down the stairs, Bruce walking sideways with his cane, to the series of rooms where the chocolate was stored.

Sami tours them around the basement. Opens a couple of the doors to the storage spaces. The one full of the rat shit has a ladder and tabletop blocking the door. She assumes nobody ever got to the hazmat cleanup. "I've been thinking, what if we knock down the walls between the closets? Bruce already determined that they aren't load bearing. Wouldn't we have comparable space to the upstairs music classroom? Maybe more? We could gut it, put in some decent lighting, a few countertops, some brightly colored decorations like big period table posters, and all of that. And presto, we have the lab."

Shawn leans into one of the rooms, takes out a flashlight, and cuts its beam across the dark inside. He examines a wall, takes some quick measurements, and works his way down the row to the next room. As he goes to clear the tabletop and ladder from the final doorway, Sami says, "Don't bother. It's identical to the others."

"OK. Well, I've got good news and bad news," Shawn says. "The good news: You could turn this into a large, usable space. It's a solid idea. Really is. Bad news: No matter what you spend, you'll never get it to code. Not for a school. Kids can't go to school underground with no windows and no proper fire exit. And, before you ask, I don't think there's any reasonable way to put in egress windows down here . . . even if you had the budget and all of the near-impossible district approvals."

"Only that little bit of bad news?" Sami's shoulders fall, followed by her head.

"That." He retracts his tape measure and hangs it back on his tool belt. "And the rats."

"Rats?" Sami asks, avoiding looking at Bruce.

"I can smell them," Shawn says. "I've been doing this a long time."

She fights back a heavy surge of tears, pretending to check her watch. But then she actually looks at the time. "Shit. I mean, shoot. I have to go. I'm gonna be late for softball practice. Dammit."

"Wait, how do we—?" Bruce starts to ask.

"Millie'll show you out." Sami sprints up the stairs.

Bruce pulls his list from his pocket and says, "I was still hoping to talk to you about my daughter's—"

Sami is about to run down the hallway crying but sees someone approaching. She whips back around and hides behind the door atop the basement stairs—just in time to burst into uncontrollable tears. She muffles her sobs with her jacket sleeve.

"Well, that didn't go so well," she hears Bruce say to Shawn.

"I'm just looking to retire. I want to help my daughter and all. The school. You know. But I've got plenty of stress already."

"I feel you. Any chance you'd like to share a nice special cigarette?" Bruce asks Shawn. "For your nerves."

"Thought you'd never ask. Not in here though," Shawn says as Sami peeks out from the darkness behind the door to see him adjusting his tool belt. "Your ponytail's a dead giveaway."

"Yeah, didn't mean in here. My Westy's out back."

Now that she's almost recomposed herself, Sami prepares for the next stage of her flight. She's going to be late getting Macy to practice. She holds her breath and slowly moves toward the door. But the other person is close to the doorway, only a few feet away from her.

Millie, the secretary, takes a couple of steps down the stairs and leans her hip into the banister, drinking a diet soda from a plastic bottle and twirling an unlit cigarette between her fingers. "You fellas got room for one more?"

NINETEEN *2014*

The old restaurant is a mess. Again. The front door was forced open and left ajar. There're a bunch of empty beer cans and spent nitrous cartridges thrown all over the floor like it's a dump or squatter space and not a place of business with profound potential. To add insult to injury, rainwater and leaves got in through the open door and soaked a stack of old drywall left over from some earlier, aborted remodel that Bruce had been planning to use to trim some materials costs.

He arrived today with ambitious plans to cut boards and nail together a second wall's worth of framing. Mel had a delivery guy who works with his family drop off some more two-by-fours. And Shawn, the old handyman who he got blazed with, left him an ancient radial saw and a couple of other tools on loan.

When high, Bruce also had a rather brilliant—if he says so himself—idea to solve Sami's problems. He intends to further figure that out today too. Ride to the rescue and have Sami owe him a big one. But he's going to have to start by cleaning the restaurant. Again.

He walks out into the parking lot and makes his way on his cane toward the spray-painted Previa up on blocks in the corner of the lot where the cracked pavement gives way to overgrown grass, blackberry thickets, and a marsh of green water and litter.

"Spazzy? What the fuck, dude?"

There is no answer. He gets closer to the minivan and sees

the portly blond man swaddled in numerous jackets and layers of sweatpants inside the hoarder's vehicle, with barely enough room for a prostrate adult among stacks of newspaper, plastic bags full of other plastic bags, cardboard boxes overflowing with cans and bottles, and a significant collection of rocks. There is bird shit all over the vehicle.

"Man. Come on." Bruce taps on the window with his cane, making sure to not get any avian flu on it. "I'm trying my best to be cool here, but you can't keep breaking into the restaurant."

"It's not breaking in if the door's unlocked." The man keeps his eyes closed and doesn't move.

"That's 'cause it's already broken. If Mel would've—"

"Where am I supposed to take a shit then, Bruce?" He pulls up onto one of his elbows and opens his eyes. He is heavyset with long blond hair, soft features, and whorls of wispy golden neck beard.

"I don't know. That's not my problem."

"I dunno either, so it kinda is your problem. That's been my private bathroom for the last two or so years. Squatter's rights. Get it?"

"Stop."

"Stop what? Eating? Stop defecating? I may be experiencing homelessness, but I'm a living, breathing human being with a fully functioning digestive tract. You prefer that I shit like any other mammal in the parking lot where you could step in it? Track it all over the place?"

"I prefer . . . I don't know what I prefer." Bruce can't be totally upset with his squatter. He wants a clear, professional-looking parking lot but would never call the cops on anyone. That's rule number one. Not that the cops would even show. But Bruce gets it. He has lived nose just above water before. He sees how it can all fall apart. How it is so hard to get back out of that hole, the sides crumbling and caving in as you try to scramble and climb your way out. "And anyway, what does that have to do with leaving the door open? Or throwing a bunch of beer and nitrous garbage all over the place?"

The man sits up fully and looks out of the Previa window between gaps in the spray-painted lettering. "Be honest with me, Bruce: Did you come out here and start all this drama just so you could smoke weed with me again?"

Bruce wants to be mad but is having trouble finding the specific emotions. "No. Totally no." He pulls a glass pipe, already packed, out of his pocket. "How'd you get the name Spazzy, anyhow? You seem pretty slow-moving."

"It's Spatzy, dude. Scotty Patzold." He opens the door, swings out his feet, and forces them into old rubber boots. "Spazzy is derogatory."

"Since when?"

"Do a better job keeping up with cultural progress and inclusion." Spatzy grabs the pipe and lighter, placing the glass against his chapped lips and the flame to the green bud. "What's your story, Captain Bruce? I sense tumult."

"Well, my wife and I—actually, hurry up and pass. I've gotta get back inside."

"To be fair, it was dark last night, and I was super faded, but . . . I've gotta admit . . . I don't see you making a lot of headway inside the warehouse there."

"Look, I'm, I don't need to explain myself to you too. But I'm trying. I'm . . ." He takes the pipe back from Spatzy, disinfects the tip of the glass with the flame, and savors a long, indulgent inhale to the point that he coughs. "I'm doing my best under the circumstances. I'm more of an ideas guy, anyway."

"What?"

"You heard me."

"Yeah, you have ideas."

"Yes, ideas."

"I have ideas too. But I can't tell you."

"OK, that's totally fine."

Spatzy motions for Bruce to pass back the pipe. Bruce shakes his head and takes another hit for himself.

Spatzy continues, "OK, actually: What do you know about quantum key distribution? Entanglement. Photon polarization. Shit like that."

"The fuck are you talking about?" Bruce coughs again as he finishes out the bowl and returns it and the lighter to his jeans pocket.

"How do you think I communicate with the seagulls in ways that are immune to eavesdropping?" Spatzy stares at Bruce, waiting for a response, but doesn't get anything from the glassy-eyed restaurant proprietor. "You also need to study up on Masonic ritual and symbolism. Look around. Open your mind. Masonic leaders built this whole city. There are signs everywhere if you only know what you're looking for, like that compass design on this building with the letter *G*. *G*: geometry, God, gimel, the third letter in the Hebrew alphabet. Three represents the Supreme Architect of the Universe—across languages."

"OK."

"SuperSonic. Like it also says right there on your hat. Listen: *S* is nineteen, *U* is what? Twenty-one. *P* is sixteen. *E* is five. *R* is eighteen. *S*, again, is nineteen. *O* is fifteen. *N* is one before that at fourteen. *I* is nine. And *C* is good old number three. You know what that means?"

"That you're way higher than I am?"

Spatzy shakes his head. "One hundred thirty-nine. You know that number? It adds up to one hundred thirty-nine." He waits for Bruce's reaction again, which never comes. "It evokes happiness for some and sadness for others. It is also synonymous with Judas, who was what? The thirteenth apostle. Get it now? In the Hebrew alphabet, the thirteenth letter symbolizes death. In tarot, it's the reaper.

On Friday the 13th, the most honorable leader of the Knights Templars was arrested by the Inquisition and the order was destroyed. But one hundred thirty-nine is not a number of death so much as the end of a cycle. And what is the end of a cycle but the beginning of another? Perpetual transformation and successive renewals. Change. Or, as I like to call it, life. That is all fairly obvious—if you only stopped sleepwalking through your own goddamn life, Bruce."

"I'll wake up tomorrow and start counting letters if you stop breaking into the fucking restaurant, Spatzy." Bruce backs away from the car and tunes out whatever Spatzy replies, but it sounds a lot like "I'll be here when you're ready to smoke more weed."

Bruce goes inside and sweeps the floor in a grid pattern, using the half-busted push broom to plow the sawdust, garbage, and dropped nails into piles and then into the warped, dented dustpan covered with old, dried gum. Or, hopefully, that's what it was.

He looks at the size of the space and the single semi-constructed wall frame. This shit is never going to happen. Bruce decides he should bluff the completion of the whole second floor. He'll nail a few planks across the staircase and make it look like it's under construction. Rather ingenious actually. He reduced the workload by 50 percent. Just like that, he essentially completed half the work. A good day overall. Ideas guy, see? Maybe he should go home and enjoy a well-deserved nap?

He takes out his flip phone and dials the city historic preservation society again. He asks for Charlie, the lady he spoke to on all of his previous calls, and gets put on hold. He hopes he has enough cellular minutes left on his phone card. He paces and drags the broom with him to pretend he is accomplishing something.

Bruce has already spent a bunch of time on the phone with these people. Based on some stuff he'd read about and seen during the hunt for a viable location for his cannabis master plan, he had the idea that he could get the school building officially deemed a part of the city's untouchable patrimony. Then Sami's issues would all go away. Poof.

In his initial calls, he was warned that the building itself was too much of a postwar box and didn't meet the architectural requirements for preservation. But eventually, he found his way to this Charlie lady, and she assured him that it isn't only about "preserving high-quality structures," but that it is also about places and things that "we feel deeply about" and "the retention of our cultural community."

Now, after some fifteen minutes on hold listening to canned Muzak and Bruce almost giving up, Charlie finally joins the call. "Thanks for your patience, Mr. Jorgensen."

"Bruce. Please."

"OK, Bruce."

"So, are we going to be able to do this?" he asks. "Save the school."

"I think it's a strong possibility." She clears her throat. "You know, what is personal for you can be just as important for the whole community."

Bruce's heart rate increases. He forgets about his trouble with Spatzy and the mess in the restaurant. For a moment, he forgets how far behind he is with construction. And the minimal amount of day-to-day help he's getting from Mel. He is going to be a hero. Or a hero for Sami, at least. And that's going to open many doors for him that are then going to prove his worth and successes to Wren. He is what he would almost call: excited. "This is great news," he says. "I can't wait to tell Sami."

"Who's Sami?"

"Head of the PTA." He's hoping to wrap this up and tell Sami the good news later today. "She's gonna be so happy. Really."

"Well, maybe she can help you with the initial forms."

"Which initial forms?"

"Go to the website and download the long-form application packet."

"OK?" He feels a small part of himself die at the word *long-form*.

"Once the application is submitted along with all supporting documents, we can start the process. I guess you could submit the initial application without the supporting documents, but—insider advice—they wait until all of the materials are in before moving forward, so you may as well pull it all together and do it at once."

"Start the process? I thought you said you thought this was going to work."

"Yes, I think it could. I'm always an optimist. To my detriment, my partner likes to say. But I have a good feeling about this. Anyway, then you have to get all of the essays, video attestations, and any other supporting materials in place. The application is a multi-step process. Again, it's a lot of work, but I'll be here to answer any questions if you need. I'm pulling for you, Bruce."

Maybe he can convince Sami to take the lead on those next steps. She seems to be on top of those kinds of things. And she'd still be happy that he had the idea. He asks, "So you approve the application, and then it's sorted?"

"Well, you have the school district's support, right?"

"Well . . ."

"We're going to need them on board with the application. If not, it becomes a whole different can of worms. Doesn't mean that it's not still theoretically possible but, regardless, the complete application has to then make its way to staff review. When and if it clears that, it will go to the Commission review. That will be the biggest hurdle, but I don't think it's impossible either. The Commission takes its time and gives everything a fair shake and deep consideration. They only meet a few times per year, so you should also really take your time and make the application as strong as possible. Collect proof of community support. All of that. And if they green-light it, you will then move toward a certificate of approval. If things go smoothly, you could have that in hand sometime in the next sixteen or maybe, more realistically, eighteen months. Two years. Tops. Although, I have seen it take three to four years or more when there's a legal fight."

"I don't think you understand," Bruce chokes his way through the dry words.

"Understand what?"

"Our what-do-you-call-it? How long we have to do this thing."

"Your timeline?"

"Yes, that. I hate to rush you, but we need this soon. It's like kind of an urgent situation. Couldn't we talk this through now on the phone, and you take it from there?"

"There are some expedited processes. For emergencies. But like how soon?"

"Well, not today or anything," Bruce says and holds his breath.

She gives him a soft laugh in response. He has the dreaded realization from her tenor that she thinks he is joking.

"We could maybe wait a few weeks. If not a month," he continues. "That's still possible, right? Under special conditions?"

"And, sorry if I'm confused, you don't know if you have official school board support or not? For one of their buildings?"

"Not yet, but . . ."

"I think, for the sake of transparency, I should let you know that if you want to preserve the building without their support, it will be a longer, more drawn-out process. Likely with a legal component. And, even if you get the necessary legal resources, rally the community, and succeed, you are saving the building in its current state, or at least certain visual and structural components of its current state, but not necessarily for its current usage. Let's say they want to turn it into a community center or bowling alley or a movie theater—it could become any of those things but just with the shell or spirit of the original building. You can't compel them to keep students at—"

"Hey, sorry," Bruce cuts in. "This is—something's come up. I've gotta go."

"OK?"

"I'll call you back though." He thanks Charlie and, much to his own surprise, kicks a hole in the sheet of waterlogged gypsum board leaned up against the wall. Then he laughs to himself. This is not him. Loose Bruce is not angry or violent. He's overcome by an urge to smoke more weed.

He'd been hoping, planning to show up to his next PTA meeting and be the savior. He was so close. But now it is gone. Just like that. Story of his goddamn life.

Bruce walks outside and spits into the wet, gray parking lot. His spine is screaming at him. He watches Spatzy come out of the bushes and walk toward his van.

"Whatcha doing?" Bruce asks.

"Enjoying my new alfresco lavatory. What do you care?"

For the first time he notices an extension cord coming out of the restaurant on the far side and running into Spatzy's van.

"What's that?"

"How do you think I charge my smartphone?"

"You have a smartphone? I don't have a smartphone."

"You should. It's basic modern literacy. Don't know how you keep up with the world without one."

Bruce breaks out his glass bowl with a new, fresh green nug in it. "Let's do this."

"You mind if I hit it first?" Spatzy holds out a hand covered in, at least, two pairs of knit gloves. "I'm a bit of a germophobe."

"Maybe you want to come inside and give me a hand with cleanup?" Bruce passes the pipe to Spatzy.

"Nah." He takes a big toke. Coughs. Exhales. "Honestly, you just got here, man. I've been here for a while. And I really prefer the vibe the way that it was." He takes two more quick hits before Bruce can wrest the pipe away from him.

"We're trying to do something special here. Something big." Bruce repacks the bowl, disinfects the mouthpiece with the lighter. "Nothing personal, huh?" He thinks about how he could kick Spatzy out of the lot and immediately realizes how unrighteous that is. He can share a little space. "Maybe I can give you a key or something if you promise to close the door, stop littering inside, and not bust up the door. And flush, of course."

"I'll think about it."

Bruce looks at the electrical again, winding its way out from the building. "I'll let you keep the electrical, but maybe we could move the van around the side? Curb appeal, right? And you can also do me a favor and keep an eye on things at night? You know, give me a call from that fancy phone if you see anyone snooping around?"

Spatzy shrugs, indifferent, as he watches a couple of gulls land atop the van and promptly squirt liquid white bird crap into the existing dried collection on its roof. "I guess. But I'm not trying to get a job or nothing, dude. You got so many rules and regulations. I thought you were Loose Bruce."

"I am. I was. I mean, I am. Again." Bruce looks back at the van and the now-squawking birds. "What are those external buildings at schools? What are they called? Where they put the extra kids?"

"Juvie?"

"No, there at the school." He and Sami had briefly discussed a variation of this idea before, but there was no place to put an out-side building. Sure as hell not on the rooftop playground. But an idea just came to him. "The small classrooms?"

"Shh. You have to learn both the art and science of how to listen to them," Spatzy quiets Bruce. He's deep into a staring contest with one of the gulls. "This one is trying to tell me something. Uh-huh. Yes. He says it's called a portable."

TWENTY   *1958*

Archie pushes his swing machine, Metro Public Schools' latest standard-issue 175 RPM electric floor buffer, down the hall at Stevenson. Now that he is a floater, he cleans and shines a different school almost every day of the week. Regardless of the location, he can taste the buttery scent of the buffer wax. He can feel its light stickiness on his skin and hair.

He slows down as he passes Mrs. Hasegawa's room. She is still here at the school, working late and stacking chairs. Again, he notices that she is not wearing a wedding ring. Same as last time.

Archie doesn't mind working as a janitor. He knows he might have achieved more in his life. Grown into something better paying. Or, in an ideal world, he might have become a professional musician—but considering where he came from and what he witnessed as a child in Mississippi, he is at peace with the mind-numbing, rhythmic tranquility of his work. He is left alone to do a job. He does it well and when it is over, he is done. Until the next day, when he starts all over again.

Being a floater is not his first choice, but it too is OK. He used to work at a single school in his neighborhood and have a schedule by which he could set his watch. When Archie's hours were reduced there due to some convoluted explanation about low tax revenue, he was pleased to round out his contract by finding additional gigs and getting shuffled around from school to school.

He knows he can work harder and more consistently than just about anyone else. He has never called in sick for a single day in his life. He'd put his floor buffing up against anyone. In the mirrored reflection of his work, he bets he could shave his face, spot something stuck in his teeth, or, dammit, a woman could even apply her makeup.

And he is fairly certain that whoever is actually paying his time cards is getting a better deal on him that the other janitors for hire. While the white guys were unionized and were guaranteed a certain number of hours, Black janitors had no such infrastructure and support. Until recently, they weren't even really welcome to work outside of the main Black neighborhood. Now they can, but there are zero guarantees. He is working as much as he can to pay rent and offer a decent future for his son, Shawn.

The work might be repetitive, but Archie's mind experiences anything but monotony during these hours. He riffs off the whir of the swing machine, the echoes in the hallway, the buzzing of the lights and composes musical bars in his head. While the job will eventually break down his hands, back, and feet, it allows him to avoid small talk, gossip, and work politics. He's pretty sure that his schedule was created to minimize the Black janitor's interaction with the student body or the rest of the regular staff in white neighborhoods. But he sees a silver lining to that.

He thinks in music all day long. Always has. Perhaps most importantly, he is not mentally exhausted when he returns home and can practice piano for another hour or two on end, unless he's working these off-hours and comes home when his son is sleeping or studying.

Shawn can get rattled by music at night. When the kid finishes his homework, he's always taking apart a radio or learning how to re-wire a lamp. He wants to be an architect or an engineer. No passion for music or the arts. But that's OK. The kid will have a completely different future than his father, and Archie is more than open to that.

Not that this town isn't racist or segregated. If it weren't for the fact that there are so few Black people here overall, it might be as segregated as the South. And he figures that it also helps that this place has no sense of its own history. There's no real fixed sense of the way things are supposed to be. A lot is being made up as they go along. Sure, there are rules and laws and the status quo, white neighborhoods, Black neighborhoods, Asian neighborhoods... but it's all up for reinvention... if not now, in a generation. Or three. And Archie's pretty sure that if he can hang on and get his son through school, he will walk in a very different world.

That's also not to say that Archie is particularly optimistic about the future state of race relations in this town, let alone in the country. But change of some sort is bound to happen, and anything is possible.

A few steps past the music classroom's door, he cuts the power on the swing machine. Not just because he wants to see her, no. He tells himself that he'd have to relocate the plug here in bit, anyhow.

Archie knocks lightly on the open door. "Hello again, Mrs. Hasegawa. Can I help you stack those chairs?"

"I've got it. Thank you," she says with her back to him.

If he didn't know better, he'd think that her voice betrayed a hint of eagerness.

She rotates toward him but seemingly only as a chair-moving necessity. "It's Mr. Barrett, right?"

Archie nods from the doorway. He's pleased that she remembers him, considering that Stevenson isn't his most frequented job site.

A few weeks back, when buffing the hallways in the late afternoon, he took a short break, very unlike him really, to play the school's piano. Just to feel it out, as nobody was around. He was playing an old Pioneer Square swing number when Mrs. Hasegawa returned to her classroom. He was concerned that he could get in serious trouble, if not lose his job, for helping himself to the instruments. But she encouraged him to continue and stood there, intently watching his hands as he played.

"It's slightly out of tune," he told her, realizing too late that it could be taken as too forward, if not an insult to her competence as a teacher.

"It's most definitely not," she said with enough of a smile to show her lack of offense.

"With all due respect, it most definitely is." He met her gaze and returned her smile until they both remembered where they were and who they were and both looked away.

They recalibrated, and he was about to stand up and excuse himself to get back to work. But she surprised him by coming closer to the piano.

"I'm a strings musician," she said. "I must admit my ongoing shortcomings as a pianist."

They spoke for some fifteen minutes, long enough for him to show her how to properly tune a piano although he didn't have time to do all of it, especially considering that she didn't have a decent tuning hammer and had only three mutes rather than a collection of six or seven different sizes.

He gave the piano a thorough dusting, started with middle C, and then set and loosened the pins to get the correct pitch. He worked by ear. It was something he was always able to hear. Ever since he was a little kid. His son wouldn't recognize pitch if it nipped him on the balls. But then again, little Shawn could already do math that makes Archie's skull hurt.

Archie went back and checked his tuning progress with major third intervals.

"I still don't see how you do that," she said.

"Practice, Mrs. Hasegawa. Lots of it." He returned to the first pin he set. "By the time you get to the end of it, you'll see that the first note is now sharp."

She nodded along in agreement until he thanked her, excused himself, and returned to his floor buffing.

And as is now apparent to Archie as he stands in the doorway of her classroom, they had spent enough time together with the piano to remember each other's names. Long enough for him to second-guess if they were standing too close to each other. Long enough to smell her shampoo and allow himself to imagine touching her hand. Long enough for him to think about her on numerous occasions, including too many times over the last couple of days when he knew he'd be coming back here, hoping to catch her working late.

With little effort or awkwardness, they launch right into a conversation about repertoire. She asks about his favorite pieces and mentions that she is particular to the romantics.

"Is that a band?" he asks to his immediate embarrassment.

"It's a musical period from the end of the eighteenth and into the nineteenth century. Dvorak, Wagner, Mahler, Ravel. That's the music that really moves me. The earlier stuff is simply too dry to have the same effect."

He tells her about how he came up playing swing, jazz, and Baptist gospel, sometimes combining all of them more than his pastor might like. He had played with a blind guy named Ray Robinson at the Rocking Chair before he changed his last name to Charles. He takes some comfort in the fact that Mrs. Hasegawa is as clueless about that bit of information as he was about the romantics.

He knows they are running out of time in their inevitably short visit. He insists again on helping her organize and close down the music room. He grabs a chair, stacks another two on top, and assures Mrs. Hasegawa that it is no bother. He explains to her that he'd had to take a short break to relocate the swing machine's extension cord anyhow. He dares, "And an artist like yourself should be making music, not moving chairs."

She tries to avert her face and hide a deepening blush. "And a musical artist like yourself should be performing rather than cleaning schools." She blushes more. "I'm sorry, I didn't mean to insult your livelihood. I have picked strawberries and milked cows. I only meant that—"

"I understand, Mrs. Hasegawa." He nods and starts stacking chairs.

"It's just that I was impressed by your piano playing. Even the little bit that I heard."

They work side by side. Stacking chairs. He moves quickly. Stacking three and four chairs at a time to her one. He has plenty of experience striking stages after shows.

He is tempted to invite her to one of his performances. Archie, in fact, plays live music with some frequency. He plays every Sunday at church. And, when he has childcare for Shawn, the neighbor lady or an auntie from church, he plays in any number of bars and underground clubs in the Black neighborhoods, sometimes even downtown. But an invite, even to some of the more mixed-race clubs, would only clarify the layers of impossibility between their two worlds.

"Are you married, Mr. Barrett?" Mrs. Hasegawa asks.

"I was. I'm, I guess you'd call me a widower."

"I'm sorry to hear that. Was your wife, was she a musician too?"

"No, ma'am. She worked for the schools. On the buses. Was a natural mathematician more than a musician. Not that she got to use much of her math stuff at work."

"I too am a widow. For some time now, actually."

"Then I too am sorry, Mrs. Hasegawa. I'm sure he was a great man to have married a woman like you."

She seems to work hard to stifle a laugh. "Your wife, was she the one?"

"I'm not sure what you mean by that."

"I mean, was she who you truly wanted to be with? Was she the love of your life?"

"Yes, ma'am. I was lucky. Or, at least for once, I followed my better judgment and made a good decision."

"Hmm, yes," she says. "I have only ever followed my better judgment. Except once. I followed my passion."

"Ah, you fell for a musician, did you?"

"Not at all. He was this and that. Do you know what a bootlegger is?"

Archie laughs. "I wasn't always just a janitor, as you can imagine."

In a lower voice, she proceeds to tell Archie that her husband, the son of an established farming family, had taken to associating with smugglers and moonshiners during Prohibition. Yet he later told her that money was less a motivation for him than what he tried to justify as something akin to excitement. He wanted to explore life beyond the normal expectations of his oppressively conservative family. Only well after his death, she found out that he was known for his talents at racing cars and driving speedboats full of Canadian whiskey to outrun the Coast Guard.

Archie tells her that he had known many a man to participate in the black market but few who had also grown up with successful parents and more conventional options.

That was a question that Masako could never fully answer, but she knew that he had been sick as a child and suspected that it gave him a different view of life. A sort of unruly, defiant desperation.

As they stack chairs, she explains that soon after they married, he would stay out all night gambling and, likely, drinking. Smuggling stolen radios and the occasional car across the border with old friends. He didn't share any of this information with Masako, hiding much of his day-to-day life from her and forcing her to learn bits of his goings-on through church gossip.

She sat in the window at night waiting for him to get home, always worried that he would get shot, get in a crash, or get sent to jail. He listened to her pleading, told her he loved her and understood her concerns. But he still never changed his ways, even when she threatened to leave him.

The only thing that pulled him out of that life was getting sent to Camp Harmony and then on to Minidoka in Idaho where, in the midst of that utter degradation, Masako got pregnant, and they vowed to rebuild their relationship. Only for Sammy Hasegawa to suffer a tragic accident and pass away shortly before their daughter was born.

They finish stacking all of the chairs in the room. "And now it is just Ruth and me," Masako concludes.

"I'm sorry you've been through all that."

"I'm sure not any more than you have experienced, Mr. Barrett."

He studies her lips, cheekbones, eyelashes. Before he can think better of it, he leans forward, wraps his arms around her shoulders, and gives her a hug.

Archie pulls back even faster. "I am sorry to have been so forward, Mrs. Hasegawa." He wishes he could explain that he simply recognized a kindred spirit and has felt so alone in these past years. He also worries that he smells of floor wax.

Without a word, she leans back into him and returns the embrace. She presses her chest deeper into his, not in what he would consider a sexual manner but trying to feel the warmth and presence of another human being.

He takes a deep inhale into the top of her dense, straight hair. The hug lasts only a matter of seconds, but it is all so far beyond what he imagined possible prior to working at Stevenson today.

They hear an abrupt throat clearing from the hallway.

"I was wondering what this buffer was doing out here all by its lonesome." The red-faced math teacher, Al Schneider, swigs from a coffee mug. "Very strange, indeed."

TWENTY-ONE   *1971*

Ruth sits in a hard, blue plastic chair in the waiting room of her doctor's office. She is half falling asleep behind an issue of *Life* with some blond actress on the cover who has an amazing, intriguing life full of excitement but still managed to get some new thing called major depressive disorder. She skims an article about heroin use among American soldiers in Vietnam.

Dr. Yamamoto isn't just her doctor. He's her mom's doctor, along with most of their church. Yamamoto probably belongs to the church just to meet new patients. Ruth would like to go to a different doctor through the university or something, but her mom keeps a tight rein on the medical insurance, and seeing a different doctor would be a red flag. After days and weeks of fretting, she decided that seeing Dr. Yamamoto is her only option. She assumes he's sworn to patient confidentiality. Or he is supposed to be.

She stares at the fish tank that divides the room. There is a generous stratum of pale dust on the top. The blue and red fish swim back and forth above a small porcelain castle and seemingly drowned diver in semi-repose wearing an old-time bronze diving helmet. A bug-eyed fish nibbles at the green tank scum flowering atop his head.

Ruth feels like shit. More specifically, her stomach is churning. Her head aches with a dull but steady pressure behind her forehead. Her skin is hot and prickly with a relentless sweat.

Ruth may have led a sheltered and tightly controlled life. But she is not dumb. Pregnancy is not impossible. It's unlikely that Larry hit a hole in one in those brief moments. She keeps reminding herself that she's had a few of these issues in months prior. There is something off. The fatigue. The hot flashes. What about when her gums started bleeding? Pregnancy doesn't make your gums bleed. To the best of her admittedly meager knowledge.

She watches the fish in the tank. Swimming in tight circles. Not knowing of the ponds, rivers, lakes, and oceans in which they could have lived. They swim past a piece of fake coral and through a window of the castle. Bubbles ascend from the diver. Ruth realizes that, at this point, none of these fish would survive a day in a larger body of water.

Glamorous actresses, who look and talk perfect, are sad about their lives. Soldiers in Vietnam, American heroes who are risking their lives for democracy and freedom, are numbing themselves to death. Injecting poison into their veins. She'd long suspected that the world she knows and the world as it exists are not the same thing.

Even this doctor's office, with its fish tank, white coats, and hair-sprayed ladies working the phones and filing the files, is nothing but a few windowless rooms with an old man walking around and guessing at what ails people.

There are so many realities and realities behind those realities, she thinks. Is it possible that there is no single one truth? She looks back at the fish tank and sees her one known reality. Through the other side, just past the blue fish, Ruth sees a warped, monstrous figure through the glass. It looks a hell of a lot like Beckham's aunt, stretched in a fun-house mirror, the grotesque lips panting and drooling. Ruth laughs to herself at her paranoia. Her imagination is so vivid that she actually startled herself. But the receptionist calls, "Mrs. Noguchi?" and the crusty old beast lurches out from behind the tank and staggers up to the front desk. Her thick ankles, full of fluid, strain against the physical limits of her hosiery.

Shit. Ruth slides down behind her magazine and holds her breath. This can't be happening. Why, of all the . . . ? She tries to get her breathing back under control. To soothe her racing mind and galloping heartbeat. She slides even lower in the chair, while listening to the old lady check in.

Ruth can't relax until the aunt exits the lobby through the door into the back bowels of the doctor's office. She keeps the magazine unreadably high, covering her face until her own name is called.

Nadine, the nurse who reeks of cigarettes, walks her back through the same door and through the rabbit warren of exam rooms. She wants to ask Nadine if it is true that the doctor is required by law to keep secret all that she tells him. But Ruth stays quiet and keeps her head down. At any moment, she could pass by an open door with the ghastly aunt sitting there and overhearing everything and anything she says.

As Ruth waits in the room for the doctor to arrive, she busies herself by ripping a small tear in the paper sheet covering the examination table. She walks her fingers a half inch to the side and tears another bit of the paper and continues on down the line, creating a tasseled fringe.

Dr. Bill Yamamoto enters the room in the expected white coat and wire-rimmed glasses and with his gray hair Brylcreemed back. He's been her doctor for years now, since Ruth's mom made her move on from her childhood pediatrician.

Ruth pulls at the paper on the tabletop, and a long triangle peels back off the surface.

"Sorry, I didn't mean—"

"Not a problem, young lady." He adjusts the stethoscope around his neck and over his shoulder. "How's your mom?"

"Fine. I guess." Her finger pulls more at the paper.

"My daughter is at Boston Conservatory at Berklee now. Credits your mom with getting her into the violin, you know? Showed her so much support. Really an inspiration, your mother."

"Yeah. For sure." Ruth eyes the wooden crucifix on the desk in the office. She gets these kinds of stories with some regularity. That's what happens when your mother is a neighborhood icon. "She changed my life like this." "She supported my kid like that." At least he didn't make the comment about how Ruth must be quite a musical talent too.

"What brings you in today?" He pushes up a sleeve to show a hairless arm leading down to a simple, conservative gold watch and tidy nails.

She remembers Larry trembling and making excuses for why it was "really OK" if she wasn't ready to lose her virginity. She told him that she was. For sure. And not just because she was mad at her mom. She grabbed him by the hips, his jeans around his knees, and guided him forward. At first, his penis missed. She didn't know what to do, if she should grab it or what the standard protocol was. She hadn't even touched it or seen an erect penis, period. She had seen a flaccid one through that one lifeguard's shorts at the beach. It was the lifeguard who'd been all in the news about saving some rich kid from drowning or something. He was up in the chair with no underwear on. She didn't mean to see it, but once she did it was too difficult to look away. She still feels guilty about the self-satisfied look on the lifeguard's face.

Fortunately, Larry somehow got the wherewithal to step in, fumble for his penis with a shaky hand, and then haltingly guide it into her. His breathing changed. In fact, she was pretty sure he wasn't breathing at all. Sex didn't hurt as much as she had been told it would. Then again, she was losing her virginity at an age by which her grandmother had already had all six of her children. And, as soon as it started, it was over. Larry shuddered, a convulsion ripping through his body, and stifled a moan or a groan or some sort of deep guttural noise.

She felt a heat discharge inside her and his penis shrink and begin to retract as he collapsed atop her. But he sprung right back up, apparently reanimated by a bolt of insecurity, if not shame. He apologized to her. That wasn't how he wanted it to be. It's that he was surprised. And wanted her to like it. He thought about it too much. His expectations were too high. His excitement was too high. He couldn't help it. He would do better next time. If there were a next time.

Maybe she shouldn't have grabbed him by the hips. She'd put him under too much pressure. Ruth was sure of it. Regardless, she wished he pulled out at the end. That was what they had discussed. What they had agreed upon. But there wasn't enough of a beginning or a middle for there to be any planned end. That one kind of snuck up on them. She didn't want him to apologize or further sully the experience. It was what it was. And she was no longer a virgin. No longer fully under her mother's control.

She encouraged him to relax and put his head down on her chest. They lay in the sticky seat of his mom's Datsun and made plans to spend time together the next day while her mom was at church.

"Ruth?" asks Dr. Yamamoto.

"Yes?"

"I asked what brings you in today."

She searches for the words but can't find the right starting point.

"Nadine tells me that you haven't been feeling well. Dizziness? Nausea? Anything that you know of that could be causing that?"

"Nope. Not really."

"Family history? Anemia? Diabetes?"

"I was sickly a bit when I was a kid."

"With what?"

"My mom says it wasn't a big deal. Fevers? I'm not really sure. She told me that I got cold easily."

"OK. Well, probably nothing to worry about but just want to be sure to cover all of our bases. We should probably start with a bit of blood work."

"What do you think it could be?"

"Hard to say. Could you be pregnant?"

"Me? No. No way. God, no."

"Well, are you sexually active?"

"What?"

"Are you sexually active?"

She doesn't answer and looks away. "Are you going to talk to my mom about this?"

"Only if I have reason to." He removes his stethoscope, winds it around the back of his hand, and then unwinds it again. "So, is that a 'yes' then, Ruth?"

She continues to look away.

"OK, well, we're going to need to take some blood." He looks like he is about to smile but doesn't and shouts through the door, "Nadine. Can you come in here and walk Ruth to the lab?"

Nadine pokes her head into the room. "Follow me, Ruth."

Ruth starts to gather her stuff.

"Before you go," Dr. Yamamoto says, "I saw Mrs. Noguchi right before you. She told me a bit about you and Beckham and your budding romance. He's quite a guy. Such a smart and dependable young man." He gives her an avuncular wink. "I told her that I'd be seeing you next."

Ruth knows that she should try to fake being pleased at the connection, but she can't find it anywhere within her. She's no actress.

The doctor says, "She's waiting for you in the lobby."

TWENTY-TWO   *1971*

Upon entering the workshop adjacent to the factory floor, Larry is struck by the fact that there are so few people here today. Only a couple of the guys from the normal crew are busy machining parts for actuators.

Maybe the others are over on the factory floor for a training? Larry remembers that it must be the monthly union meeting, which is normally outside of work hours. Schedules have been shifting a bit.

He's a little late today, but this works to his favor as his absence won't be noticed, and he prefers to skip those meetings anyway. It's not that he has anything against the union, so much as he likes the relative quiet so he can think and get things done. Larry needs to catch up with his ever-expanding list of actuator pieces. Always more to fulfill. If only he could concentrate. All he can really think about is Ruth.

He enters the wood-paneled break room near the front door, counts out some change, and drops the coins into the Coke machine. He hears a click and opens the door that releases the can. He grips it in his hand, hooks his index finger into the ring, and pulls back the tab. After a long drink of the lukewarm cola, Larry returns to the workshop floor and follows his way along the safety line to his workspace.

As he walks, he replays Ruth's story about sitting through tea with that woman, who turned out to be not his archrival's mom but his aunt. Ruth repeated every detail to him. How the woman told Ruth that she was lucky to have the opportunity to be with her nephew. How she'd won some sort of mating lottery. And that Ruth wasn't the aunt's first (or third) choice.

The aunt did afford Ruth the compliment that "at least you aren't Chinese or Korean." Ruth claimed that she then point-blank asked the aunt, "Is Beckham actually interested in me?" Without hesitation, the aunt responded that the answer was beside the point. Her nephew remains focused on work and doesn't know what he wants or needs beyond that. Regardless, it was time for him to find a wife. To start his career and become an upstanding member of the wider community. For God's sake, he is in his midtwenties. He can't stay single forever. Nobody wants to lie there sedated with their mouth open for an unmarried dentist.

The aunt added that she also appreciated that Masako is known for her dedication and hard work. That she hoped Ruth had the same sense of loyalty, diligence, and prudence. Not one of those Americanized girls who expected Hollywood romance and public kissing and holding hands, flowers, Valentine's candies, and such. But someone who would support a man with purpose and discretion and spare him and his family all of the self-indulgent complaints.

Ruth told Larry that she didn't finish her tea. Never even started it. She thanked the aunt for the honor of sharing her time. The aunt said that she expected to see Ruth at church that Sunday. And to please make a little more effort with her appearance this week. Good posture doesn't cost anything. And a little powder to lighten up your face so you don't look like an Okinawan wouldn't kill you, would it?

Ruth told Larry she kept her fingers crossed behind her back for much of the conversation with Beckham's aunt. Larry listened to her every word as they walked around the perimeter of Stevenson Elementary, shuffling along in the light rain and soft dirt. She said she knew, in her heart, she didn't want to marry Beckham. She could feel it. Beyond his aunt. And Beckham himself. And his politics.

Larry told Ruth that he has no doubt in her. In them. But he didn't mention his misgivings in himself. Many of them. Will he be a good father? A good husband? A successful provider? He never had any role model on any of those fronts. His family only knew generations of displacement, poverty, and dejection.

Over the past few days, he's been hit with a 747 of deep insecurity. Of the offense of wanting or even actually starting to believe in himself when all worldly evidence points to the fact that he is not worthy of anyone's confidence, love, or investment. Why is he the one, out of all of these generations of Dugdales, who could turn it all around? But maybe he could? And maybe he is? Or maybe he's fooling himself, like so many times in the past. Fuck.

He looks around the workshop. The tables. Machines. Shearing devices for the actuators. Test flaps. Come what may, he will give it all he has. He will make it work. Grow in the company. Push through any barriers and provide for his family. Yes, if he believes it, it will become true. Much of it is state of mind. Trusting that you might actually deserve this. That's what a successful person would say. That's what his manager, Gerry, would say. Larry is not only composed from the stories of the past; he will launch forward into his own future. On his terms. He will become supersonic.

At the end of their walk around the school, Ruth told Larry that knowing in her heart that she doesn't want to be with Beckham is one page in a bigger book. Other things would still have to change. And she had no realistic idea as to how to proceed.

"Simple," Larry said. He told her she just has to get up her nerve to lay it all out for her mom. Tell her how it is.

When she demurred, he said, "I'll help you. We can talk to your mom together. Tomorrow. At the Broiler? We'll invite her out to try the Captain's Platter. My treat."

Ruth seemed a bit unsure. OK, maybe a lot unsure. Larry could see that she was scared. But it could work. Ruth is an adult. An educated adult. And now she has him. He could give her cover to take those next few essential steps to liberate her future. Their future together. See? Here he was, daring to be optimistic and even have some self-confidence again. He savored this foreign, yet seductive, feeling.

Ruth said that she would think about it. That didn't stop him from proceeding with the plans, setting a time, and even calling to make a reservation at the Broiler, although the waitress said flatly, "We don't make reservations."

"Really?" he pushed. "Not even for special occasions?"

"Um, have you ever been here before?" she snapped back before excusing herself and hanging up the call.

As Larry sits at his cluttered workbench teeming with metal shavings, grease pencils, and old newspaper, a colleague, another one whose name Larry never remembers, passes him, jogging down the aisle beyond the walk path. "Union meeting. Cafeteria. Right now," the man nearly shouts as he continues on his way.

Larry pretends to be confused by the man's words. Truth be told, he hates meetings. Meetings of any sort. He'd rather work on actuators. Make sure that wing flaps go up and down. That doors open. That nose cones drop. Supersonic transportation ain't gonna build itself. Union meeting and dues and resolutions aren't going to build it either. Only focus and hard work will fulfill this technological destiny.

His understanding of this goes back to almost a decade ago when he took the bus downtown to see the World's Fair. Sure, not everything that he saw there turned out to be 100 percent accurate.

The model of the city under the bubble dome and all that. But the main gist, the theme, he might say, it was intact.

He came away with a taste of the future. A new America, fueled by boundless growth and new ideas about aerospace, science and technology, that would manifest right here in this city. A future that was a clean line, a perfectly uninterrupted arcing trajectory from the past to a world in which the human race, or more precisely America, would master nature and unwanted change through building new and better machines. Affluence, automation, consumerism and American strength would expand, while poverty and other social inequalities would be rendered irrelevant on a rising tide of abundance. And the Soviet Union, Sputnik be damned, would be left behind to history. This was the post–World War II era, and there was an endless runway for technology-fueled American exceptionalism and progress. For God's sake, a year after the World's Fair was when Kennedy gave the speech that initiated the whole Supersonic Transport effort.

For most of his life, Larry had this sense but no idea how he could participate in it. The Navy offered him a glimpse of hope, but he sure fucked that up at his first opportunity like a good Dugdale, didn't he? But then this job, it changed everything. It was that rising tide of abundance. It had to be. The present was obliterating the past. Ending history altogether. Giving him a chance to move forward in a way his mother and father, whoever that guy was, could never have imagined.

He realizes that Ruth is a message from the universe. He must not accept a near miss with her. He must make this work. He must tell her now. He walks over to Gerry's empty desk and picks up his phone. He looks at the poster of the starting lineup of the 1970–1971 NBA SuperSonics basketball team on the wall next to the desk and feels an invigorating sense of fate.

Making this phone call is a bit reckless, as he's not sure what he'll do if Masako picks up the receiver. He craves a smoke and scans Gerry's desk for those shitty low-tar, filtered things. The healthy ones with no taste. They're nowhere in sight.

Thank God, it's Ruth who answers after three rings. That said, he is also not sure what he's going to say to her. He sort of blacks out and just starts talking.

"Me and you tomorrow. We're going to talk to your mom. Together."

"I told you that it's much more complicated than that, Larry. I don't know."

"I do know." He impresses himself with this new decisiveness. It's as if a different, non–Larry Dugdale person has commandeered his tongue. "Well, at least, let's try and see? I can talk to her. See how it goes."

"I still don't know."

"I know this: I know that I want to be with you. More than anything."

"I, you see, there're so many things that—"

"Will you marry me?"

"What?"

"I'm sorry. I didn't want to ask you that over the phone. I don't know what came over me." His pulse pounds in his gums.

"I'm very flattered, Larry. Really. But it, this and everything else, it's all so much at once. Too much at once. I need to think about it. "

"OK, I'll ask you again in person. When you won't be able to resist my charms. We're gonna build a family together, I promise you."

A mass of machinists come through the front door, pouring into the workshop and break room. Some are shouting. He sees Ollie, Sven, Uwe, Todd. All of them. Even Gerry. One kicks the garbage can in the break room doorway, knocking its contents across the floor.

Larry puts the phone to his chest to muffle the noise and then returns it to his ear and says, "I'm gonna have to call you back, Ruth."

"Sorry, what?"

"I've gotta go. Tomorrow. Your mom."

"What's going on over there?"

"Sorry. Gotta go." He hangs up the phone.

Gerry walks past Larry and sits down at the adjacent desk. He leans back in the chair and plants his hands atop his bald head, showcasing a couple of sweat stains in the armpits of his misbuttoned dress shirt.

"They cancelled it," Gerry says, lighting a cigarette. "The fucking Congress. They pulled the plug."

Larry signals to pass him a cigarette, but Gerry doesn't seem to see or care or both.

"Cancelled what?" Larry is afraid to ask, but the words still roll out.

"The goddamn Supersonic."

"What? They can't cancel it. You can't cancel the future."

"Well, they did. Cut the funding. No warning. Just like that. Said it was a waste of money. That the engineer's last simulation failed. That we're doing some national belt-tightening. Fucking news to me, isn't it?"

Larry drops the can of Coke that he had long ago forgotten he had in his hand and leans back against Gerry's desk to steady himself against waves of nauseating vertigo. "How did we not know? The Supersonic was my life's work."

"You work on 727 rear doors, pal," Gerry scoffs.

"But, well. I basically did work on the Supersonic."

"No, you didn't. Nobody did. Not exclusively. The engineers never even built a working model. Not out of metal. They've still been modeling parts out of fucking wood." Gerry pauses for a few moments and exhales through his teeth. He looks up at the Super-Sonics basketball poster on the wall, rips it down, wads it up, and throws it on the floor. Then he gets up out of his chair just enough to kick the wadded poster for good measure.

"But it was so close. I mean, I was asked to do things here and there for the engineers. I thought . . ." Larry starts rubbing his face with his hands. "It's like we were all working on the Supersonic Transport already. That everything was moving forward. One direction. Up and up and up. Always getting better. Stronger. Faster. We were there."

"What does this mean for us? For the machinists?" Larry can't look at Gerry's face and observes the expanding pool of sticky cola on the floor.

"Done. Cut. Laid off. Outta here." Gerry makes a chopping motion with his hand and then stubs out his cigarette on his desktop. He thinks and then lights another.

"They'll find us another job here at the company though, right?" Larry asks.

"Nah, buddy. We're gone. All of us. Effective immediately. Didn't you hear anything they said at that shit show of a meeting?"

"Wait, I thought you said that we don't actually work for the Supersonic. Not yet. Right? Doesn't that mean something?"

"The whole company, the whole economy, this whole city just took a big shit. We're the guys at the bottom, Larry. You know what happens to the guys at the bottom? The same thing that always happens to the guys at the bottom, Larry. Hope you've been saving some scratch. Or don't have any serious plans for the next decade or so, kid." Gerry gets up and starts shuffling toward the door, a broken man. To the best of Larry's knowledge, Gerry had been at the company for his whole adult life. He moved toward the door with nothing more than the cigarette between his lips.

Larry follows behind him and sees others packing up work-spaces. Yelling. He sees more than one guy with his face in his hands, crying.

"We're all canned? Just like that? Seriously?" He tries to catch up to Gerry. "I've got things. Things I have to do. Need to do. This has to be a mistake."

"We were going to change everything. Alter the course of history. And the fucking Supersonic never even got off the ground." Gerry walks out into the gray late-morning light without looking back. "I guess we got our change though."

TWENTY-THREE   *2014*

Percy goes into their darkened bedroom and kisses Sami on the forehead. Her skin is cold and dry on his lips. He flips on the bedside lamp, which is the only light she can consistently tolerate these days. "How're you feeling, sweetheart?"

She doesn't answer. Doesn't even try. In their nearly two decades of marriage, Percy has never seen his wife so despondent. Sure, she's been down before here and there within the range of normal midlife emotion and perhaps perimenopause. And he's aware that she's been dabbling with some nagging, parental malaise. But this depression hit her like a plummeting cartoon piano and has had her pinned down under its weight for weeks with no relief in sight.

Percy took all of his remaining sick days off of work to be with Sami and alleviate some of their never-ending domestic responsibilities. She let him help with a few things like rushing the kids out to school in the morning. But Sami doesn't trust him to cook or do laundry or manage the complexities of the kids' after-school and social schedules. She still pulled herself out of bed—with matted hair and wearing the same sweatpants—to make dinner, drive Macy to softball and drop off Aidan at the movies to meet with his friends. Percy watched as she completed these tasks only to beat a swift retreat to their bedroom.

He hoped things would be on the mend by the time he had to

go back to work, but nothing changed. Not in a positive direction, anyhow. As she settled into increasing acceptance of her defeat, Sami's mood only darkened. She's now spending some twelve to fourteen hours per day in bed. Although every time he checks, she doesn't seem to be asleep. She is losing weight. Sami needs fresh air. Sunlight. A change of clothes. Something.

He can think of at least half a dozen friends and acquaintances whose nervous breakdowns wouldn't surprise him. Of course, he'd feel terribly for them and offer his support however possible. But he wouldn't be shocked by their troubles, especially with his experience as a mental health professional.

Sami, on the other hand . . . he didn't know she had it in her. Sami the unflappable, steady hand. Sami who always wears her same white shoes and blue jacket and has her bottomless dedication to that morass of a school. But this seems to have been a torpedo below her waterline.

And, not that it's about him, but the size of his blind spot is almost as troubling to Percy as his wife's condition. When had he become so blinkered? Especially with his own wife and family. And what does that say about him? What does it say of Percy Stalworth as a school counselor? Nothing positive, no matter how one considers it.

He asks her again how she's feeling. And, again, she doesn't answer.

The silence is punctured by two of their kids arguing in the hallway, something about a remote or who gets to choose the show. Percy announces in a raised but civil voice, "C'mon guys. Let's please try to get along. You're mother's not . . ." He balks at delivering the full explanation. They are trying to keep her depression quiet from the kids. Yet no matter their level of parental discretion, the children can still tell that Mommy is not right. The disagreement continues unabated in the hallway.

"Too easy," Sami says.

"What?" he asks, surprised to hear her voice.

"You're too easy on them," Sami says without opening her eyes. "Pliable."

"We do fine. Normally. It's that—"

"You lost your enforcer."

He wants to defend himself. Not himself so much as his parenting approach. He knows from his training that there are ways to navigate interpersonal relationships without conflict or forcing contrived absolutes. He decides that the last thing Sami needs right now is an argument with him over their different child-rearing styles and tries to soothe her by petting her shoulders and gathering her hair at the top of her neck.

Sami covers her face with her hands just in time to muffle another wave of crying. As she returns to near composure, she pulls the sheets over her head and says, "It's dead."

"What is?"

"My dream. My goal. I'm a failure. Not only a failure but a fucking failure."

"No, you're not. You still have me. And the children. You're a wonderful mother. The best."

The argument on the other side of the door tips into a screaming match. There's a meaty thud. Then a rising moan that careens over into a caterwaul of tears and someone repeating, "I hate you. I hate you so much," with increasing volume. Percy and Sami can't be sure which child or even if it's one of their sons or daughters. They've lost the ability to differentiate between hysterics. It's all an endless background track of low-level interpersonal conflict in the Hasegawa-Stalworth household.

"I've let down my family," Sami chokes.

He gently pulls the sheet off of her face and tries to convey some sincerity. "We don't feel that way at all, honey."

She gives him a pinched, desperate look as if she is suffering from abdominal cramps.

"I promise," he tries to reassure her, squeezing her hand.

"I don't mean this family. I mean my family. My original family. Sorry, that sounded worse than I meant."

He nods. Right. Yes. Sure.

"It was up to me. And I let their dishonor, their historical dishonor stand. All that I've been pushing for amounts to, well, nothing. Absolutely nothing. That's me: absolutely nothing."

"You're only one person. All of this, it's not on you."

"You can just go and walk around and happily, actively snub your family name, Percy. I have to fight to show that mine ever even existed."

"I am on your side, Sami."

"You don't understand. You can't understand. I love you, but we're not from the same place."

"Yes, actually, we are from the same place."

"Same place. Different sides of the tracks."

He swallows deliberately and absorbs the fact that if the school falls apart it won't be a momentary upset but could cause a longer-term trauma to her mental well-being. Not just in some way that he can tell her to take deep breaths and move on. This will be an open wound until the day she dies. Perhaps beyond.

"I think you should reconsider seeing a therapist," he offers. "There's Peter. He's a very thoughtful man. Very thoughtful. Very in-demand therapist. But I'm sure he could find room in his schedule for you. I could ask him at fermentation club."

"With all due respect, Percy, the last thing I need is a second therapist to tell me about why I shouldn't be upset about something they've never once had to deal with in their own lives."

Is this the beginning of the end of our marriage? Percy wonders to himself. He thought they had done such a good job of mollifying conflict and sustaining their relationship over time, but maybe he was wrong. Maybe he'd nonchalantly created a situation where she shouldered too much and now the whole marriage would be toppled—not by a direct, open struggle between them, but by her slowly amassed lack of personal fulfillment.

He considers trying to convince her to turn the page. When working with young people, the intuitive, if not clinical, approach is to look to the open possibilities of the future. Tell them that this will change. They have the power to make things different. Better. But it is not the same in your late forties. Your peak is past. Or recently past. Just around the corner, if you're very lucky and have been striving for some time. The best you can do is forget and deny. He might suggest that she get a new hobby that'll make her feel distracted, if not somewhat fulfilled in a different way. Or she could refocus on the kids. That makes sense on paper. Not necessarily in practice. He holds his tongue. Refocusing on the kids is the exact type of blundering husbandly advice that could make her even more miserable, if not enraged at him.

He is tempted to slip out and check the temperatures on his newest batch of cider down in the basement. He's proud that his cider is made with only organic, local apples and solar energy. But the key to brewing is consistency. Fermentation generates its own heat. His brewing mentor, Hank, impressed upon him that overheated yeast produces higher levels of fruity esters and heavier fusel oils, which can adversely affect both alcohol levels and the finished flavor. Unfortunately, the house's solar is still anything but consistent, which requires him to keep tabs on the heat levels.

"Did you hear what I said?" Sami's voice crackles with frustration.

"Sorry, I was—I don't know." He feels like a dick for even thinking about cider while his wife is suffering. That said, he can't let the batch spoil either.

She starts to get up and mumbles something about dinner.

In a moment of awkward impulsivity, he ventures, "No, no. I'll cook. Stay here. Am gonna do something special. Was already planning on it."

"I'm skeptical." She doesn't look at him.

"Of course." He tries to sound as upbeat as he can without being obviously fake.

To his surprise, she accepts and swings around to sit back down on the edge of the bed. She crawls under the sheets and pulls them over her face.

"You sure you don't want to come join me in the kitchen? Just to keep me company. Get out of the room?" He tries to work through and deny to himself the fact that she called him on his dinner-making bluff. Or, at least, a semi-bluff. A hedge, perhaps.

She shakes her head. "Can you turn off the lamp?"

He wants to continue to encourage her but decides not to push too hard and excuses himself to the kitchen with a small, rolling wave of pride.

An hour later he's had four ciders, burnt the rice to the bottom of the pot, set off the fire alarm, remembered that he meant to make potatoes, not rice, in the first place, and, by Sami's account, come to ask her where the pots, pans, and measuring cups are located on a total of five different occasions. "I'm sorry, I forgot you just moved in here," she said.

Dinner is a salad. Of sorts. It's the kind of thing that he thought Sami would approve of but doesn't seem to be going over too well with the kids. Greens with a couple of hard-boiled eggs and a can of tuna emptied on top. Some of the rice from the top of the pot is salvageable as a side dish but still carries a bit of carbonized aroma.

After a final and unsuccessful attempt at trying to convince Sami to come to the table for dinner, Percy takes food to her in the room. "Look, it's a salade Niçoise. Or kind of like a Niçoise." He shows his wife, illuminating the bowl with the light from his phone.

"Thanks, Percy. But I'm not hungry. And please don't bring food into the bedroom. That's your rule."

"I'm not eating that," one of the kids shouts from the hallway. "Dad, where's your credit card?"

"No. You can't—"

"Too late. We already ordered the pizza."

"But I didn't give you my card."

"We pay when it gets here."

Percy is about to protest but decides to let it go. The conflict level is already too high. He sets the bowl of salad on the nightstand next to the bed and looks out the window.

He can see the big rock outside in the dirt. Deep breath. Focus on the rock that has been there since time immemorial. In the grand scheme of things, his mortal concerns are insignificant. This is how he starts off his commutes to work on mornings when he's not motivated to ride his bike in the rain. Look at the ancient rock. Another deep breath. Yes, he will be happy with pizza, he decides. Pizza is good. Everyone likes pizza. Life is short. He does find it a bit odd that the rock appears to be illuminated from behind by a sharp, white light. One more breath.

He draws back the curtain to see what's giving the rock that spectral appearance. Headlights? He notices that there's a VW van parked on the edge of the lot behind it. Its headlights are out. Still looks to be an '80s Syncro Westfalia four-wheel drive. Percy always wanted one of those. This one would be a classic but looks a bit worse for wear.

A man comes around from behind the rock with a beaming flashlight and an extended measuring tape in one hand. He's wearing a green hat, shorts, and sandals, no matter the cold. He carries something in the other hand as he advances: a stick, no, a cane, and uses it to shoo off a couple of seagulls roosting on the rock.

It appears that the man is waving up toward him in the window. Percy looks again. Squints to focus. The man aims the flashlight right into Percy's face, burning squiggly red tracers in his eyes.

"Sami," the man says her name in a hushed shout. "Sami. Hey, come check this out."

Percy turns to his wife. "There's some dude outside calling for you."

She doesn't answer.

"Sami?"

"Bruce," she says in a monotone.

They hear him repeat her name from outside.

"Please tell me you're not having some sort of crisis affair with *that* guy."

"He's my PTA helper. Or was," she says.

"Gotcha. Well, even if you are having an affair with him. Which I want to mention that you didn't exactly deny just now, maybe we could step out and say hello. I know that sounds a little crazy, but it's never a bad idea to get some fresh air." As he starts to move around the room, he realizes he's pretty buzzed and possibly making impulsive decisions.

Sami doesn't respond.

"How long?" Percy shouts to his kids through the bedroom door.

"How long what?"

"Pizza."

"Half hour," answers a voice that sounds like their middle son.

"Pliable," Sami says from bed.

"It's Friday. Let's take it easy. C'mon." He offers her a hand. "We're getting you out of the house. Go say hi to your friend."

"He's not my friend."

"We'll be back for pizza."

"Sami," the man shouts her name again from outside. "I've got an idea."

Some minutes later, Percy's coaxed Sami into her blue jacket, even helping get her limp arms down both of her sleeves and zipping it up to the neck.

He suggests that they say hi to Bruce and then stroll around the neighborhood, around the school and the dirt parking lot really. She doesn't necessarily confirm his plan, but she doesn't refuse it either. He brings a glass growler of the cider from the last batch with them and takes a long draw on the front porch. He's really digging this Spanish-style *sidra* that he and Hank devised. They managed to get a great wild yeast strain, and the cider is more vinegary and tart than the champagne-style French cider they'd been trying to make before.

Sami grabs the bottle from his hands and takes a drink. She spits some out at first. "Bitter," she says while wiping at her tongue with the whole palm of her hand.

"Try it again. Embrace the acidity."

She takes another drink and, this time, keeps it down. "Still don't like it. But I'll embrace the alcohol."

They watch a plane fly overhead. A couple of them. The airport must be busy, it being the beginning of the weekend and all. They put the traffic into a looping holding pattern that circles over this part of town while awaiting landing clearance.

He puts his arm around her. "I'm glad you came out."

"We shouldn't leave Macy home alone."

"The kids are all together. It's fine."

They walk toward the rock on the edge of the property and the parking lot. She stops to take another drink from the growler.

"I kinda hate to admit this," she says. "But it's almost pretty drinkable. Sort of."

"Why do you hate to admit it?"

"Because you get so much enjoyment out of doing stuff that you're not good at. Or even trying hard to ever become good at." They start to walk. "I want to hate your hobbies. But they make you so . . . fucking happy. And sometimes, they even end up being decent. I want it all, and I'm doing nothing good or even decent."

He shrugs. "You need to go easier on yourself."

"Again, different sides of the tracks," she says.

Bruce sees Percy and Sami headed his way and calls her name again. They tell him to hold up a second. A few steps from their front porch, they stop and look at the school for a moment, and then she looks away. He remembers when Masako was dying. The Generalissimo. The lady ran everything with a titanium fist. She probably felt that she had no other choice. She'd had a hard life. He was well aware of that. Aware that most people had a harder life than him. That's one of the main reasons he decided to become a public school therapist. To help people who are having a rough go of it but to get to them early enough that he can make a difference and find them where they are—at public school. Only rich kids, baby Stalworths and such, can afford private therapists for any length of time these days.

That's not to say that his childhood was perfect. Money only goes so far. And, in many cases, it supplants real emotional connection between family members like the cellulose of a tree being slowly replaced by quartz to leave behind nothing but petrified wood. Percy would've rather had a genuine relationship with his father than have had his paid-for summer camps and a car and vacations where nobody spoke to each other. Not that the Stalworths actually had so much money by the time his father offed himself. And it only got worse from there.

He'd craved the bond that Sami had with her grandmother. His own youth was about showing others how great the family was, how smart and successful they all were, while coldly neglecting each other, if not cynically competing, behind closed doors.

Even if the Generalissimo was rigid and often harsh, she truly cared and became softer in her later years. At least, that's how Sami saw it. Masako was nostalgic for her teaching years and for the feeling of bringing music into the lives of children. Not all children. She didn't care much for the dilettantes or the blindly overachieving grade chasers. But her whole life made sense when she discovered an apt pupil. Someone who had that combination of talent, discipline, and willingness to learn. And she had more than a few. Sometimes one, two, or even three per year. Yet, sometimes a few classes would pass by without what she always referred to as "a decent one."

In Masako's final years, back before Percy and Sami were married, she lost her ability to see and couldn't talk much. But she could still hear. Sami was able to track down a handful of her "decent ones" from years past, mainly people with family still in the neighborhood. There was a music producer in LA who scored TV commercials and the odd TV show or indie movie. There was a woman in the Chicago Symphony and another in the local symphony. The known number of musical successes, meaning a former student of Masako's with an active career in some sort of music, was pushing seven. Ten or twelve if you include those who went on to teach music. Rumor held the numbers to be higher, but Sami could only find so many. And she convinced the guy in LA, the woman in Chicago, and the lady in the local symphony to arrange a tribute to Masako with some of the current students when they were all in town around the holidays. The school was closed for the break, but they played outside in front of the rock.

Sami rolled Masako out there in a wheelchair and whispered into her ear the surprise that was about to happen. They played a couple of her favorites. Old European stuff. Percy didn't recognize any of it. The event even drew some random bystanders, like an old Black guy who Percy swears he saw crying during the performance.

Masako listened intently with her eyes closed. It lasted only about ten minutes in total. That's all the old woman could handle. Sami thanked everyone for coming. For doing this for her grandmother. And first publicly ventured an idea she'd been discussing with Percy since they met: "Someday this won't be Stevenson Elementary. This'll be Masako Hasegawa Elementary." The children and the adults cheered. They hugged Masako. Told her what she had meant to them. Tears streamed down some of their faces.

Sami leaned into her grandmother's ear. "I am going to do that for you."

Masako nodded. Percy thought he saw her smile.

Sami fought to keep her composure and said, "I promise. I want you to know that."

Percy looks out over the lot now, remembering the day. He too was moved to the point of tears. Something he was never supposed to feel or show in Chez Stalworth with his emotionally unmoored, grandiose father, sedated mother, and cutthroat sibling.

He knew that day with Masako, in that very moment, that he would propose marriage to Sami. That he wanted to become part of her family. To leave his history in the past and start over with this woman, here where she was so grounded.

Their marriage helped him to feel like a more complete human being. To slough off as much of the bullshit as he could manage to let go of and refocus on becoming the person he had wished he could be. To build the family he wanted, with warmth and love between the parents and children.

But there were so many children. One after the next. He became unaware of months and seasons. Years were compressed to a couple of quick memories, photographs, and bullet points. He and Sami were often working in parallel. Just trying to keep it all afloat.

He always figured they would come back together when their lives and family allowed them to do so. When the time was right. He knew she wasn't always happy. Who was? No one with children, and especially not with four, was happy. And sure, she'd missed out on a traditional career. But she had the kids, the school, and the PTA, and she had this promise to rename . . .

Yeah, this is bad, he thinks. Maybe really bad. Shit, he should have known this was coming. He sees again the vague signposts of a path by which he and Sami unravel. The same signposts he's missed or ignored for years.

"Sami," shouts the man, Bruce, making his way over to them.

"Nice Sonics hat," Percy says, admiring the unswerving local pride in another fallen institution. The man nods and encourages them to follow him to his van.

Bruce talks as he walks with his cane. "I was on my way to see you. I was busy getting some information. But I was coming to see you next."

"Coming to see me?" asks Sami, walking closer to him. She signals to Percy for another drink.

"I had to review some specs first." He opens the van's sliding side door. It's dented and moves uneasily in its track. But he gets it done on the second or third attempt and gestures with his flashlight to a pile of papers on the floor of the vehicle, proudly revealing his prized assets. "Check it out."

Percy is hit with the smell of mildew and decades of stale bong hits. Yes, maybe he'd been a bit too spontaneous to suggest this encounter.

"This is my husband, Percy." Sami introduces the two men. "This is Bruce, who was doing some PTA stuff with me."

The man gives Percy another noncommittal nod. Beyond the

Sonics hat, Percy is not impressed. Well, he'd like the van too, if it received a bit of maintenance. But he tries to look with empathy toward this man who upends all of Percy's stereotypes and expectations of a PTA parent.

Bruce smooths out some large blueprint-style map on the stained, carpeted van floor. "Schematics," he says. He also has some blurry printouts from the internet, what appears to be a small amount of text smashed into the corner of the page by aggressive blocks of banner ads for fast food and mortgage refinance companies. He starts marking up the larger paper with a stubby grease pencil. "Um, twenty-two. By thirty-six. Thirty-five, really. I think that's what I got. And it gets tighter over by the rock. Eighteen. Roughly."

Percy and Sami watch, perplexed. Then Bruce puffs himself up over his cane, obviously excited to play the hero. "What do you know about mobile classrooms?"

"Like a trailer?" Percy asks.

"Like a portable. Most of the small ones are thirty-six by twenty-four, but some of the older, square ones are even smaller. The wood ones. The ones used at some of the other schools. Maybe we can get our hands on a used portable. See where I'm going?"

Sami says, "We already talked about that. Remember? Early on. The biggest challenge for the school is that it has no space. That's one of its official shortcomings."

Bruce upturns his palms and sweeps them past the rock. "What about here?"

"Doesn't belong to the school," Sami says. "Never has. We park on it because nobody's ever complained."

"See, get this: I checked. Like deep, classified, black-ops research. Even talked to a geology professor at the university. Or I left him a voicemail, at least."

"OK?"

"It doesn't belong to anybody. Weird grandfathering thing around this rock, it's called a glacial something."

"Erratic," Percy says, aware that he could be referring to the rock or Bruce.

"Yeah, that's it. Dumped here by a massive sheet of ice," Bruce continues. "Plus, there's the greenbelt behind it there. A creek and makeshift dump, really. Goes way back. Way way back. It's crazy, this bit of land sits between the other properties in all of the city maps and as-builts. It's like a black hole. Our own little Bermuda Triangle."

Percy finds himself a bit more interested but still guarded for his wife, whom he can feel starting to wake up to this man's frantic proposal.

"I'm an ideas guy . . . and this is my big idea." Bruce touches the schematic with his grease pencil. "Boom."

"Boom?" Sami leans into the van, looking closer at the papers.

A brown sedan with tinted windows rolls by slowly, pausing and then continuing past the lot. Bruce quickly pulls the van's sliding door halfway shut, almost hitting Sami. He keeps staring at the car in furrowed paranoia.

"Not bad." Sami places a hand on Bruce's shoulder, turning her back to Percy. "You sure about this?"

"It'll cost a bit more than the original remodel ideas. But it'll work."

"I can put together a school auction or something to try to cover the difference," Sami considers aloud.

Percy games it all out in his head. Bruce is onto something here, at least for the shorter term. Things might be fine. So long as they save the school and still give it the Hasegawa name that it deserves, returning a degree of honor to the family. Things will be fine.

"Mom? Dad?" Aidan shouts from the front porch of the house.

They turn to face him. He stands next to an adult they don't imme-diately recognize. Percy's adrenaline blasts through the cider haze as he attempts to identify the interloper. He sees the brown sedan parked nearby.

"Pizza's here. We need your card," Aidan shouts again.

Sami and Bruce have half reopened the van door and are poring over the schematics and printouts. Without breaking her attention from the paperwork, she says, "I'm gonna stick around and go over some details with Bruce. I've gotta call your sister. Right away."

"Dad?" another shout comes from the front porch. "Hurry up. He's waiting."

Percy wishes Sami and Bruce luck, but they're preoccupied with more pressing matters.

TWENTY-FOUR *2014*

Bruce waves back the moving truck as it reverses through the restaurant parking lot toward the main door. Wren rolls down the truck's driver's-side window and cranes her head out toward him. "Good?"

"A few more. Keep comin'." He continues his hand signaling, doing his best impression of an aircraft marshaler guiding a plane into its gate.

The truck comes to a stop while he's still directing her back, and Wren hops out. He likes the way she looks in her moving attire of old jeans and a hoodie she used to wear in the earlier years of their relationship. Her hair is tied up atop her head, giving a proper showcase for her linear cheekbones.

"Where's Sierra?" he asks, anticipating seeing his daughter today.

"She's at her speech therapy appointment." Wren pulls on a pair of leather working gloves. "If we'd met up when originally planned . . ."

"I thought we were taking a break on speech therapy until the school helps us get the insurance going?"

"Don't you remember our last three conversations? That's why I'm here. I'm redoing the basement and garage so we can rent it to tourists on that website."

"Which website?"

"Will you know it if I tell you the name?"

He shrugs. The basement was the last little refuge of his personal belongings. "You're gonna let strangers stay there?"

"If they pay, yes. Look: This's a Hail Mary. I don't want to do it either. I know change is hard, but we need to think about what's best for Sierra." She goes around to the back of the truck, rolls up the cargo door, and points to two large cardboard boxes and a bevy of rusted ski gear. "You've got tons of empty space; let's put it to use."

"I'm down to store stuff." He leans up against his cane and does a quick visual inventory of the back of the truck. "But I don't see any of Sierra's stuff here. Or your stuff."

"C'mon, Bruce. Let's not go there right now."

"Seems to me like a pretty good time to talk about it."

"It's complicated. You know that. Listen, I rented the truck. Packed it. Brought it all right here to you with a bow on it. Regardless of if you answered my calls. So, let's please not fight."

"OK. I'm, I don't think I could lift that out of there. Even if I wanted to."

She pulls out the truck's back ramp and starts loading the first box and ski gear on a dolly.

He watches, wilting into his cane. "Maybe we should hold tight on all of this. I've got some really big things afoot. Maybe you're jumping the gun moving all my stuff—"

"Jumping the gun? Our daughter needs serious help. We've been talking about this for over a year and have, so far, made negative progress with the school. Again, I know change is hard. But we have to do something. It's all part of the process."

"Which process are we talking about?"

"Fixing up the basement?"

"Are we?" He exhales and rubs his face.

She doesn't seem sure of how to react. She wheels one box into the restaurant while leaving the other outside with Bruce. He opens the top to look inside and sees his racoon roadkill ski hat. The eyeless face smiles up at him, mocking his ruin. It looks to have gotten wet and has white mold garnishing the tips of the fur. He feels as if he could cry.

Wren returns to collect the second box. Once she's dropped that off inside, she pushes the dolly back up the ramp and sets about closing up the back of the truck.

"You leaving already? Just like that?"

"Sierra's session is only an hour. I've gotta—"

"What time is it?"

"Not a typical Bruce question." She glances at her watch, then seems to evaluate his reaction, searching for a sign of what he's up to. "A little after two."

"Hold tight. Wait, I see them coming." He points to an older Land Cruiser turning into the lot. "Give me a couple more minutes."

Wren slowly peels back her work gloves, finger by finger.

"I had a breakthrough. A big idea. I'm gonna save the school. I'm gonna get Sierra sorted. Get her teachers, insurance . . . everything figured out."

"That would be amazing. But with all due respect, Bruce, you've been claiming stuff like that for way too long."

Sami lowers herself out of the SUV, one white sneaker after the next. Her hair is back in a ponytail and still looks a bit damp from her shower.

"Sami, this is Wren." Bruce performs his most formal version of an introduction. "Wren, this is Sami."

They exchange pleasantries. Wren starts to head back toward the moving truck. Saying something again about having to pick up Sierra.

"Is Shawn inside?" Sami asks Bruce.

"No, he'll be here any moment." He then shouts after Wren. "Hey, that wasn't a couple more minutes."

She slows her walks and turns back to Sami and Bruce.

Bruce then tries Sami. "Tell her why you're here."

Sami looks confused. "School planning?"

"But tell her the plan."

"Um, well, a few things." Sami appraises the estranged couple's dynamic, and then says, "Oh. OK. Bruce here, he had a great idea to fix a big problem. Now we're gonna make it happen."

Wren warms to Sami. "You're the PTA lady, right?"

"Yeah. That's what they call me. The PTA lady," Sami says, straightening up. "And mom. That's me."

"Amazing. OK. Sorry to be so forward, I'm in a rush to pick up my daughter, but—hopefully Bruce has already talked to you about this—maybe you could help us figure out some paperwork stuff with the school. IEP and insurance won't cover anything until the school confirms need. I've reached out before. So many times. And tried all of the obvious channels. But—we're in quite a bind."

"Bruce already told me all about it," Sami explains. "We've got a couple of hills to climb here first, but I'm on it. Next thing. I promise."

"Really?" Wren puts her hands on her knees and catches her breath for a moment. "That'd mean the world to me. To Sierra. Thank you."

Sami winks. "Thank Bruce. He's really been stepping up. Huge."

Shawn's work van pulls into the lot and parks alongside Sami's vehicle. He gets out, reaches back inside, and grabs his leather tool belt. "Let's do this." He beams at Sami and Bruce. He nods hello to Wren.

Bruce is busy observing Wren's building elation. Wren repeats that she has to go but thanks everyone and trades phone numbers with Sami before climbing back into the moving van.

Bruce invites Shawn and Sami inside to go over his array of

paperwork, formerly laid out on his van's floor and now on an old door balanced atop two sawhorses.

As Sami enters the creaking restaurant, her head swivels around, observing the piles of sawdust and partial framing.

"This is your place?" she asks, walking past the boxes holding the majority of Bruce's worldly belongings and then around a pile of Spatzy's spent beer cans.

"Sure is."

"What do you do here again?"

"Business."

"OK?"

"Retail, I guess. But still a work in progress."

"What are you going to sell?"

"Yes."

"Huh?"

Bruce points to the printout images of old, wooden school portables. He asks Shawn, "Do you know if any other schools have, like, a used one? Or if there's some other secondhand option out there?"

"Probably. I imagine so." Shawn rotates his tool belt along his waist.

"So, we could get one?"

"For the right price. I don't see why not." Shawn shrugs. "Where you gonna put it though? The school has a pretty tight footprint."

"Yeah, no." Bruce moves his finger on the neighborhood as-built map. "Here. The parking lot. Across the street."

"What about environmental regulations? The lot backs up onto the greenbelt. Aren't there lots of rules about that?" Sami starts to lean against the desk but thinks better of it as the door-top starts to slide.

"I got calls out to city officials, but it should be fine. For a while, at least. Long enough for them to decide to close a different school, and we can deal with the details over the longer run," Bruce says. "My building is just over the other side of the greenbelt, so I've done my research. And then some."

"Don't we need to get utilities to the portable?" Sami asks. "Kids can't study in the dark."

"I thought it through. We can run a single electrical line for the lights and fire alarms. No water. No sewage."

"Electrical is feasible," Shawn says. "Still some challenges."

"Is that hard to do?" Sami asks Shawn.

"Technically, no. I could hack something into the panel in a matter of minutes."

Bruce feels a mass of energy building in his chest. This is going to happen, he thinks to himself. All of these doubters. All these years. I'm proving my value to the community. My vision. Wren will see that it's something I thought of and made happen.

And when his retail store wins the lottery, he and Wren can go back to the good parts of how things were, but all will be for the better. Maybe this is how it was always supposed to be. He is the hero who needed to venture out into the wilderness and confront the beast that threatened his village so he could return home triumphant and changed into his fully realized potential.

"But there's no way in hell that I'm messing with the school's panel," Shawn says, looking at a blueprint of the school itself. "There's liability and all sorts of other concerns. The bureaucracy on something like that is a monumental pain in the ass. Beyond what you can believe."

"We talking weeks?" Sami asks.

"Months. Years?"

She droops. "We need it to be up and running, like yesterday."

"That's your house, right?" Shawn points to her place on the neighborhood map. "Run the electrical from your house for the time being. Just until we come up with a longer-term plan. That's easy. I can bury the line and bluff like it's legit to buy us some more time."

"Hot damn." Bruce smiles, wobbles a bit on his cane, and tries to give Sami a high five.

"I can't," she says. Leaving Bruce hanging.

"What do you mean you can't?" He lowers his hand. "I thought this was the most important thing in the world to you."

"It's that . . . we have solar. My husband insisted on it. I mean, I agree that, theoretically, it's the right thing, but we can barely run our kids' computers and the lights at the same time when it's raining."

They share a moment of noiseless frustration. Bruce can feel his old friend, defeat, stalking the perimeter. Getting ready to plant a hatchet right between his shoulder blades.

"You could run electrical from here, if you wanted." Shawn motions with his head to the old electrical box on the far wall of the restaurant. "It's technically a no-no to go through the greenbelt, but we could keep it discreet. I mean, it's not like they stop people from dumping garbage or even living down in the greenbelt. It's what? Under three hundred meters from here?"

"Meters? Wait. Are meters the same as yards?"

"No, it's more in yards," Shawn says. "Like a third more. Like three hundred thirty-three yards."

"Phew. So, three hundred thirty-three times three—wait . . ."

"A thousand feet," Sami answers. "Plug together ten hundred-foot extension cords? I think I've got two or three to donate."

"I'd run Romex straight across. No plugs. Could bring it right up under the portable where nobody can see." Shawn looks at the neighborhood map. "Cheap too. It's actually a nifty solution. I think it's less than three hundred meters."

"Less? Less than a thousand feet?" Electrical or no electrical, the distance from his future cannabis retail HQ is no longer to a parking lot but to a school building. Full of students. America's future generation. As the gull flies. He'd checked that it was over a thousand to the main Stevenson property before he pursued renting the restaurant. That was the whole goddamn point. But it wasn't far over the Liquor Control Board distance limit. He'd known that and had kind of eyeballed the measurements and then forgotten the specifics anyhow. "Wait, Shawn, are we talking to the edge of the property or the portable?"

"The portable, man. What good's it do us to run electrical to the edge?" He loops his thumbs into his tool belt and looks quizzically at Bruce.

"Sorry, guys. Give me a minute." Bruce excuses himself. He moves as fast as he can past all of his personal history in cardboard boxes, past the pile of empty beer cans, and prays that Spatzy will be outside to join him for a smoke session.

TWENTY-FIVE   *1971*

Ruth enters the kitchen to see Masako drinking her morning tea-cup of hot water and watching out the window as the sun finishes rising over the rock. A single egg boils in a small, enameled pot under the white light of the stovetop's fluorescent tube. The reflected glare assaults Ruth's retinas. At first, she doesn't notice the smell of the eggs, but soon it becomes unbearable, its stench crawling through the entire room. The scent of burning plastic? No, burning hair. No, low tide. Maybe all of them swirled together.

She's hit with another wave of nausea. Ruth turns and leans against the countertop, doing her best to conceal the fact that she's about to vomit.

She threw up before in the shower and figured she'd be in the clear by now. But she can feel her stomach issue a series of fluttering micro-contractions as the hot acid inches its way back up her throat. Ruth decides to return to her room. Best not to talk. To not even try. She should be able to stomach these smells; it's the same breakfast her mother's eaten every day for as long back as Ruth can remember.

"You'd better blow-dry your hair," Masako comments while rotating the window's handle to crank it open. "Beckham and his aunt are picking us up in a half hour. Less. Twenty-seven minutes."

Ruth inhales through her mouth to top up on fresh oxygen and then answers, "You already told me that, Mom . . . *Okasan*. When you woke me up. And again, when you rushed me into the shower."

Masako isn't paying attention. "You. Get out of there," she shouts out the window. She rapidly cranks open the window, showcasing decades of practice, grabs a dried pine cone off the sill, and throws it down to the garden below. "Move it." Two gulls depart from the beets, turnips, carrots, and spinach in her late fall garden and land on the top of the nearby rock. Still not looking at Ruth, Masako winds closed the window and says, "I know I already told you. But I can't understand why I ever have to convince you to bathe. Especially for church."

On her way out of the room, Ruth grouses, "It's not even Sunday."

"God is not a one-day-a-week affair, Ruth," Masako calls after her.

"Thanksgiving isn't a Christian holiday. It's a pagan fall bounty festival putting on a happy face to cover up the national history of genocide."

"Be that as it may, I told you today's not about Thanksgiving. Gennie Ikeda is getting married. As she is your friend and a core part of the church community, we are all going to be there. Remember? Community."

She kind of remembers spending the night at Gennie's house once when she was young. She was never actually friends with Gennie and definitely isn't now. She didn't even know that Gennie was getting married. She's sure her mom had told her, but it didn't even register. That's how much she cares.

"We can have a quiet evening at home on Thanksgiving." Masako turns off the boiling water and fishes for the egg with a long spoon.

"What about what I asked you about Thanksgiving dinner and Larry?"

"Enough. We're not talking about that. Please finish getting ready."

Later, after Ruth has had a chance to vomit again, she washes the remnants out of her hair and then gives it all a good once-over with the stylish new blow-dryer she'd finally convinced her mom to buy. The one with the wood-grain plastic casing.

Masako lets herself into the bathroom. Ruth admires the two of them side by side in the mirrored cabinet. Their hair and glasses and clothes are different, but the immutable physical similarities, the nose, the cheekbones, the chin, even their height, are identical. Ruth doesn't say anything, as she finally has her nausea under control and plans to keep it that way. Assuming that her mother is about to give her a lecture, she preemptively turns back on the blow-dryer and points in the general direction of her already-dry hair.

"You know . . . I'm tired," Masako says over the noise of the appliance. "I started working as a teacher later than most. A lot has happened. So many things. I'm tired now. I want to retire someday."

Masako gently takes the blow-dryer from Ruth, turns it off, and sets it on the counter. She starts grooming her daughter's hair with her favorite brush. "You're graduating now. You have more education than I ever had. But things are different these days. I want you to take over for me. I want continuity for all that I built. It's my legacy. And I want it to be your legacy too."

Ruth tries to look pleased about this.

"You need to start to make some big decisions for your future." Masako brushes harder.

More than you know, Mom, Ruth thinks to herself as she burps pure acid. She hears the phone ring down the hall and is pleased with the timing.

"I'll get it." Masako moves toward the door.

"No, it's for me. The one I told you about." Ruth slides around her mom, moving as quickly as she can back to the kitchen. She notes her mother's incredulity. "Remember?" Ruth knows it's the morning call she's been waiting for from the nurse at Dr. Yamamoto's office.

Ruth grabs the receiver off the kitchen wall and carries it as far the cord will go. She reopens the window and leans her head out, striving for a modicum of privacy before she finally answers. "This is Ruth."

"Hi, Ms. Hasegawa. This is Dr. Yamamoto."

"I thought I was going to speak with the nurse."

"I thought I'd have a word with you, directly."

Here it comes. She doesn't need a doctor to tell her that she's pregnant. She can feel it in her cells. Feel it in her morning sickness that refuses to be confined to mornings. Feel it in her discomfort with simply walking or moving across her house.

Dr. Yamamoto has continued to collect urine samples and prod her with needles. She knows he's about to figure it out and wishes she could come out and tell him, but she can't get herself past that threshold of actively admitting to being sexually active. The doctor would never understand about *aitsu* Larry. With a careless word, he could ruin her and her mother's reputations at the church and throughout the wider community.

She looks over her shoulder to see Masako collecting a coat from the hall closet. She remains right outside of earshot so long as Ruth keeps her voice down.

"Ms. Hasegawa, I must let you know that we got some tests back, and you are pregnant. It's early still. Usually, I'd tell you in person, but I wanted to let you know right away."

"Pregnant? With a . . . baby?"

"Please allow me to give you the same advice I'd give my own daughters in this situation: If you get married now, right away, it won't be definitively clear that you became pregnant before the wedding. The baby could've been, say, premature by a month or so. You can always say that. And I won't publicly contradict you."

She thinks about Larry in a suit. Walking down the aisle. No, screw the aisle, a park. In front of the justice of the peace. Better yet, while circling the globe on a supersonic jet.

She's not ready to get married, but with Larry, she's not actively repulsed by the concept. She hasn't seen him for a few days. She's heard rumors of terrible layoffs at the company. Last they spoke, he said, no, no, all is fine. He is so busy at work. He's been putting in nights. He is supposed to call her about their plans for Thanksgiving. Lots to talk about. Lots to catch up on. He even said he has some new records for her.

Dr. Yamamoto continues, "Society, at large, frowns on premarital intercourse. And for good reason. Listen, Ms. Hasegawa. Don't repeat this back to anyone at church, but I am an open-minded and contemporary doctor in many ways. Or, at least, I am a doctor who tries to accept and work within the realities on the ground, as they reveal themselves to us. We must remember that God is mysterious. I think, in certain circumstances with certain people, it is OK for people who are planning to get married to experiment with intercourse before they tie the knot. Preferably once they're already engaged, but you understand what I mean. You'll be spending the rest of your lives together, so it's not a terrible idea for you and Beckham to get to know each other better. It would be unfortunate to marry someone who is not, what shall I call it? Compatible."

"Beckham. Right." Even her toenails hurt.

"And I am happy to know that you two are compatible. Anyway, that leaves one other issue. I am concerned by your swollen lymph nodes, and what could be an ever-so-slightly enlarged liver and spleen. These symptoms are not specific, but I'm following up some hunches. Did you ever do chemotherapy?"

"What? No."

"What did your father die of?"

"An accident."

"What kind of accident?"

"I don't know. Something fatal. You know my mom: no follow-up questions."

"OK. Just want to do my due diligence as you're going to be a mother yourself. A good doctor can't be too cautious, right? Probably nothing to worry about, but I'll let you know what I find out," Yamamoto says. "In the meantime, I'll see you at the wedding?"

"I'm not getting married, I mean, not yet. I need to time to process—"

"Today's wedding. Gennie Ikeda."

"Oh, yes, wouldn't miss it. Couldn't miss it, even if I wanted to."

"Oh good. Gennie is only a year or two younger than you. There's still hope." He laughs, as she fantasizes about punching him in his saggy old balls.

She remembers not liking Gennie and still having to spend the night at her house. Gennie was very girly and wanted to dress up and wear makeup and do a bunch of boring things, like pretend that they were princesses or ballerinas. At least, that's what Ruth recalls. And they barely spoke by middle and high school. But she does carry one memory from the night that she spent at Gennie's house. She was uncomfortable or nervous or angry or something and came upstairs and stood by Gennie's front door, hoping that Masako would come and take her home.

Gennie's mom found her and when Ruth asked to go home, Gennie's mom wrapped her arms around her and started sobbing. She kept telling Ruth that "it's going to be OK."

Ruth asked Mrs. Ikeda why she was crying. She doesn't recollect exactly what Gennie's mom answered, but it was something

like, "Oh . . . you don't know . . . do you?" and stared at Ruth with
her mouth half-open. She followed it with a short lecture about Jesus and left the room.

Ruth hadn't thought about that night in years. But she remembers now that the words had confused and frightened her to a point
that she couldn't process them—and decided not to explore them
any further. To the best of Ruth's memory, she never returned to
the Ikeda house after that one night. But Masako and Ruth soon
joined the church along with Gennie's family. She wonders if that
was some part of the babysitting and assistance deal. She doesn't
remember Masako being particularly religious prior to that, but
what does she really remember from childhood?

Dr. Yamamoto says goodbye but then adds a final offer. "Let
me know if you'd like me to speak to Beckham directly about the
situation, and what he needs to do. I will be very private about it. I
recognize that these issues can be hard for a proper young woman
like yourself to discuss."

"No, yes, no. I'll, yeah, I guess I still don't know what I'll do."
She watches the seagulls return to the garden and snatch a fat slug
out of the beets. She hangs up the call, dials Larry's house, and
leans back out the window.

When he answers with the sound of his mom's TV game show
blaring in the background, Ruth skips all pleasantries and gets
right to the point. Or as close as she can get to the point. "The car.
Remember? Remember what we—you know?"

"I can't really hear you, Ruthie," Larry says. "Wait, hold on a
sec. Can you turn it down, Ma?"

"Your car. I had suspicions, I thought, but now I found out for
sure that I'm—"

Ruth hears footsteps behind her and pulls her head back inside.

Masako, Beckham, and Beckham's aunt stand in the kitchen,
all wearing buttoned-up coats.

"You found out what for sure?" the aunt asks through a bogus smile.

"Um, that Gennie's getting married?" Ruth attempts to match her leer and slowly disconnects the call.

TWENTY-SIX   *1971*

Larry, sheathed in a plastic rain slicker, lifts a suitcase onto the conveyor belt. It's less a lift than a throw, really. He's finishing a ten-hour shift in a heavy downpour, an hour after sunset. His muscles scream from his hands and triceps to his lower back and the arches of his feet. Sweat runs down his sides, trapped under the impermeable rain protection. His care for the well-being of each bag decreases as the shift wears on. But this is the last plane to unload, and he digs to find a final burst of motivation.

Where the hell is Gerry? he repeats to himself, as rain rolls down his face. He needs to talk to his former boss and find out the status of getting his job back or, at least, some similar machinist work. Any real job at the company. Anything with a future. Gerry has contacts in the union and lines on opportunities where they are bringing back some experienced hands.

All of this is temporary. Larry losing his job. This momentary unemployment. It's but a pothole in the road. This baggage-handling gig is, in fact, very temporary. It's helping out with extra hours around the Thanksgiving holiday, maybe up through Christmas and New Year's. Maximum. He's already put in more mind-melting, monotonous hours than he ever imagined.

The company can't simply let go of all of their talent. The people who build the planes. Sure, there are some financial challenges and far-away political decisions that can affect short-term production choices, but they still have to make aircraft, right? And to do that, they need people like Larry. They need Larry, himself. He'll restart at any real job, anywhere in the company, and build his way back to the Supersonic once it is inevitably resuscitated. He's ready to work—just give him a lane, for God's sake.

Gerry promised that they'd talk to the union rep. That they'd get their foot back in the door. Gerry was supposed to be here today, tossing suitcases side by side with Larry. But dude is nowhere to be found.

Even more importantly, Larry needs to get out of here and go finish his conversation with Ruth. Tonight. Right now, actually. About their future together. He can't lie to her, but he also can't tell her his current truth. He needs, at least, a kernel of positive news, a small inkling of some sort of career hope, to be able to convince her to build the rest of their lives together. And, either way, he sure as hell can't stand her up again.

"Any word on Gerry?" Larry asks the crew manager, Randy, again. "You check the sign-up for next shift?"

Randy is under a small vinyl canopy, seeking shelter from the downpour. He shrugs and adjusts the antennae on his walkie-talkie while sucking out something from between his teeth.

"Did he call in sick? Or maybe got put on a different crew today?" Larry asks.

Randy doesn't answer and continues to mess with the walkie-talkie. "What the . . . ?" he mumbles to himself.

Larry picks up another suitcase, a gray-green one with a metal rim. He lofts it from the cart to the mouth of the conveyor belt with a bit too much spirit. The rim dents near a corner.

"Easy there, pal." Randy suddenly realizes that Larry exists. "Place it, don't toss it. And if you're gonna throw it, then it's all in the wrists. Wrists to fingers. The bag should roll off your fingers with finesse. Treat it soft. Like a nice piece of pussy."

"*Finesse*'s a big word for you, Rand," comments another bag-gage handler, a couple of inches of wet hairy ass showing above his beltline.

"Says a guy who lifts boxes of other people's T-shirts and un-derwear for a living." Randy uses his bottom lip to grab a bit of his mustache and maneuver it down between his teeth so he can dis-tractedly nibble on the tips. He remains fixated on his walkie-talkie.

Larry checks the time again, counting the minutes until he can get out of here, get home, and get dry before meeting up with Ruth. But as soon as the shift's over, he'll first call Gerry's house from the break room and get an update on their return to work. Real work. He grabs the next bag and carefully loads it onto the belt.

"Bet you wouldn't even know what to do with a nice piece of pussy, would you, Larry?" Randy spits on the cement and returns to playing with some dials on the walkie-talkie. "Can't have you hourly fools fucking up luggage along with the rest of our reputa-tions. If I didn't have to get outta here for Thanksgiving tomorrow, I'd write you up and send you packing right now."

Larry would almost prefer getting sent home. It's true that he needs every dollar he can get, but Ruth said she has something to tell him. Something important. Hopefully it's about them spend-ing Thanksgiving with Masako. He even managed to get the holi-day off, which was no small scheduling feat and included prepaying the debt with a steady week of double shifts. Tomorrow is essential, as he needs Masako to be there when he pops the question again—this time in person.

"Chop chop, dumbasses. Last plane," Randy says. "I gotta drive over the mountains to go see my goddamn in-laws. Am sure the rain's turning to snow in the passes."

There are only a few more carts. Maybe a hundred suitcases. Almost done. One way or another, Larry is going to convince Ruth of their upcoming years together. A house. Children. At least two.

Maybe four. Dogs. A cat? Caring. Love. Support. And all of that for Masako too.

He knows Masako is going to resist at first. This other fucker, Beckman, or whatever, seems like a safer choice. On paper. But Masako only knows what's on the surface. Not what is in their hearts. Larry will do whatever it takes. He can't let Ruth slip through his fingers. He needs something now. Something dramatic. Something to save the day and keep her from being forced to settle for that dentist fuck until Larry can get his job back, find something, anything real, better. Where is Gerry, anyway?

Another 727 heads their way, slow-rolling across the tarmac.

"That for the next crew?" Larry asks.

"They're not out here yet."

"What's your radio say, Rand?" asks another one of the baggage handlers.

"It's not working." He toggles with the dials. "C'mon, you piece of crap."

The 727 turns and moves to the far end of the tarmac, the part Randy calls the apron. But it's still within their crew's zone. The plane taxis a bit more and stops under some bright lights.

"I've really gotta get out of here," Larry says. "Our shift's up."

"If anyone's leaving, it's me." Randy picks up the walkie-talkie again. "Office, this is Gate Area Two, come in. Office, this is Gate Two. What's the deal with this new Northwest Orient? A 'two-seven.'"

He gets only dead air. The whole crew turns to watch as two cop cars speed down the runway; their red and blue rotating lights twirl, but the sirens are off. A moment later, two more squad cars follow behind.

"The hell?" Randy asks no one and the whole group at once. He tries different frequencies. "Everything's shut down right. Radio silence."

For a few minutes, they all watch without saying a word. Larry squints to try to make out the details. The cop cars stay at a distance from the plane, and nobody gets out of the vehicles. Larry notices that all of the window shades appear to be closed on the aircraft.

A couple of fuel trucks line up behind the cop cars, and then Randy's walkie-talkie crackles and beeps. He steps out from under his canopy and paces in the rain while talking. Larry can't hear what's being said. He continues to fixate on the plane. Nothing seems to be happening. Probably some sort of equipment issue. The landing gear looks good. The plane touched down with no obvious issues.

"How much longer?" Larry asks as Randy returns to his covered area.

"Airport's locked down. Everybody's gotta stick around for a bit longer," Randy says, winds up, and kicks a suitcase with all his might. He tries to walk it off as if he hasn't just sprained, if not broken, a couple of toes. Between shallow breaths he chokes out, "Orders. From the top."

"Which top?" a handler asks.

"The top top." Randy lights a cigarette, which even Larry knows is against the rules considering their proximity to two five-thousand-gallon fuel trucks.

"Couldn't we say I left before you told us to stay?" Larry tries to load the final suitcases off the cart and onto the belt.

"Anybody leaves before they get here, and I lose my job."

"Before who gets here?"

Just then a squad car rolls up near the gate, and an officer in full uniform with a rain cover over his trooper's hat steps out. "Which one of you's Randall?"

Randy raises a hand, his half-smoked cigarette between two fingers. As fast as his arm goes up, it comes back down.

"Let's go, then." The cop beckons Randy forward with a black leather–gloved hand. Randy limps through the rain toward the squad car and shares a couple of hushed sentences with the officer.

Larry looks over toward the plane. Still nothing new. The whole thing is probably a false alarm. Another exercise in bullshit.

The officer leans his folded arms across the top of the open squad-car door. "I'm gonna need to escort all you boys back to the break room. See who knows what about what."

"We ain't all gonna fit in your car," jokes the handler with the sagging pants.

"Especially not your fat ass. But you're all gonna walk. Even Captain Walkie-Talkie over here. Nice and slow. Together in a little group. Like schoolgirls." The officer gets in his car, turns on the ignition, and rolls down the window. "Be prepared to stick around for a while."

Larry guesses at how long it would take him to run to the fence line. He could probably get up and over the fence before the cop caught him. Especially if he ran straight behind the group of baggage handlers so the officer would have to drive around them. Or plow right through them with his squad car. But he figures he'd probably drive around. Dude doesn't want that much death on his hands. Even a cop. And especially not the night before Thanksgiving. Then Larry remembers that everyone else here knows his name and Randy probably has his address and Social Security number on record somewhere, so that might not be his smartest move. Even if the whole thing is some stupid airport emergency test. He's sure that the shit would come down on Larry Dugdale. Like it always does.

"What's this about?" one of the other handlers asks. "Can't you tell us nothing?"

Randy looks to the officer for permission. The officer gives him a curt nod.

"Seems there's some yahoo hijacker on board."

"Goddamn commies," the baggage handler says. "He gonna fly it to Cuba?"

"From what I hear, it's some stiff in a tie and sunglasses. Demanding two hundred large or he's gonna blow up the whole damn plane. Passengers and all." The officer lets the car idle and start to roll. He continues to talk out the window. "FBI's gonna want to talk to each and every one of you. Move it. Leave the bags."

The soaking wet crew soon shares the overheated break room with another baggage-handling team from the other side of the airport. Hours pass, each man taking turns to fill out paperwork with their names, addresses, and phone numbers for an unnamed pockmarked man in glasses covered in oily fingerprints who smells of old tobacco and gin. Worst of all, the man is hoarding the one telephone on his temporary desk.

Larry paces the room from corner to corner, begging to use the phone. "I swear, I'm running out of time," he argues to the pockmarked man. "You have to give me my one call."

"You're not being arrested," the man says.

"Can I go then?"

"No."

"That phone's in here because of the union. I have the right to—"

"Why are you so eager?"

"My girlfriend. Well, my almost fiancée, you see, she—"

"Right." Through his smudged glasses, the man dissects Larry. "Which one are you again?"

As the others wait, he proceeds with another round of questions for young Mr. Dugdale about recent travels, past felonies, political allegiances, his feeling about the American government, and if he had experience with special ops or ordinance training or was ever a paratrooper.

When the man digs into why Larry was active Navy but never

served in Vietnam, he refuses to take "It's a long story" as a sufficient answer.

"I was discharged."

"Honorably?"

Larry shrugs.

"Why?"

"I crashed a Jeep into a ditch."

The man pushes his glasses back up the bridge of his nose and
loosens his already-crooked tie. "That doesn't sound like a reason.
Not during wartime."

"It was my commander's Jeep."

The man still gives him an incredulous look.

"I kinda took it without asking."

"You stole it?"

"No, not stealing. Not exactly."

The man puts the phone to his ear and makes a clipped call to
a colleague about pulling records on Larry. He stubs out his smoke
in an overflowing ashtray while continuing to look Larry up and
down. "Now go sit over there in the corner of the room. Away from
the others."

The other baggage handlers are ordered to line up at the door
and are sent home. Except for Larry. And Randy, who's told to stay
for additional questions about his temporary hire, Larry Dugdale.
They are seated on opposite ends of the room, but Larry can feel
Randy's homicidal glare boring through the back of his skull.

They wipe condensation from the windows and watch as cars
and trucks come and go but never get close to the plane. A mid-
size bus parks right outside the area illuminated by the powerful
lights. A man in plain clothes with a large handheld canvas bag approaches the plane. Then others arrive, and the man shuttles what
appear to be three or four backpacks onboard. "Parachutes," says
the cop to the pockmarked man. "Look to be civilian ones."

Nothing happens for what seems like another hour. Maybe twice that. Larry picks at his nails and imagines Ruth and Beckman on their honeymoon, sitting at an outdoor restaurant with a white tablecloth in some idealized Maui utopia. Then he conjures the same image with himself interposed into the groom's spot at the table. But the face in his mind fades back to Beckman. Beckman with his nice clothes and straight, white teeth. Beckman with a giant, golden penis breaching the edge of the table like a spectacular phallic whale, pushing away the table settings and knocking over the water glasses. He tries again, but Larry can't maintain the picture with himself in the role. Only Beckman and his appendage. He feels tightness in his chest and looks down to see a littering of white bits of cuticle across the lap of his work pants. Larry wipes away the chunks of peeled skin cells, feeling disgusted with himself.

Then, with no warning, the passengers start to stream down the 727's airstairs in a single file. Larry, Randy, the pockmarked man, and the cop all press their faces against the break room windows. The passengers keep their heads slung low and forward. They are rushed by police across the tarmac to the waiting bus.

Randy, who has only smoked and sworn quietly to himself for the last couple of hours, catches new static on his walkie-talkie. He tunes in to hear intra-airport gossip starting to leak through. "We're back on," he tells the others.

Larry tries to get closer so he can hear.

"Not you, dickhead." Randy points to him. "Go back over there."

Rumors starts to fly from crews and workers at other parts of the airport.

"Dude requested a flight plan," a voice, which sounds like Sherm in maintenance, says through the walkie-talkie. "Southeast course toward Mexico. Mexico City. Airspeed was what? . . . One hundred knots."

"That's a goddamn glide," Randy mumbles. "A hundred knots is the bare minimum to not stall out the plane."

"The Supersonic would've gone almost two thousand knots. One thousand, nine hundred eighty-five to be more accurate," Larry tells them.

"Shut up, Larry. That has nothing to do with nothing," Randy shouts.

"Max ten-thousand-foot altitude. Landing gear down," crackles through the radio. "Flaps lowered fifteen degrees."

The cop says, "He's planning to jump. Bet you a thousand bucks."

"And, get this," the voice says, "cabin unpressurized with rear exit door open—airstair extended."

"Can't do that." Larry gets to his feet.

"Bet he doesn't care what Larry the part-time baggage handler thinks," Randy says. "I sure don't."

"I work with the actuators for 727 tailgates. I know it as well as anyone out there. Trust me, he doesn't want to try to take off like that. He's gonna have to open the airstairs in flight. But I bet he doesn't know how to do that," Larry says.

"There's no fucking way he can make it to Mexico City with that flight configuration," Randy adds. "Probably less than even a thousand miles. This guy doesn't know what he's doing."

"They're gonna refuel in Reno," says the pockmarked man.

"That's a ruse. He knows we'd try to nail him there," says the cop. "He'll jump first. He might even bail right outside the city limits. Shit, he might've already slipped off along with the hostages. Hid all that cash up his ass or something."

Larry thinks back to the grinding teeth and churning diarrhea of waiting to drive the getaway car when the neighborhood guys robbed those liquor stores. You never fully forget that combination of fear and exhilaration. He ventures, "Maybe the bomb isn't even real."

"Real or not, you still screwed us tonight, Larry," Randy says.

Larry looks to the clock and comes to terms with the bitter fact that he's missed the chance to talk to Ruth. She must be in bed by now, shampooed, in clean pajamas, long asleep, and convinced that Larry stood her up, once again. That's now two times too many.

He knows that he has likely messed up any chance of convincing Masako that they should spend Thanksgiving together. Or even a few minutes on the porch. Beckman is one big step closer to romancing Ruth in the Hawaiian paradise with his expensive orthodontics and shimmering dong. Larry is one step closer to spending the rest of his life sitting on the couch with his mom, eating frozen chicken pot pies and backyard potatoes while watching *Gunsmoke* and *Marcus Welby, M.D.* reruns.

They all stay at the window as the 727 taxis back to the runway and prepares for takeoff. Larry congratulates himself on the fact that the airstairs are, in fact, closed.

"Hey, asshole." Randy turns to Larry. "I'm going to need you to work tomorrow. Early."

"You approved me for the holiday off. Remember? All those extra shifts I did?"

Randy ignores him.

Larry continues, "This, what happened here tonight, it's not my fault, Randy. At all. I promise."

"We got a hole in the schedule now to fill. The call came through earlier; I'm remembering now. I think it's that guy you were asking about."

"Which guy?"

"Gerald somebody-or-other."

"Gerry?"

"Guess so. Turns out, he hung himself on the doorknob in a gas station bathroom. Imagine that? Right before his ass was supposed to come into the job this morning. Slipped my mind ... I mean, what a day today, am I right?"

Larry feels his bowels drop. Poor Gerry. He didn't have a family. No wife. No kids. No support. This job was all he had. Larry wouldn't wish this outcome on his worst enemy, but he also somehow understands why Gerry did what he did.

He cranes his neck around the edge of the window frame and can see the green right wingtip lights as the 727 climbs into the sky.

"Can I go?" Randy begs. "The highway passes're gonna get snowed out."

The pockmarked man lights another cigarette and asks the cop, "What do you think? Is Larry here our man on the ground? The crucial coconspirator?"

"Nah, look at him. He's no accomplice." The cop lights a smoke too and sets his brow in strained concentration. "I'm gonna say: Larry's much more than that. He's the mastermind. Planned the whole thing."

Larry's heartbeat stutters and his vision darkens. He wonders if Ruth will visit him in jail, or if he'll go the way of Gerry before ever getting to the slammer.

Both the pockmarked man and the police officer burst into hyperventilating, snorting laughter.

"Can I go then?" Randy begs. "Just keep Larry. Until you get his records."

"Records? What records? We were just fucking around. These hostage things can really drag, you know."

Randy puts his head between his knees and stomps his feet. Larry thinks his boss might be crying.

"Time to go, you bums." The cop points to the door. "Happy Thanksgiving."

"I don't have anywhere to go." Larry watches the plane.

"Go jerk off in your car for all I care," says the cop. "But you can't stay here."

My car, Larry thinks. My car. Ruth and I had sex in my car. Or my mom's car. And she said on the phone that she found out that she's? . . . Oh my God.

Larry sees the last flicker of the green wing lights as they disappear into the clouds. "How much you say that dude got away with again?"

TWENTY-SEVEN   *2014*

Sami, already decked out in her evening attire for the auction, wrestles the old public-school-issued wooden ladder up against the cafeteria wall.

When tonight is over, when the last cheap sauvignon blanc has been splashed down the front of a dress, the food truck departed, the final inappropriate sex joke made between parents who don't normally share basic greetings during morning drop-off, she will have rallied stakeholders, also known as the parents and Kim, to fund the STEAM lab expansion while preserving the city's longest continuously running elementary music department, saving the school, and clearing the path for it to be rechristened as Masako Hasegawa Elementary (and Stalworth STEAM Lab, but Sami can live with that). And then, a lifetime after leaving the workforce to molder as a nurse log for her children, Sami will reenter the game with Kim's help right into a position that she could never have otherwise attained. Checklist accomplished: end to end.

She takes off the upscale leather heels she bought special for tonight's event and carefully lays them near the feet of the ladder. Regular Sami wouldn't covet such material things, but it's important that she doesn't show up in her standard attire tonight and, instead, looks the part as the queen bee of the auction. After all, she'll be seated next to the guest of honor, the city's next mayor, Kimberly Stalworth, at Table One—along with a local newspaper reporter and, supposedly, photographer who will be joining Kim and Zafar.

Sami will debut herself as a person with an important future. A person to be reckoned with. A person whom Mayor Stalworth can tap for a high-profile position befitting of her talents.

She didn't exactly tell Percy that she purchased the shoes. She justified the splurge by telling herself that she would only wear the heels indoors for this one evening and could still return them within the next ten days. No harm, no foul.

After cursing herself for wearing this evening's pocketless skirt for this last decorating session, she tucks her phone into her bra. She can't have Kim or Bruce finally return her calls when she's hanging event banners from the top rungs of the ladder and have to climb back down to the floor to answer.

That reminds her, where the hell is Bruce? He had started contributing ideas, even good ideas, and helping her move things forward. And, suddenly, he's disappeared again. He barely answers his phone. She can't get a straight answer out of him. And he should have been here an hour ago.

But that's OK. Bruce is Bruce. All that really matters is that Kim and Zafar will show up tonight and use their foundation, aka Kimberley's campaign slush fund, to make a tax-deductible donation getting them within striking distance of their estimated construction goal of a hundred thousand dollars—and a reasonable showing of parental donations will put them over the top.

Or no, wait, Kim changed it yesterday to the opposite of that. She wants to see how much the school parents can raise first, and then she'll donate the difference. "Don't overcommit if you don't have to," Kim told Sami. "That's a key efficiency driver."

Either way, Sami has Kim's ace up her sleeve, and that guaranteed outcome is what's kept her going through the tumultuous organization of this undertaking. She has already prepared a giant thank-you poster for Kim, which contains a handful of education-policy messaging points dictated by Kim's PR director. Sami even remade the sign a second time to be sure that the design adhered to the campaign color palette.

She also sewed a bright-green felt STEVENSON ELEMENTARY: FULL STEAM AHEAD banner with an awkwardly rendered school Super Seagull captaining a big nineteenth-century-looking ship full of puffing smokestacks. She refolds the banner, gathers a box of plastic pushpins, and double-checks the stability of the ladder on the waxed and buffed floor.

This has been a big push. She expected it to be a significant commitment, but why couldn't she focus on being the brains behind the auction and not have to hang all of the decorations too? By herself. Or contract the thematically incongruous Inca Trail Peruvian food truck and unbox the shelf-stable hors d'oeuvres on the folding tables. Or borrow the damn tables themselves. Or oversee the procurement of every single auction item from Café Djibouti coffee cards and donated floral arrangements on up to the "Full STEAM Ahead" Alaska cruise. Or run all ticket sales and accounting.

She imagines the answer to her auction problems lies in her better learning how to share responsibilities. Yet, one cannot delegate a large amount of volunteer work for the auction if only Bruce volunteers, and he doesn't answer his phone or show up on time and, when he does, tends to have his fly down or a pants leg tucked into a sock. Therefore, the only realistic answer is to put her head down and make it happen . . . much like being a stay-at-home mother of four.

Whenever Sami wavers, she comes back to the fact that the historical misdeeds against her family must be corrected. Or mitigated. At least recognized. And she is the only one who can do this, with the impending rededication of Masako Hasegawa Elementary, the living legacy of her grandmother's life's work.

Sami repeats her practiced series of deep breaths until the urge to leave Bruce another voice message passes. This auction, this effort, it's all worth it. She'll make it worth it. And people will recognize that Sami Hasegawa-Stalworth is someone who matters—a force to be reckoned with.

She jams the box of pushpins into the elastic waist of her skirt, clenches the green felt banner between her teeth, and starts climbing the ladder.

Sami arrives at the second rung from the top of the ladder and is still too low to reach the required height. No self-respecting decorator would pin the green felt banner over the Stevenson Green section of the wall. That's obvious. It needs to go over the Stevenson White, some twelve to fifteen feet off the ground.

She makes up her mind and steps to the top rung, testing at first with one foot and a trembling thigh and then committing to balancing herself at the top. Yes, here she is. High enough. Good enough. Making it happen without anyone's help.

As soon as she stops shaking, Sami extends her arm as far as she can and presses the plastic pushpin through the green banner.

It won't go into the cafeteria wall. She tries again to no avail and wonders if the wall is paint atop cement. Or cinder blocks. Most of the building is wood, but anything's possible in these older public school buildings.

She pushes again, the plastic hourglass head of the pin denting a purple crescent into the pad of her thumb. The pin bends. Then breaks in half.

Sami falls forward, slamming her cheek and underarm against the wall. The box of pushpins ejects from the waist of her skirt, opening midair and raining down on the floor below. The ladder rocks, then wobbles, and its feet start to slide back, away from the wall. She visualizes the next moment as the ladder shoots out from under her and her stomach accelerates up through her head as her body plummets to the floor.

Guests will arrive to discover her shattered corpse with a pair of fabulous, not noticeably worn high heels in the middle of an otherwise-undecorated cafeteria.

Sami slides a few feet down the face of the wall, dragging her cheek along the Stevenson Green—and then snaps to an abrupt halt.

The banner drifts to the floor. Sami keeps herself pressed against the wall, the cool paint on her cheek until her breathing calms. Yes, cinder blocks. She can feel them through her face. As soon as she is sure that the ladder is not about to continue its slide, she looks down to see that the feet of the ladder rode over one of the shoes, devouring it under the weight. But stopping the slide.

Sami clears herself back off the wall in a slow, vertical push-up and puts her injured thumb in her mouth, applying a steady pressure between her molars. Both to nurse the pain and to stifle a barrage of swear words that she can feel working their way up her throat.

She feels her cheekbone to make sure she's not about to get a bruise for the night's big event. The results are not yet conclusive.

She climbs back down to the floor, navigates around the fallen pushpins like so many tiny land mines, and removes her new shoe from under the ladder. It's obliterated. The leather toe looks like pennies stretched on a railroad track, and the heel is ripped clean off. She could cry. But that's not going to help her make it through the evening.

Sami calls Bruce. He doesn't answer. She checks the time. She tries again. No answer. She almost leaves an angry, scolding message but focuses on Kim and the fact that she will put her hefty thumb on the money scale. All will be OK. She will try Bruce again in five. And, if not, she'll try his wife.

She takes a photo of the cafeteria table closest to the makeshift stage. Table One. With its plastic flowers and a construction paper cutout of a steamship. She adds the caption: *Our table for tonight! Looking forward to it, sis!!!* and then thinks better of sending it. Kim can't sit at a cafeteria table made for elementary school students. Sami is going to have to do better.

While thinking on it, Sami straightens the ladder and wedges the broken heel back under its right foot. She considers for a moment and then shoves the other shoe under the left side. May as well get some good use out of them before they head to the landfill. She locates duct tape in the cafeteria's kitchen, takes the green banner in her teeth, and starts to climb the ladder again.

TWENTY-EIGHT   *2014*

Bruce nears the school cafeteria door, sweat collecting under his Sonics hat. He knows he's late for the auction setup. He gets it. Sami already called and texted him to the point that he is no longer checking his phone. He is well aware. Aware that he wasn't able to sleep last night. That he sat in the apartment thinking through a million and one ways that he could wriggle out of the auction. Out of the PTA. Sabotage his own portable plan to save his weed business. He's thought through a few different forms of subterfuge. But he still can't figure how to do it without letting down Wren. And, for that matter, Sierra.

Fuck, it's all too much. How did this become so damn stressful? Helping out with the PTA auction was supposed to be a reason to get out of his furniture-less apartment. To better facilitate and improve Sierra's school experience in a demonstrable way. And, in the process, prove some things to Wren. So many things to Wren.

But now there are other considerations. Between this and other things that he needs to prove to Wren. And to the whole world. Mutual exclusions. Things that must be weighed and considered.

And Sami wants everything from him: right now. Suddenly, he is back in the well-worn territory of undershooting expectations. Outsize ones at that. It's as if Sami plagiarized Bruce and Wren's marital script, adapting the tragic romance into their own grinding procedural.

He tries to bend his ruminations toward his usual gripes about the ascendancy of technology, quantitative reasoning, data-driven decision-making, and the neoliberal profit motive. None of this is going anywhere good. Not here in this city. Nowhere. It's stripping all of the joy and creativity out of life, but to what end? An illusion of greater control over results and vaster wealth for the soulless number crunchers? It's enough to make him wish he hadn't lived past twenty-five. He's pretty sure that the world stopped improving in any demonstrable way at some point in the mid-'90s anyway.

As he shifts his cane to his left hand so he can pull open the cafeteria door, the stray hairs in Bruce's ears and along his neckline go rigid, attuning themselves to the footfalls of work boots sprinting across the pavement behind him. He hears the contours of a man's shouts between labored breaths.

A shot of bright white electricity ripples down Bruce's spine. Adrenaline he hasn't tasted since well before his fiftieth. Really since the herniated discs. The cortisone shots. The vertebral fusion.

He lets go of the door handle and spins around to locate Sierra, trailing him by a couple of paces. A mass of tangled hair bouncing as she skips. He does a quick take of the school entrance and surrounding brick exterior, evaluating escape routes and potential dead ends.

"You? Hey," the man yells, slowing to a jog, but well inside Bruce's comfort zone. Bruce grips the cane, both a sign of his vulnerability and a potential delivery mechanism for blunt force trauma.

Bruce pulls Sierra toward him to maximize the gap and jumps diagonally across her to better face whatever comes next. It must be said that he has an immediate sense of shame about the inelegance of his flat-footed landing.

"Oh, man. Shoot. Scared ya, huh?" The man comes to a stop and rests his hands on his knees, trying to catch his breath. He wears heavy canvas overalls and a craft beer–brand hoodie strewn with light-colored dog fur. He has expansive shoulders, a long goatee without a mustache, and a mouth of dull, wandering teeth. He holds a couple of pages of paper in his left fist. One of those yellow triplicate sheets. "You, uh, doing a little babysitting today, Pops?"

The babysitting question is one for which Bruce has never determined a proper answer, at least one that doesn't sound defensive, sad, or overly earnest. He should have worked out the perfect, cutting response by now. He had meant to come up with one, but as Wren says, follow-through is not his forte.

He feels his heart skipping every other beat and has to check that his hands aren't fluttering. "The heck do you want, dude?"

"I went to the wrong—is this door open?" The man, or kid, as Bruce revises, waves the triplicate papers and uses his head to nod to two silver beer kegs and a hand truck down the street. "You know where the PTA ladies're at?"

Bruce tells him he'll sign the paperwork. He also looks for an opportunity to explain that he knows his way around a keg. When he was a young buck living the life up in the mountains, he was rumored to hold the regional record for the longest uninterrupted keg stand. He developed a proprietary trick where he used the tip of his tongue to regulate the flow of the beer up and over the back of his palate, so he never choked on the carbonation. These diminished days, he can't really drink beer because it makes him congested.

"Gotta be a PTA signature," the delivery guy says and puts his index finger on the papers. "Event hosts. State Liquor Board rules."

"Yeah, I'm helping out with the auction. A bit. As like part of the PTA."

"You're in the PTA?" the delivery guy surveys Bruce from his Sonics hat and ponytail down to his cargo shorts, duct-taped sport sandals, unruly toenails, and back.

"Just as a . . ." Bruce can't be sure, but it seems like the guy is about to laugh at him. He wants to explain all of the layers of reasons that have brought him to this point but can't muster the motivation and trails off.

The man gives Bruce a shoulder slap, which he feels resonate into L4 and L5, but he tries not to wince. "Least I won't have to teach another housewife how to tap a keg. Right, dude?"

Bruce is buoyed that the man has recognized him as a kindred spirit, if not as a former party legend. This should indicate that their interaction has already found its bottom and is on the rebound.

"By the way"—Bruce remembers what he wants to say—"it's called parenting, not babysitting. And a father can parent just as much. Should parent just as much. It's not for special occasions. That's, like, our duty. As fathers."

His phone starts buzzing again in his pocket. He's sure it's Sami. He doesn't care if she's running the auction or has been head of the PTA for millennia or whatever. This is like the hundredth time in the last few hours, not that he's counting.

The delivery guy offers the papers to Bruce and pats the numerous pockets in his overalls until he finds a ballpoint. "I get it . . . the babysitting thing. I got three rug rats myself, brother. It's that, I thought . . ."

"Thought what?" Bruce braces his hip against the cane and grabs the papers and pen. He scans for the signature line, but his phone keeps ringing. "Hold on." He curses under his breath and answers the phone.

"You see the email?" It's obviously Mel. Bruce knows the voice from a mile off. But there's something different. He sounds like the Old Mel. Wild. Hyped. Ecstatic.

"You OK?" Bruce asks.

"I'm more than OK. I feel like my uncles at Christmas open bar."

"You been drinking?"

"Don't worry about me. You see the email?"

"What email?"

"Check your email. Now." Mel hollers like he's riding bareback in a rodeo, hanging on for dear life. "Loose Fuckin' Bruce, that's what I'm sayin', Loose Fuckin' Bruce. The SuperChronics live again. You did it, man."

"I'm gonna call you right back, Mel." Bruce switches off his phone and turns back to the delivery guy. "You were saying?"

"I was thinking—sorry, but you're a bit—aren't you in, like, your forties?"

"Something like that."

"Don't take this the wrong way." The man lets his laugh go and motions his head toward Sierra. "I, I thought you're her gramps."

Bruce stares at the delivery guy for a moment without answering or finding a grain of comedic value in his misunderstanding. He hands the paperwork back to the man and follows it with a little pat on the chest. "Door's straight ahead. Get it signed inside. I got other business to attend to."

Bruce taps Sierra on the shoulder and starts walking back toward the Westy across the street by the rock. "Change of plans." He moves as quickly as he can on the cane. They need to get out of here before Sami spots him.

He tries not to admit it to himself, but he can already feel that his clumsy jump re-aggravated his spine. Normally he'd be looking at numerous days of bed rest, painkillers, and self-pity. But the good news blasts right through it all.

He unlocks the door to the Westy and starts his laborious process of climbing in right as Wren's Camry pulls into the spot next to him. Shit. "Hey. Great timing. We came out to meet you," he says as he relocks the van door and pockets the key.

"Sami called me," Wren says. "Said she couldn't get ahold of you or something?"

"No, no. All under control. Let's all go inside."

TWENTY-NINE   *1958*

Masako peeks through the small wired-glass window in the classroom door and sees nothing and no one in the hallway. She opens the door and slides the homemade wooden wedge under its base. It's Wednesday. The second Wednesday of the month. This should be the day. She is sure of it.

"You have the house key?" she double-checks with Ruth, who slouches in her chair, a book bag hanging from one shoulder.

"We're the only family I know who locks their doors during the day," her fifth-grade daughter says.

"Here." She takes the house key off of her key ring and presses it into Ruth's palm. Masako looks over her daughter's shoulder to see out into the hallway again. Nothing. But she thinks she might hear the distant whirring sound of the floor buffer. Maybe not. She could be imagining things. "Off you go. See you after I finish closing up my room."

"I can stay and help."

"No, go do your homework."

"I don't have any homework."

"Practice your violin then. How do you expect to become proficient, if not good, when you never practice on your own volition?"

"Yes, *Okasan*." Ruth walks off, her shoulders still rounded. Masako is concerned about Ruth's overall lethargy. She will take notes. Keep a journal to share with the doctors and the specialists when she next sees them. Thank God for the health insurance she receives as a state employee. She takes a quick moment to appreciate that it makes all of this possible.

But she is distracted by the sound in the hallway. Yes, the floor buffer. For sure now. She wants to stick her head out and confirm that it's him, but she also doesn't want to be too forward.

As he gets closer, Masako takes a quick pass at the beginning of Dvorak's Symphony No. 9 on her violin. The "New World" one, with its Native American influences and appealing melodies.

"That's beautiful," a voice says from the hallway.

She looks up, as casually as possible, to see Archie pushing the swing machine. Masako puts down the violin and stands. "Come in, I'll show you."

Archie turns off the buffer and starts to step into the room but hesitates. "Last time, that teacher . . ."

"I explained the situation to the principal. All a big misunderstanding. Come in please. I insist."

Masako gives Archie a hug. Something she'd been thinking of since she last saw him. It's fleeting as he rapidly backs off, she hopes because he is nervous and not because he is displeased to see her. She wants to hold on longer. She smells the floor wax on his skin and feels a light perspiration of hard work when her hand touches the back of his forearm. "You look dressed up today."

He looks down at his maroon, broad-collared shirt and thanks her for the compliment. "We have a gig right after my shift. All in matching colors, you know. Trying to give the band more of a style. A feel."

"I'm sure it'll be great." She is not sure what else to say. She'd like to go to the show but realizes that is out of the question for reasons on top of reasons.

"The music . . . what you were playing. Oh boy. That was really something," he says. "Such complexity. I've never played something like that. Where do you even start?"

"I'd love to show you. Do you have a decade to practice? Give or take."

"For you, yes. But I only have about five minutes today before I have to get back to making that hallway floor shine like glass."

She hands him the sheet music. "Take this with you. It's interesting to see what all goes into it. We can talk about it next time I see you."

He thanks her and beams.

"Fold it and put it in your pocket to take home."

"Oh no, I couldn't fold that. I want to keep it the way you gave it to me. Such a special piece of music and all."

"Just do it. You can't work while holding it, right?"

"I'll run out and put it in my car. Nice and safe. And then I can grab some special music for you too. We'll call it a swap."

"I don't know." Masako feels prickly heat flushing across her face. "I'm not very familiar with popular music. Plus, you don't have much time."

"It's OK. I was already planning to give it to you, when the time was right. I can be back in two minutes. One minute. I'll run."

She goes to say no, but he's already gone. He wasn't exaggerating about running. She watches him through the classroom window in a sprint out to his work van by the rock. He retrieves the sheet music he was looking for in no time and slams closed the sliding door, which spooks a handful of gulls atop the boulder.

As the gulls spin upward, one squirts out a long ribbon of hot white bird shit that streams downward, splashing Archie right across the shoulder. He stops running and turns around.

Even from the classroom, Masako can see white stain on his maroon shirt.

Archie returns to his van and tries to clean himself with rag.

Don't do it, she says to herself. You'll smear it. He drapes a light jacket over his shoulders and resumes his sprint back to the classroom.

He reenters the room and tries to hand Masako the music. She takes it, graciously, but before even reading it says, "Please, let me wash that for you, Mr. Barrett."

"Archie, please." He hesitates. "Wash what?"

"I saw through the window." She nods toward the small, porcelain drinking fountain in the corner. "I've helped kids wash off worse between classes. You'd be amazed by how many girls menstruate for their first time at school or the number of boys who still aren't properly bathroom trained."

"But we only have a few minutes."

"Now. Please." She beckons for the shirt. "Here, I'll close the door if it makes you more comfortable." As it doesn't lock from the inside, she jams the wedge back under the closed door as hard as she can.

He unbuttons and removes his maroon shirt to reveal a clingy white tank top undershirt. She does her best to stay fixed on the soiled outer shirt as he hands it to her. But Masako can't help but notice the sharp lines of definition between the muscles in his arms and shoulders. She allows her imagination to conjure ideas of the lines bisecting the muscles down his abdomen and between his chest and torso. Sure, she is most attracted to him as a musician. But as a former farm laborer herself, she appreciates the effect of all that physical work. She likes a man who takes care of himself. A man who isn't a smoker or drinker and can see the physical potential within himself.

She pinches and folds the fabric of the maroon shirt on either side of the spot of impact and wets it under the trickle of the drinking fountain. "There is a bar of soap in my bottom desk drawer. Can you grab it for me?"

As he gets the soap she says, "Tell me about the music, before we're out of time."

He hands her the soap, which she massages into the stain. He then holds up the sheet music so she can read it.

"'Confession Blues'?"

"This is an original. I played it with Ray Charles at the Rocking Chair. See it's all in braille here?" He runs his finger along the raised bumps. "See my handwritten notes all along the side here? Went on to be his first hit. Have it. It's a gift."

"I couldn't. How will you play it again?"

"Ray played it blind, so I'm sure I'll manage. Keep it. I insist." He sets the music on her desk along with a second sheet. "There's another one I included that I just played with this kid and his band. They didn't really know how to write music, so I helped them out. It's rough but there's something special there. Something different."

"What's the name of the band?"

He glances quickly at the sheet again. "The Velvetones."

As she rubs together the two folded parts of the shirt, she thinks about letting Archie know that she has never heard of the Velvetones and only heard of Ray Charles from him. She also wants to dance around the other big issue on her mind but has never been good at holding back or avoiding her true thoughts. "Sorry if this is too forward, Mr. Barrett . . ."

"Archie."

"OK, sorry if this is too forward, Archie, but what happened to your wife?"

He stands up straighter. "She became very sad after our son was born. Not sad about Shawn so much as sad about the whole world and her place in it. It was all too hard for her to take."

"I'm so sorry." She wishes she could hug him more and give him the comfort he needs. But he stands at an appropriate, if not disproportionate, distance from her, overcompensating for his semi-clothed state.

"Unfortunately, some of us simply aren't equipped to round the big corners that life presents." He buries his hands in his pockets and rotates his shoulders forward, locking out his arms to obscure his exposed chest. "And your husband, Mrs. Hasegawa? If it's not too forward."

"Masako. But you can call me Macy like the others do."

"I like Masako."

She finishes washing the shirt and starts waving it in the air for a quick dry. "An accident, unfortunately." She walks the shirt over to him to show off her handiwork. "Still wet. But it'll be good by the time of your gig."

"What kind of accident?"

"More of a cosmic accident really. He had finally straightened out his life when—"

"Hey," a voice shouts through the classroom's exterior window.

Archie grabs the shirt out of Masako's hands and covers himself with it as much as he can. They both turn toward the voice.

"What is this?" Bev Donahoe, the class monitor, raps on the window. The math teacher, Al Schneider, stands right behind her in the landscaped bushes. "Whatever this is, it's not OK."

"Why are you standing in the bushes?" Masako asks.

"We're coming right over. Don't you dare go anywhere." Bev marches off.

Moments later they are pounding at the classroom door. Al presses his hysterical, reddened face to the wired-glass door window and shouts, "Why is this locked? This is against the Stevenson code of conduct."

Masako picks up the sheet music off of her desk and waits for Archie to get fully dressed. She then kicks out the doorstop. "This is not what you think. He was just showing me—"

The door swings open, and Al grabs the music from Masako's hand. "'Confession' what? 'Blues'? I sincerely hope you're not planning to teach this, this garbage, to our children."

Archie starts, "Excuse me, but—"

Masako cuts him off. "Please. This is my fault."

"Did he threaten you, Macy?" Al hounds her.

"No, I—"

Bev turns her back to Archie and presses herself close to Masako's face. "We all hoped you'd actually attempt to fit in here, Macy."

"I'm going to have to report you to the principal. Again," adds Al. "There're no third chances around here."

"Libby and I really pulled for you, Macy," Bev says. "But this is too much. Way too much."

"This is a misunderstanding. I was—she had nothing to do with this," Archie says and moves toward the door. "I'll be going. This my fault. Please leave her alone."

Al steps out of his way but makes a spectacle of wadding up the Ray Charles sheet music. He's about to destroy the second one when Archie snatches it out of Al's hand.

On his way out into the hallway, Archie attempts one last glance at Masako. But she stays focused on her own feet. He grabs the floor buffer and starts pushing as fast as he can.

"Leave it. You're done here. You can count on that," Al shouts after Archie.

Once they hear Archie's footsteps disappear, Bev folds her arms across her chest and says, "We're gonna give you one last chance, Macy. Give us one good reason we shouldn't go straight to the principal."

"Please." Masako takes everything she feels and rams it down into the iron casket that holds so many of her other emotions and dreams from her youth. "I can change. I will change. I need this job. For my daughter. I'll be what you need me to be. Please."

THIRTY   *1971*

Ruth stirs in her bed. She is not sure why. Maybe she heard something. Maybe it's because the sun is coming up. Either way, she'll have to be up soon for church's Thanksgiving event.

It hasn't been a restful sleep. She can't be sure she was ever really asleep at all. She might have been lying here and willing herself out of consciousness with indeterminate results.

She cried for much of the evening yesterday. And at a few other points during the night. Larry promised. He promised her. Right to her face. And he did it again. He stood her up. Without so much as a call or explanation.

Ruth has thought through every scenario. Every permutation. Either he is dead. Killed in an unfortunate accident like her father. Which is possible but unlikely. But possible. Or he must know that Ruth is pregnant and, like expecting fathers since the dawn of humanity, freaked out and ran away. Her sweet, well-intentioned, hapless Larry Dugdale with his dark eyes, seagull tattoos, rock band T-shirts, and sad attempt at a mustache. She has decided, after much consideration, that the latter scenario is much more probable. In fact, in must be what happened.

He said he was going to marry her. Or wanted to marry her. She repeats it to herself. She heard it right out of his mouth when he called from work. Larry was going to ask her mother. She wonders if she'd imagined that. Or twisted his words to convince herself that she was loved and desired. No, he said it. For sure.

She almost understands him crumbling before the specter of impending fatherhood and all that it entails. Ruth feels the pressure herself. Larry never came out and said it to her directly, but she's pretty sure he lost his job. She'd even asked him, and he'd been evasive with "Trust me, I'm figuring some stuff out" and "I'll have good news to tell you soon."

She knows that, in an ideal world, Larry wants to be with her. But this is not an ideal world. Far from it.

And now she is going to have to spend Thanksgiving with her mother and start the day with a church visit with Beckham and company. To make matters considerably worse, she and Beckham are to meet privately with Reverend Saito. Masako assures Ruth that it's just a formality, a talk that the Reverend likes to give to all potential young couples in the church. Ruth doesn't know who arranged the meeting, but it's a good bet that it was Beckham's aunt or the aunt in collusion with her own mother.

Still lying on her back in bed, Ruth places a flat palm on her lower abdomen. She holds the hand in place, waiting for a sign, a kick, something. Nothing happens, but she can feel that her body is changing. A heat. Or growing firmness. Slight discomfort to the touch. She's not sure. But considering Ruth's relative slenderness (although not as slender as her mom might desire), she imagines she's days away from starting to show the earliest hints of her pregnancy. It's still too soon to be obvious to others. But she can see it in the intangibles. And if she can see it herself, she knows that Masako won't be far behind. She never is.

Ruth is startled by a blunt thud at the window. Yes, that was exactly what awoke her before. She springs to her knees and peers through the glass to catch a glimpse of a man sprinting back behind the rock. With some focused squinting, she can make out the tips of battered sneakers as the man crouches for cover. She knows it's him.

Ruth slides open the window a few inches. Slowly, so as to not disturb her mother in the adjacent room. She puts her face to the window and looks again for the shoes. She can't yell to him, but perhaps she can give him a signal. Something with her hands. Or she could mouth words to him. But the tips of the sneakers are gone.

As she closes the window, she sees a couple of pine cones on the exterior sill. One has off-white lined stationery secured around it with a yellow rubber band. She feeds her right arm out the open window and reaches as far as she can along the sill. She touches the edge of the paper-covered pine cone with her fingertips and stretches every joint in her arm to try to get a couple of her fingers around it. Ruth wonders how much a person can lengthen their appendages through sheer will. She gets a finger on it, but the pine cone slides forward and off the sill.

Crap, Ruth curses to herself, batting away any sense of reflexive guilt. She doesn't have the angle to see where the pine cone fell, but it must be in her mom's garden below. There is no way she can go downstairs and out the door without her mother hearing it. Instead, Ruth acts like all is normal. She takes a leisurely shower, stabilizes her morning sickness, and gets dressed for church.

Ruth waits to get down to the kitchen until her mother has woken up and finished eating her hard-boiled egg. She finds Masako with her head out the window, looking down into the garden below.

"Mom?" Ruth channels her fear into a tone of urgency.

"What?" Masako pulls her head back through the windows. Her curlers still in. "What's the matter?"

"It's—we've gotta go, they'll be here soon. You still have . . ." Unable to locate the noun during one of her spells of brain fog, she waves her hand in a circular motion in front of her mother's head.

"I've got lots of practice. I can get them out fast." Masako leans back out the window and shouts something out it.

"What are you doing?"

"Damn gulls in my garden." Masako backs out of the window and turns to look at Ruth. "And you? What are you doing? Aren't you going to eat any breakfast? And why do you have your coat on already?"

Ruth stares downward to evaluate her attire. "Just getting ready for church. Don't want to be late."

"I guess there's a first time for everything." Masako turns back to the window. "I'm going to run out there quick."

"No. Why?"

"Since when do you care about my garden? You're the girl who boasts of having a black thumb."

"I've got it. I'll do it for you. You go get ready."

Masako cocks her head to the side and evaluates her daughter with a hard face of mounting incredulity.

"I've already got my coat on." Ruth moves toward the door. "And also, I want to give Beckham and his aunt a . . . a squash. You have squash out there, right? You know, very fall. Autumnal. For Thanksgiving."

"I can do a better job than you at picking good ones."

"It's about the thought. The intention. I want it to come from me."

"Good to see you coming around." Masako nods, her cheeks and brow line softening. "They should be here in a few minutes. I'll meet you up front."

Ruth crouches over the garden and selects the ugliest, wartiest gourd for her favorite aunt. This is my intention you, you—bitch, she says to herself and feels a cathartic glow. Ruth thinks she could get used to this. *Bitch*—she tries it again.

While down in a squat, she locates the paper-wrapped pine cone among the vines and slips it into her coat pocket. As she carries the squash around to the front of the house, she reaches into the pocket and removes the rubber band.

Ruth sees the gray BMW pulling to a stop in front of the house. Beckham is driving with his hands firmly planted at ten and two. He does a proper over-shoulder head check while parallel parking.

She opens the note in her palm and looks down at it.

> *Dear Ruth,*
> *Meet me at the rock at midnight*
> *December 1st*
> *We will leave together*
> *Get married*
> *In Maui*
> *(or wherever you want)*
> *Trust me*
> *Please*
> *Trust me*
> *I will do whatever it takes*
> *I mean it*
> *I love you*
> *and our baby*
> > *Always & forever,*
> > *Larry*

Ruth jams the paper back into her pocket as Beckham exits the vehicle to present her with a single rose in cellophane. He greets her with an uninspired "Good morning."

She pushes the lumpy squash in his direction. "For your aunt. But you can share it, if you want."

There is little conversation during the ride to church. Masako tosses mindless small talk and unanswered questions into the void. Ruth notices how Beckham seems to be trying to strangle the steering wheel with flexed, white knuckles and the sudden, total lack of engagement between the aunt and her now-sullen nephew.

They all sit together in a row of four at the Thanksgiving service. Reverend Saito preaches from his wheelchair. He goes on and on. Something about forgiveness and perseverance. Ruth thinks it has a very *issei* tone. All of that *gaman* sense of enduring the unbearable with patience and dignity, stuff that her mother had absorbed from her own parents and tried so hard to pass along to her. Truth be told, Ruth is barely listening.

First and foremost, she's hoping that Dr. Yamamoto, who sits with his wife a few rows up and to the left, doesn't notice her or feel the need to make awkward small talk with her or her mom after the service. But she's also thinking about Larry. About his hand running down her side, over her hip, and along her thigh. December 1. At midnight. Larry is right: She can pull the rip cord on all of this. This church. Beckham. This life. Her mother's expectations. All of it. Just like that. She's an adult. An independent person. A woman with her own ideas and dreams.

But, she reminds herself, Larry stood her up again to meet with her and her mom. How can she really trust that he'll be at the rock? This has happened more than once.

She goes back and forth until the service wraps up. Church-goers file down the stairs to the basement for another potlatch.

Beckham's aunt reminds Ruth of her and Beckham's meeting with the Reverend. As they walk back toward the church offices, the aunt follows.

Beckham gives her a harsh look, but she continues behind them. He stops, turns, and says, "No."

She puts a hand to her chest. "But Beckham?"

"Please go eat. I'll see you after."

She moves toward the basement stairs, stumbling forward on her short legs in a dejected shuffle.

Ruth and Beckham enter the Reverend's office to find Saito in his wheelchair behind the desk. "Come in." He beckons and then signals for Beckham to close the door behind him. "Take a seat, please."

As they sit down in the two chairs facing the desk, Ruth sees Dr. Yamamoto standing motionless a few feet behind the Reverend's shoulder. Stomach acid rushes up her throat.

"Dr. Yamamoto and I thought we could be of some service." Saito looks beyond the young people toward some point on the wall above the office door. Ruth wonders how good his vision is these days anyway. "Often, a big challenge requires a unified response."

Yamamoto takes a few rigid steps forward so that he is flush with the Reverend. "Usually, I discuss this kind of stuff at my practice. But I thought that we could bring together a medical and spiritual component here. That is really the only way to heal the whole person."

Ruth turns to Beckham and the words spill from her mouth, "Listen, I'm, um, you're not the uh—"

"Please, Ruth. We'll handle this," the Reverend interrupts her. "There are times in life when the individual must let the community catch them and break their fall. Not everyone has this privilege. Ruth, we know you are a modern woman. A new generation. But there are also times when elders know best. Please, listen with open hearts and minds."

Dr. Yamamoto starts again. "Beckham, as you might have assumed or you two might have discussed, Ruth is pregnant."

Beckham doesn't answer. He looks to Ruth as if he is trying to swallow. Then he opens his mouth, but no words come out.

"No need to explain the obvious, son," Dr. Yamamoto says. "We are all family here."

Although Beckham stays fixated on the Reverend, Ruth can feel the young dentist's radiating sense of dread nipping at her skin.

"Of course, we don't encourage these things. Or officially condone them. But they do happen, young man," Saito says, leaning forward in his chair. "This shall not be shared outside of this room. But Dr. Yamamoto here had a child out of wedlock during the war. Shore leave in Hawaii. With a *haole*. A pretty darn good-looking *haole*, at that. But still a *haole*. And what they used to call 'not the marrying type.'"

The two old men share a quick, nearly lascivious laugh that reinvigorates Ruth's nausea. The Reverend continues, "But you can do the right thing, son. I've counseled your aunt for a long time about you not expressing interest in viable brides. About spending all your free time with that colleague of yours. I explained to her that some young men simply go through these fleeting phases."

"I told you . . ." Beckham stammers. "We were—we had a lot to study. Dentistry stuff."

"We all have phases. Not totally unlike when young Private Yamamoto was fornicating with white women of questionable repute. We all make missteps. I told your aunt that when it came time to marry and have children and become an upstanding member of your community, that you would do the right thing. That you would grow out of it. And, in the end, your aunt had nothing to worry about with you. Am I correct, Mr. Beckham Wong? I'm sorry, Dr. Beckham Wong, DDS."

Beckham crumbles in on himself while somehow still maintaining upright posture.

"But there's another issue, Ruth. There's no easy way to tell you this," Yamamoto downshifts to a more somber, professional tone, "but you have leukemia."

The floor drops out from under Ruth. She watches her own life, a movie on a screen, from afar.

"Together, you two can beat it," Yamamoto says and then puts his hand on the Reverend's shoulder. "As a community, we will beat it together."

"Leukemia?" she says, or tries to say, as she careens into the abyss below.

"I did a little poking around and tracked down some records. Turns out your old pediatrician was a med school buddy of mine. Both attended on the G.I. Bill. Anyway, you've been in remission for a long time. But you were first diagnosed at four."

Ruth falls faster and faster. Her childhood flipping by in front of her eyes.

"Will she be able to have the baby?" Beckham asks.

"There will be some very hard decisions to make. But remission is possible. Again." Yamamoto's hand quivers on the Reverend's shoulder. "Ruth. Did you not know about this?"

Ruth has no idea where to start. She reaches toward words in some place above and out of her sight.

He adds, "We could have figured this out a lot faster had you told me about your father's history of leukemia."

"Accident," she finally finds her tongue. "He died in an accident."

"Not according to your medical history. Or his death certificate, for that matter."

The best she can do is slowly shake her head.

"I'm going to need to have a word with Mrs. Hasegawa about all of that. Leukemia isn't often hereditary, but there's been some interesting genetic research coming out in the last couple of years. I'm going to bet you have Li-Fraumeni syndrome, which would increase your risk. Fascinating stuff, actually."

Ruth reaches terminal velocity where she feels as if she is floating, seemingly no longer subjected to the rules of gravity.

The Reverend leans across the desk and places a hand atop Beckham's hand. He nods for Ruth to give him her hand too. When she doesn't respond, Beckham grabs her hand and passes it to the Reverend. She doesn't resist. The arm is not her own. This body is not her own. Nor is this life.

Saito says, "The doctor and I discussed this, at length, and feel that the best course of action is for you, Beckham, to do what we all know you need to do."

"Which is?" Beckham asks and looks furtively at Ruth, still without turning his head.

The Reverend places Ruth's hand atop Beckham's and caps them both with his own veined and liver-spotted hands. "The time is now."

THIRTY-ONE   *1971*

Larry waits for the cleaners to gather their supplies and wheel their cart and vacuums off the plane. Blood throbs in his Adam's apple as he makes his way down the aisle and then slips Gerry's old leather briefcase under seat 29F. He spins around in his best Navy-trained about-face and starts back up the aisle to exit the plane. Less than five minutes total. Ahead of schedule.

As he's leaving, Larry catches the gleam of the case's chrome buckle in the corner of his eye. He can't be sure if it's an actual reflection or his imagination, but he decides that he needs to inspect the briefcase one last time. Make sure he grabbed the right one or that it looks legitimate inside or whatever. Larry crouches down and cracks it open. Yes. All is still in order. The paper towel rolls painted red, with a nice gloss to really make the color pop. A handful of insulated wires connected to nothing. A big (dead) twelve-volt battery. His mom's alarm clock. She never gets up on time for anything anyway.

He found the battery and wires in a junk pile at the empty lot down the street from his house. The hardest thing to find was the paper towel rolls. He and his mom don't have such disposable extravagances at home, so he had to liberate them from the restroom at the airport and meticulously roll out the paper and remove the center tube. He was not one to waste the paper towels, so he re-rolled the spools as best as he could and jammed them into the dispenser, even though they could no longer be extracted in any reasonable fashion.

Once he has triple-checked his handiwork, Larry jogs back to the front of the plane—pausing at the door to the jet bridge. Still only five minutes. Five and a half. He's OK. He just has to be sure to keep everything else on time.

Fighting every impulse in his body to sprint off the plane, Larry makes sure that no one is coming down the gangway. The stopwatch ticks louder and louder in his brain. He has a little more than a half an hour to do all that must be done and get his ass back here to seat 29F.

The jet bridge is clear, so he moves briskly off the plane, across the initial few yards of the hallway, and out the side door, back down to the tarmac below. Already dressed in his work coveralls, he blends right back into the baggage-handler work crew below the plane.

"Where the hell were you?" Randy shouts at him.

Larry puckers his lips, gently pinches the tip of his coverall's fly between an index finger and thumb, and arches his back in what he considers to be the universal sign for male urination.

"C'mon, Lar," Randy scolds. "First shift's almost up. Get to it."

As soon as the final suitcases are loaded into the hold, Larry grabs his oversize canvas duffel that he'd held on to from his Navy days and punches out his time card. Rather than exiting to the employee parking lot, he doubles back into the airport, the bag slung over his shoulder. He goes into the men's room, pumps a small, frothy mound of liquid hand soap into his palm, and locks himself in the bathroom stall.

Without using a mirror, he lathers his face and makes quick, somewhat painful work of his mustache with a plastic safety razor. Larry removes his coveralls to reveal his best Sunday attire below: his grandfather's ill-fitting suit jacket, pants that end well above his ankles, and a clip-on tie. He carefully folds his coveralls and stuffs them into the duffel bag.

Fourteen minutes. He has to move faster.

Larry puts on a baseball hat. A green one for the new Super-Sonics basketball team. A baseball basketball hat, he laughs to himself. What will they come up with next? And he tucks the longer back of his hair up into it and puts on a pair of black Wayfarer sunglasses. Or ones that look like Wayfarers that he bought at the gas station.

He stowed the briefcase on the plane because he's done his research and knows that since the Thanksgiving eve incident, they are installing a magnetometer at the airport. None of the other baggage handlers knows if it's operational yet or not, but he studied up a bit on the technology. They've been used for years to check that there're no pieces of metal, either spikes or broken pieces of saw blade, in logs before they get milled into lumber. This civilian version they've been talking about is a four- or five-foot-long tunnel, and they're suggesting making all air travelers walk through these things now.

He looks around and doesn't see anything. Truth be told, he can't see that well out of the scratched sunglass lenses. Larry's pleased to find no line at the check-in desk. A coiffured blond woman in a red airline uniform with an off-center, tiny hat greets him. "Hello, sir. Do you have a reservation?"

"I got one." He digs into his pocket and passes her the folded ticket, pleased with himself that he planned ahead.

She accepts the paper and reads it slowly and methodically, a bit too slowly and methodically for his taste and time pressure. "Welcome, Mr. Carnahan."

"Gerry, please." Larry stands in profile to her and obsessively kneads his brow below the lowered brim of his green hat.

"Flying to Portland today, Gerry?"

He grunts a vague confirmation.

"The plane is loading. You're cutting it close. Do you have a bag to check?"

He shakes his head no. His impulse is to engage her with a joke about not trusting the baggage handlers but opts to forego any non-essential banter.

"Good. Phew, I'll radio ahead. But you need to run."

He turns and starts to head toward the gate.

"Wait, Mr. Carnahan. Come back."

He feels his heart inside his Adam's apple again. The world slows. Does he stop? Make a break for it? He decides to pretend that he didn't hear her and keep moving. Cocking his head slightly, he sees her say something to the woman next to her and then start to move toward him, walking faster and faster until she exits out from behind the counter. He picks up his pace. She increases to a sort of loping jog in her high heels.

Fuck. Where did he go wrong? He thought he'd been so careful. Planned so well in advance. Why is he always thwarted before he can accomplish anything? It's always the same. He considers bolting out the front door of the airport. He can still abandon this plan. There's nothing illegal about buying a ticket and not using it. But, for God's sake, he's never even flown in a plane before and is using every cell in his being to not face that overwhelming, ass-puckering, penis-shriveling terror.

Although, if all works out according to plan, he will never even get off the ground.

"Mr. Carnahan. Please stop," she yells after him. A few passersby around him look at the shouting woman and then at him, the one person in her direct path.

He decides that it's better to try to talk his way out of it rather than let her chase him. He turns to face her.

"You forgot . . ." She pants. "You forgot your ticket." She hands him the piece of paper with a shaky hand and then leans down to adjust her nylon on a smarting foot. "Seat 29F. Now: run. Fast."

He lights his last cigarette and smokes it hands-free while sprinting through the terminal. His tension starts to ease. He should have planned better for smokes. Larry dealt with the emotional side of this the only way he knew: to pretend it wasn't happening.

To his surprise, there is no magnetometer tunnel to pass through. There is a single sleepy officer in his dark blue uniform sitting on a stool in the hallway. Larry reasons that if the airport and airlines and America's formerly Preeminent Aerospace Company don't learn from their mistakes or improve their security, they deserve what's about to happen to them.

When he arrives at the terminal side of the jet bridge, he sees that another woman in the same red uniform is starting to pull a faux velvet rope closed across the gate. A second person, a man in a red waistcoat and trousers, stands behind her.

"Hold on," Larry shouts, rather conspicuously, as he runs toward them. "Wait. One more."

"Got your ticket?" asks the man.

Larry holds up the boarding pass for a brief read, and they wave him through. The smoldering nub of his cigarette still rests between his lips. He starts down the bridge toward the plane, the nearly empty duffel bouncing on his shoulder.

"Actually, wait," he shouts back at the ticket takers and then takes this smoke out of his mouth so he can speak more clearly. "Please."

"Boarding's done, sir."

"I need one minute. Please just one minute. I know you won't be flying away in one minute, right? There's still lots to do before takeoff. Please. I have to make a call. A very important call."

The woman looks at him skeptically.

"For love."

"Let me guess: true love?" Exasperated, she reopens the rope at the gate and waves him back through.

He digs in his pocket with his free hand and asks the woman. "Can you loan me a dime?"

"Are you serious?"

"Here's a dime for true love," the man says to Larry in a smoker's croak and tosses him a coin. "Make it fast, pal. Pretend . . . pretend real hard that you're about to miss your flight to Portland."

Larry drops the coin into the pay phone, dials the number, and busies himself locating a bit of open sand in the ashtray's forest of cigarette stumps. He stubs out his butt and admires the lush cream-iness of the sand as the call goes through.

"Yes?" Ruth answers with a guarded tone that makes him as-sume Masako is standing over his shoulder.

"It's me."

"Carrie?" she asks.

"Carrie? No, me." He looks to the man and woman at the gate and lowers his voice. "Larry."

"Yes, Carrie. How are you?" Ruth asks.

"Oh, cool. I get it. Code names. Even better, rhyming code names. You're so smart. I'll call you . . . damn, what rhymes with Ruth?"

"Where have you been?"

"I'll tell you everything but can't right now. I promise. Did you get my note? I need to know that you got the note."

"I got your note. I want to meet up, yes . . . as planned. You're doing good though?"

"I'm doing something big. Something for you. For us. For the baby. Our baby."

"Beckham proposed," she says with a thin, strained happiness. "I thought I'd share that . . . big news."

Larry falls up against the pay phones. The world spins. Or they say the world is always spinning, so Larry wonders if he's stepped out of time and space and the world keeps moving on.

"Last chance, pal," the man in red says.

"Hold your horses. I'm having a moment here." Larry tries to pull himself together. He asks into the phone, "And what did you say?"

"Yes, marriage. Very exciting. Uh huh," Ruth says.

"Right now, sir," the female gate attendant says and holds the gate rope clip in her hand.

"I'll make this work. We'll leave this all behind. Together. Me, you, and our baby. Promise me you'll be there at the rock."

Ruth doesn't answer.

"Sir, I'm serious," the gate attendant says. "Last chance."

Larry must know her answer and tries again. "Tell me you'll be there, Ruth. Oh shit . . . sorry, didn't mean to use your real name. Give me a sign. Something."

"OK," she says. "I look forward to it." She whispers something to someone near her. Something about "my friend from school." Then she says back into the phone, "Bye . . . Carrie."

"I love you." He hurls his words against the dial tone and bursts into tears. Beckham proposed? What the fuck? And to make matters worse, he can't even start to entertain the idea of voluntarily entering a tube of metal that flies off into the atmosphere at thirty thousand feet with no way off that doesn't involve parachuting skills or splattering into human paste. He realizes he is going to die. They are all going to die. People weren't meant to fly high above the ground in man-made birds. He knows this. He works on planes every day. Or used to. Even if he's never been on one.

Stick to the plan, he repeats to himself. Snap out of it and stick to the goddamn plan, Larry, and you don't even need to think about parachutes. You won't even need to leave the ground.

He considers screaming "help." But to whom? Ruth? His mother? His ancestors? It doesn't matter, as his tongue can't seem to form additional words. His fingers scratch at his own face and chest, trying to find something to hold on to. His breathing gets faster and faster. He can't get enough oxygen into his lungs. The more he breathes, the dizzier he gets.

His eyelids are pressed shut with every bit of strength in every muscle in his face. Maybe he can scream without words, but he is breathing so fast that he can't even form a sound.

Larry doubles over, resting his hands on his knees, and opens his eyes to find himself level with the ashtray. He realizes that a simple cigarette can fix all of this. He wills himself to dig a smokable butt out of the sand and repeatedly attempt to light it with quaking hands until he's able to extract a single drag. He does that with another butt. Gets two drags. And then another. Until he feels the internal fortitude to put one foot in front of the other and walk to the gate and get on the plane, all that way to seat 29F.

The man in red steps between Larry and the rope. "Sorry, sir."

Larry's vision clarifies, and he starts to rediscover his voice. "No."

"It's too late." The man shakes his head.

"I have to."

"I can't."

"Why didn't you warn me?"

"We've been telling you for the last ten minutes as you've been walking in circles and shouting and crying," says the woman as she beckons to someone somewhere behind Larry. "Using some pretty unnecessary language."

Larry rehearses in his head how after the money and parachutes are delivered, he'll pull back on his jumpsuit, slip off the plane with the confused, panicked crush of released passengers, and walk away through the baggage-processing zone to a blissful, worry-free future with his true love and their child.

Sure, it won't be totally worry free. It won't be endless money that he demands from the Aerospace Company. He doesn't want to be greedy or ask for too much. Just the equivalent of finishing out the next year of his original contract. Plus, a month or three of buffer to cover any unexpected costs. And baby costs, of course. But it will be enough for them to get set up as a family and for him to then pursue an honest career he can be proud of again.

He sizes up the male gate attendant in red and decides that now is his time to rise to the occasion. To be the man of the moment. To not let others once again dictate his destiny. He imagines himself as a seagull flying higher and higher into the sky, takes a deep breath, and states in an even voice, "OK, well, call the plane and tell them to stop. I need to get on."

He thinks again of Ruth. Her perfect kindness and unrivaled beauty. The only bad part is that she is now engaged to that dumb fucking dentist, and everyone will think that their child is his child. He is stealing Larry's family. His whole world. This cannot happen. "I have to get on that flight," he yells.

"We told you: it's too late."

The whole room starts to vibrate. Sweat flops off Larry's forehead. His stress rises, like magma up a volcano, pushing into the top of his skull until it finds a way out. "I know my way across the tarmac. Let me through. I can catch the plane." He tries to run around the man to enter the gate.

The man grabs at the sleeve of Larry's jacket. "Sir . . . you can't."

Larry bites the man's hand, shrieks as loud as he can, topples the rope, and starts sprinting down the gangway. He hears rushing footsteps behind him in the corridor. Or are they in front of him? Or is that an echo? Larry doesn't get a chance to see before the hurtling body collides square across his rib cage, folding him in half. Larry catches only a flash of a blue uniform as the air rushes out of his lungs and his vision tightens to black.

Is this death? He thinks of Ruth, the rock, of them together in Maui with their child—before he loses all sense of self and unloads his bladder into his grandfather's suit pants.

THIRTY-TWO *2014*

Sami doesn't know if it should even be called a stage. Maybe more of a dais. A rostrum? It's not a podium; she's sure of that. Or let's call it what it is: an old black tablecloth stapled atop a wooden shipping pallet.

The surface rumples when Sami walks on it, so she steps carefully, almost tiptoeing, across the platform in her same old nothing-special-even-for-this-special-occasion white running shoes. She knew she should have spray-painted the plywood black, but it came down to time for that or sourcing a decent seating option for Kim and the other VIPs at Table One. And she'd made her decision.

While the other auction attendees sit knees up like grasshoppers on affixed benches along the rectangular cafeteria tables made for elementary students, Table One is a full-size round dining table. In fact, it's Sami's dining room table. She rolled it over in the final hours to give Kim and her entourage the seating they deserved. She carried her own dining room chairs too. One by one.

Beyond the reporter, Kim had promised to bring along another two power couples. Sami was assured that they were important local citizens. Very philanthropic folks who care deeply about public education.

But they never materialized. Even Zafar begged off right before the event due to unexpected work commitments and Elise texted on his behalf that, of course, Sami would still be in the most capable of hands with the city's next mayor. For now, Table One is down to Kim and her assistant, who both sit up front facing the dais—regardless of whether their faces are buried in their smartphones or not.

Well, Percy's at the table too. Sami moved him there to help balance out one of the empty chairs but still made sure to sit him as far away from his sister as possible. Like across the table but not so directly across that they had to look at each other.

Sami leans in close to the mic and welcomes the thirty or so parents and teachers and the one VIP to the auction. She hopes that no one can see her facial bruise from the banner-hanging mishap under the multiple layers of foundation makeup. Words come out of her mouth. She says a few things, somewhat convincingly and with an upbeat tempo, until she hears a volley of "we can't hear you"s from the around the cafeteria.

"Don't stand so close to the mic," someone yells.

"Maybe it's off?" a person who sounds a lot like Monica asks. Sami steps back, tangling her feet in the black cloth covering and nearly tripping. She attempts to talk into the mic from an angle but then abandons it altogether and shouts her welcomes again to the attendees of the first annual Stevenson Elementary Full STEAM Ahead auction.

She maintains the charade and doesn't say a word about the impending school closure. She almost goes there. Every cell in her body tells her to scream out to the whole room that this is it. The last chance. That if they don't work together, it won't matter if the school is called Stevenson or Hasegawa or Stalworth Inc., there won't be a second annual Full STEAM Ahead auction because there won't be STEAM, a music program, or even a school. Their kids are going to be shipped off to here, there, and everywhere. Scattered to the winds of the callous, bean-counting district.

Sami swore a blood oath of secrecy about her insider school-status information to Principal Doucette, whose opinion she no longer cares about and whose dumb face she can see right now in the crowd. But she signed a for-real, binding nondisclosure agreement with Kim, who is the only opinion she still cares about and who will make everything possible tonight.

While continuing to talk to the crowd with some boilerplate about how excited and honored she is that everyone made it out this evening to support such a good cause as continuing the school's legacy while simultaneously helping the school evolve to better fit with the times, Sami waves to Great-Uncle Bert, whom she hasn't seen in years but who insisted on coming out of respect for his departed cousin, Masako. She should have moved Bert along with Percy, but she didn't want to add a senior in a wheelchair to elite Table One. She feels guilty about it. No way around that. But in such an event, one must make some hard choices in the name of optics.

Sami admits to herself that she is nervous. OK, freaking out. Mildly if not significantly. She tries to soothe her nerves by admiring her decorative work about the cafeteria. The borrowed folding side tables have vases of cut flowers from neighborhood gardens alternating with fanned-out disposable platters of salami and sliced cheese hors d'oeuvres along with stacks of paper napkins in assorted school colors. As the PTA couldn't pay a guarantee to the Inca Trail Peruvian food truck, it too delivered its last-minute regrets and opted instead for a downtown sporting event. But it was OK. She'd made do. As always.

At least, Elise confirmed that the STEAM petition is in motion with the district to shelter Stevenson from closure. The paperwork takes a while to process, so they already submitted it based on the future Stalworth Lab in the portable classroom. The path is clear. Now all they have to do is actually pay for and erect the lab, throw in a few cross listings, and they're all but guaranteed that the district will have to shutter a different school. Then Sami can get back to renaming Hasegawa Elementary.

Sami must focus on these fundamentals. This setting of the table for the meal that Kim is about to deliver ... even if, currently at this event, her sister-in-law seems otherwise directed or disengaged.

Sami decides to get Kim off her screen by formally introducing the evening's VIP and plugging her mayoral candidacy. She leans back into the mic, remembers that it's not working and shouts, "It's my great honor tonight to introduce a very special person who has graced us with her presence, someone not only near and dear to my—" but stops short when she sees Kim put her phone to her ear. Her sister-in-law then says something into the phone that sounds a lot like "hold on a second," gets up from her seat, and makes her way out the cafeteria door.

Sami has no idea what to think. She watches through the window as Kim intermittently passes by, pacing back and forth, gesticulating with her free hand. Goddamn. Sami wishes she weren't so reliant on this one person. She wishes that all of American society didn't suddenly seem to rise or fall at the unreliable behest of self-serving rich people. She'd like to blame Reagan for all of it, but it was probably always that way.

If this world were fair or moral or had made any progress over the last generations, the school should be preserved due to the civic value of its musical past or its role as a cultural and historical site. Why can't anyone do the right thing and simply give all of the expropriated land back to her family? She wouldn't use it to turn a profit ... she'd keep it as is—with a quick name change, of course.

It shouldn't even be a battle. Not one that is waged down at Sami's grassroots level. But it requires Kim, with her Mothership backing, or some other act of God to save the place. It's a shame they never stumbled across a mammoth tusk or some other indispensable historical artifact on the property.

She wonders if she could get her hands on a tusk and bury it on the land to stop development. Maybe Bruce has some black market connections who could make that happen, but she imagines that bankrolling a portable classroom and light remodel is more afford-able than ice-age ivory. For now, it has to be Kim. She is the one and only way.

Sami realizes that she is staring out the window and hasn't said anything new to the audience. She can't be sure if it's been a mat-ter of seconds or minutes. Either way, she hears the chatter of the crowd's attention turning away from her and toward itself. If things aren't already full-on awkward, they will be in a matter of moments.

"Hold tight, everyone. Enjoy your beverages. We have beer and some wine at the folding table. Then we'll come back and auction off the Café Djibouti coffee cards, a month of endless sweet-and-sour wings at the Peking Castle, and private music lessons with Ms. Monica Barrett. All the way up to the big kahuna item of the Alaska cruise to Skagway, like the gold miners who put this city on the map."

Sami makes her way between the tables toward the door. She passes Principal Doucette who sits by himself, scratching some crust off his pants leg, as Millie, the secretary, abandoned the seat-ing chart and is now holding hands with Shawn at Table Three, alongside Monica and a number of the other teachers. There are two tables dedicated to parents. It's a fraction of the school com-munity, but Sami is still pleased that they showed. Not a terrible turn of events considering that, a few weeks back, she had but a single PTA volunteer.

Before she steps outside, Sami glances at Bruce and his wife, Wren, seated near each other but apparently inhabiting different dimensions. Bruce is drinking from a red plastic cup and staring into the distance. She can't figure him out.

She walks out into the cold and sees her breath as she utters her sister-in-law's name.

Kim puts a palm up in her direction and mouths, "Hold on."

A big, soft blond man with long hair and the look of someone without regular access to a shower steps between the two of them. He cradles a brown paper Food King grocery bag under his arm.

"Can I help you?" Sami asks as formally as possible. Kim stares at the man like she knows him but is likely judging Sami and the school on account of having such shabby guests.

"Is Loose Bruce here?" the man asks, clearing a few strands of hair from his face and blinking enough times that Sami must turn away to not feel like she too is staring.

Jesus Christ, Bruce. What now? she thinks to herself. "Um, do you have a ticket? This is a private event. For, you know, parents and teachers."

"It's cool. I've gotta talk to Bruce." The man proceeds toward the door.

"Wait. Hold up, I can go get Bruce to come out and—" Sami waves at the blond man to come back. "What's in the bag?"

"Cash."

"Cash?" She notes that he's wearing, at least, three pairs of layered pants.

"It's an auction, isn't it?"

Sami is about to insist on inspecting the bag. You can never be too careful at schools these days. But Kim hangs up her call and says, "Unfortunately, sis, something's come up."

"Come up?" As she tries to process this, Sami sees that the blond man has disappeared inside the cafeteria.

"Yes, thanks for the invite. Really appreciate it." Kim starts making her way to her vehicle. "Gotta run."

"You're leaving? What about—"

"What about what?"

Sami realizes that Kim already has her purse and jacket folded under her arm.

"Follow up with Elise about any details," Kim says without looking back. "Am putting out fires. I'll be in touch."

Sami stands outside the door. Dumbfounded. She pulls herself together to go inside and talk to Elise, but the assistant also comes out the door.

Sami heads her off. "Elise. Hey. I was on my way to talk with you."

"Where's Kim?" she asks Sami.

Sami shrugs. "Something, someplace important. Fires to be put out."

"Guess I'm gonna have to call my own ride to get home." Elise rolls her eyes and starts messing with her phone.

"Wait, you can't go too," Sami begs. "You're supposed to help the school. Remember? Finish up what Kim came here for."

"Listen, honestly, I think it's already finished." Elise hits a button on her phone. "Nice. Only two minutes out."

"I don't care if you stay for the whole evening. Just commit to the donation. I thought Kim wanted it to be a public announcement. But, you know, whatever works. Just write the school the check. We can do it real fast. Right here. Right now."

"Take a hint, for God's sake."

Sami suddenly feels very small, very alone.

"Kim's been talking with the developers all night," Elise says and rests a hand briefly on Sami's shoulder. "Turns out a solid campaign donation from their consortium is worth a lot more than having her name on some public school lab. Zafar was the one really geeking out about STEM anyway."

"Was she, uh, going to tell me this?"

"Sure, eventually. Maybe. I'm sure she drove up their donation number sky-high. She's so gifted at brinksmanship. I've learned so much from her. Oh, here's my ride." A rideshare car pulls up, and Elise opens the door and gets inside.

Sami grabs the door handle to stop Elise from closing it. "What about the STEAM petition to save the school? That's already in motion. What about an actual portable? An actual lab?"

"Sorry, but that's for you to figure out now. Knowing my boss, she's guaranteed her payout, either way."

"Are you fucking kidding me?"

"Easy with the language." Elise pulls on the car door until Sami lets go of the handle. "Kim did ask me to tell you she would still like to honor your job offer when she becomes mayor. She continues to appreciate your loyalty and support for her candidacy. And, of course, please remember that you are under a strict NDA."

Elise pulls closed the door, and the car drives off. Sami looks back into the cafeteria through the window. People have continued to drink and are swaying, talking loudly, and getting more animated. Sami feels her chance to honor her grandmother and her family's legacy peel away. Dread worms through her veins. She too considers fleeing but walks back inside, watching herself put one sneaker in front of the other, and heads straight for the dais.

"Hi, all. Some things have changed," she addresses the crowd in her loudest voice. "I need your help. The school needs your help. We have to rise to the occasion in a big way and figure out how to raise money for the school. I hate to be the bearer of bad news, but if we can't do that, the school is likely going to shut down."

A groan ripples through the crowd. Doucette leans forward in his chair and shakes his head.

"We're gonna have to think outside of the box. And come up with some serious cash."

"What about the Alaska cruise?" one of the teachers asks.

"There's, well, there isn't actually an Alaska cruise." Sami's voice cracks as she does her best to not cry in front of everyone. "I was trying to make the auction look bigger than it is. And I assumed it wouldn't come to that."

Percy approaches Sami from the side, places his hand gently

atop her forearm, and whispers in her ear, "Let's think this through. See what we can figure out with small donations."

"I already did that math," she says. "Would be thousands from everyone here. Not gonna happen."

"I've got something," Shawn announces to the room. He gives Millie a kiss on the cheek and rises from one of the back tables. "Hold tight. I'll be back in twenty . . . thirty minutes. Max."

Bruce looks out over the restless auction crowd while working on his third, maybe seventh, IPA. Not his favorite, but that's what they have tonight. Well, that and a growler of some weird homemade cider that some neighbor left out on the back table. That was repellent too. Not that it stopped Bruce from finishing it.

He chokes back another mouthful of room-temperature IPA and wonders how such a noxious, bitter beer became a mainstream, if not dominant, beverage of choice. He can no longer breathe through his nose. Bruce squeezes the plastic cup until its rim cracks.

He misses the good old days when all you could get in town was Rainier or Olympia, of which the main difference was the packaging. If you ask Bruce, now it's these people who are watered down. Sure, most of them moved here from elsewhere, but they went to the same colleges, live out the same goals in slightly different houses, and work in different departments of the same big companies. Their homogenized lifestyle and lack of imagination, for that matter, are offset by an excess of consumer options so they can publicly differentiate themselves by adopting bewildering, superficial preferences like claiming to enjoy varying gradations of strange, sour piss beer.

"Easy, Bruce." Wren wipes at her sleeve. "You splashed me."

He apologizes and finds a paper napkin to dab at the beer

droplets on her sweater but mainly takes in the moment of un-guarded, up-close contact with his wife. He falls into her gaze, traveling through the early years with Sierra as a baby, the death of Wren's mother, when Wren landed her first sales job, when the teachers first called them into the classroom to "voice concerns" about Sierra's educational progress, when the doctors starting batting about a possible diagnosis, tears, fights, joy, and even their road trip to Ocean Shores that was as close as they'd ever come to a honeymoon.

He thinks about how much they've been through together, how much they've shared and how much more they could have together, should have together. He wants nothing more than to share the astounding news of the lottery and all that it will do for them as a family if Wren only permits him back into her orbit.

He feels sorry for Sami at this frantic moment but can also see how the lack of VIP attendance at the empty round table up front will make his decision for him. No harm, no foul. Except for the impact on the neighborhood. And the schoolkids. And his own daughter. And all of her potential at the school. Which, of course, won't do him any favors with his wife either. But hopefully, that's something that they can remedy later. Once his weed business is up and running.

And, while he's at it, what the hell is Spatzy doing here at the auction lurking against the back wall with a grocery bag looking all sketchy and shit? He knows it's his fault as he told his parking lot lodger about the auction, but Bruce can't be bothered to talk to him. Not now. It's all too much. Too much on top of too much. Bruce's plan is to pretend that he doesn't notice that Spatzy's here until the auction is over . . . kind of like his current "What? Sorry to hear that things fell apart, such a shame" approach to the whole event. He's running out the clock.

"What can we do to help save the school?" Wren asks Bruce,

breaking him out of his ruminations while gracing him a few more moments of her direct attention.

"How should I know?" he says, immediately regretting his defensive glibness. He has to bottle up the urge to tell her about his impending personal success. He may not be the most tactful man in the world, but even he recognizes that now isn't the right time. Not tonight. Bruce knows his wife well enough to predict that she won't be able to process that news, no matter how positive, through her haze of anger and sense of righteous indignation. He'll have to wait for a better chance to tell her that he made this crazy thing happen. Through strategy, dedication, and hard work. Something big. With big implications. For all of them.

Wren turns back to face the stage. "This can't happen. Sierra needs this. We need this."

Both Bruce and Wren look up at the sound of the opening door. Shawn runs back into the cafeteria, waving to Sami. A piece of paper in his free hand.

"Excuse me a second," Bruce says to Wren with a gleam of purpose.

He notes the perspiration dotting Shawn's forehead as they convene near the door.

"This belonged to my father." Shawn hands the paper to Sami, propping himself against the corner of the table to catch his breath.

Bruce looks over Sami's shoulder to read the faded paper with handwritten musical notes. "The Velvetones?"

"From when my dad was much younger. Most of the stuff he collected later on was what he called the romantics. Dead white dudes."

"What's this then?" Sami squints at the page.

"See these initials here?" Shawn points to the penciled-in letters *J.M.H.* in the corner.

Sami shrugs.

"James Marshall Hendrix."

"Jimi?" Bruce asks.

Shawn nods. "Velvetones were his first band."

"Jesus," Sami exhales.

"Better than Jesus," Shawn says. "At guitar anyway. My father played a gig with him at a synagogue when Jimi was a teenager."

"Are you sure? I mean, that you want to do this? Donate it?" Sami asks, her face pinched in anticipation.

Shawn looks over at the table where his daughter is seated. "Yes. My father made me promise to never sell it. He wanted me to do something special with it. This feels right. For the school. The kids. For my Monica. For Millie."

Only as they break from their huddle does Bruce step back enough from the prevailing momentum to grasp that he is not sure this is a good thing. Probably the opposite. For his business, at least. He starts to say something, come up with some reason why they might need to think on this a bit more or reconsider, but he sees his wife's wide-eyed eagerness and sits back down beside her without a word.

"What're you guys up to?" Wren asks.

He smiles, weakly.

Sami takes the stage along with Monica. They're greeted with cheers and whistles from the crowd. A few people get to their feet. Then more. Soon most of the room is standing. Millie and two teachers, who apparently got a good head start on the sauvignon blanc, are already climbing atop the tables to dance.

"This donation is on behalf of my father, grandfather, and the whole Barrett family." Monica holds up the sheet. "We have here an early piece of music my grandfather composed with local music royalty . . . Mr. Jimi Hendrix."

Principal Doucette, one of the last people seated, stands up and mumbles something about needing to go to the bathroom. He gets a quick round of boos on his way out and heads down the hallway in the opposite direction of the restrooms.

Bruce doesn't want to look too closely, but he might just be witnessing the school community starting to bond. He swallows hard and feels the fear breaking back through his alcohol fog. What to do? What to do? What is right? What is . . . he totally forgets what he was thinking about . . . yeah, no, he's still solidly intoxicated.

Bidding starts small. A hundred. Two hundred dollars.

Sami's ancient uncle stands up from his wheelchair and shouts, "Four hundred."

"We have four hundred," Monica announces and pumps her fist in the air.

"Dedicated to my cousin, Masako Hasegawa, who in a different life should have played Carnegie Hall," the uncle continues to yell, between sips from his plastic cup.

A parent, or perhaps a teacher, whom Bruce doesn't recognize puts up her hand.

"Is that four fifty?" Sami asks.

The woman nods her head.

"Do we have five hundred?" Monica follows.

The uncle starts to raise his hand but does some counting on his fingers and drops back down into his wheelchair, occupying himself with his beer.

Others starts to sit down. Here and there. Then en masse.

Bruce is hit with a potent combination of relief and immediate guilt. He can feel his face blushing hot red. He's not a religious man. Never has been. But he asks the universe for a sign, something to point him in the right direction. Tell him how to navigate this choice, what his role should be in all of this.

Spatzy raises his hand.

You've gotta be fucking kidding me, Bruce thinks.

"You, um, sir?" asks Sami. "That's five hundred?"

"No."

"OK then. Please only raise your hand to bid. Anyone else? Anyone? Five hundred? Going once . . ."

Spatzy raises his hand again. Bruce realizes he's going to have to deal with him, if not drag him out of here. Although Spatzy's a pretty big dude, and Bruce is not sure if he could manage any dragging in this state.

"You again," Sami stumbles over her words. "Sorry, but—"

"Not five hundred." Spatzy doesn't look up from the floor. "Five thousand."

There is a collective gasp throughout the room. Followed by a belch for which no one takes credit but which came from Spatzy's direction.

"Screw it, ten," he announces in an uneven voice, looking into his paper bag.

Sami and Monica start to hug each other but look again at the bidder and freeze up in a moment of obvious disbelief.

"Hold on a second," Bruce says to the crowd. He limps over to Spatzy.

He gets up close in the blond man's ear and whispers, "Don't mess with these people. This is hard enough for them already."

"I'm not messing with anybody. Should I offer fifteen? It's a virtuous number meaning curiosity, intuition, and self-awareness." He leans over Bruce's shoulder and shouts to the room, "Fifteen."

There's a smattering of cheers, but people react with more confusion and muted incredulity at this point.

Spatzy mutters to Bruce, "That's the highest I can go."

"Are we talking about cents or dollars here?"

"I'm a thirty-third-degree Scottish Rite Mason and sole keeper of a Freemason fortune of Klondike gold dating back to the founding of this city."

"No, Spatzy. You live in a Previa in the parking lot of my weed store."

"Don't you see it? Thirty-third degree. Thirty-three? It's a special double number, a master number, meant to guide and support humanity. It's the most advanced on this spiritual path, earning it the grand title of Master Teacher."

"Master bullshitter. C'mon, let's step outside. Apologize to these people. Get some fresh air." Bruce loses his whisper and grabs Spatzy's shoulder.

He brushes off Bruce's hand. "You're right. I may have exaggerated the Mason stuff. Sometimes, I have some challenges determining what's going on inside my head and what's going on outside of it."

"OK, can we step outside then? I'll apologize to the people for you."

"I was actually one of the first four programmers at Mothership. Back in the late seventies." He opens the top of the grocery bag to show Bruce stacked hundred-dollar bills among other wadded-up cash.

Before Bruce can weigh the personal and professional implications, he gives Sami a thumbs-up. Why a thumbs-up? Was he suddenly swept up in this burgeoning sense of collective pride and possibility? He'd like to think not. But can't be sure.

"Going once . . . going twice . . . sold to Bruce's shockingly generous friend along the back wall."

Clapping and whistling ensue. Bruce sees parents and even someone who looks like Sierra's old second-grade teacher dancing on the table alongside Millie.

From the stage, Sami calls for a quick break. She and Monica come down to talk to Bruce and Spatzy.

"Thank you on behalf of my family. And the school." Monica hands him the sheet music.

Spatzy refuses to take it. "It has to live here in the school. In the music room." He passes the whole paper bag to Sami. "Most of it's there. Gotta go grab the rest from my van."

"This is a huge leap forward. But we still have a long way to go." Sami thanks him profusely, and then she and Monica head back to the stage.

Over the next hour of increasing excitement, desperation, and inebriation, they sell the endless sweet-and-sour wings, music lessons with Monica, and the coffee cards, all at solid, marked-up prices.

When the auction items are exhausted, Sami proposes the Hail Mary option. "What's the chance that everyone here could come up with two thousand bucks per person? Or maybe only a thousand?"

A few people are able to do it. Three, to be exact. Including Sami and Percy. They're the only ones Bruce recognizes.

Wren and Bruce come up with a hundred.

"Anyone else? If we're gonna make this happen, we have to do it together," Sami pleads from the stage. "This is our last chance." Monica is still at her side.

They get a couple more. People cheer but Bruce can see Sami's downshifting energy. She's coming to accept that the gulf is unbridgeable.

"Wish I could help more," Spatzy mumbles to Bruce and Wren at their table. "My wife keeps me on an allowance."

"Your wife?" Bruce asks.

"She doesn't like me making impulsive, large donations and whatnot."

Bruce doesn't have time to process this before Sami makes an announcement from the stage.

"Well, my friends, we went down swinging," Sami says, no longer able to hold back her tears. She and Monica put an arm around each other. "But we've really come together tonight. And while we're losing our school, we've regained our community. Oh, and by the way, please never vote for Kim Stalworth for mayor."

Wren starts to cry too. "Poor school. Poor Sierra." She places her hand on Bruce's knee just below the hem of his shorts.

His heartbeat goes on a quick hiatus. Bruce feels the contact of her hand touching his skin. He looks down to see that it is, in fact, happening, this crossing of personal and physical boundaries. Then he looks back up to see her suffering. Tears welling in the corners of her eyes. Her lips tight, fighting to maintain a facade of composure. He looks back down at her hand again, and the words rush out of his mouth. "I have an idea."

"I'd never ask you to sell your Westy," she assures him.

"Better. I won the lottery," he says with a mounting sense of duty and purpose mixed with an impulsive disorientation. He stands and shouts toward the stage, "Hold on, Sami. I have an idea."

"Like the *lottery* lottery?" Wren says in a hushed voice, pulling him back down by his sleeve.

"The cannabis retail lottery."

"OK? Cool? And that's what?"

"You see, I had this plan. Rather ingenious, really. It was, well, I can explain that later. The point is, we could sell this retail license to an investor. Enough to save the school and still give us something left over. I swore I'd never do it, but I can talk to Mel—"

She hugs him, face first. Crying into his neck. She pulls back and says to him, "This is the Bruce I've been trying to find again."

As Bruce stands up, he gets a better sense of how drunk he actually is. He takes a few breaths to stabilize himself and makes his way up to the makeshift stage alongside Sami, beer in his hand instead of his cane. Up close, he can see that Sami's mascara has streaked into the heavy foundation on her cheeks. He whispers into her ear what he intends to do.

He taps the mic to make sure it's working. No luck. He takes out his flip phone and dials Mel. He announces to the crowd, "I've got a surprise for you all."

He nods to his wife from the stage. The call to Mel rings and rings. There's no answer. He hangs up and tries again.

Spatzy comes up to the side of the stage. "I remember now what I came here to ask you. Or tell you. Tell you, ask you."

"Not now, Spatzy."

"Mel stopped by. Said he's sorry. Didn't know his aunt already had a contract out on the property before you applied to your lottery thing. He had no idea. Really. He told me I gotta move too. You got an extra parking spot at your apartment? You think your Westy could tow my van over there? I just spent all my money."

Bruce does not give himself the chance to feel the rage flaming over every inch of his being and dials Mel again. "I'm gonna keep calling until he answers. C'mon, Melchor. Goddammit. We're gonna fix this. We have to fix this."

"We had about forty-two beers together. Give or take," Spatzy says. "Kept talking about how it's the same rat-fuck developers who're gonna flip the school."

Bruce spikes his phone on the floor, smashing it into a dozen plastic shards. He tries to flee the stage but twists his feet in the black drape and flops off the side off the pallet, tossing his IPA in the air.

Spatzy takes much of the beer to the face but holds his ground, breaking Bruce's fall with the pillowy cradle of his ample bosom.

PART V   *1903*

Siab knows his eyes are not as accurate as they used to be. He squints, looks again, and, indeed, the man is exactly who he thinks it is. He recognizes, all too well, the awkward Boston who staggers into the far edge of the clearing.

Siab wants nothing more than to kill Erasmus. He dreams about it frequently, even if the repercussions would be catastrophic for him, his wife, and, most importantly, the land. But by showing up right here, right now, Erasmus is really tempting him.

"Hello there, old boy," Erasmus hollers at the last Duwamish landowner in town. He pauses to cough and then catch his breath. He walks toward Siab and the big rock at the center of the clearing. The gulls know by now to move out of his path.

Siab gives Tietsa the three-part whistle. He thinks better of it and tells her to bring him the rifle first. Then to go into the house and put the fir beam across the door.

He checks over his shoulder to see if there is anyone else on or near the property. Witnesses. No, nobody. Just Siab, Tietsa, and Erasmus. Well, there's the immigrant family who help with the daily labor. They're resting in their tents out along the tree line. But they wouldn't say a thing.

He thinks through his options and figures the steps involved in burying Erasmus fast enough to deny that they had any idea about the mysterious disappearance. The laborers could help. And

Erasmus is sure to have had plenty of other enemies who wished him harm. Not to mention his known entanglement with the poppy and all that comes along with that.

"Still pulling up tubers, eh?" Erasmus reaches the middle of the clearing.

Siab and Tietsa always planned that their children, fully grown, would move home and take over the Duwamps Hill farm. Hold on to the land for the grandchildren and then the grandchildren's children and so on—however long was required. Siab and Tietsa's son and daughter should have already returned by now. But their son is in poor health from a broken leg that was never properly set. He struggles to provide for his family out on the reservation and has taken to alcohol to soothe his melancholy. Their daughter's husband committed suicide and left her with four children.

Neither of their children knows the first thing about farming. Or, at least, that's Siab's understanding. He hasn't left the farm or seen his children since they were young and entrusted to the care of relatives out in the comparative safety beyond the city.

Siab would never admit it, especially not to Erasmus, but he is tired. They have continued their ceaseless obligation, even as their backs weakened and knees locked up. One of Tietsa's thumbs is frozen in a permanent crook. Farming has become too much for them. Even with the help of the laborers.

But the old couple cannot leave. Must not leave. Not until they find someone who can care for the land.

Siab grabs the rifle from his wife and cocks it. He tries to do it all in one fluid and intimidating motion, but his rigid wrists don't allow it. "I heard you're finally going to try to take my land."

"Who told you that?" Erasmus coughs until he spits out a small amount of vomit. "Sorry, I stopped taking my medicine again. Not an easy enterprise. Not at all."

"I heard it from the lawyers and police and other snakes who gave us your absurd eviction papers." Siab notices that his wife hasn't gone inside. He motions again for her to go but can tell from the firmness of her expression that she will not be convinced. Tietsa steels herself alongside her husband as he levels the gun at their neighbor.

"You don't understand," says Erasmus, lowering down enough to peer, curiously, into the rifle barrel, perhaps inspecting the bore.

"No, you don't understand," Tietsa says. "Or you'd never show your face here."

"I can't keep living like this," Erasmus pleads. "I need you to free me from the curse. I need you to free me so that I can fulfill my destiny."

"What curse?" asks Tietsa.

"You know, the bird. The damned seagull. It was an accident, for God's sake."

Siab shakes his head and keeps the rifle trained on Erasmus. "I can't do that."

"Why not?"

"Because it's not a curse. It's only a bad feeling. A feeling that you're a problem. That you're what you'd call an asshole."

"Yes," says Tietsa. "Only you can free yourself from that."

"I know the curse exists because I have lived it." Erasmus leans forward to catch his breath. "Am living it."

Siab lowers the gun. "Only an asshole would try to take the most important thing from us and ask me to pardon his guilt."

"It's the lawyer. Not me."

"He used your name."

"Sloot will take your land under my claim or another. That's why I came to talk to you."

"Thanks?" Siab points the rifle at Erasmus's chest again.

"Please, Sam." Erasmus drops down to his knees. "I will

immediately deed the land back to you, you see? Well, to a care-taker. Legally, it can't be an Indian. Maybe in my son's name? He's currently a toddler and with my dear former wife, God knows where, but . . ."

Siab laughs for lack of locating a more appropriate reaction or emotion.

Erasmus presses his forehead to the barrel of the gun. "Either shoot me or free me from the curse. Please. If you spare my life, I will leave the city and dedicate the rest of my time on this Earth to creating something of value for humanity. I have a vision of a flying airship."

Siab is so tired of hearing the ridiculous words fall from this man's mouth. He stares down the sight of the rifle to the center of Erasmus's head and considers his intuition telling him to pull the trigger.

"I don't want to always bring more misfortune," Erasmus cries. "We can never give up this land. If necessary, we will die here."

Siab looks at Tiesta for her confirmation. But she turns away.

Truth be told, Siab was counting on or, at least, had hoped for the whole city's collapse by now. It was not an unreasonable as-sumption, especially as he'd witnessed its disgraceful beginnings too. But the discovery of their shiny gold was wind to a wildfire. And the damned city kept reinventing itself and growing and re-inventing itself again into flying boats or whatever this madman is talking about now.

When Tietsa returned from her last trip to speak with their children about the farm and to meet their grandchildren for the very first time, she also told Siab—in no uncertain terms—that she wanted live out her final circles of the seasons on the peninsula: with their children. That her whole life has been in service to the farm, to their ancestors, to maintaining the sacred land.

He understood her sadness but reminded her that it is their duty. It is about so much more than their life or how they are feeling in the moment.

"They need us too," she said. "Not our ancestors. Our children. Our living children. Our grandchildren need us. And I need them."

"But we must await the Changer," he says to his wife while still keeping his eye trained on the barrel.

"He appears in all different forms, great and small. You know this, Si'sia."

Siab's cheeks flush at his childhood nickname. He lowers the hammer and pulls the gun away from Erasmus's head.

Erasmus collapses to the ground. "Fine. You want more? Have it. Have the Masonic Hall I'm building across the creek there. Have it all. I'll deed the whole top of the hill to you. All of it. All I have."

Siab and Tietsa share a skeptical glance. She asks, "How can we be sure the rock is never desecrated?"

"I don't know. Some sort of special designation. A trust to the city? A citywide rule against disturbing erratic rocks over a certain size? I will see what I can do. You need a caretaker, though."

"We don't trust you. Or your son. Never met him, but he's probably an asshole too," Siab says. "With all due respect."

Erasmus struggles up to his feet. "Who do you trust, then?"

Tietsa calls over the mother and father of the immigrant family. The woman is pregnant and shifts side to side as she walks.

They speak quietly to Siab and Tietsa.

"The decision has been made. They will take care of the land until change comes again and our relatives return," Siab tells Erasmus. "Now go prove that you can do the right thing."

"And the curse?"

"That's for you to fix."

"Please, Indian Sam."

"Sure, you're free now." Siab rubs his palms together and hesitantly waves them over Erasmus's face. "Whatever you want to hear. Go."

"Thank you, old boy," Erasmus says as he retreats, smiling, from the property. "Count on me, Indian Sam."

The farmhand wife whispers something to her husband in Japanese. The husband places a hand on her pregnant belly and says to the old Duwamish couple, "We will name our first child after you."

THIRTY-FOUR

Ruth stands facing the rock until the sun comes over the horizon and the seagulls fly away. Her feet hurt. Her ankles hurt. Legs. All the way up. Holding both hands to her belly and with tears winding down her face, she finally gives up and heads back to the house.

Ruth tiptoes through the flagstone entry and returns to her room before her mom wakes up. She changes back into her pajamas and puts the duffel bag that holds her favorite clothes and albums into the depths of her closet. She takes the note that she'd left for her mom off of the made bed, rips it up into indecipherable confetti, and puts it at the bottom of her wastepaper basket. As her nausea mounts, she heads to the kitchen to make a tea and adds both turmeric and ginseng that she bought at the hippie health food store.

Dr. Yamamoto wants her to start chemical treatment now for the leukemia. But that would mean the end of her baby's life.

There is no question for Ruth. Until the baby is born, she will rely on natural medicines to combat her illness.

As the tea steeps, Ruth calls Larry's house. The phone rings and rings. No one picks up.

Beckham is her next call. The aunt answers, and Ruth insists that she wake up Beckham and put him on. The aunt is hesitant but responds to Ruth's newfound, commanding tone.

"I want you to know that I am not going to go through with this," she says as soon as Beckham comes on the line.

"With the baby? I really think you should do the treatment."

"With the marriage."

"But you're not well."

"I'm well aware of that."

"Where will you go?"

"Not sure. Maybe my Uncle Bert's. For a while."

"You are going to marry that girl," the aunt yells from somewhere near Beckham. "What will everybody think?"

"Enough, Auntie," he says away from the phone.

"It's an embarrassment," the aunt shouts.

"Goodbye, Beckham," Ruth says. "I wish you the best."

She takes a sip from her tea, shuffles down the hall, and straightens up her posture before she knocks on Masako's bedroom door. "Mom? We need to talk."

"Hold on. I just got out of the shower." Masako opens the door. A towel wrapped around her head.

"It's back," Ruth says to her mother.

"What's back?"

"You know. Just like my father."

THIRTY-FIVE   *1972*

Using the armrest of the lone chipped-white Adirondack chair as his makeshift desk, Larry signs the letter, folds it into thirds, and slides the paper into the envelope. Although his twice-daily pills often leave his lips sticking to the fronts of his teeth, he conjures enough saliva to lick and seal the envelope flap with tortured precision.

Going all the way back to when, as a child, he first wrote and attempted to send letters to the father he'd never met and never would, he's recoiled at the flavor of the envelope's gummed adhesive. These days, it barely registers on his taste buds. Larry's unsure if his dulled senses are due to licking so many envelopes these last months. Or more side effects of the pills of assorted colors, shapes, and sizes. Or the cascade of cigarettes, one of which he stubs out now on the armrest.

As is his routine, he aims with a trembling hand to extinguish the glowing red cherry in the same small black circle as his last smoke and the last three thousand before that. He doesn't want to ruin the chair, but the spot keeps getting larger and darker and is dimpling the damp wood.

Standing up, he steadies himself and looks out over the little orchard of twisted, fruitless branches he's been caring for. He's storing some scion stems of heartier apple varieties in plastic bags with wet sawdust and sphagnum moss and plans to graft them in the next week or two before the rootstock fully wakes up from dormancy. He could even have some decent cider apples by next season—but will thankfully be long gone from this place by then.

Larry looks past the trees to the metal security fence to the mountain peaks and the city that he imagines must lie somewhere beyond. Wearing his soft, gray institutional slippers, he shuffles back inside the building and on to the mail room.

He spends his whole week waiting for Friday. After lunch, the mail is sorted into the patient's boxes, and he is always the first in line. Larry runs his hand around the dusty interior of his cubby and buries his weekly disappointment under a practiced ritual of affixing stamps to a new batch of his handwritten letters to his mom and, of course, Ruth.

Larry places them in the outgoing mailbox, says a short prayer, not to some deity, but to Ruth herself, that the letter, or any of his many letters, will find its way to her hands, his own mom's hands or even her mom's hands. He then heads back outside to his orchard, away from the TVs and the card games and all the other certified crazy people.

He waits to cry, or get as close as he can to crying on his medications, until he sits back down in the chair, lights another smoke, and looks out over the skeletal trees, the mountains, and the horizon. Only allowing himself a contained few moments of desperate sadness, he sets about rebuilding his improbable hope that he'll hear back from Ruth the next Friday.

Larry is well aware of how dark things can get when he loses faith that he will ever see her again. He was still in a holding cell when the clock struck midnight on December 1. Ruth was, he knew, waiting at the rock: alone, confused, and, above all, disappointed in him. Larry asked the airport police, or whoever they were, for a lawyer or a phone call. Like he'd seen on TV. But, once again, he was never put under arrest or granted any of the supposed rights that come with that. His next impulse was to kill himself, but short of cracking open his head on one of the cell walls, which he tried half-heartedly and with little to show for it, he had no viable options.

As soon as the authorities learned of his earlier military discharge for "misconduct and erratic behavior; suspected schizophrenia," he was brought straight to this facility on a desolate piece of grassland somewhere outside of town. The exterior looked like a weathered clapboard house with numerous sprawling additions, but the interior was somewhere between a budget-challenged rural hospital and a minimum-security prison. He was never told exactly where he was, but he thinks he's out on the peninsula—with Ruth, and now their baby, far beyond the mountains and water.

The thought of their eventual reunification was, and is, the only thing that pulls him back from his bleakest considerations. Upon arrival at the hospital, he played nice and did everything he was asked. He was cooperative during his intake. He met with panels of nodding doctors. Met with groups of other slack-jawed patients. He volunteered to use his horticultural talents to spruce up the orchard.

As it became apparent that good behavior wasn't going to soften this stint into a temporary hold or short-term evaluation, he asked repeatedly to leave. Tried to leave. Pleaded. And eventually pondered escape but never got near the fence.

He still attends all of his group meetings but speaks only if forced. They keep the windows open during the sessions, as the cold wind keeps everyone awake and makes it less obvious who is wearing diapers.

He has a doctor or some guy with a white coat whom he meets with in an office that smells like hard candies and roach spray. The

credential on the wall behind the desk is for a Dr. Richard Kellerman, but Larry has purposefully never learned the name of the old
stiff with military posture, bottle-thick glasses, and a fondness for
the "marvels of American chemistry."

The doctor, for his part, is supportive of Larry's gardening (all
parts not involving shears or other metal tools), is hesitant about
his letter-writing fixation, and insists that Larry must admit that he
is psychically disturbed and come to terms with these disabilities
if he is to ever truly commit to preparing for a return to the wider
world. "Denial is futile," the doctor says with a thin smile in every
goddamn meeting, as if the rhyme makes any of this humorous.

He reminds Larry that sane people know when they aren't doing well. It's a sure sign of mental illness when one is unaware of
how far gone they really are. Yet, the doctor can provide no good
answer for Larry's question of how anyone knows if they are both
sane and doing well—perhaps they are simply in love.

Larry is told that he must state the words *schizophrenia* and
schizophrenic. Own them. Then he'll start to build the requisite
trust with the doctor that he'll proactively maintain his medication
regimen and learn to self-manage his condition in a way that will
qualify him for release.

He knows he did what he did at the airport for a reason, and
that reason was not him being crazy. But every time he tries to
explain his predicament, Larry watches his doctor stop paying attention and return to tapping his pen on his clipboard. Today, the
quack taps the pen and adds in the flourish of a melodramatic head
swivel to check his clock.

"Fine, I'm schizo-whatever," Larry shouts at the doctor. "I'm
bananas, I admit it. All I want to do now is take good care of myself
so I can see Ruth and our baby and be a productive member of society. Now and forever."

The doctor considers for a second and removes his glasses. "Nice try, Larry. But you're going to have to do a lot more soul-searching to convince me that you're sincere, my friend."

Larry makes sure to tell the man that they are not friends. Quite the opposite. He can't process what all of his words mean as they pour from his mouth, but it's clear from the doctor's expression that Larry's made an immediate, if not significant, step backward. He tries to apologize, but the doctor refuses to further engage with his irate patient.

Before he can make things worse, Larry excuses himself from the office. He takes one of his marker pens (no hard points allowed) outside and starts writing another letter. He reasons that if he can just explain things to her in the right way, Ruth will find it in her heart to forgive him for not showing up at the rock. Just as she had done after he stood her up at the Broiler. Maybe she'd even come to visit him with the baby. Maybe if the doctor sees him with his family, he will finally understand that it's not all in Larry's head.

He stares at each blank page, contorting his brain to devise the right words to explain to Ruth what happened. Actually, it's not hard to explain what happened. That's easy. It's why it happened, why he'd made the decision that causes him to hyperventilate and run back to his shared room to unknown hours spent face down on his rough, bleached sheets and slender mattress.

Larry spends days dreaming up elaborate excuses for his actions, many involving Beckham's aunt, others blaming CIA mind control, mistaken identity, or an implausible amnesia narrative that he borrows from a TV movie he once saw with his mom. But he never has the heart to write any of them on the paper.

In the end, the best he can do is be honest and beg Ruth for her forgiveness and to say that he tried, for them, for their family—but came up short. Again. And promise that even though she has no reason to continue to trust him, he will find his way back to her and the baby. He swears his life on it. His ancestors' lives on it.

Larry understands Ruth's disappointment. He is sympathetic to her anger. He fears she is now forcibly, or, even worse, happily married to a wealthy dentist, passing off their baby as the child of this other man. But if she'd only read his letters and hear him out . . .

Another Friday arrives and, once again, he is first in line to get his mail. And, once again, his cubby is empty. He returns to the Adirondack chair and speculates if the existing branches of the apple trees could hold the plummeting body weight of an incarcerated, debatably schizophrenic half-Duwamish mental patient for long enough to do what needs to be done.

Instead of testing out his hypothesis, he starts writing a new letter to Ruth.

Bruce parks the Westy in front of his old house and walks his daughter up toward the front door. His spine is still killing him, and he moves step by step up to the stairs on his cane.

Wren paces on the porch, phone to her ear. As they approach, she pockets her phone and stares at Bruce, tapping the back of her left wrist with growing intensity.

"I'm sorry?" he says, halting his progress one step from the top.

"No, you're on time," she says. "Early, even. Who are you?"

He reaches into the cargo pocket of his shorts and produces a digital wristwatch that Sami gave him. Not that he's looked at it today. "Still plain old Bruce Jorgensen, I guess."

Wren gives Sierra a hug and holds the door for their daughter to enter. "Can you stick around for a few?" she asks Bruce.

He freezes, transfixed on the threshold of the doorway, knowing each creaking floorboard, the smell of the kitchen countertop compost bin, and the placement of every light switch that lay beyond.

"Just to strategize our next steps with Sierra's school stuff. Not to—"

"I'd love to. And I will," he hesitates. "But I can't right now."

She looks down to the parked Westy on the street below and sees Spatzy reclined contentedly in the passenger seat. "I see."

"It's not like that. I'm helping him move. And he said he might be interested to bankroll my privacy glasses. Either way, it's a really long story."

"Always is, Bruce."

"No, seriously. Truth is, I have to get to a PTA meeting."

"I've been trying to call Sami about Sierra's paperwork, and no word. Nothing."

"She's taking some personal time. I'm actually, well, I'm taking over the PTA from Sami. I mean, she asked me to head it up for her. Am organizing the community of other parents to advocate for our kids in the next steps, if the school really does close. Fight the man and all that, you know."

"Wow. OK then, Mr. PTA Dad. I guess I'll be calling you instead of Sami about paperwork from now on. Wren grabs the back of his hand and squeezes it with intention before she heads inside. "We'll talk. You know where to find me."

It's not much. But he's pretty sure he's glimpsed proof of life, the surviving embers of their marriage. The ones that he could feel were there but hadn't been able to verify. But they are there, and they are just enough. He's reminded to always trust his intuition. To never listen to the naysayers.

He sidesteps his way down the front steps, as fast as he can, to the Westy and gets in the driver's side. He double-checks to see if Wren is watching him from her window. No such luck.

"Let's go," he says to Spatzy. "Gotta get your ass home."

Spatzy passes him a yellow plastic lighter and a glass pipe packed tightly with purple-green buds. "Special delivery for Loose Bruce. One deluxe order of superchronic."

Bruce waves him off and shakes his head. "Nah, man. Duty calls. Today's a new day."

He inserts the key in the Westy's ignition. The engine rumbles and then dies.

Sami sets about making her teacup of hot water and a hard-boiled egg for breakfast, as she does every day, while watching the backhoes break ground out her kitchen window.

After decades in the cabinet in the school's main office, the framed photo of her grandmother sits on Sami's windowsill, well-dusted and with its glass polished to the point that Sami can admire her own reflection atop Masako's portrait.

Percy tries to get her to do something else, to move away from the window, to try to return to her job search, to go on a short vacation, to do anything other than watch the demolition. But she feels it her obligation to see every moment. To bear witness to this turning of the page. A new chapter away from her family and their past.

They've already closed and ripped up the street for cables or sewer or whatever. Today they're digging up the parking lot next to the rock. Scraping away the hard-packed dirt.

Sami knows she fought. She tried with all that she could. But she can't stop thinking that she could have done more. Rallied the wider community in a different fashion. Raised money far and wide. Just done something, anything, differently.

In the end, she failed. There is no way around that. And this demolition is the direct result of her failure. She thinks of her grandmother and her family before that. She thinks about the students and the teachers. Sami wishes some act of God, some force majeure, would stop this so-called progress and return everything to the way it's supposed to be.

The backhoes dig closer and closer to the rock. And then, suddenly, the work stops.

Sami presses herself closer to the window. A foreman, or some man not in coveralls, is called over to peer into the excavated hole. A few others try to see what the commotion is about near the rock but are chased away.

She wonders what they've struck. Buried treasure? That mammoth tusk she'd wished for? Oil? A dinosaur bone? She looks at the photo of her grandmother and begs, please, anything to stop this wrongheaded progress.

The area around the rock is cordoned off, and the laborers, including the backhoe operator, are sent to the far side of the worksite.

A couple hours later, a dark-windowed sedan arrives, and two men in suits dirty up their leather shoes to get a better look at whatever it is that they see buried beside the rock.

They converse with the foreman and then pace around the hole, at once speaking through pursed lips and gesticulating wildly with their hands.

This is it. They found something. Is it something that can put a stop to this insanity? Something that will return everything to the way it should be, the way it used to be? Sami wonders. Yes?

Nope.

The men in suits return to their vehicle and speed off. The foreman jumps into the backhoe and sets about hastily filling in the hole by himself.

Sami turns away from the framed portrait of her grandmother and drops her head into her hands. The hard-boiled egg and teacup of water sit cold on the countertop.

THIRTY-EIGHT   1975

"Get your ass in here. Now," the nurse, his hairy upper arms and love handles straining against hospital whites, shouts out the back door into the orchard. "For God's sake, Larry, it's pissing rain."

Larry no longer writes outside, not that he writes much inside either these days. The burn hole ate an ashtray into the chair's armrest, which filled with rainwater and slowly rotted out the whole right side. Same thing happened to the left side, a year later. His feet have worn a depression in front of the chair, killing the grass and giving Larry his own little doormat of mud. He looks for a new spot to put out his cigarette but realizes that the rain has already done that for him.

He waits a few more minutes, ignoring the nurse, and then stands up, looks out over the orchard to the mountain peaks beyond, and returns inside the building.

"I've been calling you for ten minutes," the nurse says as Larry passes him in the doorway.

"Couldn't hear you." Larry keeps his head down.

"Right. C'mon, dish duty. You're late."

"Checking my mail first."

"'Course you are," the nurse says as Larry shuffles along.

He tells himself he'd still write more if he only had stamps. The doctor felt that mail had become too much of a self-defeating obsession and, while he never fessed up to it, had choked off Larry's supply of stamps over the years. Instead, the doctor steered Larry toward gardening and even let him teach some of the basics to other patients in a weekly horticulture class.

Larry has an envelope to send today, though. He's run out of words to say the same things to Ruth, to profess his love to her, so he's started drawing. Gulls, rocks, skylines, salmon, jets, jets with variable-sweep wings, jets with canards, jets with no wings, clams, actuators, mushrooms, crabs, babies, marijuana leaves, mountains, more gulls. He frequently puts them all on the same page at the same time "like manic wallpaper," as the doctor once categorized the drawings—even though Larry keeps them hidden under his mattress and today is the first time he's considered sharing them with anyone.

Even if she doesn't write back, hopefully Ruth will show his latest sketches to the baby. Or the kid. Whoever they are and however big they are. He imagines his little Ruthie or Larry Jr. sucking their thumb and studying the drawings to learn about who their father is. This message from beyond that he never received from his own old man.

As he nears the mail room, his mind starts to stampede with the improbable hope that this time, for once, he will receive a response. He goes to his cubby, arm extended, and runs his hand around the interior.

Today is no different from last Friday. Or any Friday before that.

Battling back his tears, he goes to place his envelope in the outgoing mail but remembers that he doesn't have a stamp. He knocks on the door to the back room and asks the orderly, the new sweaty one who got stuck with mail room duty and does his best to avoid Larry, if he could float him a stamp.

"You know I can't do that," the man says while still sorting packages.

"Just this once."

"You said the same thing last week."

"And you didn't give me one last week."

"And I'm not gonna again."

Larry starts to head back outside in the rain and away from all of these people. The ones who look at him and judge him and try to break him over and over again.

"Hey," the orderly calls after him. "You know who's Dugdale? Mr. Dugdale?"

Larry explains that he does. Quite well, in fact, and persuades the man to hand him a large, brown envelope, too big for the mail cubby.

The name on the return address at the top reads: MRS. MASAKO HASEGAWA.

Larry is hit by a wave of lightheadedness. He flattens his back against the wall and sucks down a series of frantic breaths. As soon as he's reasonably confident that he's not going to faint, he thanks the orderly, grips the oversize envelope under his arm, and races out the door. Better to read it in the rain than let any of the people inside see his treasured letter or try to take it away.

So much comes flooding back. Things he has tried to remember. Others he has tried to forget.

He sits down in the wet wooden chair, faces out to the trees, and works himself up to opening the letter. He runs his finger under the flap to preserve the envelope, slides out the pages, and rests them on the knee of his hospital pants. Larry reads out loud in a strained whisper:

> *Mr. Dugdale,*
>   *I have thought about writing you for some time.*
>   *First off, you need to know that my dear daughter and the most important person in my whole life, Ruth*

Hasegawa, passed away three years ago to the day I am writing you this letter.

She died here at home. I would like to say that she passed peacefully, but it was more complicated than that. I will never be the same.

I recently read your letters to Ruth. All of them. I can now see that you loved her. I don't fully understand why you made the decisions you did. Or what was happening in your head. I am sure I was hard on you. I have been hard on everyone, myself included. But I was trying to do what I thought was best for Ruth and to give her a life that was less difficult than my own.

For a long time, I was angry about you and how you left, and probably at myself too for how I treated you. I wondered if I had, in fact, created this situation. But now I no longer have the time or energy for those emotions and stories I told myself. I want to share a few things while we still have time.

You have a daughter named Sami. She is young and energetic and healthy. I have thought so much about Ruth and all of the mistakes I made and have looked deep inside to not make them all over again. People rarely get a second chance. I never gave people a second chance. But, somehow, I got a second chance to raise a child.

It is hard work. Often too-hard of work for a woman of my age. But after losing Ruth, Sami is the one thing keeping me here in this life.

Ruth had hoped to introduce Sami to your mother, but she became too frail. She left me your mother's address and made me promise to visit her. I delayed for a long time. I'm not sure if it was because of grief or anger or nerves or pride or all of them together. For that I am deeply sorry.

I recently took Sami by your mother's house to meet her. Marie has not lived there since shortly after you did. As this might be news to you too, I thought I would share that the neighbor told me she could not keep up with the cost of living in the city and had to move out to somewhere across the water. I tried to track her down. I have found no phone number or address.

A young blond lady now lives in the house. I apologize that I forget her name, but her family name is Jorgensen. Her aunt and uncle live next door and help her rent her house so she can better get by with her young son, who is only a little bit older than Sami. The blond lady said she knew you too. We even had a good laugh as she said she had gone to the movies with you a couple of times before you joined the Navy. From the way she talked, I think she was once sweet on you too.

She and I shared some stories about raising children by ourselves. The children played together. They got along, yet quarreled, as if they were siblings.

As I left, she gave me the stacks of letters that you had sent to your mother. I went home and read all of the letters. Then I went down into my basement, opened the shoeboxes full of unopened letters that you'd sent to Ruth, and stayed up all night reading every single one of them. They gave me a better sense of who you are and could've been as a father.

You will be happy to know that Ruth never married Beckham. She told me that he was not Sami's father, and she would never accept a dime from him or his family. He and his best friend from dentistry school moved to San Francisco right after graduation to establish a new practice. I never heard from him again.

His aunt, for reasons I still don't understand, has kept up appearances at the church that he and Ruth were, in fact, married and that Beckham only left town due to his overwhelming sense of grief. She even told people that he was supporting his daughter from afar and paying regular visits. I do not attend the church anymore.

Your beautiful daughter, Sami, is named after my late husband and Ruth's father, Sammy Hasegawa. He was a good man and, at times, a not-so-good man. An imperfect person. I guess that we all are. Regardless, it was so very hard for Ruth to never meet her father. She told me that you never met yours.

I fear that Sami will never know her father either. This is why I am writing you. Obviously, I have not seen eye to eye with you in the past. But maybe we can change that.

I would understand if you hate me and never want to see me again. But if you are open to us coming to visit you, please write me back and let me know. Otherwise, I will leave you in peace and hope that you will find it in your heart to come and meet your daughter after you are released.

Sincerely,

Mrs. Hasegawa

He reaches back into the envelope and removes a large black-and-white photograph. It is a picture of Ruth cradling the baby in her arms. Kissing bald little Sami on the forehead. Ruth looks slender, maybe too slender for someone who has recently given birth. But her expression is of profound joy. He can't begin to understand the overwhelming beauty of the baby.

Larry weeps hot, thick tears that mix with the rain on the letter and photograph.

He, at once, feels the darkest chasm of loss joined with such love, such a sense of belonging to something so profound and real. He puts the photo to his chest and embraces it as if it were Baby Sami herself, and he were protecting her from the rain.

He will find his way home, to raise this child. Together with Masako. By himself. Whatever it takes.

That night he writes a long, inspired letter to Sami and Masako, asking them to come now, tomorrow, whenever they can. He fills page after page, his marker pen struggling to keep up with his thoughts, ideas, and hopes. He puts the pages under his mattress, right next to Sami's photo and Masako's letter, so he can send it when the mail goes out next Friday. He requests an emergency appointment with his doctor.

When the appointment is granted two days later, Larry meets the white-coated man across the desk in the same room as always.

Before taking his seat, Larry announces, "I've come to terms with the fact that I'm not OK, mentally speaking. I am . . . schizophrenic. I suffer from . . . schizophrenia. Did I pronounce that right? Anyway, I now understand that. Clearly. But I have gotten much better and would never again do the stuff I did to get in here in the first place. I was in a bad place. It was wrong. I see all of that now, and thank you, doctor, so very much for helping me to get to this point. Showing me the way back to being a regular member of society. Regular as can be."

The physician looks over the top of his glasses, evaluating his patient. His sizable head wavers atop its neck and then starts to nod. Larry likes where this is going.

"I believe you, Larry," he says. "Thank you for taking this big step."

"Then what's the next step?" Larry asks, sitting down on the front edge of the chair and leaning forward, ready to stand back up, walk out of this office, out the front door of the facility, and keep on going.

"Same as always. We are on the path to healing," the doctor responds.

"But when can I go home?"

"If you are not well, you are in the right place. For now, at least. Right? And you've done such a nice job in the orchard with the other patients."

"What about next week? Does that work?" Larry realizes why they won't let him have a sharp writing utensil, as it would already be buried in the doctor's jugular.

"It's a process, Larry. It's taken you a long time to get you to this recognition. Now is when we really start to heal."

"How much time?"

"That depends. But I think it's safe to say that it will still take a while."

"Can I get some stamps then?"

"Sorry, no."

That night, Larry climbs out the kitchen window that he'd pried open with the steel splash curtain rod he purloined from the commercial dishwasher during his shift. He leans the sodden remains of the Adirondack chair against the trunk of the most successful and robust of his apple trees, pinches a lit cigarette between his lips, and makes his way onto the strategically grafted branches that now grow right up to the back fence. He crawls along the base of a single branch until it gets too thin for his weight, and then balances each foot on different branches, with his hands holding two thinner grafts above.

The further out he gets, the more the branches bend underfoot. He reaches with the tip of his right big toe, stretching for the top of the fence, but needs to get another six or eight inches closer. As he creeps forward, the branches buckle, and he hears a loud crack behind him. Larry thinks he sees a light turn on in one of the facility's common rooms.

If he gives up and turns around, he could probably get back into the kitchen before anyone realizes anything is amiss. He is frozen, unable to make a decision until there is another cracking sound, now closer, and the branch starts to give way under him. Before he can think it through, Larry lets go of the twigs, puts his palms together over his head, and dives toward the fence line.

He catches the top of the chain link with his chest and feels the metal points razor down his skin and catch in his abdomen. He hangs, folded over the top of the fence for a moment, then kicks up his legs once, twice, three times until he flips over onto the far side, landing hard on his shoulder.

Larry watches his cigarette fizzle out in the mud a few inches from his face, while regaining his breath and scanning his body to make sure nothing's broken. He staggers to his feet, locates the outlines of the mountains in the darkness, and runs toward them.

It's slower going then he'd like in the waterlogged grass, so he turns onto the closest road—which, fortunately, looks to be the same way toward the mountains. Toward the water. Toward his child.

His vision adjusts to the darkness, his heart doubles its pace, and his lungs pump ever-larger quantities of cold air in and out of his scraped, bleeding chest. He will give up at nothing and has the searing motivation to run all the way to Sami's doorstep. He'll swim if he has to. Climb a mountain.

But he doesn't make it very far running down the potholed, dirt road with a separated shoulder and a possibly sprained ankle in institutional slippers before security locates him in the headlights of their station wagon.

Dr. Kellerman, as Larry is forced to formally address him moving forward, doubles Larry's medicine so that he is no longer a threat to himself or anyone around him. He loses all gardening and mail privileges, not that he can do much with the tremor in his hands or read much with such clouded memory. And he has all personal items confiscated, including the unsent letter and drawings under his mattress, lest he use anything to try to flee or convince others to assist him.

Larry descends into himself, falling further away from the outside world. A gauzy veil obscures his sense of division between days, months, and years.

It's just him in the chair, the trees, the mountains, and his cigarettes. There are no mirrors in the facility. But as he flicks his butts into the bits of pooled rainwater atop the mud patch by his feet, he catches the contours of his reflection and knows that his child must no longer be a child.

Sami waits for Bruce in front of her house as planned. She's surprised when he rolls up in his VW van less than fifteen minutes late.

He opens his driver's-side door and gives her a hard time that she's still wearing the same white shoes and blue rain jacket. She responds that, after all of these years, he should have come up with a new joke.

"Why mess with a good thing?" he asks.

"That's how I feel about my shoes," she says, walking up to the van. "I can't believe this thing's still running. It's even older than you."

"You'd never believe what you can learn on the internet," he says. "Sierra and I installed a used Subaru EJ22 2.2-liter engine. Right in the comfort of our own driveway. Doesn't have as much juice as the EJ25 I wanted but less prone to head-gasket problems."

She smiles, not really sure what he's talking about, but notices his ponytail is gone. His whole head is shaved. Bruce steps out of the van without a cane anywhere in sight.

Sami's concerned about him walking the full distance over to the event. It's not far. Adjacent to her house, really. But they have to make their way around the block of condos to get to the new entrance on the far side. "You sure? We could drive."

"Years of physical therapy and the odd hot yoga class have done wonders for my core strength." He pats his abdomen with a palm and climbs down out of the vehicle.

She can't tell if he is being sarcastic or not. Such detection has never been her forte. As they start to walk, he tells her that none of this progress would have been possible without having found sobriety first. He hasn't even had any social bong hits since forever. And he never would have been able to commit himself to long-term sobriety had he and Wren not reunited after the failed auction, rededicating their lives to each other. Sami has a creeping sense that Bruce is being ... completely earnest..

Sami and Bruce had a good, and often fruitful, working relationship for a few years in the mid- to late 2010s, when he was head of the middle school PTA, and she was appointed to the vacant spot on the school board that opened up when the former board member seriously thrashed her sister-in-law, Kim, to become mayor of the city. Before Macy got to high school, before Covid, and before Sami burnt out on the politics, bureaucracy, and all of that.

"Wait, I almost forgot . . ." he says and jogs back to the van. She can't quite believe how fast he can move. He returns with a couple of T-shirts, a small stack of stickers, and a ski hat. He hands it over to Sami. "From my personal stash."

Sami will have to mail it to Macy at college, halfway across the country, but will earn major points with her daughter for tracking down the last of Loose Bruce's Ski Hut gear, which, she's been told, sold out online some weeks prior.

She thanks him and stuffs the swag into her nylon purse as they continue their walk back around the condos. He tells her that his Ski Hut has never been and never will be as profitable as a weed store, but he is both stoked and honored to own—or own 51 percent—of the tiny shop that he and Melchor originally opened out of three shipping containers and an all-season tent in the parking lot of Mel's aunt's mixed retail and apartment complex.

Sure, their commercial neighbors—the smoke shop, the twenty-four-hour massage place, the rapid-serve sandwich chain—strike the perfect balance of seediness and corniness. But regardless of the strip mall ambience, Loose Bruce's Ski Hut is one of the very few remaining ski shops in town without deeper-pocketed backers and is widely regarded as keeper of the underground vibe. A rare throwback to purer, radder times and the culture's independent past. Maybe even the whole city's more idiosyncratic, independent past.

Bruce tells her that he never did get around to manufacturing his privacy glasses—she doesn't remember those or might have blocked the whole episode from her memory. Nor has he ever moved a ton of skis, boots, or poles. He simply can't compete with the discount volume pricing of the big boys. But the store is turning a steady profit off its Loose Bruce's Ski Hut–branded trucker hats, beanies, T-shirts, and various sizes and shapes of stickers bearing the little caricature logo that Sierra drew a number of years back: Bruce's ponytailed head crowned by his raccoon hat. She even got the old soul patch just right.

He's not quite sure how it happened, but his cartoon visage stumbled its way into viral underground credibility with backcountry skiers, outdoor fanatics, municipal chauvinists, and a variety of preening baristas and bartenders. From there it pushed through to an avalanche of teenage action sports poseurs from LA to Boston and back—and even a handful of corporate dads with roof boxes on their SUVs. In Bruce's estimation, it's become some sort of sought-after talisman for authenticity strivers and nostalgia traffickers. Social media has something to do with it, and—no matter how many times Sierra tries to explain it all to him—he still doesn't get it.

Bruce concedes that it's all a team effort. Spatzy set up the website and does odd jobs around the shop when he feels like showing up. Wren keeps the books. Melchor manages custom branding and printing. They sold out of Loose Bruce merch twice so far this year, and he's filled orders for as far away as Austria and Australia.

As they walk, Bruce and Sami continue on about life, children, and the weather. She almost tells him that, now that she and Percy are empty nesters, she's thinking about writing a book about the history of her family. But she doesn't want to jinx it. She'll keep thinking on that one for now.

They make their way around the condos, which are all glass and metal with a few composite panels and tasteful hardwood accents. Near the roofline are big green block letters that spell out the name THE SUPERSONIC, with a stylized jet logo flying off toward the heavens. She's not even sure what that's supposed to refer to.

The building's developers weren't able to dynamite, dig out, or otherwise move the rock as they would have liked due to some strange, grandfathered city bylaws that no one could really explain and that seemed to go back to the early 1900s. They gave up and built around it on three sides—the condo's walls rising above the boulder like smooth, aluminum bluffs. A skirt of bright green artificial turf extends out from the base of the rock. The resulting mini-park serves as a lightly used outdoor space for the condo dwellers to quickly puff on their vapes or take out their dogs for a late-night piss.

From what Sami can tell, most of the people who live in the building are young Mothership employees and other recent arrivals who sign leases sight unseen and then spend most of their lives in front of screens. Half of them left during Covid or the subsequent tech downturn. But now there's a new wave of them. A beehive repopulating its colony after the spring thaw.

"I'm coming to terms with the fact that the newcomers never really return to wherever they came from," Sami says. "They just pass down their title to the next newer newcomers."

Bruce thinks for a moment, sucks his teeth, and says, "Yeah, maybe things never go back to the way they used to be—nobody can even agree on what used to be. There's only now, change, and then, like, the next now. Fuck it all, right?"

Sami and Bruce enter the area by the rock just in time for the ceremony and make their way up to the front of the small crowd of twelve or so people. They both kiss their waiting spouses and say hello to Shawn and Millie, who've come back to visit from retirement out in the suburbs.

Sami watches Bruce's daughter, Sierra, as she stands to face the group. This was her doing, after all. She and her younger generation, online activist friends or whatever they call these people, who watched all those online videos she made teaching them to play music. Then she got them to sign that petition she started as her extracurricular high school project. The one where Percy signed on as her faculty sponsor.

Sami knows that Sierra, who has come so far with her expressive language and speaks so eloquently in her online videos, still hates talking in front of live crowds. She makes a short, efficient speech. She thanks Percy and her parents and briefly introduces her mentor and music teacher, Monica, who'd used some of the remaining community auction funds to start a small music school and, thereby, altered Sierra's life. Sierra also pauses to thank the people who came before them on this land.

"We weren't able to officially change the neighborhood name back to its original Duwamps Hill. Yet. We'll keep on fighting. Even next year when I'm at college," Sierra says to a round of applause. "But, in the meantime, we did chalk up an initial victory . . ."

A representative from the mayor's office removes the green drape from over the bronze memorial plaque jutting up from the turf next to the rock: HASEGAWA FARMS SQUARE.

Sami listens as the mayor's representative then reads aloud the smaller inscription, including a brief mention of the family farm-worker who went on to become a teacher at the elementary school that later occupied part of the land. In this moment, Sami has never felt less conflicted about rallying all of those votes against her sister-in-law for mayor a decade back.

The crowd claps, and people turn their attention to small talk. Bruce gives Sami a brotherly nudge with his elbow. She tries to smile through her clashing emotions. It's true, this isn't exactly what she wanted or how she wanted it. It isn't the path she'd hoped for. But, hell, who gets that? If we're lucky, we get to stick around long enough to appreciate the path we've actually walked. She puts an arm over Bruce's shoulder and gives him a grateful, if somewhat stiff, side hug. Maybe she'll write that book about her family after all.

As the attendees start to funnel out of the narrow Hasegawa Farms Square, an old, gray man with a wispy mustache stubs out a smoke and pushes his walker up between Sami and Bruce. He wipes at his watery brown eyes and asks Sami in an uneven voice, "You Ruthie's kid?"

Sami nods, trying to place the old man. Then she looks to Bruce, who shrugs.

She notices what appears to be an ancient, bled-out maritime tattoo of a bird on the old man's forearm. Is that a seagull? Hard to tell at this point.

"I read in the paper. About this." The old man works to get out the words.

"You were friends with my mom? With Ruth?"

"You could say that. Yes."

Sami tries to decipher the stories worn into the deep creases in the man's face and to somehow understand her own sense of familiarity. She might be wrong, but she is pretty sure he is about to start crying.

Suddenly, she finds herself fighting back her own tears. "I'm Sami." She touches the man on the back of his arm, atop the bird tattoo.

"I know," he says.

Before Sami can respond, she is distracted by the squawking gulls behind her. She glances over her shoulder to see the flock atop the big, egg-shaped rock.

If she didn't know better, she'd think that one of the seagulls was staring right back at her, Bruce, and the old man.

It cocks its head in their direction before it wheels off into the leaden, overcast sky.

ACKNOWLEDGMENTS

While *Supersonic* is a work of fiction, it was important to be as accurate as possible with various historical and cultural details. This was guided by the invaluable support of several people with lived experience and historical expertise.

Upon beginning research, I called Duwamish Tribal Services and was immediately referred to David Buerge, the tribe's "unofficial official historian." David graciously met with me over the course of multiple years and reviewed draft after draft of material. Duwamish Tribal Services director Kristina Pearson was generous with her time and read and reviewed the completed manuscript.

Others who helped me breathe life into these stories and characters include Alison Miller, Jerry Cohen, and Fred Moody. While Masako is not based on Claire Suguro, my decision to make the character be the first local public school teacher of Asian descent was inspired by Claire's groundbreaking career. I am more than honored to have grown up knowing Auntie Claire, and I considered her family.

A huge thank-you to my insightful editor, Harry Kirchner, who believes in me and makes this whole process feel like an adventure with an old friend.

And my agent, Jennie Dunham, who is wise, patient, measured, and everything I am not. Thank you for always keeping an eye on the long game.

To my friend and mentor, Johnny Evison. This book would not be what it is without your support, inspiration, and all-around big-heartedness. Please read all his books.

Thank you to Dan Smetanka at Counterpoint. You are a force. To Megan Fishmann and Rachel Fershleiser, who conjure the magic of connecting the book with readers. And to Laura Berry, Yukiko Tominaga, Wah-Ming Chang, Dan López, Lily Philpott, Vanessa Genao, Dan Goff, Alyssa Lo, Lena Moses-Schmitt, Ashley Kiedrowski, Madelyn Lindquist, and others at Catapult and Counterpoint, who make it all happen. Thank you to Seana Hayden at Penguin Random House for getting *Supersonic* into all the bookstores I love.

To the talented Zachary Cole and Jon Strickland, for their early reads and feedback. Also Sonia Vargas, Nathaniel Schleimer, Spencer Thun, Alex Prindle, Cynthia Brothers, Aki Ueoka, and J. Baab, for specific insights throughout.

To my friends at Third Place Books: Seattle is lucky to have you.

Last but not least, to Tábata Silva Kohnstamm, James Kohnstamm, Linda Baker Kohnstamm, and Edward Kohnstamm (1940–2024). RIP Dad. I love you forever.

© Brian Smale

THOMAS KOHNSTAMM was born and raised in Seattle and still lives in the same house he grew up in—now with his wife and two children. He's a career-long freelance writer and has run his own video and animation studio for over a decade. *Supersonic* is his third book. Find out more at thomaskohnstamm.com.